A FISTFUL OF CREDITS

CREDITS

STORIES FROM THE
FOUR HORSEMEN UNIVERSE

Edited by
Chris Kennedy and Mark Wandrey

Seventh Seal Press
Virginia Beach, VA

Chris Kennedy/Seventh Seal Press
2052 Bierce Dr.
Virginia Beach, VA 23454
http://chriskennedypublishing.com/

Publisher's Note: This is a work of fiction. Names, characters, places, and incidents are a product of the author's imagination. Locales and public names are sometimes used for atmospheric purposes. Any resemblance to actual people, living or dead, or to businesses, companies, events, institutions, or locales is completely coincidental.

Editor: Chris Kennedy
Co-Editor: Mark Wandrey
Cover Design: Brenda Mihalko
Cover Image: Ricky Ryan

A Fistful of Credits/Chris Kennedy. -- 1st ed.
ISBN 978-1942936701

This book is dedicated to all the readers who support us, and to the scifi authors who paved the way so that today's authors can do what we love. This book is for you.

"And when He had opened the fifth seal, I saw under the altar the souls of them that were slain for the Word of God, and for the testimony which they held. And they cried with a loud voice, saying, "How long, O Lord, holy and true, dost Thou not judge and avenge our blood on them that dwell on the earth?" And white robes were given unto every one of them, and it was said unto them that they should rest yet for a little while, until it was fulfilled that their fellow servants and brethren were killed, as they had been."

— *Revelation 6:9-11*

Preface by Chris Kennedy

This book was born in the same place as the rest of the Four Horsemen Universe—in a bar. Mark and I were talking about the universe, and where we wanted to go with it, and we realized the galaxy was a lot bigger than we were going to be able to flesh out on our own any time soon.

We needed help.

So we asked some authors we knew, and some we just sort of knew of, if they'd like to help us expand our universe by writing a short story set in the universe. We were overwhelmed at the response—it will take us several books to accommodate all of the authors who immediately said "Yes!" when we asked them to participate. Like us, they found the universe a lot of fun and couldn't wait to jump in.

We gave them a short primer on the universe and sent them on their way with only two points of guidance: it had to be set in the Four Horsemen Universe, and it had to be good. As such, these 14 tales describe the highs and lows of life on the battlefield, as well as in the streets and alleys of the Four Horsemen Universe. While some deal with mercenaries, others introduce readers to members of the other guilds and organizations, and even a vagrant living on the street.

Edited by universe creators Mark Wandrey and Chris Kennedy, "A Fistful of Credits" includes all-new stories by a variety of bestselling authors—and some you may not have heard of...yet. Authors Brad R. Torgersen, Christopher Nuttall, Terry Mixon, Doug Dandridge, Paul Corcoran, Jason Cordova, Jon Osborne, Kevin Ikenberry, John Del Arroz, Kacey Ezell, Christopher Woods, Charity Ayres, Mark Wandrey, and Chris Kennedy take on various aspects of the universe, giving you additional insight into a galaxy that isn't at war, but definitely isn't at peace. One thing is for sure, though—anything's possible if you have a fistful of credits.

Mark and I are indebted to the authors who participated in this project for their time and talents, and to Dr. Charles E. Gannon for the foreword.

What makes Dr. Gannon worthy of kicking off this book (i.e., Why should you listen to him)? You name it; he's done it. He's been selected as a Fulbright Fellow at Liverpool University, Palacky University, and the University of Dundee. He has written outstanding fiction, including two New York Times Best Selling series: the Starfire military SF series and Eric Flint's Ring of Fire series. He has also written award-winning non-fiction, including his book, "Rumors of War and Infernal Machines" that won the American Library Association Award for Outstanding Book. He is a member of SIGMA, the "SF think-tank" which advises intelligence and defense agencies, and he was one of the featured speakers on Discovery Channel's second installment of "Curiosity," titled "When Aliens Attack." A better question might be, what hasn't Dr. Gannon done?

Better than any of that, though, Dr. Charles E. Gannon is just a heck of a guy, and I'm proud to know him. Once in a while, he even lets me call him, "Chuck."

Take a look at what Dr. Gannon has to say—he knows what he's talking about.

Chris Kennedy
Virginia Beach, VA

Foreword by Dr. Charles E. Gannon

It's the Twenty-Second Century; the galaxy has opened up to us as a hyperactive beehive of stargates and new technologies, and we suddenly find ourselves in a vast playground of different races, environments, and cultures. There's just one catch:

Humanity is pretty much at the bottom of the food chain.

We do have one commercially viable asset, however: our willingness to fight for pay. And there is plenty of fighting to be done in a universe that is not so much governed by rule of law, as it is balance of terror. In a setting that evokes and blends elements that resonate with elements of Pournelle's Falkenberg books, Mass Effect, and even a Star Wars-meets-Warhammer 40K vibe, conflict is omnipresent. But that conflict doesn't conform to the predictable shapes of a single, expansive war of contending states, ideologies, or even species. It is a constant fractal churn of battles and invasions, double-crosses and surgical strikes, all fought in the pursuit of one overarching objective: power.

Whether that power is measured as influence, security, technology, resources, or money varies, of course. Because this is a galaxy-spanning Warring-States period, with every planet and every race jockeying for position and, in some cases, survival. Humanity is one of the latter. But fortunately (and ironically, and even sadly), we Humans are quite accustomed to combat—and our visceral, close-range experience of it makes us more ready for its vicissitudes, horror, and grief. So although our technology is rudimentary and our knowledge of surrounding space extremely limited, four mercenary groups— The Four Horsemen—nonetheless survive long enough to start bringing in the currency necessary to upgrade our planet into a minor power that can survive being dropped into the shark-tank that is the

Milky Way. This then, is space opera at its most energetic, with a compelling mixture of technological wonders and limitations thrown in for good measure. (And you'll have to read it for yourself to find out what I mean with that cryptic comment.)

However, the editors of this series have also achieved something else: they have not merely compiled a selection of great stories; they have curated a collection of great writers in the genre. And that is probably worth the cover price alone. Here's what I mean:

One of the great things about the age of electronic publishing is that, if you are a book lover (and since you are reading this now, I'm pretty sure that means you) you always have more to read. Not only are traditional publishers producing record numbers of books, but small presses and indies are creating a non-stop monsoon of them in every genre, according to every taste and preference. There's only one drawback:

Finding the ones worth reading.

It's been said that when everyone is shouting, you can't hear anyone. It's a little bit like that in electronic publishing. Now that everyone with a computer can independently write, edit, package, publish, and market their own books, there is no reliable way to know where the good stuff is. You can stick with the traditional publishers—but if you are a regular reader with very specific tastes, you might run out of material pretty quickly. Or given their prices, you might run out of money. On the other end of the spectrum, there are some books out there that, just by looking at the misspellings on the cover of the book, you can be pretty sure will not warrant investing any time in— even if they are free.

But what about the immense bulge in the middle ground, the trackless expanse of tantalizing titles and cover art and blurbs that succeed in catching your eye but fail to tell you what you most want to know: will I like it? How do you find the good, even the best work that suits your taste when there are so many people putting it on the market?

The answer is, quite literally, right in front of your eyes. The co-creators of this series—Chris Kennedy and Mark Wandrey—are examples of indie-powered cream rising to the top of their electronic subgenre. They have written and succeeded—critically and financially—amidst the endless thickets of internet publishing. They understand what it means to write for a target audience with specific interests, and since you're perusing this now, it also means they know how to find and connect with those readers.

But they have an even rarer skill: the ability to find, and recruit, more excellent writers who are cut from the same cloth. And they are able to gather contributors from the full spectrum of that environment: from well-established authors associated with traditional imprints to indies who might have gone under your radar—until now. So they are doing more than bringing you great fiction. They are bringing you great authors to discover, to follow: they are expanding your access to more of the military-themed space opera that you love best. If you doubt me, just turn to the table of contents and take a look at the names you find there. And then read the stories and see if you haven't found at least half a dozen new authors to follow.

But why believe me? And why are you reading a stupid foreword instead of starting your journey with the Four Horsemen of this troubled and almost apocalyptic future?

So—turn the page, damn it!

Dr. Charles E. Gannon
May 22, 2017

Chris' Introduction to:

The Last Alpha

by Mark Wandrey

Anyone who follows Mark on his boards will know of his long-running dispute with his publisher over story size. Generally, Mark likes to view a final word count in the same manner a bull views a red cape—it's something to charge past as quickly as possible. "The Last Alpha" is one of those stories, as it is (by more than 10%) longer than any of the other stories in this book. It's also one of the best, which is why I let it stay that length.

Mark is a Dragon-nominated author who writes scifi and zombie apocalypse and is the Co-Editor for this book. Although we're officially co-creators and have spent countless hours on the phone and online hashing it out, the Four Horsemen Universe is originally Mark's brainchild, and he will always have 51% of the decision on all matters for how it runs. If you think antimatter is a real "thing" that ought to be in the universe, you can blame Mark for its exclusion; I used my 49% to its greatest effect, but was denied. Want to see where the universe started? You can get the first contact story for free at his website: http://worldmaker.us/.

His contribution to the anthology, "The Last Alpha," takes a look at the effects that joining the Galactic Union has had on Earth society, as seen by the last man to return from the Alpha Contracts. After more than 100 years of fighting, is it time for him to settle down into a life of luxury, or will he have to walk tall?

You may want to remember Zeke, too, as you haven't seen the last of him...

THE LAST ALPHA
by Mark Wandrey

Part I

The Return

The flyer banked over the Smoky Mountains, dropping below Mach as it fell into the city's traffic control pattern. The 700 nautical mile flight had taken a boring 40 minutes, and Zeke had spent it looking through some of his old digital photos and thinking about his short time in Houston. It had been 10 years since he'd sent anything to be stowed there, and the storage unit had been so rusted, he'd had to pay the owner $500 to cut the door down, then another $1,000 to shut up about what was inside. The contents had been packed into a mobile cargo module and were awaiting his final decision on their disposition.

"Cash when we land," the pilot said through the partition. Zeke just nodded. The man scowled and went back to his controls.

It would have been impossible to hire a robotic flight. You can't smooth talk a robot with cold, hard cash. This guy, though, had been another matter. The little plastic safe in the partition held a single 1,000 credit chit, its tiny red diamond shining a promise to the cabby. The safe could only be opened if they both thumbed it at the same time. The driver hadn't wanted to go, not even for a stack of five crisp new $500 dollar bills with Barack Obama's face grinning like an idiot on each one. No surprise the chit did it, though; that little piece of plastic was worth more than $10,000 in US dollars. A credit could buy you dinner from a robochef, a buck wouldn't buy a stick of gum.

They were low now, under 5,000 feet, and he could see the Tennessee River twisting and turning below. The crumbling remains of old Interstate 40 were still there, and the gleaming superconducting rails of the southern trans-continental maglev roughly followed the same path, though without the curves. You couldn't turn hundreds of tons of train quickly when it was traveling faster than the speed of sound.

As luck would have it, he spotted one of the high-speed transports. It swept gracefully around a curve and slowed before it went through a tunnel. Zeke could just make out the bow shockwave of the engine unit as it came out the other end, accelerated, and shot ahead of them. As his flyer passed over the last ridge, he finally saw his destination: Chattanooga. The maglev train slowed below Mach again before it went through the city...but not by much.

The cabby headed for the destination his passenger had specified when they took off. Seeing they were on final approach, Zeke put away the ancient digital viewer in his sole piece of luggage, an equally venerable Osprey duffel bag, and zipped it up. He checked that everything was in its place under his leather bomber jacket and zipped it up as well. He still hadn't gotten used to how loosely the jacket fit compared to the way his memory said it should.

The cab banked, and rotor blades extended from the top of the fuselage. The cab transitioned to helicopter mode, flared, and set down in the big red-painted landing zone; the flexible signs saying "Danger – VTOL Zone – Keep Back!" rocked in the rotor wash from the flyer. The cabby kept the hydrogen-powered fuel cells hot.

"Okay, you're here," he said, and he put his thumb on the safe release. Zeke looked at the flashing red light on the safe and considered. A thousand credits was a thousand credits. The driver's cocky look slowly morphed into one of concern. "It was a good ride, and fast..." he said in a mulish tone. Zeke looked out of the tinted canopy of the flyer, noticing a few shabbily-dressed pedestrians staring at the flyer sitting with its blades still spinning. They seemed mildly curious.

Zeke pressed his thumb to the safe. The door on the other side popped open, and the canopy released. He didn't wait for the cabby to say anything or offer any thanks. People would do stupid things over that kind of money.

He walked quickly away from the flyer to reduce the chance of mischief and was rewarded by a quick blast of chop wash as the cab screamed into the sky. As the wind eddies died out, he fished one of his hand-wrapped cigars from the faded leather jacket and bit off the end. A poorly-dressed woman slowly pushing a FedMart shopping cart gave him a look that was somewhere between disgust and outright loathing as he used an alien-manufactured plasma lighter to ignite the pungent stogie.

"You aren't supposed to smoke," she muttered, loud enough for him to hear. He exhaled a huge cloud of smoke in her direction, smiled, and nodded. She accelerated slightly.

The departure of the flyer had scattered tiny tornadoes of garbage and leaves in its wake. Zeke strolled down the sidewalk a few blocks until he reached his first destination. The old building had started life as a train station and was a center of rail commerce so important in the 19th century that it had become the stuff of songs. Later, in the 20th century, it became a hotel and convention center. Then, as time and mismanagement took its toll, housing for indigent people. Some research on the Aethernet enroute from Houston had indicated it was a FedMart distribution center, but he quickly saw that was out of date. The entire structure had been looted and burned to the ground.

He examined the ruins of the historic Chattanooga Choo-Choo for a few minutes, trying to imagine how it looked when he'd last seen it. He walked over the long-fallen 'Do Not Cross' tape and through some of the vacant structures. Eventually, his needs fulfilled, he walked back out.

At the street, he found a pair of young men trying far too hard to look inconspicuous. He gave them a quick assessment and came up with a very low number of possibilities before he walked the rest of the way out to stand between them.

"Whatcha lookin for in there, grandpa?"

Zeke puffed on his cigar and regarded them with a calm, cool gaze.

"Doncha know that smoking is bad for you?" the other asked.

Puff, puff. Zeke walked away.

"Hey! You don't walk away from us!"

"Yeah, you know who we is?"

Zeke stopped and turned, examining the punk. About 20, maybe 25, undernourished, and with long, greasy hair that was half in dreadlocks and half in cornrows. He wore some sort of military surplus jacket which bulged noticeably and combat boots with steel tips. Cheap metamorphic tats covered both sides of his neck. One looked like a fire-breathing dragon, the other a butterfly with fangs. Cute. The other punk was less colorful, but they both looked confident and hungry. He shook his head.

"Weez wit the TVG, muthafucka." Zeke cocked his head. "You knows, Tennessee Valley Gangstas!"

"Yeah," the other said.

Zeke grinned, gave a little chuckle, and turned to walk away. A second later, he heard their footfalls.

* * *

There wasn't much he remembered about the city. That, in and of itself, wasn't a surprise; he'd been gone a long time. The changes, though, weren't from the natural progress of growth and evolution of a city, so much as its decay and decent into barbarism. He strolled down Market Street, noting places he remembered. Porker's Barbecue, home of some of the best brisket he'd ever eaten, had ended its life as a check-cashing place before being condemned. The Patten Towers, where he'd once had an apartment, had suffered a similar fate to the Choo-Choo; only a burned-out husk remained.

As Zeke got to MLK, he saw a pair of police cruisers parked at the corner of 8th street, and he turned left before they could see him. One of them might have caught a glimpse of him, but he wasn't too worried. What was one more drifter in this decaying town?

On Broad Street, the Starbucks was amazingly still standing. He walked down to take a look, then realized it was like the one in the Houston Starport, a robotic vendor. He figured the taste wouldn't be any different, so he went back to MLK and continued west. He was heading for a specific destination, though he didn't know why. It couldn't still be there, not the way the town looked, but he persisted. His feelings of bitter nostalgia got more intense with every step.

As Zeke approached the corner of MLK and Carter streets, he thought he caught a whiff of hot grease and baked goods. It wasn't possible, yet there it was—just across Carter from him. The City

Café Diner looked almost the same. The memory felt like a shot to the gut.

"Huh," he said in amazement. A sound made him turn, and he saw the police car whiz by on Broad Street, heading south. He crossed Carter and went up to the diner. It had changed after all.

It had always been in the corner of an old hotel. The space was leased from the building owner, and the café had been known far and wide for its cakes and pies, but they'd made a mean cup of coffee and some great omelets, too. The hotel was gone, demolished at some point, and the café was a standalone structure now. Its walls were hardened, and the entryway had a robotic guard built in with heavily-armored shutters and blast grates which could be lowered. It reminded him of some areas of Startown. The parking lot held a dozen ground cars of questionable utility, most showing more rust than paint.

"Your business," the robot said in passable English. He was impressed as it looked like an Oogar design.

"I'd like some coffee," he said. The robot considered him, and he considered it. Roughly humanoid, it was nine feet tall with two heavily-reinforced arms. One held a stun baton, and the other a shield. On the shield was a faded but readable sticker: "Robot Sentry License 8-771-A – City of Chattanooga," and the date it was renewed.

"A balance of at least fifty dollars is required for entrance," the robot informed him. "Cash or credit?"

"Credit," he said, and held out his Yack. The Universal Account Access Card had a scan-enabled ID code and was linked to a bank account. The robot's laser swept across it, then the machine slid aside on its track.

"Welcome to the City Café Diner," it said, but pronounced Café as "Kaf-ee". The door opened, and he went in. The interior was unchanged; it was decorated in mid-nineteenth century diner style, with lots of chrome, red plastic upholstery, and checkered vinyl flooring. It felt like home. Zeke grinned like a kid.

"Yeah?" asked a woman half his age from behind the bar where a pair of women were drinking sodas and talking.

"Coffee?" he said. "Maybe a piece of pie?" The big rotating display was still there, and while the number of options seemed to have decreased, there were still a lot of tasty-looking confections. She examined him with a critical eye, and he could tell she was wondering if her Oogar surplus robot was on the fritz. "I can pay," he said, cutting off her concern. She grunted, took a menu, and led him to an empty booth. He dropped his bag on the seat and plopped down. The place was so familiar it hurt. He'd practically grown up here.

There were maybe a dozen people in the place. Owing to the minimum solvency needed to get in, the clientele was better off than the few people he'd seen on the streets, although they still seemed well-worn. The woman handed him a battered old slate with the menu. As Zeke glanced at it, he was surprised to realize he was hungry. The images of the food looked as good as he remembered, so he selected pancakes, eggs, bacon, and orange juice. The menu said coffee was complementary with any complete meal.

"Bacon is synthetic," the waitress warned, then shrugged, "our source for real bacon was shut down by protestors two weeks ago."

"Protesting what?" he asked.

"Animal rights. Where you been? The Supreme World Court is about to grant a stay on slaughter of all farm animals." He looked at her as queerly as she'd looked at him. "Where you been, another planet?"

"Or thousand," he mumbled. "Fake's fine." He touched the order button and was told his breakfast would be $125 dollars. He touched his Yack to the slate, which beeped. The waitress seemed surprised, but she took the slate and walked off. A minute later a serving robot buzzed over on quiet tracks and delivered his coffee. He'd had better, but not many times. "Ahhh," he said as the hot liquid hit his throat.

He was just finishing his pancakes when the door buzzed, and a pair of cops came in. He'd been half-expecting that when they raced by heading south. They were both past middle age and had that sloppy look of cops who didn't take their job seriously. They had new multi-function slug guns on their belts and expensive shoes. Pretty spiffy for a dump like Chattanooga. The one wearing stripes went over to the waitress, and, after a minute, she pointed at him. They sauntered over.

"Yack?" the one with corporal stripes asked.

"Is there a problem, officer?" Zeke asked.

"He said, 'Yack,'" the sergeant said, and he dropped a hand to his gun. Zeke's eyes narrowed, but he handed it to them, slowly. The corporal snatched it from him and used a wrist scanner on it. He took a slate and examined the readout.

"Randy Snyder?" the corporal asked. Zeke nodded. "Says here you're from Wichita, Kansas. What you doing in Chattanooga?"

"Traveling," Zeke said. "I was looking for Wichita and got lost."

"Don't be smart with us," the sergeant said. "You the one who beat up those boys back by the Choo-Choo?"

"Don't know what you're talking about."

"That so?" the corporal asked. Zeke nodded. "You messed up those TVG boys pretty good."

"I might have seen a couple men down that way," Zeke said. "They looked kind of clumsy. Maybe they fell face first onto the sidewalk a few dozen times." He'd seen the cameras mounted in their hats, and knew he was being recorded. He considered his timeline and decided he was fine. The forged Yack was better than anything you could buy on Earth. It would hold up for a few days, at least.

"I figured you'd say something like that," the sergeant said, then gestured at Zeke. "Give him his Yack back." The corporal did as instructed. "You best be careful around here, Mr. Snyder. In fact, after that incident, it would be best if you just got in another flying cab and left."

Zeke nodded as if he were accepting good advice; instead, he was noting they knew how he'd gotten here. Obviously, he'd been watched since his cab set down.

"Have a nice day, officers," he said as they headed towards the door. Through the window next to him, Zeke had a narrow view of the door, but it was enough to see the officers outside talking with six punks, all dressed like the other two he'd beaten the shit out of an hour ago. One of the punks passed the cops something, and Zeke thought he caught a red glint. He nodded again and finished his coffee as the cops overrode the robot, and the six gangers filed in. The waitress looked alarmed.

"You can't be in here," she complained loudly, "we paid already!"

"Shut up, bitch!" one yelled back. Zeke noted which one. The last piece of bacon went into his mouth. Not bad, for modified plant proteins. He'd had a hell of a lot worse. The gang members moved down to surround his booth, and the patrons began to flee out the exit. The gang watched them leave. When the last one was out, the waitress retreated into a back room, and a loud buzzer sounded. The shutters all clattered down, and an armored door closed over the room she'd gone into. The ornate cake display was covered by a drop-down shield. Good, he thought.

"You messed up Rocker and Tonka," one of them said.

"We gonna mess you up, real bad," the one who'd yelled at the waitress added.

"Only chance," Zeke said. "Walk out the door, while you can."

"Or what?" another asked, after they'd all stopped laughing. "You gonna bleed on us, old man?"

"Or none of you will be walking anywhere." Their faces went from amused to angry. He reached under his shirt and drew out a coin affixed to a chain. It was made from old, tarnished metal, and had a female Mongol horse archer in mid-stride in relief. The three facing him saw it, one went pale.

"Scoot, man," he said towards the leader, "we better go."

"You gone fuckin mad?" Scoot asked.

"Dude, that's a Golden Horde challenge coin. I saw one on a Tri-V show in school."

Zeke nodded and looked Scoot right in the eye. "He's right. So again, just walk out. Your call."

"You a Four Horsemen, old fart?"

"No," he admitted, "but they owe me a debt."

"See?" Scoot asked. "Even if he was some badass merc, he's old and shriveled up. Let's do this."

"Your choice," Zeke said. The kid who'd recognized the challenge coin took a step back, but Scoot went in, right hand shooting in low at Zeke's ribs, a long, razor-edged carbon-fiber knife in his hand.

Zeke caught the man's hand with his left hand, arresting the momentum an inch before the blade reached his coat. He squeezed and crushed every bone in Scoot's hand. The sound of snapping bones was hideously loud, as were Scoot's screams. Several of the gang drew firearms. Zeke rotated his body and pulled Scoot in front of him, and the bullets punched into the gang leader's chest. Zeke pushed up and out of the booth, using Scoot's body like a battering ram to send the men flying.

Less than a minute later, he was working out a kink in his shoulder as he walked over to a booth and knelt next to it. The kid who'd recognized him was cowering there, shaking uncontrollably.

"Please don't kill me," the kid begged. Zeke reached in, lightning fast, snatched the kid's left foot, and dragged him out of his hiding place. He screamed like a girl as Zeke hoisted him off his feet and held him one-handed completely off the ground.

"Your friends upset me," Zeke explained. The kid looked at the diner from upside down; five bodies lay sprawled around the interior. "I didn't mean to kill any of them. Sorry about that." The kid was turning red-faced. "I need to know who you work for."

"The cops paid us," the kid moaned.

"No, I don't mean the cops." Zeke reached behind his back with his free hand and drew a half-meter of blackened combat knife. Alien script was laser etched into its alloy surface. "Who's your boss? Give me a name."

Five minutes later the shutter opened on the back room, and a set of eyes looked around for any signs of movement. Not finding any, the door rotated up. The waitress, two cooks, and the owner who'd been in back doing paperwork came out carefully. The waitress gasped when she saw the TVG gang members scattered, sprawled, and broken. There were copious amounts of blood on the floor, and a cleaning robot was making macabre, bloody swirls as it tried vainly to clean the carnage. To all their surprise, the old man was back in his booth sipping the half-finished orange juice.

"More coffee?" he asked. The waitress just stared in stunned horror, so he raised his cup and waggled it impatiently. A long, bloody black knife sat on the table, across the empty breakfast plate. The coffee robot was near the service area, its little rubber wheels spinning in a puddle of blood, unable to reach him. The waitress didn't move, so the owner picked up the coffee pot and carried it over to refill Zeke's cup.

"Much obliged," he said as he took a sip. "Ahh." He put the cup down. "Can I ask you something?"

"S-sure," the owner answered, managing it with only a sight stammer.

"This establishment was once owned by the Avander family?"

"Yeah," he said, his face scrunching up in concentration, "but that was like seventy, eighty years ago."

"What happened to Molly Avander?" The man told him. Zeke took in the information, then nodded. "My thanks. The back exit still next to the freezer?" Surprised, the owner nodded.

Zeke got up and stretched; the kink in his shoulder still hurt. The big knife disappeared, then he took his shoulder bag and went around the bodies, the blood, and the frustrated cleaning robot and walked back behind the counter. The cooks moved out of the way; he slid by the waitress. She looked at him with eyes wide with terror.

He stopped at the counter, fished into a special pocket in his bag, and took out a credit chit, sitting it gently on the counter.

"For the mess," he said, "and probably the lawyers." Then he was gone. The owner walked over and looked down at the plastic Galactic Union credit chit, a tiny red diamond embedded in see-through plastic in its center. It was a 5,000 credit chit. They found the youngest gang member where Zeke had left him, unconscious and hung upside down by his shoes from a coat rack.

A few blocks away Zeke decided he couldn't stay on foot. The town was so poor, though, it didn't seem right to deprive one of the denizens of their transportation. He passed under the partially collapsed Highway 27 bridge toward the old Mitsubishi dealer, only to discover it was now a Binnig dealer. Of course, this one didn't sell CASPers, combat assault systems, personal; instead, it sold robots much like the one probably still trying to clean up the blood in the City Café Diner.

A motorcycle was parked out front; it was probably only half his age. It seemed well-maintained, so he went into the dealer. The bike belonged to the service technician. He hadn't wanted to sell, but a 1,000-credit chit changed his mind. Another hundred got him a gas voucher and a helmet.

Zeke took the time to disable the tracking device, then slung his bag across the low saddle, fired up the bike, and got on Highway 27, heading north. There were no other vehicles, and he found out why when he reached the P. R. Olgiati Bridge. Only one span remained standing over the Tennessee River, and it was cracked and crumbling. He went across it at nearly 90 miles per hour. Back in town, he heard the first sirens.

He exited the abandoned highway on the other side of the river, turning left on Manufacturers Road. When that intersected Cherokee Boulevard, he found the first signs of commerce other than the Café. A few desultory businesses clung to life here—fix-it shops, fast food robots, and a government welfare office. While he waited for a light, a police car cruised by. It was modern and well-maintained, unlike the other cars. He nodded to the cop behind the wheel, who nodded back. A scanner was on the roof, mounted next to the light bar. The cop didn't hit the brakes or turn on his lights. No facial recognition out on him yet. Sloppy.

When the light changed, he crossed the intersection where Manufacturers turned into Velma, took a right, went a few blocks, took a left, and quickly lost himself in side streets. He drove slowly, just under the speed limit to avoid drawing undue attention. There were quite a few bikes about, and many were better than his. Despite how many credits he'd gone through, it was a good choice.

It took ten minutes of zigzagging to reach his destination. Zeke waved to the groundskeeper as he pulled into the information spot at the Chattanooga Memorial Park and looked up what he needed, then he was back on the bike and driving around the twists and turns of the old cemetery. He found the grave in only a few minutes.

"Jenifer Avander," the gravestone read. He knew the birthdate of his daughter well. The date of her death was there for him, too—over 60 years ago. She'd died young, only 43 years old. There was no indication of why on the grave, and the Aethernet hadn't had anything on her. She was born before it was established, and the public records for Chattanooga were a wreck, just like the city.

Zeke took out a fresh cigar and lit it. Next to Jenifer's grave was another labeled, "Molly Greene." His ex-wife had returned to her maiden name at some point after he'd left. A simple marker, just like their daughter's. The date of her death was only a year later. The sound of a leaf crunching in the fall grass made him slip a hand under his coat.

"I'm not armed," an older voice said. Zeke turned his head to see the gardener standing in the trees a short distance away. "I was just watching. Not a lot of people come here anymore. You looked a little rough, and we've had some try digging up bodies for loot."

"Grave robbers?" Zeke asked, a big puff of smoke billowing in the chill breeze. The old man nodded, though Zeke realized the guy was probably young enough to be his grandson. He looked at the cigar and gave an almost sly grin, like he was seeing something that he had fond memories of.

"You kin to them?" the man asked. Zeke nodded and looked back. "I know the family." That brought his head around quickly.

"Tell me," Zeke said.

"Well, things was looking pretty good around here when I was in grade school, oh 75 years ago. Molly Greene there owned the City Café Diner, just off downtown. Nice place, still there as a matter of fact. I went there with my family every Sunday for breakfast. She was nice. Well, she was never happy after her husband went and died in them first merc wars, so she eventually sold the diner. She went to work at the Sequoyah fusion test plant, up where the nuclear reactor was before them protestors got it shut down in the twenties."

"They wanted to put one of the really big plants there, only it ended up being put in Atlanta instead." He shrugged. "Politicians and stuff. Business flocked down thereabouts, not here. Businesses started to dry up. All that merc money started making people lazy. Government had money to give people stuff. Why work? Free food, free cars, free TVs; you name it! It was the durned lottery every day! Only then it starts getting expensive to buy stuff, and the government cuts back. All the jobs moved away. Some not even to other countries, either, but to other planets! I hear tell we used to fuss about Mexican aliens. Shit, that ain't nothing compared to a talking ten-foot-wide spider!"

He cackled at his own joke and shook his head. Zeke thought the geezer wouldn't be laughing if he'd ever met a Tortantula in person. The alien spiders had particularly poor dispositions.

"So our town slowly died," the gardener continued. "Most people left, only wasn't no place to go, was there? It wasn't just Chattanooga going down the drain, but the whole country. Shoot, darn near the whole planet!" The man shook his head, then spit in the grass. "All that money, and the government just shoveled it out to people for junk. Then the magnetic train went through without stopping, and things really went to shit. That damned TVG gang uses the city as a base, no one wants to live here, cops is workin' for them...it's just never ending—"

"What happened to Molly?" Zeke asked. The man shook his head and seemed to remember Zeke was there.

"Huh? Oh, well her daughter took up with some nefarious character from Atlanta 'bouts. Had a kid I think. Anyway, there was a turf war, and she died in the gun battle when her scummy husband tried to shoot it out. I think the kid was killed too. Molly couldn't handle it. She hung herself about a year later."

Zeke sighed. That filled in one of the pieces he was missing. It also started a small fire in the pit of his stomach. He knew what he needed to do now before he left for good. He glanced at the third grave for a long moment as the gardener went back to rambling about welfare and aliens. Finally, he interrupted him.

"Thanks for the information," Zeke said and headed for the road nearby where his bike rested.

"Hey mister," the gardener called after him. "What's your name, and why you wanna know about them Avanders?"

"Zeke," he said over his shoulder, answering the first question but not the second. He brought the bike to life and rode off without another word. The gardener walked up and examined the two graves the stranger had been standing in front of. The sound of his motorcycle was fading in the distance as he looked at the third grave. "Dr. Ezekiel Avander," it said; he had died almost 90 years ago. "Lost in the Alpha Contracts under the employ of mercenary company Whitewater Intl."

"Ezekiel..." the old man mused. He turned to catch a glimpse of the departing stranger, but the bike was long gone.

Part II

Loose Ends

Zeke lay in his cell with no arms or legs, lying in his own filth, trying to eat some of the half-rotten garbage his masters had slid under the door with a shovel. He hadn't been able to clean himself for a week, and he knew he was in danger of becoming seriously sick, but calling out only earned him a beating. When the door flew open, he only barely got his head out of the way. A huge reptilian creature looked down at him in disgust.

"Work now," it said.

"I need to clean," he said, not looking his keeper in the eye.

"Work now," it insisted.

"If I don't clean up, I'm going to be too sick to work," he persisted, taking a chance. But if they didn't let him clean himself now, they never would once the work started. He could eat in there without his arms or legs, but relieving himself had negative side effects he loathed. The jailer examined him for a minute, its wide nostrils flaring, then snapping closed at the putrid stench. "If you left me an arm I wouldn't fucking stink like this," he snarled, and instantly regretted it.

"Cho-to!" the jailer barked, and his assistant shambled down. Another slave like Zeke, Cho-to enjoyed his captivity, because he oversaw the other slaves. He liked hurting people. The four-armed humanoid Lumar was seven feet tall, and about as smart as a nine-year-old Human. Almost. He stared down at Zeke with malevolence in his eyes. "Clean it, give it limbs, dress it, and deliver it to the labs."

"Master," the Lumar said, bowing deeply in order to be shorter than the five-and-a-half-foot tall reptilian. When the jailer walked away, Cho-to's grin got even bigger. "I clean," he said, showing teeth filed to points. Cho-to had started his illustrious career in the exciting field of slavery as a pit fighter. The Lumar disappeared and returned with a firehose.

"You sadistic fuck," Zeke said in the alien's language. Cho-to's face turned to rage, and the hose blasted out at its full, skin-burning power. Zeke screamed and tried to breathe.

Zeke sat up in bed with a strangled cry, gasping for breath and covered in so much sweat he almost thought he was back in that cell. He struggled to control his breathing, putting his head between his legs. The last time he had that nightmare was at least a month ago, shortly before returning home. A sign of anxiety, he thought, as he got up to shower.

An hour later, he sipped coffee and watched as a police cruiser hummed by. It was the third one in 20 minutes. In the two weeks since his incident at the City Café Diner, the heat had turned up an order of magnitude. The cops finally realized his Yack was a forgery when they back-checked on Randy Snyder, who had died when a tsunami hit Laem Chabang five years ago. He'd tossed the Yack in the Tennessee River after draining the account.

He watched through the flop's cracked window as the police car slid past. Its scanner mast was extended, and that meant they knew he was in the area. They'd been closing in as sightings came in. Not a lot of old drifter types riding motorcycles. He had been through three bikes so far. He'd ditched the first a day later. The second when he'd come out of a bar to see cops examining it. His third one was a block away, and there it would remain until found.

He'd used them to finish his reconnaissance and learn more about his home town as it existed today. The only two employers were the fusion plant, which provided power for most of Tennessee and Kentucky, though just barely, and the FedMart distribution center. The first had a hundred workers, mostly professional, the latter employed a couple thousand people and twice that many robots to move entitlements around the region. TVG hijacked about one in fifty robotic transports, by his best estimate. The police caught the hijackers, maybe twice a year. It was a big news story, but never seemed to lead to bigger catches.

The other thing he found was an alien-made manufactory, a huge one-piece robotic factory which took raw materials and produced finished goods. It had been purchased by a local consortium which went out of business before the group could bring it online. They'd wanted to build fliers in the manufactory. He'd gotten through the pathetic security at the bankrupt facility and had figured out the problem in only an hour. Another piece of the plan fell into place.

He went about making sure there was no physical evidence to link him to this place. After years of dealing with highly advanced Galactic Union tech, it wasn't hard. As he worked he thought about the leader of this gang, the TVG. Last night he'd verified who it was. No one knew the leader's real name...but Zeke did.

Zeke shouldered his bag and headed down the back stairs. An old Dodge pickup truck sat there idling, a curl of smoke from the exhaust.

"Hey Zeke," the driver said.

"Hey," he said as he slung the bag into the cab and climbed up. The Binnig mechanic, Joe Brown, had proved quite helpful, and amazingly willing to break the law. "What's the word?"

"Came in today." Zeke looked at him hard. "No kidding. Boss messaged me." Zeke grunted, but Joe saw the little grin. "Shit's gonna hit the fan, ain't it?" The grin got bigger. "Let me help."

"No," Zeke said.

"I can drive a—"

"I said 'no,'" Zeke said, glaring at the kid, "and I meant, 'no.'"

"Cool, fine," Joe said and put the wheezing truck into gear. It was made over a century before and preferred actual gasoline, not the synthetic alcohol mix. As the kid drove, Zeke slid the mask over his face. He was Asian today. He had been black yesterday, and if needed, he would be American Indian tomorrow. The masks cost almost a thousand US each, but were well worth it, as they were undetectable by the tech the local cops were using.

The masks were so good he'd used one two days ago to masquerade as a Binnig deliveryman to drop off a package at the police loading dock. He did it late at night, when only the automatic systems were there to greet him. The mask's synthetic retinal pattern defeated the sentry, and he'd delivered the box. He grinned when he thought about the look on the receiving clerk's face when the man came in the next day to find an empty box. Of course, it wasn't empty when Zeke dropped it there.

The drive only took ten minutes. Like most days, there was only minimal traffic on the Chattanooga streets. Most people were on foot or on bikes, even with snow flurries in the forecast. There were a few barely-functioning gas-powered vehicles, like Joe's ancient Dodge, and a few more electric vehicles, all of Human design, humming along. They passed three police cruisers. None turned in pursuit, so the mask did its job. Halfway there, Joe pointed up to where a pair of police fliers were patrolling a route over the dying city.

"More of those every day," Joe said. "You kicked over a hornet's nest." Zeke just nodded. He fished a cigar out of his pocket as they approached the Binnig dealership, and Joe parked behind it, next to the shop door. Zeke climbed out and lit the cigar. It was only two steps from the truck to the door, which opened as he approached.

"Zeke-san," the man who was holding the door for him said, bowing slightly.

"Tokuzumi-san," Zeke said, bowing in return as he entered. The other man had learned to tolerate the cigars. "It is here?"

"Hai! Arrived late last night." Joe came in, locked the door, and led the way into the pre-delivery service shop. Crates were lined up along the far wall, opposite the big roll-up delivery door. They all bore the logo of Binnig Industries and had "Industrial Robotics" painted on their grey plastic sides. "I am amazed you could arrange this," Tokuzumi said when they reached a crate next to a work bench.

"Galactic Union credits can do amazing things," he said. "Can I see?" Tokuzumi gave a little bow again, and he worked the release, pivoting the plastic door of the container upwards. The object inside just barely fit, with heavy padding on all sides so it couldn't move. A note was taped to the front. The Japanese technician took the note and handed it to Zeke.

"Zeke, I hope this does the trick. Best I could arrange on short notice. Serial number is null, so it can't be traced. Could only send it bare, just as you see. But I suspect you can do a lot with it, just the same. For old times." It was signed Sansar Enkh, with a stylized "GH" written next to the signature.

Zeke spent a few minutes removing the packaging and examining what his credits had purchased. It was both better than, and less than, what he'd hoped.

"And your intentions with this, Zeke-san?" Tokuzumi asked.

"I think you know full well what my intensions are."

The man looked at him critically. "You understand my concern," Tokuzumi said; "my business, my company's business here is at stake. Binnig's reputation as well. It is a risk."

"It is," Zeke acknowledged. "Were the extra parts in the other containers?" He gestured at the other identical boxes.

"Yes," Tokuzumi confirmed, "enough to build a robot that would fit in here. A piece in each one so the weight would not be noticed." Zeke nodded. "I would guess it is not possible then to stop you."

"No," Zeke said, "and frankly, you shouldn't want to."

They backed the pickup into the shop, loaded the cargo into the back, and covered it with old tarps Zeke had found in alleys over the last two weeks. It would look like just another beater carrying trash. When they were done, he went to his duffel bag and gave Tokuzumi a five thousand credit chit.

"For your risk." The man bowed and accepted it. It was more than he'd promised, because Tokuzumi didn't know about the delivery Zeke made in the man's delivery truck. He'd need it for lawyers, if things didn't work out. Zeke next held out a thousand-credit chit for Joe. "For the truck." Joe laughed and shook his head.

"Shit, I done took enough of your money. That truck ain't worth fifty credits." He held out his hand. "Good luck." Zeke shook it and left, tossing the cigar into the ditch and putting the mask back on as he got in the truck. They watched him pull out in the street before closing the roll-up door.

* * *

Zeke spent the afternoon working. He stopped at the anonymously-rented storage unit where he'd had his personal container shipped. The modular facility had installed the unit in an empty space, and it opened to his retinal scan. There wasn't room inside for the truck, so he backed the bed of the truck inside to work. It was starting to get dark when he finished and pulled out of the storage facility. He dropped his cargo at the planned location and headed downtown.

He parked the truck two blocks from the police station in an alley, but within view of the big, modern building. He pulled a shade over the windows that mimicked an empty truck and started opening boxes. As the sun was setting, he was ready.

Zeke didn't use his pinplants—implants in his brain that allowed him to access computer networks and store data—very much. He'd never liked them, but they were a requirement of service with the Golden Horde, so he'd gotten them. The problem was his expertise with them wasn't the best, and inside the Aethernet, you were vulnerable. The police usually had the best hackers in their employ. This time, though, he was ready.

He loaded a high-end scrambler program and accessed a local node of the Aethernet. The program informed him he had about ten minutes. More than enough. He used the pinplants to dial a number.

"Chief Forrest," the voice answered.

"Chief, my name is Zeke." There was a pause.

"Why do I care who you are? And how did you get this number?"

"You care because your officers only know me by the name Randy Snyder, and I got it from a friend."

"You're a wanted man," Forrest said. "You killed four citizens, and maimed two others."

"Technically, they killed themselves," Zeke pointed out. "I did maim those two, though. All me." The line was silent for a moment. "I know you're attempting to trace this, so let's be brief."

"Sure, what's on your mind?"

"How long has TVG been paying your mortgage, Captain?"

"Fuck you," the man growled.

Zeke laughed. "I watched your men pay the punks who attacked me. I recorded it on my pinplants. I've been documenting your men as they helped the punks take extortion, operate whore houses, run drugs—both domestic and alien—and generally be anything except police. You use minor gangs for wetwork like you tried on me in the diner, and you take coin from the TVG boss directly to facilitate his robbing, stealing, and general asshattery all over the region."

"You're one dead motherfucker," Chief Forrest yelled into his phone.

Zeke laughed again as he heard the policeman snarling impotently on the other end. "Tell you what; I'm going to oblige you. I'm coming through your front door in ten minutes, and I'm going to personally shoot your fat ass dead. How's that?" he cut the connection and burned the account he'd used. The scrambler program said he'd had less than a minute. His heart was racing; that was exciting! He pulled the shade back and waited, checking his watch. The first police cars came screaming down Market Street two minutes later, and in another minute, they were racing in from all directions. As the ten minutes was almost up, Zeke nodded and turned to the array of slate computers he'd set up in the passenger seat. He checked a connection and activated the link. In the police building, a PA began to blare Zeke's voice.

"Attention Chattanooga Police Department. Your chief has been taking thieves' and murderers' money for years. Many of you know this and endorse it. You are no better than he, and many of you are worse. You have one minute to leave if you don't want to suffer the same fate as Chief Forrest." He severed the connection and burned that Aethernet account too.

There followed a minute while several dozen officers either ran or walked quickly from the building. A small number of civilians working late ran as well. Zeke could see more than a few react to insults hurled at them as they went by officers standing in the doorways with armor and assault rifles. Then that minute passed.

"Time's up, Chief," Zeke said, and turned to another slate with two buttons on it. One said "ARM;" he touched it. 20 little red indicators turned to green, and the next button went from amber to red: "FIRE." He pressed it.

The box he'd delivered contained 20 Zuul-manufactured demo drones. They were designed to spread out, head down in a building, locate structural points, and hide. He'd loaded each one with a five-pound block of K2. The blast was substantial, but tamped by the drones. He'd done that to reduce the risk of injury to any civilians nearby. The result was a near-perfect controlled demolition. After a series of shudders, the Chief looked up in confusion a second before the 12-story police headquarters came down in a continuous column of death and destruction.

Zeke started the truck and pulled into the street. As he turned he could see the former 12-story building was now less than two. There would be precious few survivors. He nodded as he watched the cloud spreading in the rearview mirror.

* * *

During the drive back across town, he smoked a cigar with the window down. He didn't worry about the police. Zeke estimated that out of a department of 200, fewer than 20 remained. But they were the 20 worth saving. A small part of him felt remorse for the good ones who'd died in the building, either too afraid to run or just too stupid.

He reached his destination and slowed the truck as he approached what had been an exclusive neighborhood when he grew up. Lookout Mountain overlooked the city and was once where the most expensive houses stood. If you looked up from the city center, the neighborhood atop Lookout Mountain dominated the skyline. In the mid-21st century it had been dominated by cheap, high-rise apartment buildings. Little more than a slum now, there was still one huge mansion on Scenic Highway, surrounded by 20 acres, which he was going to visit.

The truck wheezed its way up the Ochs Highway, approaching the tabletop-type mountain. Once a scenic country drive, it had been lined with mini malls and convenience stores before the economy collapsed after first contact. As the climb became steep, the road switched back and split. One way went to the top of the mountain, the other became Red Riding Hood Trail and sloped down into nearby Georgia. It was that corner that dealt him his first setback.

A couple of junk cars were across the road that hadn't been there earlier in the afternoon. Zeke brought the old pickup to a jerky stop and eyed the cars suspiciously. Sure enough, a half dozen men came from either side, having hidden behind several dumpsters and a half-melted bus stop shelter.

"Whatcha want up here, old man?" the first to arrive asked.

"Wanna score some sparkle," Zeke answered, adding just a touch of twitchiness to his manner. A working streetlight was only a dozen feet up the road, and he shied away from its glow to add to his performance. "You got you some sparkle?"

"I look like a fuckin sparkler?" the punk asked and took a half-hearted swipe at Zeke, who ducked without making it look like an overly hard effort.

"S-sorry," Zeke pleaded. "C-can I go up the mountain and get some?" The others were all holding back, not seeing anything strange. They'd obviously set the roadblock when Zeke blew up the police station. This was a delay he couldn't afford. When the leader of the TVG realized their protector, Chief Forrest was no longer drawing breath, they'd pull back into their rabbit holes and fortify. One of the others suddenly spoke up.

"Hey!" he barked, "That's him!" Zeke spat when he recognized the kid from the diner. He'd only shaved off a few pieces of skin and left the kid alive. Now he regretted that decision.

"Sorry," he said to the one who'd walked up to his door as Zeke pulled the trigger. The .54 caliber Bulldog revolver's roar was muffled because he'd fired it up against the door from the inside. The round passed through the inside panel, the window, the outside wall, and still had enough energy to blow a dinner plate-sized chunk out of the punk's chest cavity. He looked surprised as he fell.

Zeke raised the gun and blew the head off the one he'd spared weeks ago in the diner. He didn't want him explaining anything to the other scumbags before Zeke's job was done. He hit the gas. The old truck shuddered and roared forward with a squelch of tires on damp asphalt. There was a disorganized roar of various pistols, rifles, and shotguns that tore into the body, cab, and fenders of the truck.

He counted on their incompetence to get him through it, and it was just that sort of gamble that usually bit him in the ass. A .32 caliber full metal jacket round fired from a 150-year-old pistol aimed at the truck's rear tire passed through the rear window and took off most of Zeke's right ear.

"Son of a bitch," he snarled. He aimed at the trunk of the smaller of the two junk cars blocking the road, and just before impact snatched up a grenade from the passenger seat and pitched it out the shattered left window, back toward the now-running gang members.

The truck tore through the more modern and lighter junk car, and the grenade exploded, killing several gang members and giving his now dangerously-sputtering truck a little kick in the ass. A few more rounds bounced off the truck, but he'd taken the fight out of the group.

With the last of the truck's life, he reached the top of the mountain road, turned into an alley between two decaying low-rent high rises, and let it die. He was done with it, anyway. He scooped up his shoulder bag, fished a sterile wound dressing out, and pressed it to his face. That stung. Then grabbed a grenade off the seat, pulled the pin, and dropped it back in. He was a block away before the truck went up in a ball of fire.

* * *

The mansion was the only well-lit building in the area. Bad move, Zeke thought as he stomped in that direction. Might as well advertise! As he moved through the trees, he could already see light armored cars and hundreds of gang members. They buzzed around like angry hornets. Between the demolition of the police station, the attack on their sentries, and the explosion of Zeke's truck, their leader rightly realized trouble was coming. They just didn't know how big.

The first gang member who heard something took a long time yelling to get the others' attention. By the time he had it, they didn't need his help to see it. Eight feet of carbon/metal alloy war machine strode out of the woods and stopped just outside the eight-foot reinforced chain link fence. They all fell into a stunned silence.

"Holy shit," someone said.

Zeke brought the CASPer's PA speakers to life, and his voice boomed. "I'm here to talk to your leader," he said. "We can do this the easy way or the hard way." He saw the parapets of the four-story mansion begin to fill with gang members armed with all kinds of weapons imaginable. The interior Tri-V on his combat suit strained as it classified levels of threat from zero for nothing, to ten for deadly. It marked a half dozen as five, the highest present. All were on the armored personnel carriers. "What's it going to be?"

Fifty feet away an older gang banger, a rare thing for that profession, laughed and raised his ancient AK-47. A string of 'pings' sounded as the 7.62 rounds bounced harmlessly off the chassis. A half-second later, 100 guns were roaring, and Zeke thought it sounded like the inside of a tin shed during a downpour.

"Guess it's the easy way," he said, and flicked off the loud speakers.

More than 100 targets were identified, most firing or trying to fire weapons at him. The scene looked like an old WWII epic he'd seen as a kid. He leaned forward, the haptic suit he wore translating the actions into movements, and the huge suit walked into, and through the reinforced fence.

The Mk 8 CASPer his old friend in the Golden Horde had broken a dozen laws to send him didn't have any of the weapons he'd used in the merc company; that would have been far more difficult to send. So Zeke had dug into the container of purloined weapons he'd smuggled back from off world and improvised.

On his right arm was a miniature chain gun. Zeke triggered it and played the weapon around the house's perimeter, mowing down dozens and sending even more running for their lives. A .50 caliber Browning in one of the armored cars opened up, one of the threat level five weapons, and the rounds walked in toward him. Zeke hefted the Oogar-manufactured recoilless rifle and felt the shudder through his suit; the armored car was nearly torn in half.

He sidestepped more .50 caliber fire, reloaded the recoilless, and fired again, then three more times. The armored cars were done. A Molotov cocktail soared over his head. That wouldn't do, the suit could be overloaded or shorted out from burning gasoline. He cleaned out the entire area where the throw came from, its flight trajectory analyzed and given to him by the suit's computer.

Heavy fire came from the roof. He marked the roofline with his eyes, dropped the now empty recoilless, and raised his left arm. The medium crew-served chemical laser whined as it fired, and he worked the pulse across the top of the house. Architectural features were sliced off, wood caught fire, and several heads rolled down the roof. He reloaded the laser with the only other charge he had for it and noted he was going to run out of ammo.

"I don't have time for this shit." He used the suit's scanners on the house. Only one room, top floor towards the city, had people not moving around. "That'll be him," he said. Zeke triggered the CAS-Per's jumpjets. The half-ton steel war machine roared into the air and angled toward the house. He dropped a half a dozen K bombs, smallish grenades, into the courtyard below, to keep them busy.

Zeke cut the jets, and the suit hit the house like a wrecking ball, smashing through roofing, metal reinforcement, and beams. He kissed the jumpjet controls slightly, just to be sure he didn't over penetrate, bent his legs slightly, and came down with a thunderous crash in the boss's office. He might have gone through that floor too if he hadn't first roasted, then crushed a poorly-placed guard.

The room held a dozen of the boss' most elite people, armed predominantly with pistols and rifles, but a couple had the first lasers he'd seen. With reflexes born from years of combat in the CASPers, he scanned the room. The man behind the desk was huge, muscled, scarred, and looked scared to death. The rest were a motley collection of rogues and thugs, until he came to one who looked surprised, but not freaked out. *Bingo*, he said.

The temporary shock caused by the arrival of a thousand-pound suit of combat armor was broken, and a dozen guns started to come up.

"Not so fast, kids," Zeke said and aimed the laser at the man he'd picked out of the crowd. "Twitch and he's toast. Literally."

"Who gives a fuck about him?" The man behind the desk stammered.

"You do, because that's your boss."

"B-bullshit!"

"Fine, I'll just waste him then." Zeke leveled the laser at the man's Adam's apple.

"Stop," the man ordered. "Okay," he said and slowly raised his hands. "If you wanted me dead, I'd be dead."

"Boss," the thug behind the desk said.

"No, Hoss, it's cool."

"Yeah, Hoss," Zeke said, "get the others and leave." The big guy looked half-panicked and glanced imploringly at his leader.

"Do as he says," the boss said. He looked scared, but not terrified. Good, Zeke thought. He slowly walked around behind the desk, the CASPer's laser emitter tracking him with deadly precision, and put a hand on Hoss' shoulder. The leader was about 30, naturally thin, and had intelligent eyes. He considered the visage of a merc combat suit in his inner sanctum, and laughed. "Go on," he said again to Hoss, who slowly rose.

"Smart man," Zeke said. "Go. I'm not going to kill him, yet. We need to talk."

"Whatever you say, boss," Hoss said. Despite his obvious fear of the huge combat suit, he glared daggers at Zeke as he left.

With reluctance, the surviving guards moved out the door. Zeke watched in the suit's displays, and could see the hall was already jammed with dozens of gang members. The doors slowly closed. They were alone. With a pop and a hiss, the cockpit of the CASPer released and rose in two pieces to reveal Zeke inside, a bloody bandage on the side of his face. The boss looked curious and surprised.

"They told me you was an old man."

Zeke nodded. "Yes, I'm old," he said, "and disappointed."

"Huh?"

"I'm disappointed in you," Zeke said. "I'd expect better from my kin."

"What? Who *are* you?" the boss demanded.

"Ezekiel Avander," Zeke said; "Dr. Ezekiel Avander." The boss's jaw fell open, and he openly gawked. "Yeah," Zeke said, lowering his head and looking at the man from under bushy eyebrows. He pointed with the suit's arm at a portrait on the wall. It was Zeke, his wife Molly, and their daughter Jennifer.

"Ezekiel died in those first contracts, 90 years ago!" the boss complained.

"I went on the *alpha* contracts," Zeke corrected, "and *almost* didn't come back. I was a slave for 70 years, then a merc for 20. I was going to come back and retire, but you changed my mind." The boss looked at him in a swirling mixture of amazement, anger, and confusion. "I honestly expected better of my grandson, Zebedia Avander. Official report was you died. Took me a while to put the pieces together."

"They call me Zeb now," the boss said. Zeke shrugged. He'd been a little flattered when he found out his daughter carried on the family tradition of Z-named boys. Zeb looked at the portrait and back at Zeke. There was little doubt. The man in the CASPer was older, but still obviously the same man. "How?"

"The HecSha who held me were really good at nanites and nano-biology." He shrugged again. "I was already a physician and a biologist. Between making tailored nanovirus for them, I tinkered. I guess you can say I found the fountain of youth."

"So now what?" Zeb asked spreading his arms wide in surrender. "Grandpa?"

"Zeke is fine," he said; "it's best if most don't know who I am." Zeb looked surprised when Zeke disconnected his haptic leads and crawled out of the suit. "I think it best that TVG come under new management."

Zeb looked gob-smacked. In minutes he'd gone from leader of a huge gang to displaced by a long gone dead ancestor? "What?"

"You haven't been thinking like an Avander," Zeke said. "This small-time shit is foolish. You got the organization and some man-power, but you're going about it all wrong. So, I'm taking over."

"What makes you think I'll just step aside?"

"I don't want to kill my own blood," Zeke said, stepping up to within inches of his grandson, "but don't think I won't." He picked up a small marble statue of a naked woman from the desk and crushed it in his cybernetic hand like it was an empty pop can. "Do I make myself clear, sonny?" He blew the dust from his hand and looked at the man.

"Perfectly," Zeb said, looking away.

"Good." Zeke pushed past his grandson and took a seat in the ornate office chair. It was the same chair he'd last sat in almost 90 years ago. It felt good. He drew out a cigar, his last one on hand, fished the trusty plasma lighter from a pocket, and brought the stogie to life. Zeb looked askance at the growing cloud of smoke. He appeared despondent and resigned. You don't run even a small criminal empire without being able to read the writing on the wall.

"So now what Gran-, I mean Zeke? You gonna just toss me aside?"

"Don't be stupid." Zeke chuckled and blew a smoke ring. "You're a great organizer. You turned that bunch of scum into a group who'd fight and die for you." Blood dripped from his ruined ear onto his shoulder, and he sighed. "No, Zeb, I'm going to run the show, but I have big plans for you. Never been in jail, right?" Zeb looked confused, but shook his head. "Excellent. Besides, I'm 132 years old. I don't want to do this forever, but my talent is obviously needed. You help me run my plan, get things going, and you take over in 10, 20 years, tops."

"That's a long damned time," Zeb complained.

"You don't think I'm going to let my only blood die of old age, do you?" The younger man's eyes widened when he realized what Zeke was offering. "Yeah, exactly. Do we have a deal?" He stood and held out his hand. Zeb considered for almost a second before he took it. The younger man got the first look at his grandfather's intricate cybernetic hand and marveled at it. "Now the plan." Zeke spent a minute explaining what he had in mind. Zeb's bemused look slowly changed to interest, and then a huge smile crossed his face.

"You know how much all that will cost?"

"A lot," Zeke admitted. "We'll have to expand your network, carefully, and be much more selective. Plenty of money to be made. Bring me that bag?" he said and pointed at the open CASPer. Zeb did as he was told. "This will get us started," he said and took out a stack of six one-million credit chits. Zeb shook his head in amazement, and Zeke beamed. "Golden Horde pays good. Okay, call the boys in and let's talk."

"What are we going to tell them?" Zeb asked.

"We're going to tell them the truth," Zeke said. "We're going legit. We've got the one thing that people will pay any amount of money for, and that they will come from the ends of the Earth to obtain. Not only that, but we're the sole supplier—we can name our own price."

"I don't get it," Zeb said, shaking his head. "There's nothing here; this place is a shit hole. What could we possible give people that would make them want to come here?"

"We can give them the one thing everybody wants more of." Zeke smiled. "We can give them life. And we'll sell it to them, for a price." Zeb looked confused, but slowly a smile spread across his face as Zeke puffed on his cigar and quietly chuckled.

Epilogue

A New Day

Zeke stood on the balcony of his family estate and enjoyed the renewed view of Chattanooga. The two high-rise buildings between Avander Estates and the city had been demolished the month prior. Most of the mountain's ruined and decaying buildings were going, one at a time.

In the city below, the new police station was going up. After the state investigation was concluded, and the blame placed on international drug traffickers thanks to anonymous informers, a new chief had been elected. The candidacy was unopposed, and Zeke had been sure of that. Chief Zeb Avander was overseeing the rebuilding of the city police department. It was an important job as the manufactory was opening this month. A lot of his money had gone into it; trying to get the alien pharmaceuticals manufactory to make fliers had almost ruined it. By this time next month, though, it would be turning out the first age-extending nanite treatments from Avander Pharmaceuticals, a division of Avander Intergalactic.

Zeke was happy with the progress he'd made, and continued to make. Businesses all over the Tennessee valley were delighted to pay Avander Protective Services to keep the gangs under control. And Avander Transportation was paying for the new maglev station which was going up on the ruins of the old Chattanooga Choo-Choo station. Yes, things were coming along fine. But he had to get back to work. The governor of the state was due that afternoon. Zeke felt it was high time for Tennessee to have a Starport, and he knew right where to put it. Puffing a cigar, he went inside and closed the doors.

# # # # #

Mark's Introduction to:

Breach of Contract

by Terry Mixon

Terry is one of those extraordinary authors who, like myself, decided that going our own way with self-pub and small press was more attractive than the traditional presses. His efforts have been rewarded with multiple bestselling mil-sf and urban fantasy stories. His series include the Empire of Bones Saga and the Humanity Unlimited Saga. A former non-commissioned U.S. Army officer, Terry also worked at NASA's Mission Control Center at the Johnson Space Center for space shuttle and ISS mission support. What hasn't Terry done? Why, write a story in the Four Horsemen universe. That is, until now.

Terry's story, "Breach of Contract," follows the possible ramifications of not playing fair in a universe where someone can legally hunt you down for revenge. The Four Horsemen universe might appear like a Wild West town, with no laws or protectors, but they're out there. They just might not do what you expect them to, even if you're the good guys.

Find out more about Terry at http://www.terrymixon.com/.

BREACH OF CONTRACT
by Terry Mixon

Anton Kolenchenko slipped into his tiny passenger cabin and immediately regretted not announcing himself. He'd meant to teach his younger partner a lesson about keeping her guard up at all times. Instead, she'd taught him about the importance of knocking.

Jackie O'Hara had just stepped out of the compact shower in the corner. The morphagenic tattoo of a Japanese dragon she'd commissioned—over his strong objections—when she'd graduated high school currently sat on her left buttock. The beast seemed to be leering at him.

The petite girl turned toward him and smiled without a hint of self-consciousness as she wrapped a towel around herself. The cloth did nothing to disguise her slender beauty. Perversely, it enhanced her innate sexuality.

He sternly reminded his body that she was completely off limits.

"There you are," she said cheerfully, seemingly unconcerned that he'd seen every inch of her naked body. "I was wondering where you'd gotten off to."

"I apologize for my discourtesy," he said contritely. "I should have knocked."

The short redhead shot him a quizzical look as she wrapped a second towel around her hair. "It's your cabin, too. Why would you knock?"

He gestured toward the shower. "In Russia, it's considered rude to stare at a bathing woman."

"You were staring? That's sweet."

He felt his face reddening even further and decided to stop digging a hole for himself.

She gave him a wide smile as she sat at the compact vanity. He wasn't quite certain the aliens who'd designed the interstellar cruise liner had envisioned the shelf as such, but it worked well enough with the small mirror his partner had added.

"You should know by now I have zero body modesty," Jackie said as she started putting her makeup on. "I grew up in a nudist colony, for God's sake. Having men ogle me isn't one of my hang-ups.

"Besides, you used to be an FSB agent. Didn't you guys spy on everyone? Surely you've seen plenty of naked women before."

"More than I can easily remember, but I hadn't known them since before they could walk," he grumbled as he plopped down on his bed. "You take great joy in tormenting me, don't you?"

Their small cabin had the equivalent of two twin-sized beds, a shower, and just enough storage to hold their clothing for a week. As huge as the ship was, you had to pay through the nose for even the smallest cabin. Their cover identities didn't allow for any extravagances.

"I kinda do," she said slyly. "I considered squealing 'Uncle Anton' and running over for a big hug. Should I put my hair up in pigtails and dig out the lollypops?"

He blanched. "Don't you dare!"

She laughed, her voice like the soft tinkling of bells. "You are so easy, Anton! I promise I'll stop teasing you. For now. I assume you have some new information. Spill."

Relieved to move past the awkward situation, he got down to business. "The party is still on for tonight, and our mole managed to get us on the approved guest list. I just picked up the chip with our invitation."

Jackie's grin turned cold. "Yes! Now we'll get the bastard!"

While understandable, her enthusiasm still chilled him. There was far too great an opportunity for this to go horribly wrong. If the target caught them, the consequences would be extreme. He accepted the risk for himself, but he was determined to protect Jackie.

"Don't get carried away," he said repressively. "You can't allow your rage to blind you. This operation is critical to our overall success. We must approach it cautiously and methodically. We won't get a second chance."

She nodded, smothering her enthusiasm. "You don't have to tell me that. I know this is the best chance I'll ever have to get the bastards that killed my father. Believe me, I'm the most dedicated person for this job. That's why you hired me, isn't it?"

"Technically, I didn't hire you. As Sean's heir, you inherited your father's ownership stake in the Dire Wolves. Your share is equal to mine, though I have managerial control. That's what paid for those fancy pinplants of yours. And if anything got you selected for this mission, it's them."

Not that the defunct mercenary company possessed anything other than its name. They'd lost all their assets when Sean and the rest died on their last mission.

Still, the company name had opened doors for him to perform contract intelligence work for other mercenary companies. Half that income had gone to his orphaned partner's daughter.

Jackie took a deep breath and nodded. "And those pinplants will make the bastards pay for what they did to the Dire Wolves and my father. You can count on that. I've been working toward this my entire life. I won't screw it up."

When she spoke like this—so quietly angry—she sounded just like her dead father. Anton missed his old friend so very much, even after two decades.

But he needed to thread a narrow path between taking the revenge they both thirsted for and putting the young woman he deeply cared about in deadly peril.

Yestrellian Corporation had already proven themselves to be treacherous. If the two of them made a mistake today, they'd pay with their lives.

Jackie reached out and took his hands in hers. "I'm ready for this, Anton. I won't let you down."

"I know you won't," he sighed. "I just can't help worrying."

"Who is it that always tells me the best cure for worry is to plan for every possible contingency? Let's go over everything one last time."

"I trained you right," he said with a chuckle. "The plan is simple, though the details might end up being complex.

"Nedget Xarbon is the chief executive officer at Yestrellian. He just finished negotiating a very lucrative contract this morning and is in a celebratory mood. As is his habit, he's publicizing the deal by inviting all the notables on the liner to a party. I suspect the real reason he does this is to make certain everyone knows how rich and successful he and his company are. Our mole has access to the guest list and has inserted our cover identities."

Jackie nodded. "And it's my job to be arm candy while we get close enough to the bastard to steal his login credentials from the chip he uses to identify himself to the company computers."

Anton nodded. "Exactly. Once we have that, our mole can access the corporate computer systems above his clearance level and get all the data about the mission Yestrellian hired the Dire Wolves for.

"I hope he'll find enough evidence of wrongdoing to get the Mercenary Guild to revive the contract and invoke the penalties for breach of contract."

"The Galactic Union pisses me off," Jackie snarled. "How can they live with themselves when they let rich scumbags kill with impunity?"

He shrugged. "They remind me of what I've read about the old United Nations. Relatively toothless and headed for a rude wakeup call one day. On the plus side, if we get away with this, we'll be able to use the one thing the Union holds dear over our enemies.

"The contract they signed with the Dire Wolves had a clause allowing the investigation of circumstances under which the parties held up their end of the deal. If we can prove intentional wrongdoing, they'll have to pay a significant penalty."

Her eyes glittered. "As if they don't have enough to pay it off. I want to see the bastards bleed."

"And that fills me with dread. There is a ceiling to our success. The Mercenary Guild has a limited ability to punish Yestrellian. Only what is in the contract itself. They can't take action against the people responsible, only the company.

"Still, the penalty would be quite stiff. Such a loss, combined with the public embarrassment, will likely cause the Yestrellian equivalent of the board of directors to fire Xarbon. He won't come out of this unscathed."

"And you call that justice?" she hissed. "He killed my father and all your friends."

"Justice? No. For all the Galactic Union's talk to the contrary, I never expected to see justice; I'll settle for revenge. The target almost certainly betrayed us for money and enhanced reputation. That's what we'll take away from him."

He held onto her hands when she tried to pull away.

"As satisfying as killing someone would be, it would lead to retaliation. I don't want to hear someone killed you in the dead of night and made it look like an accident. They'll know exactly who did this to them. The records at the party will ensure it.

"There almost certainly won't be any retaliation for corporate espionage and taking the contract dispute to the Mercenary Guild. Not any more than trying to harm the two of us financially, anyway. You have to accept that there are limits to what we can accomplish in our quest for revenge."

She nodded slowly, not speaking.

He sighed internally. He knew how headstrong she could be. They'd already been over this ground several times in the extensive planning they'd done for the mission.

Anton had to keep a firm grip on the reins or she'd do something remarkably stupid in her thirst for vengeance. She was all he had left of his old friend.

"I'll get us something to eat while you finish getting dressed," he said after a minute. "I know you're not happy with the situation, but it's for the best. Just this one time, I beg you to trust me."

Jackie closed her eyes and took a deep breath. "I've always trusted you. You win. We'll do it your way."

He wished he believed that to be true, but he was a spy. He knew people lied all the damned time. Even when they thought they were telling the truth.

In the heat of the moment, Jackie might still do something stupid when the aliens that killed her father were right in front of her. He could only pray he'd trained her well enough to pull this off, or they'd both be dead.

* * *

Jackie felt her gut tighten as Anton led her toward the liner's ballroom. Years of planning, hard work, and pain had brought her to this moment. She knew how much was riding on her performance tonight, and it made her stomach churn.

She'd known she'd eventually face the people who'd taken her father away from her, and that she'd have to smile politely while she got the evidence to damn them.

Without looking, she knew Anton was walking beside her in the wide corridor with an expression that said he owned the ship. The man exuded confidence. She only wished she felt half as poised.

Her memories of her father were fuzzy. She'd been very young the last time she'd seen him. It had been at a party he'd thrown for the mercenary company he and Anton had formed.

She had no idea what they'd been celebrating, and it didn't matter. All she knew was her father had been happy. He'd had his arm thrown across Anton's shoulders and was telling him some story with a grin plastered across his face and a drink in his hand.

Anton had been his usual dour self, seemingly uncomfortable with the contact between him and his friend. He'd never been the outgoing member of that pairing. The man had trouble displaying emotion, though she had no trouble reading him.

He'd been there for her when her father had failed to come home. Not openly. Her mother would never have stood for that. The woman's incandescent rage at her husband's loss had focused entirely on Anton Kolenchenko.

So, he'd become a covert part of Jackie's life. Turning up in places her mother would never have expected him to be, teaching her skills that would horrify the woman.

As far as her mother knew, Jackie was off studying computers. She'd never understood her daughter's interest in the devices, but she didn't see any harm in allowing her to pursue their mastery.

That view would have quickly changed if she'd had any inkling of who Jackie's teachers had been. Criminals and hackers, spies and the seamy underbelly of society. Not just Earth society, either. Jackie had worked closely with various aliens spread across the Union, many that were members of various crime syndicates.

No, her mother wouldn't have been happy about that at all.

In addition, Jackie's trust fund had paid for a fortune in implanted computer technology and related hardware that her mother had no idea lurked inside her daughter's head. The gear was cutting edge—even on the galactic stage—and had cost an unspeakable number of credits.

Anton had been working just as hard on his end of the operation. He'd cultivated contacts inside the Yestrellian Corporation over the last two decades. That patience had paid off. They now had a mole positioned close to the chief executive.

With the codes she was going to steal tonight, the mole would be able to use his access to get them every file they needed to ruin Xarbon's life.

It all came down to tonight. She had to come through, no matter what it took.

"Relax," Anton said softly. "You're stalking."

Jackie took a deep breath and let it out slowly. "Sorry. I'm just thinking about everything that brought me to this place."

"Put that all out of your head. Focus on the here and now. We'll deal with the past once this is settled."

Jackie nodded and focused her attention on their surroundings as a distraction.

She thought the journey from their very modest accommodations to the part of the ship reserved for the wealthiest passengers said a lot about the Galactic Union. The bare metal bulkheads had transformed by stages as they passed through areas frequented by ever more well-to-do travelers.

First came the cheap, fake paneling, then real wood, and finally rare woods with subtle highlights that probably cost more than her pinplants.

The worn carpeting gave way to thicker, richer textures before being replaced by polished stone. Jackie had no idea where the builders had found the stuff, but she'd love a kitchen counter made of the pale gray stone with bright streaks of silver. It was gorgeous.

Even in the section of the ship reserved for the most powerful, the area closest to the ballroom stood out. Small alcoves hosted what appeared to be works of art in various mediums. Many well-dressed guests lingered, taking in whatever message the work represented to them.

Then they came around the bend in the corridor, and she saw the ballroom entrance.

She took one final deep breath and made sure her game face was on. This was it.

The wood used for the doors was dark and covered in what appeared to be hand-carved scenes of great celebrations. The detail work had to be amazing close up. Perhaps she'd have a chance to examine it more closely before they left.

Unsurprisingly, Yestrellian security had a significant contingent at the entrance. They were screening all the guests. The overt aspect of that meant checking their identities against the guest list. The more subtle angle was scanning them for weapons of all kinds.

Anton's deft touch on her elbow steered her to one side as they approached the security contingent. That brought them in front of a diminutive being that vaguely resembled a chipmunk. A Flatar. Fur covered his—at least she assumed he was male—exposed arms, neck, and head.

His hands were narrow, and he had exceptionally sharp claws at the tips of his digits. She imagined they would leave some nasty scars in a fight.

While dressed in what looked to be some type of formal clothing, the security man wore a belt containing a pistol and other accoutrements. He wore a translation pendant on his collar.

Anton and she also wore pendants that would translate every bit of alien speech into something comprehensible. It wouldn't do much good to go to a party where you couldn't understand anything.

The guard glanced at her for a moment and then focused his attention on Anton. His attitude toward her seemed dismissive.

"Invitation?"

This was the moment of truth. If everything went according to plan, they'd go right in. If there was something wrong with their entries on the list or something else tipped security off, they'd be making a rather hasty exit and hiding out until departure.

Anton reached into his jacket and pulled out a data chip, which he handed to the guard. The being plugged it into a handheld device, which beeped. He pocketed the chip.

"Enjoy the party," he said as he gestured toward the ballroom door.

Anton inclined his head and led Jackie inside.

The tension that had been building inside her drained away a little. The first potential point of failure was behind them.

Inside, the sheer scale of the room and the varied number of people almost overwhelmed her. The ballroom was larger than any space she'd ever seen before on a ship. No wonder the ship was so large—it would have to be to generate spin-induced gravity for the space. It was far larger than she'd anticipated, and much more richly decked out than anything she was prepared for.

Rich tapestries covered the wall like she'd imagine in an old king's throne room. The stone floor was even more ostentatious here, with veins of what looked like precious metals streaked liberally throughout it. Full-size statuary filled every nook and cranny, and she wondered what they did with it when the ship maneuvered.

The guests were even more impressive. Jackie had traveled through the Galactic Union numerous times while acquiring her hardware and training. She'd rarely seen so many species represented in one place before, and the exceptions had been a couple of bazaars on major worlds.

Those places certainly hadn't included the social classes represented here, either. These people were movers and shakers in their societies. The wealthy and powerful. Just the kind of people the head of an influential corporation would want to associate with.

To her surprise, there actually seemed to be dancing taking place in the ballroom. Of course, the method of that varied per species, but they somehow managed to work with the soft music coming from the live orchestra beside the dance floor. In fact, multiple species made up at least half of the dance pairings.

Anton drew her toward the side of the room containing what looked like a grand buffet. That surprised her, too. With so many different species present, how could they possibly satisfy such a wide variety of potential snackers?

Better yet, would they have anything she would find appealing or even non-toxic?

Her guardian gestured toward a section of one table. "Those are fit for human consumption, but I'd stay away from about half of the offerings. Just because it won't kill you doesn't mean it tastes good."

"Thankfully, I'm not here to have an enjoyable meal," she responded softly. "Though, I suppose I need to get something so that I don't look out of place. What would you suggest?"

He pointed at a silver bowl. "Spread some of the paste on the crackers beside the bowl. I think you'll be pleased with the combination."

She eyed him suspiciously, but took several crackers and covered them with the paste. "What exactly is this?"

"We don't have time to get into that," he said somewhat evasively. "We'll be able to pick up a few glasses of alcohol at the end of the table. Trust me when I say that you'll find the taste to your liking."

Uncertain she fully believed him, she nibbled on a paste-covered cracker and found the flavor was really quite good. It reminded her of seafood, though in a mild sort of fashion. The cracker also had a definite flavor that was similar to fresh bread.

Pleased, she grabbed more of each and followed Anton as he stepped up to what appeared to be an alien sommelier. The being was tall, gaunt, and his skin reminded Jackie of a shark. His smile showed off teeth that did nothing to dispel her impression.

She didn't catch what Anton said, but the man produced a bottle of white wine from Earth. He poured the pale liquid into clear glasses for them.

A sip confirmed it was wine, and that it was exceptionally good. It complemented the flavor of the crackers and the unknown meat, enhancing them even more.

Anton led her to the edge of the room where they could see all the occupants. Jackie had no idea how many were present.

"That's him up at the head of the room," her partner said quietly.

Jackie hadn't needed him to tell her that. She'd spent an inordinate amount of time studying their target. She'd wanted to know everything she could about the man who'd killed her father.

Nedget Xarbon was a Gtandan. The species was somewhat taller than humans on average, with a vaguely porcine appearance. Their noses were very reminiscent of a pig's snout, to her thinking.

It was impossible to see from this distance, but she knew his skin also sported the same sort of texture and hair as a pig. Not a cute little potbelly pig, either. A boar hog. All that was missing were tusks to complete the imagery.

But he wasn't a pig. Well, not physically anyway. Analogies only went so far when concerning alien species.

Xarbon stood inside a small cluster of others. Every once in a while, a new individual or group would make their way to join him while others wandered off.

"How long do we wait before we present ourselves?" she asked as she sipped her wine.

Anton shrugged slightly. "Long enough to allow his security to relax. They're watching us."

Jackie didn't see anyone staring at them, but that hardly meant anything to people with galactic technology.

Her pinplants detected a number of connected devices in the room. Since the ship was still in hyperspace, they weren't attached to GalNet, but that didn't mean they weren't powerful.

She flashed an overlay across her view and immediately saw which guests were connected to the ship's local node, or at least had devices attached to it. That included virtually everyone in the ballroom.

It also included the room's security. No common area of the ship was completely without surveillance, and the ballroom was thoroughly covered. The feeds were encrypted, but what was the use of having all her training if she couldn't tap into them?

She'd already practiced on other areas of the ship and had familiarity with the standard protocols used aboard the liner. The ones protecting the feeds in the ballroom yielded to her in moments.

A dozen hidden cameras watched various areas of the huge room. Some swiveled to provide a wide-angle view, while others targeted subjects of interest.

Trade guild rules allowed public monitoring in the visual spectrum, but were more restrictive of audio. She supposed they figured that if you could see it, it was fair game. Amping up a microphone to listen in on private conversations—even in a public space—was forbidden.

That was why the two of them felt comfortable speaking softly to one another. The low-powered audio jammers they both wore added some reassurance, too.

Someone had indeed targeted them with one of the cameras. Jackie wasn't certain which of the individuals in the room was receiving the telemetry—or even if they were present—but she and Anton had obviously attracted some interest.

"I see what you mean. Do you think it's going to be difficult to introduce ourselves?"

He shook his head. "No. The entire purpose of this gathering is to allow anyone to come bask in his presence. The thinking is that anyone who has enough juice to wrangle an invitation is worthy to make Xarbon's acquaintance. One never knows exactly who will prove useful in future negotiations."

She watched the ebb and flow of people seeking out Xarbon's company. Many stayed only for a few words, but others lingered. Jackie doubted they were exchanging anything more than pleasantries, but there was definitely some kind of subtle power game at play.

Each person stayed as long as they felt they could comfortably do so or, perhaps in a few cases, overstayed. She watched as Xarbon's security team discreetly edged one of the latter out of the cluster gathered around their master.

"I'm going to have to get close to him," she said softly. "The equipment's range is quite limited."

"That shouldn't be a problem. His race shares a variant of humanity's habit of kissing hands. Particularly with females in their society. I'm not certain, but I believe there may be an aspect of domineering involved. Gtandan females seem to have something of a second-class citizenship."

Somehow, that didn't surprise her. Even if it hadn't been a species-specific behavior, she suspected Xarbon was something of a sexist. Their mole inside the organization indicated that the only females on his staff filled subservient positions to similar males.

She'd use that to her advantage, if possible. He'd dismiss her and focus his attention on Anton. So would his security group. That should allow her to get closer than they'd prefer. She'd only need a moment.

The video feed stayed on them longer than she'd anticipated, but it eventually moved on to other guests.

She wondered why they were so interested in the two of them. Was it because they were human? Perhaps his security was worried about the potential aggressiveness of one of the few mercenary species in the Galactic Union.

Only slightly more than three dozen species were warlike enough as a group to provide units to the Mercenary Guild. Humans were not as individually powerful as many of the others, but they'd developed something of a reputation in the last ninety years.

The Dire Wolves had never been widely known—even inside mercenary circles—but Anton had gained enough experience to know how many species felt around a race capable of bringing wholesale destruction down on their heads. He'd shared that with her as part of her education.

True, most humans in galactic society were nonmilitary. That was helpful. It meant Yestrellian security might have a general worry, but no specific concerns about the two of them.

"It's time," Anton said. He set his glass down on a handy table, his wine hardly touched.

Jackie decided her wine glass would make a handy prop. She took one last cracker in her free hand to nibble on as her mentor led them toward the target.

No one raised an eyebrow as they joined the outer circle of people around the target. He was still half a dozen meters away from her. Far too distant for the illegal reader in her right hand to even sense his Yestrellian Corporation identification chip, much less prompt it to disgorge its precious contents.

Its range of response was only a few inches from the target's dominant hand. That prevented anyone from casually cloning it.

When an authorized individual needed to authenticate his or her identity, they could lay their palm on a scanner and it would prompt the chip with a preprogrammed challenge.

One couldn't have employees sending out their classified credentials to everyone they passed while about their daily business. The challenge and response prevented that type of occurrence. Only an actual Yestrellian security system would elicit an answer from the chip.

Luckily, their mole had provided the necessary signal for her own chip to demand his code.

The plan was for Anton to make introductions. He'd be using their false identities, of course. It wouldn't do for Xarbon to know who'd come calling before they had proof of his perfidy. As nauseous as it was, she'd allow the target to snuffle her hand.

That was what Anton had meant when he'd mentioned the aliens had a custom similar to kissing hands. Gtandans used their big noses to sniff people in formal situations. Culturally, that might have something to do with their poor vision. She really didn't know.

At least it was hands and not crotches.

Anton deftly made conversation with those near them as he slowly shepherded her into a closer orbit around the target. She smiled and nodded at appropriate times, using her wine glass as a shield against making some kind of mistake.

Her companion was well versed in interacting with significantly more alien species than she was. He'd had decades of experience and his background as a spy helped him understand all the intricacies of dealing with them.

Finally, the two of them made it to the inner circle. The two closest members of the security team scanned them discreetly. Undoubtedly, others in the cluster surrounding the target had done the same. Otherwise, they'd never have made it so close.

Anton smiled at the target and extended his hand. "It's a pleasure to make your acquaintance, Mister Xarbon. I've been hoping to do so for quite some time. Edgar Richards," he added, giving the executive his false identity.

The alien took Anton's hand into his own and raised it to his snout as he bent slightly at the waist. Jackie thought that looked weird with a guy doing that to a guy, but there was no accounting for aliens.

Xarbon released Anton's hand and smiled at him. "I find it pleasurable to make your acquaintance, as well. What did you say your name was? Richards?

"Odd. I'm certain we've met before, but that's not the identity I seem to recall. Yours is certainly not a scent I'd easily forget. You're not a businessman. You're a mercenary. Why would you lie to me?"

Jackie saw two of the security men tense. Oh shit!

In about two seconds, the goons were going to drag them somewhere and ask lots of inconvenient questions. She'd never have the opportunity to get the code she needed to access the Yestrellian computer systems.

She tossed her wine in the closest guard's face and punched Xarbon in the nose, an action virtually guaranteed to get him to grab her wrist.

He howled in pain, but someone dragged Jackie away before he could grab her hand.

She shrieked in rage and frustration. She had to get to him or everything was going to fall apart!

Two of the guards quickly subdued Anton and pulled him back. Others swarmed in to move everyone away from the Yestrellian executive. The room had gone silent as everyone stared at the confrontation.

Xarbon stared at her as he held a cloth over his bleeding snout. His expression hinted that he thought she'd gone insane, but that didn't stop him from smiling widely.

"This party had been growing progressively more tiresome. I should thank you for providing some much-needed entertainment. What do you think, Jardis?"

"For once, I agree with you completely," the being holding Jackie said. "This should be fascinating."

Jackie finally looked at her captor and was somewhat shocked to see another Gtandan.

"Perhaps I should make introductions," the executive almost crooned. "This is my brother Jardis Xarbon. He and I rarely get a chance to visit, so I was pleased he could join us for this leg of our journey. Senior enforcers with the Peacemaker Guild rarely get vacation time."

He said that last with a tone of relish.

Dread filled her as she stared at the porcine being holding her. If this truly was Xarbon's brother, and he was an enforcer for the Peacemaker Guild, Anton and she were in very deep trouble. Not only had they failed in their mission, but they'd probably be visiting a Gtandan prison in very short order once they arrived.

They were so screwed.

* * *

Their captors hustled Anton and his young partner out of the ballroom and down the corridor. No one spoke as they took a lift to one of the poshest decks on the liner. No doubt, that was where Xarbon was staying.

They trooped their prisoners through an extravagantly ornate suite of rooms and shoved them into what looked like a private office. The guards forced them into chairs built for Gtandan butts. To say the seats were uncomfortable would have been something of an understatement.

Xarbon showed Anton his teeth. "As I recall, you once visited me in the company of a mercenary group I hired a number of years ago."

Anton stared into the executive's eyes unflinchingly. "You expect me to believe you remember my scent after twenty years? That seems a little far-fetched."

"My people's sense of smell is quite formidable, but you are correct that a normal member of my species wouldn't be able to recall meeting you after such a long time.

"I, on the other hand, have what you might call an eidetic sense of smell. I never forget the person associated with a particular scent."

The executive put his hands on his hips and cocked his head. "I'll have to check my records, but I seem to recall your mercenary company failed to accomplish the task I set out for them. Everyone died, I believe. If so, how are you sitting here in front of me?"

"That is an excellent question," Jardis Xarbon said. The translation pendant rendered the enforcer's tone as deep and slow. "And while I cannot wait to hear the answer to it, I have a few questions of my own.

"Starting with, what did you hope to accomplish by confronting my brother? I've examined the scanner readings obtained when you entered the ballroom. You aren't armed. This was not an assassination attempt."

"We came so that my companion could see the man who killed her father," Anton said.

"And who might her father have been?" Xarbon inquired in a polite tone as he looked Jackie over.

"Colonel Sean O'Hara, commanding officer of the Dire Wolves."

The Gtandan seemed to think for a moment before smiling even more widely, showing them his blunt, yellow teeth. "I remember now. I tasked your company to settle a dispute. Not only did they fail to do so, they were so inept that my enemies caught them before they'd even arrived and destroyed them in an ambush.

"Unfortunate, but hardly surprising considering the record most of you humans have fighting competent opponents. I suppose I hold some responsibility for their deaths. I should have hired someone able to actually carry out the mission."

Jackie tried to stand, but a guard shoved her back down into her chair. She glared at the alien. "You betrayed them. I don't know exactly what you did or why, but you killed my father."

Xarbon laughed. "So melodramatic! Oh, this is far more entertaining than I'd imagined! A confrontation to accuse me of terrible crimes you couldn't possibly prove.

"It sounds like something out of an entertainment stream. Only those don't end with the 'heroes' being dragged off to serve time in a Gtandan prison."

The alien glanced at his brother. "I assume the fact they're operating under false identities is a crime of some sort, is it not?"

Anton couldn't think about both of them as Xarbon. He and Jackie had settled on the target's last name as his identifier, so he needed a new way to reference the new member of the target's clan. Perhaps simply Enforcer Jardis.

Enforcer Jardis nodded. "Altering a Universal Account Access Card violates Trade Guild policy. If they have modified their UAACs, they will face significant penalties."

"Then I shall leave them in your hands, dear brother."

"Is that all?" Jackie shrieked. "Are you such a coward that you won't even face me? Fight me, you bastard."

Xarbon had taken a step toward the exit, but stopped. "Why would I possibly do that? That implies some level of guilt. I did nothing wrong. It is you who shall pay a penalty for failure. Much like your father."

"If that sense of smell of yours is so good, you'd better take a good sniff so you'll recognize me when I come for you," the young woman swore. "Which I will."

Anton wasn't certain what she was doing, but it sounded as if she was still trying to achieve their original goal. He couldn't imagine what use the information would be now. By the time they got out of prison, the corporate codes would have undoubtedly changed.

The executive stared at Jackie for a long moment. "I do believe you are the kind of being that might appear in another few decades to aberrantly attempt revenge for an event that was not my fault. Perhaps I *should* remember what you smell like."

He took her hand and jerked it up to his nose, twisting her wrist in an obviously painful manner. Anton watched her grit her teeth in pain and rage, but thought he saw a glimmer of triumph in her eyes. Perhaps she'd gotten his identity code after all.

"Now, I must be off. I undoubtedly have many curious guests. Thank you again for making my party so much more exciting than I had anticipated. I'm certain it will pay dividends for me and my company going forward.

"Good luck to you, and I certainly hope you haven't committed any other crimes my brother will need to tack on additional sentences for. That would be an even worse tragedy for you."

Anton watched the executive and his guards as they left the room. The only person remaining was the brother. The Peacemaker enforcer.

Most people from Earth didn't know much about the Peacemaker Guild. The Galactic Union required a set number of individuals join the guild to assist in enforcing the peace between the various planets and guilds that made up the Union. They often pursued wanted criminals that fled particular worlds, usually for a fee. Perhaps he could use that to Jackie's advantage.

"Enforcer Jardis—if you'll forgive my manner of address in keeping you separate in our minds from your brother—this ill-conceived idea was mine. There is no need to involve the girl.

"She's barely an adult. One blinded by grief. Do we truly need to involve a child in this mess? I'm more than willing to confess everything and accept responsibility."

The Gtandan focused his attention on Anton. "That would depend upon the full tally of your transgressions. I'm not without compassion. You've made some serious charges against my brother. Do you have any proof or is this merely wild speculation?"

Anton suspected he and Jackie would disappear if he said he had such evidence. Blood was thicker than water. The Peacemaker Guild might be the Galactic Union's equivalent of a national police force, but this was the target's brother.

"No," he admitted.

"Yes!" Jackie hissed.

"Be quiet!" Anton told her firmly.

The alien turned his attention to Jackie. "No. I want to hear what she has to say. If you have proof, it is your duty as a citizen of the Galactic Union to provide it to me."

"You'll forgive me if this sounds indelicate, but he's your brother," Anton said. "What would keep you from making us disappear and any evidence with us?"

The Gtandan showed Anton his teeth. "To begin with, there's my oath. I don't know what you've heard about the Peacemaker Guild, but we take a very dim view of those who put anything else before their oaths to enforce the peace. If my brother has done something that violates Merc Guild policy, it could create a dispute that upsets the peace.

"I've heard how many humans view the Union. Corrupt and free-for-all. Where someone can pay enough money to get away with virtually anything. You've probably also heard that the Peacemaker Guild pursues individuals based on payments made by their accusers, have you not?"

Anton nodded. "That more or less matches the stories I've heard."

"I suspected as much. I'll even grant you that the stories are true, to a degree. But in the law, degrees are critically important."

The alien turned his attention to Jackie again. "Those who swear out charges against someone do put up a fee to pay for the criminal's capture and return. What you might be unaware of is that we can and do release the charged individual if we discover the charges are untrue. I might add that those swearing out false warrants usually find themselves in significant trouble.

"As I said, the Peacemaker Guild ensures the peace is kept. That's why each world provides a set number of people to join our ranks. No one species dominates our guild, so we must all work as one to hold the Union together."

He turned to Anton. "As to your other charge, yes, Nedget is my brother. That doesn't mean he won't be held accountable if he's done something wrong. If you have proof he violated his Merc Guild-sanctioned contract, there will be consequences.

"I believe this is the point in our conversation where you either produce your proof or recant your accusation. If you want to see justice done, if you want me to show mercy to your young associate, lay your evidence before me now."

Anton sighed and slumped a little. "We hadn't gotten our hands on the proof yet. We were going to acquire it on Gtandus. I know your brother keeps records of every business dealing in the Yestrellian corporate computers.

"I paid someone to install a chip reader in my companion's hand. It's designed to capture your brother's corporate security response.

"My intent was to gain access to the Yestrellian headquarters building, obtain a copy of any evidence, and bring a complaint against him with the Mercenary Guild for breach of contract."

The Gtandan enforcer seemed to consider his words as he looked Jackie over. "That explains the little charade about him remembering your scent. Very clever."

He looked at her a moment longer and then returned his gaze to Anton.

"Leaving aside the fact that you have just admitted to another very serious crime, why would you only seek to have the Mercenary Guild find his company in breach of contract?

"While that would be undoubtedly painful for his company, and likely disastrous for his career, Nedget would still be free."

Anton shrugged. "We humans have learned to keep our expectations low when it comes to the Galactic Union. Most of you see us as savages and use the Union's laws against us.

"Hell, I almost had to cut off my right arm to get a clause into the contract that allowed the Dire Wolves to investigate our employer if the mission went badly."

The enforcer nodded. "Negotiating effective contracts can be challenging. Yet, you say you negotiated a clause allowing you to investigate the conditions that resulted in the adverse termination of your contract? How was it phrased, precisely?"

"That hardly matters," Anton growled. "Yestrellian declined to give us any access to the records on their system, and the planetary courts refused to enforce the clause. I'm sure that was another case of money doing the talking."

The Gtandan grunted. "I can see where that would be an obstacle. It's unfortunate your plans this evening didn't work out as you had hoped. You're actually closer to a potential solution than you realized.

"My brother never knows what information he will require during a negotiation. He keeps a complete set of his corporate files with him on all trips off world. It's on a slate in his room as we speak." The alien gestured toward the door.

"I have no idea how you would have gotten into his suite, but I suppose you might've been resourceful enough to make that happen. Then, of course, you'd have had to defeat the security system on his room to gain access to his slate."

Enforcer Jardis looked steadily at Anton. "It's a shame there's no proof of my brother's wrongdoing. I don't particularly like him all that much. He's been something of an ass to me my entire life."

After a long moment, the alien stepped toward the door. "I'm going to question him more closely about the events in question. Unfortunately, I expect he'll completely deny everything and will want me to follow up on your UAAC violations. As I mentioned, the penalties are quite severe.

"Since my brother has guards outside this suite and his personal rooms are secure, I feel no qualms about leaving you here while I investigate further. When I return, you should be prepared to deal with the consequences of tonight's events."

* * *

Jackie shifted her eyes to Anton as soon as the door closed behind the alien. "What's happening? What's he doing?"

Her partner shrugged. "He's playing some kind of game. He either wants to catch us in the act of breaking into his brother's slate, or he wants us to stew while we wait for him to return and arrest us."

She surged to her feet. "We've got to get the information before he gets back! If he's going to arrest us, we won't be any worse off for trying. For whatever reason, he's giving us a chance to get the proof we need."

Anton didn't stand. "We shouldn't rush into this. If it's a trap—"

"Then you've warned me," she said, cutting him off. "This is my chance to make the bastard responsible for my father's death pay. I'm not going to let that slip away. Come help me."

He sighed and stood. "I hope you're right."

The office door opened when she approached and the common room seemed to be empty. There were four other doors leading away from the larger area. One of them led to a kitchen and another to a multi-species rest room.

One of the remaining rooms undoubtedly belonged to Xarbon. The other probably held either his assistant or his guards.

Only one of the doors opened at her approach. "I'll take a quick look inside this one while you see if you can unlock the other door," she told Anton.

The man never went anywhere without his tools. Frankly, she was astonished their captors hadn't searched them. Yes, the guards had scanned them for weapons at the ballroom, but that didn't mean they were without resources.

It took Jackie less than a minute to determine the room belonged to some flunky. The clothing was definitely not up to Xarbon's credit balance and—unless he dressed as a female in the privacy of his own quarters—the person staying here was of the opposite gender.

She returned to the common area and found Anton still hard at work on the locked door. "How's it going?"

He grunted. "Someone did an exceptionally competent job of selecting the lock for this door. It's proving most vexing. I think I should have it in—"

The door slid open.

"—just a moment," he finished.

Jackie didn't wait for him to look inside before she entered. The clock was ticking. The peacemaker could already be on his way back.

The belongings in this room were definitely consistent with someone like Xarbon. It only took her a few minutes to find where he'd hidden his private slate at the back of his closet. A closet, by the way, that was larger than the stateroom she and Anton were sharing.

The slate was an exceptionally high-end model with all the bells and whistles. It had an external data storage cluster that was undoubtedly spacious and well-protected. This was where she would see if the code she'd stolen did the trick.

She arranged the slate on the sleeping pad and powered it up. As soon as it prompted her for authentication, she sent the Gtandan's stolen credentials.

Even before she'd had a chance to exult in the access the codes granted her, she heard disaster approaching. The suite door leading from the common room to the corridor slid open.

"How could you have been so stupid?" she heard Xarbon demanding. "These people are criminals. What kind of enforcer leaves criminals alone in his brother's quarters?"

Whatever else the executive might have said cut off when Anton closed the door. "It has a manual lock, but that's not going to hold for very long. Did you get in?"

"I'm in. Keep them off me as long as you can."

Jackie accessed the slate through her pinplants. They were the best that credits could buy: fast, with incredible throughput, and far more capable than the basic models.

With the co-processing and additional storage space in her head, she could search the drives much more quickly than a normal person. If there was any evidence of Xarbon's betrayal on this slate, she'd find it.

As focused as she was on the task at hand, Jackie still heard the pounding on the door. They'd figured out where she and Anton had gone. It wouldn't be very long before they overrode the manual locks and forced the door.

There was so much data. An entire corporation's worth. Searching it would take years for a normal person. With all the specialized hacking programs she'd picked up on her trips into the Galactic Union and her top-of-the-line capabilities, she was able to locate all references to the Dire Wolves in thirty seconds.

And there it was. A complete record of Yestrellian Corporation's dealings with the Dire Wolves. Everything from the contract to recordings of each of their meetings. Hundreds of files.

Knowing her time was short, Jackie copied everything into her internal memory.

As the files began copying, she looked for the one with the most recent timestamp. It turned out to be an after-action report of some kind. It was dryly written in corporate speak but held exactly the kind of shocking revelation she knew had to have existed.

At that moment, the door to the cabin crashed open and armed guards rushed in. Jackie verified the last of the files had finished copying and sent a command to the slate to re-encrypt the drive cluster with her personal code. No one would be erasing any data on it now.

She'd barely done so before the guards dragged her out into the common room. A pair of them held her arms painfully behind her. Anton had four. Playtime was over.

Xarbon stood glaring at Anton, ignoring her as if she were only a sidekick. His brother, on the other hand, focused his attention on her.

"I must say that you've proven more resourceful than I'd given you credit for," the executive snarled at the ex-FSB spy. "Now you've broken into my private quarters and attempted to access confidential corporate files. I can't begin to imagine how many years you've just earned yourself in a Gtandan prison."

Anton glanced at her, no doubt wondering if she'd found anything useful. He nodded when she smiled triumphantly.

"Actually, I'm not certain that's true," she told the Gtandan executive. "It's probably been a long time since you've reviewed the contract your company signed with the Dire Wolves. Did you know there was an audit clause?"

The alien made a gesture with his arms that she couldn't read. Maybe it was his race's equivalent to a shrug.

"So what?" Xarbon asked. "That doesn't excuse your actions. It only allows you to petition for access to the company files."

"Not petition," Anton disagreed. "The language is quite clear. It authorizes the Dire Wolves to review the files associated with their contract and their mission in cases where they suspect some kind of inappropriate conduct."

Jackie smiled. "Just in case it's not obvious, we suspect inappropriate conduct."

"That doesn't excuse corporate espionage and breaking other laws," the executive snarled. "It means you can approach a planetary court to compel access."

"Planetary courts in your pay," Anton said. "I filed the appropriate paperwork, but you paid the judge to ignore the law."

Xarbon smiled wickedly. "I suppose that's one way to view the situation. It still does not give you the right to do any of this."

He turned to his brother. "I am, of course, pressing charges. You'll take them with you when you leave. I trust you'll keep better track of them this time."

Jackie cleared her throat. "Before anyone gets carried away, I should mention that we're contacting the Mercenary Guild as soon as we come out of hyperspace to raise the issue of your breach of contract.

"I found the proof I needed to prove you intentionally betrayed the Dire Wolves in contravention to your signed agreement."

She used her pinplants to send the relevant file to the networked video screen. "According to this report—which was sent directly to you—your people used the Dire Wolves as a misdirection to one of your competitors. You made them think a third party had hired my father's company to attack them."

"So? Misdirection is no crime. That would be true even if the files you claim as evidence weren't completely fabricated. Someone turn that video screen off."

Enforcer Jardis held up a hand. "No. I want to see what this report says."

"You can't possibly believe her," Xarbon snarled. "She's a common criminal, and I'm your brother."

"Then the evidence will back your claim," Jardis said flatly. "Continue, Miss O'Hara."

She swallowed. "Your brother told the targets the Dire Wolves were coming in exchange for signing the trade agreement he wanted. He never intended for the attack to succeed. He just needed the target to believe a third party was after them.

"He arranged for my father and his people to walk right into an ambush. And I mean that literally. Your brother gave them the Dire Wolves' planned flight path and highlighted the best place to surprise them."

Jackie glared at the executive. "The Mercenary Guild takes a very dim view of outright betrayal and breach of contract. The penalties spelled out in the agreement you signed with my father—"

"Are irrelevant," Xarbon interrupted. "The contract was withdrawn because the mercenary company failed to even make an attempt to complete the work I contracted them for. They never even arrived in the target system and no one can say with any certainty exactly what happened to them."

"I know what happened to them," she said coldly. "You murdered them. Just as surely as if you'd put a gun to the back of their heads and pulled the trigger."

Xarbon gestured toward the door. "Everyone get out. This farce is over."

His brother didn't move. "It's over when I say so, brother. I find the evidence presented thus far to be compelling. I want to read the rest of this document and see what else these two have to sustain their charges."

The guards holding Jackie tensed when a dozen beings walked through the door leading into the corridor.

Xarbon glared at the newcomers. "What is the meaning of this? Get out!"

"These are my associates," Enforcer Jardis said. "They're here to make certain everyone remains civil while I complete my investigation into these accusations."

He walked to the monitor and began reading the document more closely. He gestured for Jackie to scroll it as he reached the bottom of each page.

Once he finished, she replaced it with a copy of the contract. She highlighted the clause that allowed them to pursue access to the files for an audit.

The enforcer turned back toward his brother. "You disappoint me, Nedget. You didn't even try to conceal your involvement in this terrible crime. You actually acknowledged receipt of the secret report. Talk about corporate policy taken to ridiculous extremes."

Xarbon sneered at his brother. That was the only word Jackie felt was appropriate for the expression on his face.

"Don't you dare lecture me! I've achieved success beyond your pathetic dreams. I won't allow a disgrace relegated to chasing criminals for pocket change to lecture me. None of this means anything. By the time we finish docking, all of this will go away."

"We shall see," Enforcer Jardis said thoughtfully. "In any case, as a duly-appointed enforcer of the Peacemaker Guild, I find that you have violated your contract with the Dire Wolves mercenary company.

"I am officially changing its status to fulfilled and finding you in breach of contract. I realize that I should technically classify the final condition as lost, but that wouldn't be fair considering your betrayal.

"All the relevant financial penalties are now due. Including, I might add, the payment in full for the mission itself. Based upon the language and precedent in contract law, that is going to be a substantial amount."

"I will, of course, challenge that before the guild," Xarbon said coldly. "You can rest assured that no payment will be made during my lifetime. These documents are falsified."

"Again, we shall see," Jardis said agreeably. "By my order, I am also placing you under arrest for complicity in the murder of every member of the Dire Wolves under Gtandan law."

"To preserve evidence for your trial, you will be held in close confinement aboard this ship and not allowed communication with anyone until after my agents seize the official files from your servers at the Yestrellian Corporation. I'll take the slate from your room as well."

The enforcer gestured to his men. "Take them away. Remember, no messages in or out."

Jackie expected some form of resistance from Xarbon's security team, but they released her and allowed the enforcer's people to herd them away.

Once the three of them were alone, the alien smiled at her. "Contrary to what my brother believes, I find the evidence you've presented to be most compelling. He will pay for his crimes and so will everyone involved in this tragedy.

"While I can certainly understand how the Galactic Union often appears to many of its citizens, not everyone is out to take whatever they can. Though the Peacemaker Guild does take money to keep the peace, even between the guilds, that doesn't mean justice is for sale."

They stood in silence for a moment before she spoke. "I hope you're telling me the truth. I grew up without my father because of your brother. My partner lost everything he'd worked for and all his friends, too. No amount of compensation will ever change that."

The alien nodded. "Yet I can tell you feel satisfaction at seeing justice done. I meant every word about how impressed I am with your capabilities and determination. I've begun researching you more closely and feel that I already know enough about your character to feel comfortable making you an offer.

"The Peacemaker Guild isn't just about pursuing and arresting criminals. Some of us are also tasked with gathering information and doing clandestine intelligence work. Such are my normal duties, so I have some appreciation for the skill it took to gather this information under such adverse conditions.

"I believe you could make a difference in many lives if I could convince you to assist me. The pay is terrible, the benefits so-so, but the satisfaction of seeing the guilty brought low is heady. Allow me a few days to sway you."

The offer came out of the blue. Jackie had never thought about what she would do if they actually accomplished the mission. She wasn't a mercenary. Hell, at this point, neither was Anton.

If they actually received the money for the breach of contract in the mission, she'd never have to work another day in her life. How boring would that be?

Anton shrugged. "It seems my schedule has opened up. If Jackie is willing, I'd like to hear your offer. To learn more about what you do."

Enforcer Jardis clapped his hands on their shoulders and nudged them toward the door. "Excellent! All of this has made me hungry. Let's find a quiet corner and refresh ourselves while we take the opportunity to get to know one another."

# # # # #

Mark's Introduction to:

Paint the Sky

by Jason Cordova

I first met Jason at a LibertyCon four years ago and was immediately struck by what a dynamic character he is. I've wanted to write with him ever since, but as fate would have it, things just haven't worked out. I was thrilled to find out from Chris that Jason was locked for this anthology. Jason's bestselling works center around Kaiju, and if you've read my book Cartwright's Cavaliers, you know they have a fond place in my heart. He has also released "Wraithkin," the first book in the Kin Wars Saga series, through the same publisher as the book you are reading. The second book, "Darkling," should be available soon.

The story Jason presented us tells the tale of a man who believed that simply buying the hardware for a merc company in the Four Horsemen universe was the key to instant success, and finds out that's *far* from the truth. But we also find out what a few men in CASPers (Combat Assault Systems, Personal) can accomplish if they don't have any choice. Along the way we see just how nasty life can be in a universe where it's quite literally dog-eat-dog.

Find out more about Jason at https://jasoncordova.com/.

PAINT THE SKY
by Jason Cordova

"Five?" Mulbah Luo asked incredulously as he stared at the bursar. "We only have five CASPers?"

"You heard me correctly," the man across from him said, his face grim as he matched the steely-eyed business man's gaze. "And what we have aren't even Mark Eights. They're Sevens."

Mulbah sputtered for a moment, completely flabbergasted. He had expected the cupboard to be thin, but not entirely bare. He should have listened to his personal accountant's advice before he bought the majority stake in the formerly-defunct mercenary company.

"Nobody goes into receivership in the mercenary business anymore, Mr. Luo," the attorney had stated many months before. Mulbah had been so enamored by the idea of owning his own mercenary outfit, though, that he had steamrolled through the attorney's objections and bought the former owners out. Much to their obvious relief, he recalled in hindsight. They had been almost broke, which was rare in the mercenary business, so it had been a fairly cheap purchase for the CFO turned mercenary company owner. Most companies were either fairly wealthy or completely destroyed. Getting an intact one, well…that had been the ultimate coup.

Or had it?

He pinched the bridge of his nose and exhaled slowly, counting backwards from 20 as he tried to rein in his infamous temper. The Kakata Korps, formerly *Mercenarios Ojo de Tigre*, had just had its headquarters relocated to Liberia from Seville, Spain. It had taken him purchasing a full-sized warehouse outside the city of Monrovia to hold all the equipment that had come with the takeover. He had thought he was getting a treasure trove of gently-used military equipment. According to the sellers, he had. They had failed to mention just how ancient the "gently used" equipment had been, though.

He felt more like a man getting a belt sander applied to his rear end the deeper into the inventory he delved.

"Sevens are obsolete," Mulbah muttered as he ran the calculations through his head. He had no idea just what sort of equipment would be needed for the contract he had bid on, but he had wanted to make an impression on the other mercenary units out there. His idea had been simple: take a low-risk, low-reward job and overwhelm the simple, non-violent aliens with his arsenal, then reap the rewards of a solid reputation down the line with more lucrative contracts and more overwhelming shows of force. With any luck, he had figured to replace one of the legendary Four Horsemen as top dog. Eventually.

Now? He shook his head and grumbled under his breath. "All we have is about a company's worth of advanced combat armor and the five Mark Seven's. It can't get any worse, Zion. It cannot get any worse."

"Uh, sir?" Zion Jacobs interrupted, his face still dour. He was one of the few administration men he had brought in with him who had passed the Mercenary Service Track, and though he was unfamiliar with the new company, his smarts and quick thinking had impressed Mulbah long before. "You also lack transports."

"We can rent transports," Mulbah replied instantly. He had already figured *that* into the costs, at least, since interstellar travel through the gates was pretty much a given. In fact, most of the money from the current contract would eventually cover the transportation costs of moving his company through space.

"I meant that you have no transports to the surface of the planet you're supposed to go to," Zion calmly explained. "The drop-pods we have were fitted for Mark Fives. You're going to have to land on the planet proper."

Mulbah felt the all-too-familiar pulse of the large vein on his forehead, and knew he was about to explode. His hands shook, and he made a visible effort to not lose control. He took a few more calming breaths before he dared speak.

"Do you have any *good* news?"

"The CASPers all are equipped with dual MAC's," Zion answered quickly, referring to the Magnetic Accelerator Cannon that was the staple of all mecha in the field. "Double the firepower, so each suit could potentially be worth two."

"Then subtract that bonus due to the CASPers' skeletal structure and design being obsolete. It's not cost-effective," Mulbah growled through clenched teeth. He was sliding down a slippery slope and was desperate not to lose control of his temper. He did not want to leave a poor impression but was not certain he could hang onto it any longer. He began to count his heartbeats between each breath to calm down. "But still, they use less power than the newer models. So I guess that's a bonus."

"Their power plants have been recertified recently and are in excellent working order," Zion confirmed.

"Yes," Mulbah nodded, his mood improving ever so slightly. "Good. Let's end things on a positive note."

"One final thing," Zion said as he read the final page on his slate. He looked up from the hand-held device and offered his new boss a grim look. "Not a good note. I'm sorry. You received a summons for court in the United States. Anne Arundel County in Maryland, to be precise. Apparently, your wife is divorcing you."

Mulbah's primal scream of rage and despair echoed through the mostly-empty warehouse.

* * *

"So that's the new boss, eh?" Antonius lifted his head as a faint scream came through the ventilation shaft. He glanced at the digital clock and swore. He pulled out the euro note from the breast pocket of his flight suit and passed it over. His team lead accepted the money and tried not to look too smug. "Two more minutes."

"One day you'll be as wise as I am," Samson noted sagely. "I pay attention to the *chee-chee-polay*. The man has a temper. I thought he would snap long before now."

"The CASPers aren't horrible," the third member of their little party said as he clambered down from behind the Mark Seven suit. He lovingly patted it on the arm. "It'll hold up in a fight, obsolete or no."

"Khean, you can find good in anything," Antonius complained in a good-natured tone. He waved a hand around at the limited inventory. "This isn't enough to get any job done. Not even babysitting a diplomat in a peaceful region of space."

"They never promised at MST that any of this would be easy," Khean reminded them all. The Mercenary Service Track, adopted from the American model, had been initiated by the Liberian government after the Alpha contracts had decimated most of the world's elite fighting forces. The Liberian government had squandered millions on training barely adequate mercenaries, but then had decided to simply ship them off to the United States instead. Most of the country's populace approved of this action, since the government had a poor reputation for doing anything well. "Still, better than what the Alpha contracts walked into."

"Amen, brother," Antonius agreed.

"Here he comes," Samson called out *sotto voce*. The other two men scrambled into position and stood next to their machines as the lean, well-dressed man walked in.

Mulbah sized up the employees as he walked into the open area of the warehouse. Most of the warehouse had been partitioned off with temporary dividers so equipment could be stored and located with ease, but the five Mark Sevens were simply too big and were stored in the largest open space left over. This, unfortunately, was in the back corner of the warehouse, far away from the entrance.

The movers had been careful with the equipment, however. The boxes containing advanced combat armor and weapons were neatly stacked and organized. The floors had been swept clean, and the maintenance crew had their work stations looking almost spotless. Once more, he was surprised by the former owners.

"Hello boss," Samson dipped his head quickly as Mulbah strode into their area, the bursar hot on his heels. Samson offered his hand as the men approached. "Samson Tolbert. I am the team leader."

"So, you're the head pilot of the mecha?" Mulbah nodded as he took in the brawny, muscular man. "How do you like them?"

"Pilot? Oh, no sir," Samson shook his head and laughed. "I am your head mechanic. This is my team. The little guy is Khean Waring. The mouthy one with *craw-craw* on his junk is Antonius Karnga."

"Piss on you! I'm clean! The doctor said so!" Antonius protested loudly.

"So where are the rest of the mercs?" Mulbah asked as he looked around.

"Uh, they left when they stopped getting paid, boss," Samson explained carefully. "About four months back, I think. We're still here because we got paid in full in advance. We're good negotiators."

"What? Nobody mentioned that!" Mulbah nearly shouted.

"Sorry, boss," Samson said in a low voice.

"No, I'm not yelling at you; I'm sorry," Mulbah exhaled and looked around. It took him a moment to cool down. "Are the suits operational at least?"

"They're in good shape," Antonius answered as he bounded over to one and gave it a solid rap on the arm. "These mecha might be old, but they are well-taken care of."

"They're good to go for up to eight hours, boss," Samson stated as he eyed his compatriots. "We also have reserve packs to do battle-field recharges. Drop them in from orbit as needed. That was a fun custom build. The Spaniards might not have known how to run a company, but they did listen to their mechanics."

"Could be why they never got around to replacing these," Khean said off-handedly. "We told the old bosses constantly that these were almost as good as the Mark Eights."

It was just about an unmitigated disaster. Mulbah was ruined.

"It's not all that bad, boss," Samson tried to reassure him. "The mecha can do most jobs in a pinch, as long as they are familiar with the oddities of the Mark Sevens. The armor is a little tougher but the machine is slower, so the mecha pilots will not be able to counterat-tack an enemy position easily. Defensive? These mecha can do that job, boss. I promise."

"It's not hard," Antonius confirmed. "Just need smart pilots who know the machines as well as we do. Not hard, just not always cheap."

"I'm ruined," Mulbah muttered in despair.

"Hey, wait a minute," Khean interjected. He pointed at the mecha. "These machines are *solid*, boss. The advanced combat armor? In pristine condition. The other weaponry stored over in the armory? Okay, it's old, but it's good stuff. We take pride in keeping everything in good order here. What were you expecting, new stuff? Boss, the Spaniards didn't have the capital to buy new stuff. They sure kept what they had in good shape, though."

"I was hoping to be the first successful Liberian mercenary company," Mulbah said as he looked at his four employees. "Better still, the first African one to succeed. I wanted to have people remember Liberia for something other than civil war. I want to build something here, like our ancestors dreamt of when they emigrated and founded the country. Doing this with only four employees? Impossible."

"That's a noble dream, boss, but mercs are expensive to pay on a salary," Antonius said. "Most of the soldiers were paid on a job-to-job basis. It's why the Spaniards went broke. But you say this job is easy, so you can hire mercs at a low rate and stick them in suits. Then it is a matter of watching the aliens do their thing and using the mecha as some sort of overwatch. Might not even need more troops if the job is small enough."

Mulbah thought it over. It would take more time to investigate thoroughly and hire new mercenaries for the job. Hiring a company-sized cadre of men and women would be almost impossible with his constraints, so he would need to focus his efforts and energy on the mecha. He swore. He needed more time, but time was something he did not have. It was too narrow a window in which the contract had to be fulfilled. Kakata Korps was already on the clock, and he had not a moment to spare.

Where could he find enough qualified mercs to man the suits though? He furrowed his brow and silently mulled it over. He could potentially grab some on the way out from a random merc pit and run the risk of them being unreliable. Or, he could go through the old rosters and call to see if any wanted their old jobs back. Neither scenario was going to be cost-effective, though. Both would definitely be time-consuming, a commodity he simply did not have. Plus, each man would need to be custom-fitted for their haptic suits, which meant waiting for them to join the company to make certain each fit correctly.

He was done. He was going to fail as a mercenary company owner before he even began. There was simply no way for him to find enough men to pilot the mecha, much less—

From out of the blue, inspiration struck him in the head like a thunderbolt. The solution was right there in front of him. He looked at the bursar and the three mechanics and felt a wide grin form on his face. The grin was that of a madman, and there was an excited glint in his eyes which terrified his new employees. Every member of a merc company was required by law to pass through MST and register as a merc with the guild, no matter what their final job with the company would be. Hell, *he* was registered with the guild as a merc. The fact that he owned the company meant little to the guild in the grand scheme of things.

Mulbah could not help it; the idea was *too* good to ignore. It would require quite a bit of planning, most of which he had no idea how to accomplish, and would also include figuring out transport to the surface of the planet, but...

"So...any of you want a pay raise?"

* * *

The Liberian-born, American-raised college graduate couldn't pronounce the name of the planet his mercenary company was supposed to go to. He was barely able to say the name of the species he was hired to protect during the upcoming four weeks, though he could handle the standard name other aliens called them—the Kertoschii. He did have coordinates to the world, though, which the captain of the hired vessel had no problem finding. While he didn't entirely trust the MinSha—humanity had never truly forgotten their attack on the Middle East—he was a driven and determined man who was not about to let a little alien prejudice get in the way of making a lot of money. Plus, the MinSha captain was as big a capitalist as he was.

Mulbah felt the pressure of his new company's first contract weighing on him and knew that he was growing angrier and more stressed with each passing second. He needed to protect a small, very specific area of the planet for four weeks. Four weeks on a planet whose name he was pretty sure he couldn't translate to English, with a species whose physiology was completely foreign to him. He wasn't even sure if they had bones in their lumpy, bulbous bodies. There were a lot of hisses and random clicks in the planet's name, as spoken by the natives, but thanks to the rudimentary translation process it came out as "Hot Ball of Fiery Piss."

Three minutes on the surface, and he understood why the name fit perfectly.

Except for the poles, the planet was hot and humid throughout, with varying fungi growing amidst short, flattened tree groves. There were three continents and many small islands, and roughly half of what was considered "dry land" was marsh. The thick air was oppressive and overbearing, and Mulbah could have sworn he saw bugs the size of small cats hovering in the shadows of the trees. The ground was soft and muck-filled, appearing solid until one stepped on it. Water appeared as if by magic and filled every single footstep he made. It led to the appearance that the mecha was creating small lakes in its wake as it moved. The sun was hazy due to the high humidity, and constant thunderstorms loomed in the distance.

The area where the aliens needed his protection was closer to a swamp than a marsh, with standing water in random patches, and a thorny underbrush covering most of the dry areas. Frog analogues hissed noisily, and other creatures scuttled across the ground, oblivious to the giant mecha in their midst.

Mulbah met the leader of the people who had hired him and was surprised to find the entire race consisted of a singular tribe. He was even more shocked to discover they had only recently been admitted into the Union, and this was the first contract they had offered. He was mildly confused and had many questions, but he knew he had to portray the calm and collected head of a merc company.

He had not read up on the aliens beforehand, outside of their needs and his obligations to ensure the contract was fulfilled. This was a mistake, he realized, after it dawned on him that he had no idea whatsoever how to properly greet their leader. He wasn't even sure which end of the alien, which resembled a wet trash bag with eyes and weird appendages sticking out in all directions, he was talking to.

"I'm Mulbah Luo, CEO of Kakata Korps. And you are?"

"My name is Zxkyabllob. You may call me Bob."

"Oh...okay."

"We're a very modern people."

Mulbah was at a loss. He had known the aliens would be, well, alien, but he had not expected to have a conversation with a walking trash bag who had multiple eyes and random protrusions. The alien stuck one out at him and Mulbah, hoping that he wasn't about to grab a reproductive organ, accepted it and, not knowing what else to do, shook it.

"We are familiar with Human customs thanks to the GalNet," Bob said. "I understand the 'shaking of hands' is a customary greeting. We marveled at this idea and decided to use it to make you feel more comfortable with us. The GalNet has provided us with much information on your species. We find you fascinating."

"Thank you," Mulbah said and dipped his head a little. "You are most considerate."

"We have never used hands before, either," Bob continued as his eyes shifted from the front of his body to the back. The alien began to slide away, so Mulbah followed. "Typically, if one offers an appendage, they are signaling their desire to become."

"That's...interesting," Mulbah said. He had no idea what Bob was talking about but he still held out hope that he hadn't just grabbed alien mating equipment.

"We have places for you to sleep," Bob said as a new appendage slipped out and pointed to their right. Mulbah peered off into the distance and saw rudimentary huts. "Our research suggested that men of your culture sleep in huts. Fascinating idea. Will these suffice?"

Mulbah nodded. "The men will do fine in these. Your atmosphere is very similar to our own, except a little thinner with higher doses of nitrous oxide. It makes us sound a little different."

"I have read that your species descends from the water yet does not reside in it," Bob continued as they moved past the huts. "Why?"

"I...don't know," Mulbah admitted. "Evolution works in mysterious ways."

"It does, it does," Bob burbled happily. "We formed from creatures of the water long ago, and we kept their shape and traits. Now we become and it is good."

Mulbah simply nodded. He didn't need to understand them, only to do his job.

* * *

For almost four weeks it was the same routine every day. He and the rest of his Korps would don their mecha (minus the one man who pulled overwatch during the night) and trudge out into the murky swamp and stand around. While Bob assured them the aliens would only come during a storm, Mulbah was taking no chances. He and his men maintained their post for eighteen hours straight before trudging back to their huts and removing themselves from the mecha. They would then sleep, and do it all over again in the morning.

"Nothing," Mulbah muttered as he scanned the small area for the millionth time, every sensor on the Mark Seven active and tracking. He could not quite figure out what the aliens were doing, but they appeared to be having a large gathering of some sort.

Every dawn, in fact, the aliens proceeded to almost mimic the routine of the Korps: they would wander out into the small swampy area and stand around, then scan the sky and look for something. They would interact with one another in ways that only trash bag aliens could, and then, at dusk, they would move back to an area where it was not as wet. There, they would huddle together and make odd keening sounds in the darkness. It reminded Mulbah a little of how some of the bush people in Liberia would gather around a large fire and sings songs of the day.

Today seemed to be a little different. Far in the distance, thunder crackled and boomed, and he could almost feel the burnt ozone from the lightning strikes. It was purely phantasmal sensations, he knew, but Mulbah could not shake the feeling the air was foreboding and ominous. His eyes drifted from the skies to the aliens he was guarding.

They were more nervous than usual, he noticed as he truly *watched* the proceedings for the first time. The ones he had tagged as males were continuously looking upwards towards the sky while the others were clustering closer and closer together in the knee-deep muck. The bulbous, blob-looking creatures were mewling and keening in an eerie tone. It grated on his nerves, and he almost turned off the auditory receptors in his suit.

"Boss," Samson's voice was pitched soft despite the comms links being perfectly tuned. "Are you seeing this?"

"I am," Mulbah subvocalized back. He zoomed in on the activity, and his eyes widened as he realized just what he was watching.

"Are they…giving birth?" Samson asked.

The keening suddenly stopped, and every single alien female turned to stare at one particular female. Everyone, males and females alike, backed away as the body of the chosen female rippled. The female dropped to the ground and shuddered violently. Her translucent skin rippled, and she began to emit a soft blue glow from deep within her body. The blue glow grew brighter with each passing ripple as the alien began to cry out in a low, mournful squall. The others followed suit and with one final yowl, the alien melted into the ground.

The glow was almost blinding but it slowly began to grow more subdued the longer Mulbah looked at it. He gasped as a small blue figure unfurled from the ground and began to stretch slowly out.

"It's beautiful," Khean whispered as blue glow wings unfurled from the body. Mulbah could not argue with the man. Terrifyingly Human-like, it looked very fragile and delicate to the touch, a veritable sculpture of a ballerina. Oversized eyes and elongated ears reminded Mulbah of an elf. The creature had no mouth, but for some reason this was not very disturbing. Mulbah simply marveled at the stunning creature before him.

"We are in our wetskins for many years until it is time to become," Bob explained in a hushed, awe-inspired whisper. "We are unsuited for becoming until we shed the wetskin. Then we become."

"She...became?" Mulbah asked, his reverie broken by Bob's voice.

"Yes."

Thunder rolled louder in the distance. Lightning began to strike random trees as the storm moved closer. A deep sense of dread began to form in a cold part of Mulbah's soul. There was something brewing, something darker than the coming storm.

"Antonius," Mulbah switched to his secure comms and woke up their last man, who had been on overwatch the night before and had only been asleep for a few hours. "Something's not right. I need you in your suit."

"This is one bad storm, boss," Samson said as the booms grew louder and closer. The alien who became was looking around, partly in confusion and partly in fear. The beautiful features were twisted in agony, and a primal terror enveloped it. Mulbah might not have been one of the aliens, but even he recognized fear.

"I don't think that's a storm, Samson," Mulbah replied. The sky went almost completely black as the thick cloud cover blocked out the sun. A few fat drops of rain splashed against his mecha as the storm finally moved over them.

"They come," Bob said as thunder and lightning crackled across the sky, ripping through the clouds and creating ghastly shadows with every flash.

All eyes, alien and Human alike, looked skyward now as the thunder continued to rip through the thick clouds. It rolled continuously, without end, and Mulbah started to wonder if it was thunder he was hearing or something far worse. To the naked eye there was nothing to be seen. He activated his scanner to see what was really out there. He managed not to gasp in horror and shock as the HUD began to display everything the LIDAR, his Light Detection and Ranging system, was picking up.

Hundreds of...*things* were descending on their position at a rapid rate. The little blips on his LIDAR were homing in directly on the patch where the females gathered with their newborn. The females formed a defensive circle around the newly become, but experience told Mulbah that outside of growling and trying to block the raiders, there was little the females could do to protect their youngling.

Realization dawned on him. Bob had been reticent as to *why* they needed protecting during a special time. It had not made sense a month ago, but now it was perfectly clear. They weren't there to protect the aliens from predators or resources from rival mercs while they mated. They were there to protect the sole child from slavers.

Rage boiled up from deep within his heart. He had seen the evils of slavery first hand, having grown up in Liberia, when hundreds of rescued children from Ghana were transported through Monrovia on their way to various nations to begin new lives. He had seen the emptiness in their eyes and the scars, both physical and emotional. His own childhood, while a happy one, had the dark stains of what his people had done to one another over the millennia.

Being Liberian, he understood tribal relations and family. Being American as well, though, had shown him that children were a precious and irreplaceable commodity for family, community, and a species as a whole.

He swore the only way the raiders would get the newly become was over his dead body.

"Paint the sky," Mulbah ordered, and he started firing upwards at the oncoming raiders, his dual MACs pouring an amazing number of rounds into the descending mass. The others followed his lead and began to fire as well, their suits tracking targets and eliminating them as quickly as they locked on. What had started as thousands of attackers began to rapidly decline as the systems of the mecha tracked and eliminated the raider threat.

As quickly as the blips had appeared *en masse* they were now scattering, trying to run from the unholy amount of firepower that was now directed and focused upon them. Mulbah could only imagine what was going through the invaders' heads as they faced armed opposition for the first time. They moved east of Mulbah's position and tried to regroup, but he didn't give them the opportunity. He continued to pour fire into the unseen aliens, relying on his instruments. The others spread out in a half-circle, their concerted fire unrelenting as they continued to shift targets with each eliminated enemy. The alien raiders clustered about a kilometer away before they disappeared from his sensors.

"Cease fire!" Mulbah called out. His men stopped attacking and waited for additional orders. He waited for a moment, uncertain. He had anticipated the enemy breaking and fleeing from the overwhelming amount of fire; he had not expected them to go to ground.

"Orders?" Samson asked, his voice supernaturally calm. If Mulbah had not known any better he would have assumed the massive former mechanic was far away in a safe location.

"Not sure what we're dealing with," Mulbah replied. "Anyone get any good readings?"

"Power signatures are too low to be Zuul," Khean answered almost immediately. "Whoever this is, their mass is very small since those engines don't have a lot of power."

"Or they are extremely efficient," Samson countered. Mulbah nodded.

"They've gone to ground, which means they've given up the one advantage they had over us," he said. He motioned at the aliens, who were huddled together and watching the Humans silently. "We need to protect these people at all cost."

"No idea who or what we are dealing with?" Zion asked, nervous.

"There are thirty-six other mercenary races out there," Mulbah said as he cycled through his MACs and reloaded them. "So, who knows? Quite frankly, I don't care. The Union has no rules on slavery."

"This is *legal?*" Khean asked, his shocked tone carrying easily through the comms.

"It's not genocide, so why not?" Mulbah growled as his anger and rage began to bubble forth. This time, though, he did not hold it back but instead used it to fuel him. His mind raced as he analyzed the situation. "Watch the north and south for flanking maneuvers. We don't know what we're dealing with, but if they are typical pirates they won't come straight at us."

The group waited in stony silence as the storm abated, the calm disquieting to each man. It was deathly silent in the swampy area, save for the raucous noise caused by the mechas' movements. It was strange, but Mulbah, having grown used to the noise of the CASPers, managed to tune them out and listen to his surroundings.

Khean, who was on the far right of the group, screamed suddenly and was abruptly cut off. His suit dropped off Mulbah's HUD as quickly as the scream ended. Mulbah whirled but saw no sign of the suit or of Khean. It was as if ghosts from the swamp had taken the young mercenary.

"Anybody see it?" Mulbah asked with a hint of nervousness in his tone. He had expected an ambush, but not one where a suit could be taken out without a sound being made. Did the raiders have technology which allowed them to go toe-to-toe with the CASPers? He shivered despite every effort not to.

"Nothing, boss," Samson said in a calm, collected voice. "Khean? Answer me. Are you hurt?"

"I'm up," Antonius suddenly announced. "Pursuing you now, boss. Be there in a minute."

"What took so long?" Mulbah asked as he turned to look around the swamp. There was still no sign of Khean but he knew that eventually, if the young man was dead, the emergency transponder would go active for suit recovery.

"Just one of the perks of being a mercenary," Mulbah whispered as he silently prayed for his fallen battle brother. He hoped for the best but knew, deep down, the young mechanic was more than likely dead.

"Goddamn suit," Antonius growled as he finally joined them. "Sorry boss. Had to readjust."

"Ammo check?" Mulbah asked.

"Green," Antonius replied instantly. His voice was cold and distant. A result, Mulbah guessed, from hearing Khean fall. "Full loads with tracers."

Mulbah blanched. "Tracers?"

"My own concoction," Antonius admitted. "I like the visuals, and most aliens, from what I hear, haven't dealt with tracers before. If they use their eyes to fight, it's going to terrify them."

"If they don't?" Mulbah asked.

"Then it burns when it hits," Antonius said off-handedly. "Either way, someone else feels a lot of pain."

Mulbah could not fault the man for that.

"Contact," Samson called out as he began to fire. Mulbah turned slightly and tracked the target as Samson killed it. More shadows flitted away from them, remaining out of sight. Mulbah quickly designated the targets as what they were looking for on his HUD and the LIDAR began to track them as it identified the alien raiders.

Samson strode over to one he had managed to kill and picked it up with one hand. He brought it over for Mulbah to investigate.

It was definitely not native, Mulbah decided as he inspected the dead raider. It was over two feet in length, not counting the tail, and resembled a gecko from back on Earth. The scales were a deep gray color, and the belly of the dead lizard alien was a lighter shade. It blended perfectly with the hazy gray that permeated the swampy area. It had a stumpy tail and was fairly muscular. It even had a sort of body armor, though that had obviously been worthless when faced with the Human weaponry.

The rest of the mercs drew closer together as they turned their attention back towards the swamp. Mulbah took one last look at the lizard before he tossed it into the muck, to eventually be devoured by the creatures who were native to the planet. The ooze and the insects would eventually turn the corpse into liquid, and then it would be fully acclimated into the world.

Mulbah was determined to keep the rest of his men from sharing the same fate.

"Weapons?" He growled as he rotated his suit and angled to cover the rear.

"Swords of some sort, boss," Samson replied. "Some kind of glowing thing. Almost as big as they are. Turned off when dropped. They also got some kind of blue war paint or something. Looks strange."

"More hostiles incoming," Mulbah said as his LIDAR picked up a large group of lizards gathering at the base of a large rock formation.

"Mob rules," Antonius said.

"Never seen anything like that before," Zion spoke for the first time in days. Mulbah had almost forgotten what the bursar had sounded like.

"You don't get out enough," Mulbah commented as hundreds of the lizard aliens gathered around the large rock outcropping.

One lizard, bigger than all the others, lifted a glowing weapon that was as big as the two-foot lizard and shrieked in challenge. Mulbah looked closer and saw that what Samson had originally thought was blue paint on the raiders was flapping loosely due to the winds of the storm. Mulbah frowned and had his display zoom in. He could now see that it looked more like an animal skin than a piece of clothing. It also had the same faint blue glow that the newly become had.

Mulbah's stomach dropped to the pit of Hell as the final piece of the puzzle fell into place. The aliens weren't kidnapping Bob's people to force them into slavery. Bob's people—the smart, industrious, and caring aliens—were nothing more than hunting trophies.

Black rage bubbled up and obscured his vision. A dark and primal scream tore at his throat. The MACs came up and seemingly aimed of their own volition at the leader of the raiding party. The two MACs spewed forth hundreds of rounds in mere seconds. The sustained fire shredded the lizard, and most of its body simply evaporated from the intense fire.

He did not hesitate a moment as he continued to pour fire into the raiders, whose armor was no match for the gunfire of the MACs. Even with Khean and his suit down, the remaining mecha were more than a match for the raiders, who had not expected any resistance. *Why should they*, Mulbah asked himself as he waded deeper into the muck, eliminating lizards left and right as fast as they appeared. *They've never been challenged before.*

The lizards finally realized they were outmatched and tried to retreat the way they had come. Kakata Korps refused to let them. What had been hundreds of raiders were now down to maybe two dozen, and the lizards were in full flight as Mulbah and his men chased them through the muck and water. One by one, the lizards met their demise at the hands of the newest Human mercenary company.

Mulbah was merciless in his execution of the few remaining survivors. The Union had no laws regarding slavery, but the laws of how a member could treat non-members was black and white. He would harbor no surrender or parleys with the creatures. They were vermin in need of extermination.

Mulbah checked his LIDAR; the only returns were his four remaining suits and Bob's people. He took a deep, shuddering breath and turned back. He began to slowly trudge to where he had left Bob and the others behind.

It took him over an hour to reach the small area where he had last seen them. He checked his clock and blinked, surprised. He had been out hunting the raiders for almost six hours. No wonder he was so exhausted.

"Contract is fulfilled," Mulbah gasped as he knelt down next to Bob and the alien who had become. He did a quick head count and saw that every single member of Bob's people had survived. He smiled in spite of his weariness. The contract called for the protection of the tribe, with a small bonus for ensuring every single member of the tribe survived. He had fulfilled it to the letter.

"I agree," Bob nodded as two of the other males moved towards them. "We will reclaim the dead. Your payment has been made. We thank you for accepting the contract and wish to offer you another contract in the future."

"I don't think those lizards are going to mess with you anymore," Mulbah said confidently. He then reconsidered his future business plans and smiled. "But Kakata Korps would happily accept any contracts you may need. We can even offer a discount for a long-term contract to give us exclusivity."

"This is joyous news," Bob burbled as his form jiggled happily. "In ten cycles the becoming process shall begin anew and we will be in need of your services once more. At less cost? Splendid!"

"Wait. Cycles?" Mulbah asked, confused. "You mean, like lunar cycles?"

"Oh no, that is too soon," Bob laughed as his eyes shifted from the front of his "face" to about where his stomach would be. "We become faster than most members of the Union, but primitive species outpace us. I meant solar cycles. Ten years is the term you would use."

"Son of a bitch..."

* * *

"Khean's family will be well taken care of," Mulbah promised as he looked at the partially-destroyed CASPer as it was loaded into the holding bay of the MinSha transport. The aliens were respectful and stayed out of their way, possibly surprised the five-man company had succeeded. Four-man now that Khean was gone, Mulbah mentally corrected himself as he watched Samson and Zion struggle to move Antonius' damaged suit on board. The mouthy bastard had been knocked around quite a bit in the battle, but he had managed to pop out of his suit relatively unscathed.

"His family will sing his praises and paint the sky with his memory," Antonius agreed as he watched the two men move his suit. Once it was secured in the bay the others moved their own suits into position. They were quickly tied down and secured firmly in place before the men exited their suits. Extraction in a nonemergency could be a slow process, but the mechanics knew the machines better than most pilots and had it down to an art form. They were cleaned up and ready for the trip back home in less than ten minutes. Antonius continued, "They will share tales in the bush of his heroism and use the stars to tell his story. And they will use the insurance money to take care of themselves for generations."

*Paint the sky…*Mulbah had not heard that term in years, not since he had left the land of his birth and journeyed to the land of opportunity. He had found much in America, more than he had thought he ever would. He had been given an education, a chance, and a hope for the future. His ties to his homeland were stronger still, though, giving him purpose and drive. His father and his grandparents had both taught him that hard work could overcome anything.

However, it was on a piss-ball world at the ass end of the universe where he had truly found himself.

"I was going to use 'The Lion Roars' as our motto," Mulbah said as Zion and Samson joined them. He looked at each man; all were nodding. "But after this mission, I decided on something else. Something more…us."

"You are going to use something weird, right boss?" Samson asked with a restrained sigh. Mulbah's smile was wide and amused.

"Of course I am."

"I knew it."

"Paint the sky?" Antonius asked.

The other men nodded. Mulbah grinned. It was all right, in the end.

"Let's paint the sky then."

# # # # #

Mark's Introduction to:

Surf and Turf

by Jon R. Osborne

To say I've known Jon "Oz" Osborne a long time is to say the day is long. I first met Oz nearly 30 years ago in Indianapolis, back when I just called myself a writer but was really a courier/pizza driver. Now there's an ocean of time and experience we've shared. Though we moved apart, our friendship never ended. Jon's ben writing as long as I have, but unlike myself he never quite got that push to get out there and get published. I needed to give back on this one, so I pushed. And here you have his first printed work, and I think it's a darned fine one. (Note from Chris—I agree!)

Jon presents us a story of a merc unit operating on one of the thousands of worlds in the Galactic Union, a planet inhabited by many races. The leader is the heir to a small but prestigious merc company, who like many of us, had no interest in the family business. Earth draws its fortunes from the merc trade, but many still are not interested in that life. Here we meet one such man, and how the universe doesn't always listen to our wishes, but rather our destiny. We're going to see more of Jon.

Find out more about Jon at https://www.facebook.com/lordoz.

SURF AND TURF
by Jon R. Osborne

"Here's your cerveja, Papi Bear." Talita set the bottle, already beading with condensation, on the worn table next to the collection of printouts and slates Bjorn had in front of him. "What are you working on? You've hardly flirted with me all day. I'm beginning to think you don't love me anymore."

Bjorn Tovesson III looked up, a smile tugging up the edges of his bushy beard. Normally he exchanged entendre-laden banter with the curvaceous little Brazilian waitress while drinking at Tio Ramon's. The hole-in-the-wall bar served as his unofficial HQ. He knew nothing would come of the repartee as Talita made no secret of being a lesbian, frequently having to tell amorous patrons she didn't like boys. But as soon as Bjorn had stepped into the Brazilian cervejaria a year ago, she'd taken to the hulking mercenary commander. Sure, he'd been disappointed when he found out she had a girlfriend, as had many of the troops in his command, but it was just as well since she was much younger. Flirting with the green-eyed cutie was a safe diversion and gave him a friend to talk to outside his merc outfit.

"Sorry princess, I didn't mean to ignore you." Bjorn set down a slate to pick up the beer. Cold and crisp, just the way he liked it. "Our contract term is coming up; I need to figure out if we're going to renew it and stay in garrison here."

A garrison contract on a relatively safe world was by no means lucrative, but Bjorn had spent the last year rebuilding the Berserkers after a spectacularly destructive and costly victory. The Eosigi had hired Bjorn's Berserkers to break the siege on their industrial complex on Moloq. The sieging forces happened to be dropping in additional units to break the defenders of the complex as the Berserkers launched their assault. Quick thinking and bold tactics had turned what could have been a total rout into a victory, but it was a costly victory. The Berserkers had lost almost a third of their total manpower, half of their CASPers, and a pair of dropships.

Once the Eosigi stopped trying to weasel out of the various clauses of the contract, the payout had been spectacular. The offer had been lucrative because the employer was gambling that Bjorn's Berserkers would do enough damage to weaken the siege forces without actually beating them. The Eosigi had planned on interdicting the system's emergence point with a different mercenary force, which arrived too late to stop the reinforcements.

Some of the older officers, ones that had served under Bjorn's father, Bjorn Tovesson Jr., had counselled the offer was too good to be true. The ones that survived the battle on Moloq didn't say 'I told you so.' They didn't have to, even if no one could have predicted the arrival of the Jivool mercenaries to reinforce the siege forces at just the wrong moment.

The last year had been spent working a garrison contract on Vishall, a water world in the Coro region of the Tolo galactic arm. The K2 primary cast an orange glow and appeared about a third larger in the sky; it also kept the one small landmass situated in the tropic zone pleasantly warm. In addition to extensive aquatic agriculture and some mineral extraction, the main city, Vishall Plex, had a bit of tourism from species that enjoyed balmy beaches.

Although the world was owned by the H'rang, the population included a fair number of aliens, including Humans. The H'rang, somewhat lazy and rather paranoid felinoids, were happy to farm out the work they didn't want to do themselves. Much of this involved operating the fleet of aquatic harvesting boats, as Humans were a lot less expensive than robots resistant to ocean conditions. As the Human work force grew, more Humans followed, filling various niches that supported their fellows.

The H'rang hired mercenaries to protect Vishall because it was a significant source of food, and they were worried about rumors of mysterious raids over the past couple of years. They hadn't been especially generous in the contract, but it had given Bjorn's Berserkers time and a relative haven to rebuild and train the new troops hired to replenish their ranks.

"Papi Bear, you can't leave." Talita sat in his lap, pouting and fidgeting with the bear claws that hung from his neck. She batted her green eyes at him, made even brighter by her caramel complexion. "Who will make me laugh? And who would get your cerveja?"

"Nothing's decided yet, princess." Bjorn shifted her on his leg, hoping she wouldn't notice what her presence was rousing. He'd rather wile away the hours with the vivacious waitress and cold beer than pore over the details of the potential contracts, but merc companies that stayed garrisoned too long ran the risk of losing their edge. Then again, Bjorn thought, it was a lot safer; you were less likely to be sending a bunch of your men to their deaths.

"Hey, Chica, quit wasting time with that old Quixote. We want cerveja."

Talita sighed, hopping up and going to the new arrivals a few tables over. Bjorn took a moment to admire how she filled out her cut-off shorts then turned back to his work. Whether the Berserkers would remain on Vishall had been a subject of rampant speculation.

Some of his troops were in the bar, as usual, but they knew better than to pester him. They'd know as soon as he made up his mind; maybe they'd get an inkling once he'd narrowed down the potential contracts and brought in the senior officers for their opinions.

On one hand, the Berserkers had a lot of green troops. Trying to replace two companies' worth of troops meant a lot of cubs fresh out of the merc academies on Earth and Karma. Cadre troops now made up a third of their ranks, especially in the CASPer platoons. Sure, the past year had been spent on training, but training wasn't experience under fire. More garrison time meant more time to train. More time before Bjorn had to face ordering them into danger.

"I told you, I don't like boys!"

Talita's voice snapped Bjorn out of his reverie. A quartet of tiberones, Latino youths from the Human barrio, were hassling her, like their namesake sharks, circling. The presence of the Berserkers generally kept the local gangs in check. Bjorn's troops were quick to come to the defense of local businesses, especially those that catered to the mercs. But even after a year of cracking heads, occasionally some didn't get the memo or thought the mercs' reps were Tri-V hype. The Berserkers in the bar were now watching Bjorn. They knew how this would play out.

"Boys, drink your beer and leave the chica alone," Bjorn rumbled. The tables between him and the troublemakers emptied. Bjorn figured that wouldn't be the end of it, but he felt like he should at least give the punks a chance to wise up.

"Ey, old man. Shut the fuck up." The largest took a few steps towards Bjorn's table. The other three tiberones chuckled and made supportive noises. Bjorn tried not to roll his eyes.

"Don't make me bounce you to the curb, Chico. And I'm not that old."

Ramon, the bartender, quietly removed the few breakables from the bar, shaking his head. Locals got themselves and their drinks out of the way. Meanwhile mercenaries pushed back to watch like it was some Tri-V on the Aethernet. If there had been a hint of a competitive fight, there would have been betting. They knew this would just be an object lesson.

"Ey, you're old enough to be my padre."

"Yeah, ask your mama about that, Chico." It was reflex, too easy an opening for Bjorn to pass up.

"You think you're tough, Quixote?" The Alpha tiberon marched over to Bjorn. The kid was almost 20, a little taller than average, and lean. "I hear you garrison goons are no better than the rent-a-cops at the commerce-plex." The other three chuckled more, goading alpha.

Bjorn stood, slowly and deliberately. Breaking two meters and 150 kilos, he loomed over the punk. Morphagenic tattoos on his bare right arm came to life, tribal patterns swirling to make way for a rousing bear. Bjorn hoped the Alpha backed down when he saw he was out-classed. Well, he mostly hoped, sometimes these punks needed a reminder. Ice blue eyes glared down form under bushy eyebrows.

"Don't poke the bear, boy."

Alpha flicked out a mag-knife, the blade snapping from the hilt as he slashed at Bjorn's face. To his credit, the kid was fast, probably the veteran of several street scraps, but not fast enough. Bjorn had fought creatures that would make these punks wet themselves. Bjorn's left hand snagged Alpha's wrist in mid-swing, stopping the knife cold. Alpha tried to pull back, finding his arm trapped in an iron grip.

"Chico, you must be a special kind of stupid to pull a knife on an armed merc in a merc bar full of mercs." Bjorn glared down at the tiberon, whose bravado began to melt as his companions sidled toward the exit. Bjorn increased the pressure on the wrist to a bruising level. "Now, I could make a mess, thrash you around like a ragdoll, and break your arm for good measure. Or you can drop the fucking knife and get the fuck out."

The knife clunked to the floor, the blade clicking into the hilt as it fell. Bjorn released the tiberon, watching him warily in case he wanted to do something stupid to save face with his retreating amigos. The young man's eyes flicked to the knife on the floor. Bjorn shook his head.

"You guys come back here, or give anyone grief, I will make you regret it. If you're lucky you'll only end up in traction." Bjorn flipped back his leather vest, exposing his sidearm, a massive Heckler and Glock 12mm pistol suited for his equally-massive hands. "I've got too much work to piss around with filling out forms on why I had to plug some barrio piece of shit. Don't make me change my mind."

Alpha backed up a couple of paces. "This place sucks, anyway." Alpha stalked out, catching up with his compatriots who were already safely out in the street.

Bjorn sank back into his chair and picked up his beer. Stupid kids, you'd think they'd know by now not to mess with this bar. Everyone else went back to their drinks, and the buzz of conversation returned.

"I could have handled those meninos, Papi Bear." Bjorn never tired of hearing Talita's lilting accent, even when she was scolding him. "I'm not, how do you say, a damsel. I handled tiberones before you got here, and I handle them again when you're not around."

"Sorry, princess. Habit."

She ruffled his hair, a little longer than the buzz cut he traditionally maintained. Another side effect of being in garrison too long. Despite his shaggy Viking beard, he liked to keep his hair short.

"It's okay, Papi Bear." As she bent over to scoop up the dropped knife, Bjorn knew he wasn't the only one in the bar watching. Talita took the knife to the bar, where Ramon dropped it into a box full of similar relics of poor decisions by patrons.

Bjorn took a swig of his beer, looking back at the forms and slates awaiting his attention. Not the life he had planned for himself, but one many would have thought inevitable given that his father and grandfather had run Bjorn's Berserkers. He'd had other dreams in his youth, and had once worked hard to make them come true—despite his father's wishes.

Earth, Alaska, 22 years ago

They had been trudging through the snow for four hours, each carrying 25 kilos of gear. The temperature was barely below freezing, meaning the snow wasn't light and fluffy. It fell in fat flakes, bringing a hush to the landscape. People might have thought the view scenic—snowy woods with mountains in the distance. To Bjorn, the hours his father had wasted trying to bond with him in the hopes he would forgo his aspirations of going to college on a football scholarship were just a cold, wet pain in the ass.

Bjorn had just finished the football season of his high school junior year, a season that ended with his team winning the state championship. Large, muscular, and surprisingly fast for his size, he had offers piling up from schools down south—he'd demonstrated an uncanny ability to read the opposing offense and had been the bane of every quarterback he had faced.

This distressed his father, who counted on Bjorn as heir apparent to take over the Berserkers. His grandfather, Bjorn Tovesson I, had retired last year, and Bjorn III was Bjorn Junior's only child. Fortunately, Grandpa had stayed out of the dispute. Bjorn didn't know how he'd handle it if both his elder namesakes ganged up on him.

By default, Bjorn had been enrolled in the Mercenary Service Track in grade school and kept in it. His participation and excellence in football had just been considered good physical conditioning and team-building exercises until it began to open doors.

"You know, I could swing it so you could take your VOWS assessment this summer," his father rumbled, breaking what had been an hour-long silence. He turned back towards Bjorn so the thick hood wouldn't muffle his voice. "Given your fitness and grades, it wouldn't be hard. You could at least see what you score."

"I'm already getting offers from Top-10 schools." Bjorn met his father's gaze, even though he was a couple centimeters taller and had an extra twenty kilos of bulk. Big ran in the men of the Tovesson family. "Full-ride scholarships, which pull the teeth out of your 'not on my dime' crap."

"What about after school? Four years, then what?" His father turned fully towards him. "What if you blow out your knee or something? So much for your free ride."

"Dad, we've been over this before, about 100 times." Bjorn's voice rose, stoked by resentment for the last four hours. "You're just pissed because I didn't drink the merc kool-aid, like you did with

Granddad! Could something happen to me playing ball? Sure. But at least I'm not going to get my head blown off on the football field!"

His father's expression went from icy scowl to eyes-wide in a split second. "Look out!"

Bjorn hadn't heard the Kodiak bear behind him until it burst out of the brush in a spray of branches and snow. Bjorn turned and backpedaled, trying to bring his hunting rifle up while getting out of his father's line of fire. His father sidestepped to the left, bringing his rifle up. Normally a headshot would be foolish, but it reduced the chance of hitting Bjorn. Besides, his father was a combat marksman, not your run-of-the-mill hunter.

"Shit!" Bjorn heard his father's curse just before the rifle went off; his father's left leg disappeared into a snow bank and caused him to topple as he pulled the trigger. The bullet took the bear's ear, but that was it. The bear snarled and shook its head, a spray of saliva from its fangs. It bought Bjorn another moment to back away and pull his own trigger. His hurried shot caught the bear in the neck, the bullet passing through. Now it was good and pissed as it lunged forward and clawed at him, tearing the rifle out of his grip.

Bjorn caught a glimpse of his father trying to regain his footing in the snow, one leg still sunk below the knee. Unable to free his leg, his father brought the rifle to his shoulder. Another swipe of a massive paw caught Bjorn's thick parka and his web gear, spinning him around and leaving a trail of stinging gouges along his side. Bjorn heard his father's rifle again as the beast eclipsed his view, and the bear's stinking maw came for him, its breath hot and fetid. The teeth closed over his left sleeve, and his arm exploded in pain.

Bjorn's right hand found the huge Heckler and Glock pistol that had been a Christmas present from his grandfather and pulled it free.

He remembered the boom of the gun drowning out his own screams and the bear's roars. He hit the snow as something warm sprayed him. His father's voice faded as the snowscape turned dark.

Now

All three of his slates lit up and his phone buzzed, snapping Bjorn back to the here and now. The slates flashed with a priority alert. Picking up the largest, his tactical slate, he slipped the earpiece into position and answered the call, while syncing the slate to his command channel.

"Near Space Control has reported a breach in orbital security. Eleven objects have entered the atmosphere, all projected to splash down east of V Plex." His aide, Captain William Hawkins, paused for breath. A map appeared on the tactical slate, showing the estimated landing zone. "Surface defenses are coming online, but these things have very low signatures. We have to expect some will make it down."

"Sound general recall. All troops muster with their units, immediately." Bjorn scanned the feed on his slate. Someone must have been asleep on the hyperspace emergence watch for these things to make it all the way to reentry before being detected. Behind him, he could already hear his troops vacating the bar as their own devices delivered alerts. He looked again at the projected paths of the inbound objects versus the topographical maps. Barring pulling up at the last minute, they'd still be several klicks out to sea when they splashed down, avoiding the surface-to-air defense emplacements that ringed the island. "Tell the officers to be ready for a virtual conference in 30, three-oh, minutes. I'm on my way."

Bjorn quickly scooped the extra slates and paperwork into a satchel and slipped his tactical slate into its holster. He grabbed his leather jacket off the back of the chair and shrugged it on. The Berserkers' logo with the motto 'Valhalla Awaits' was emblazoned on its back. As an afterthought, he gulped down the remainder of his beer.

"Papi Bear! What is happening?"

"Time to earn my pay, princess. Odin willing, you'll only hear some fireworks." Bjorn paused as she hugged him tighter than normal. The bar was three klicks inland, high on a rise where the terrain sloped up to meet the plateau that formed the bulk of the island. Fairly safe, at least at first, but no guarantees. "You and yours should get as high and far from the beach as possible, just to be safe though."

"Don't get yourself killed." Talita reached up and tugged playfully on his beard. "I would miss my favorite customer."

"Not planning on it." Then he remembered something Talita had mentioned over the course of his camping in this bar. "Does your cousin still own that big laundry?"

Talita looked puzzled. "Si. My primo, he owns three now."

"Good. Call him up, tell him to dump all his bleach in the storm sewers. Then he needs to call any other laundries tell them to do the same. I'll pay double to replace the bleach."

"Why?"

Bjorn looked seaward. "Because crabs hate chlorine."

Alaska, Then

"What happened?" Bjorn managed to croak. His mouth was dry, and he was vaguely aware that pain circled like hungry dogs, probably kept at bay by drugs and nanites. As his hearing returned, Bjorn could make out the tell-tale beeps of medical monitors. He cracked his eyes, squinting at the sterile brightness.

"Thank Frigg!" His mother came to his bedside. "Sweetie, can you hear me?"

Bjorn nodded weakly. "Where am I?"

"Providence Medical in Anchorage."

A few disjointed memories returned. "There was a bear."

"Not anymore," Bjorn's father rumbled from the door, filling the frame. "You blew his fucking face off."

"BJ." Short for Bjorn Junior, mom was the only person who could get away with calling Bjorn's father that.

His father rolled his eyes. "He's not ten. If a Kodiak couldn't kill him, an f-bomb from his old man won't. While I was trying to get off my ass out of the snow, you pulled your sidearm and shoved it under the bear's chin while the damned thing was trying to eat you. You put three rounds into the sonavabitch's skull. I'm proud of you, son."

It only took getting mauled by a bear to hear his father say that.

"And I'm sorry, son. If I hadn't fallen, if I'd been paying attention…"

"BJ, it was an accident. Trip knows that." Trip had been Bjorn's nickname from his mother, after Bjorn the Third.

Bjorn tried to flex his fingers. He felt his right ones budge, but not his left. Then he realized he couldn't feel his left arm. It seemed like every part of his body was a dull ache but the left arm. "My arm?"

"Don't worry, son. You're getting the best care credits can buy."

Now

Bjorn pulled his motorcycle up alongside the black and gray command rumbler, an eight-wheeled multi-terrain armored fighting vehicle that served as his mobile HQ. He absently rubbed the tarnished Thor's hammer pendant that hung on a synthleather cord with a half dozen bear claws. Dropping the kickstand and killing the engine, he swung off the motorcycle. He thumped up the ramp into the mobile command post, reaching for the locker that held his haptic suit.

"Commander." Captain Hawkins didn't salute Bjorn per combat protocols. Never give a sniper intel on who he should shoot. Hawkins had been with him for as long as Bjorn had been in the Berserkers.

"Bill, what do you have for me?" Bjorn watched the screens come to life as he shucked his leather jacket, then boots. He kept undressing down to his boxers, heedless of the rumbler's hatch being open. Modesty was a luxury, and he didn't have the time or give a shit.

"Five objects made it through the defensive batteries and splashed down five clicks east of the beach. Based on optical and radar, it looks like they are Xiq'tal drop pods." Maps and images flashed up on the Tri-V screens.

"Fucking crabs. I thought so." Bjorn stepped into the haptic suit which would let him pilot his CASPer battle armor. He struggled a bit with the magnetic zipper, another side effect of a long garrison stint. Once this was over, he'd need to up his PT regimen, maybe put in some time working out alongside the troops. "This means it's a first wave. Someone else is planning on joining the party once the Xiq'tal have shaken things up and worn us down."

Captain Hawkins nodded as he scrolled through the data on his slate. Out of all the mercenary races, the Xiq'tal were reputed to be one of the dumbest, but they were almost as good as Tortantulas as shock troops and far less expensive. They were amphibious, which made them particularly useful for assaulting coastal targets. Called crabs for their resemblance to the Terran creatures, the typical Xiq'tal trooper was two meters wide, with six legs, a pair of fighting arms ending in large claws, and a pair of manipulator arms. Real nightmare fuel. Add to that a weapon pod wired into their nervous system, and fighting a crab was like fighting a small armored vehicle that wanted to eat you. "They're watching for emergence signatures and scrambling orbital patrols."

"The same bozos that missed the crabs coming out of hyperspace to begin with? Someone's ass is getting docked a shit-load of credits." Another merc outfit handled orbital and emergence point defense; the Berserkers' flying assets were recon and assault transport only.

Hawkins nodded, continuing to parse data and cast the most important ones to the Tri-V displays. "They probably dropped running silent, coasted in, and course-corrected halfway from the La Grange point. Most of the time they would have shown up on sensors as small carbonaceous asteroids, maybe a meteor shower."

"I bet the crabs jumped the gun, probably got fucking hungry. Someone should have known better or thought they'd wreak enough havoc it didn't matter." Bjorn slid on the headpiece and made sure the contacts aligned with his pinplants. "What's the civilian sitrep?"

"Civil authorities are clearing the beach and trying to get civilians off of the streets. They are evacuating the neighborhoods adjacent to the beach." The beach and the port were the only parts of the land mass that sloped down to the ocean. The rest of the shoreline was a cliff that rose up to the plateau. "The seaport has been closed, and incoming vessels are being waved off. Fortunately, most of the aqua-agriculture boats are already out to sea. Non-essential personnel are being cleared out of the industrial complex."

Bjorn looked at the displays one more time before climbing down and striding toward the next rumbler in line. Captain Hawkins fell into step, continuing the briefing and reporting on the disposition of various units as they arrived at their assigned zones.

"Owlbear already has flyers and UAVs watching for incursion attempts along the cliffs as well as watching for the Xiq'tal to surface."

Bjorn nodded. Captain McCain commanded Owlbear, the scout company. He was a veteran from when Bjorn's father ran the Berserkers and a survivor of Moloq. He knew his business when it came to running the recon company so Bjorn let him do his thing. The last thing Bjorn needed to do was gum up the works by making competent officers wait on his go-ahead to do their jobs.

Two small reptilians peered around the back of the rumbler, el-Sha armorers. They were responsible for working on Bjorn's CAS-Per, Left Hook, named for the augmented left arm structure. The meter-tall aliens scampered ahead of Bjorn up the ramp into the rumbler.

"Everything good to go, boys?"

Both lizards nodded their green heads and gave Bjorn a thumbs-up. While they understood Human speech, they needed vocal-translators to render their hisses and clicks into something the Humans could understand.

"Left Hook load out per Bjorn Boss instructions," one of them said through the translator. He had given up trying to tell Hek and Vek apart, though somehow Hawkins always knew which one was which.

Bjorn looked over the Binning Mark 7 before turning around and going through the contortions required to climb through the clamshell hatch into the battle armor. Once in and the system confirmed connection to his haptic suit, the hatch closed and his Tri-V HUD lit up, creating a virtual view around his CASPer. He felt the slight buzz as his pinplants linked his mind with the on-board computer. He swept through the status displays for his suit, then mentally shrank them to one corner of his field of view.

"Bruin Command Actual, on line." As Bjorn received his comm check confirmation, he brought up the battlespace display. "Bettie, can you read me?"

"Loud and clear, Bruin Command." Bettie was the battlefield tactical computer. Most decent-sized merc units had a battlefield tactical computer. "Updating your battlespace and networking all company commanders for sitrep."

The captains of the other five companies reported in, all were already standing by. Like Bjorn, the captains of Kodiak and Grizzly companies were in CASPers, the other captains in their command vehicles.

"You all have the reports on the Xiq'tal. They aren't here to capture an objective, they're here to fuck shit up and chow down on us dirt-monkeys." Bjorn brought up the map, highlighting areas as he gave commands. He'd been pissed about the pinplants when he first found out they'd been installed while he was hospitalized, but now they were invaluable, and using them had become second nature.

"Grizzly Company, you're in charge of protecting the seaport and the industrial complex, Ursus Company you're supporting them from their left flank. Owlbear will have eyes on the right flank to make sure the crabs don't try to get creative on the cliffs there.

"Kodiak, you're holding the beach, Polar, you're supporting them from the wall along the promenade avenue." Bjorn was thankful for the short front the terrain created. When the crabs hit, they'd hit hard and try to push through to get into the urban area behind the beach and the industrial area past the port. Crabs didn't like shooting matches, even with the weapon pods they had glued to their carapaces. They liked up close and personal fights where they could be terrifyingly effective, especially against unaugmented opponents. Unlike Tortantulas, though, they wouldn't fight to the last. Like most aliens, once a fight became unwinnable, they'd roll over and live to eat you another day.

"Auggies need to bear the brunt of the attack." Augmented infantry were those using battle armor like CASPers. The Berserkers were equipped with a mix of Mark 6 and Mark 7 suits. Not top-of-the-line, but a lot less expensive since the Mark 8s came out, and more than capable of standing up to Xiq'tal troopers. "The rest will provide support fire; make sure everyone knows to treat the Xiq'tal as enemy vehicles."

The crabs' carapaces would stand up to small arms fire and were naturally refractive to energy weapons, but enough brute force would crack their shells, and enough joules of energy would burn through. That meant using anti-vehicle weapons and munitions, which greatly limited the amount of useful weapons and ammo among foot infantry. Bjorn dismissed the conference to let the company commanders relay orders and deploy their troops.

"Captain Hawkins, make sure Bruin Charlie and Delta are ready to swing to either front." The rumblers in those platoons were Combat Assault Systems Vehicular, nicknamed Casanovas, armored fighting vehicles. They would be able to quickly reach the beach or the port from Bruin Company's position.

Alaska, Then

"I can't play football?" Bjorn's voice had returned over the past day, which he had spent sleeping and learning about the extent of his injuries and the ensuing treatment. He was only alive because his father had been carrying his military trauma kit and had been able to call a med-flyer to evac them. The nanites in the trauma kit had stabilized Bjorn enough to survive until they reached the hospital. Part of him wished he had died out in the snow with that fucking bear; his life was over.

"I'm sorry son. I know how much that means to you." His father actually sounded sincere.

"Just focus on your recovery, sweetie." Bjorn's mother had always encouraged Bjorn's athletic aspirations, in part because she didn't want to see her only child die on some alien world. Sure, that meant that when Bjorn's father was done running the Berserkers they'd have to sell out rather than passing it on to Bjorn, but all the credits in the galaxy couldn't replace your child.

"Look on the bright side, son." His father's smile tugged at his beard. "After you finish physical therapy, you can still take your

VOWS. You'll still be eligible for mercenary work once you get back on your feet and back up to snuff."

Bjorn tried to clench his left fist.

Now

Half an hour had been spent watching the battlespace update as units moved into position. Data from those units, as well as previously deployed scout units, fed into the computer, which was watching for the first signs of the Xiq'tal scuttling out of the deeps.

Finally the first tell-tales appeared on the map as crabs swarmed out of the water around the piers in the port. Some of them doubled back onto the piers to attack the mercenaries firing down into the water while others tried to make their way towards the manufactories in the industrial complex.

Bjorn watched the updates as his men engaged the Xiq'tal. "Bettie, what's the latest feed from the beach units?"

"Last incoming feed was updated 15 seconds ago. No change, no enemy contact."

There had to be more crabs than this. A pod, which acted as a combination dropship and submarine, typically carried 100 Xiq'tal troopers. Bjorn scanned the battlespace, checking the units engaged on the piers. All were augmented infantry, the unaugmented troops providing fire support from the defensive walls surrounding the industrial zone. Bjorn would rather be on offense, looking for the weak point or lynch pin in the opposing force, like when he used to hunt down opposing quarterbacks. But for now he'd have to look for the blitz.

"Grizzly, don't let them pin you down on the piers, they're trying to break through to the industrial complex." He sent a mental instruction to Bettie to highlight the relevant zones on the map. "Be advised, Owlbear reports some of the crabs are carrying ack-ack pods, so you'll need to do this the hard way." Jumping over the Xiq'tal would normally be the fastest way for the CASPers to get across the battlefield, but the flying armor would be easy targets in the sky if they stayed up for more than a few seconds. They had already lost a handful of UAVs and a flyer that didn't get out of the firing envelope fast enough. The last thing they wanted to do was get brought to ground among the crabs, even in a CASPer. While the battler armor was tough, the crabs loved trying to pull the suits' limbs off.

The beach was still quiet. Bjorn didn't like it. "All you guys chilling on the beach, keep your eyes peeled. Hawkins, send Charlie and Delta to hit the crabs at the piers, Zones 5 and 6, try to give those CASPers an opening to push out."

The units barring the way to the manufactories had started taking casualties, but not heavily. They were well placed and started pouring fire as soon as the crabs were in range. Bjorn watched the enemy rate of attrition versus the pace of their advance. On the other side of the battle, the CASPer units on the pier pushed into Zone 6 en masse, not only blunting the crabs' charge but pushing them back into Zone 5. Tell-tales appeared in the battlespace as commanders gave their troops their orders and targets. The Casanovas got into position and opened up on Zone 5, their magnetic accelerator cannons pouring a deluge of armor-piercing rounds into the massed Xiq'tal, punctuated with the occasional missile explosion.

Then a wave of crabs burst from the surf along the beach, water spilling off their grey carapaces. Half again as many as the invaders that had hit the port, this force had to scuttle from the water across an expanse of open sand. The Berserkers used that opportunity to pepper the crabs with missiles and MAC fire. Unaugmented infantry stationed along the promenade wall and on top of the buildings closest to the beach fired squad support machine guns and portable missile launchers into the crabs further back in the surge.

The crabs responded with flechette launchers and propelled acid grenades. Neither were long-range weapons and posed little threat to the CASPers at the forefront of the fight, but the closest unaugmented infantry, hunkered down behind the wall behind the beach were susceptible to acid grenades popping off over their positions. Fortunately, automated anti-ordnance weapons were picking off most of the Xiq'tal grenades in mid-flight, raining acid down on the beach but not the unprotected troops.

Bjorn spared a glance at the seaport fight. The crabs had tried to pinch off the CASPer units before they could get off the pier but had reacted too slowly and suffered heavy losses from the Casanovas. Now the CASPers were hitting the rear of the Xiq'tal, breaking up the crabs' assault and wreaking havoc. The Xiq'tal liked to use their largest fighting claw as a shield, which they couldn't when attacked from behind.

Several blinking icons along the beach front drew his attention. Another wave of crabs had emerged from the water near the beach, one of them notably larger than the others. Upon the arrival of the larger Xiq'tal, several crabs simultaneously peppered the unaugmented positions with grenades. Guns began to go offline as acid misted down and corroded sensor elements and tracking gimbals. The crabs surged forward, ignoring the threat posed by the CASPers; several Xiq'tal were killed while their comrades clambered past. Bjorn had the best video feed of the fight zoom in on the new arrivals.

"Fuck, a king crab." Bjorn knew they were rarely deployed; whoever had hired the Xiq'tal would have paid a premium. Their presence made the Xiq'tal more coordinated and much more deadly. In the battlespace, he flagged the new arrival 'QB,' "Get the unaugmented infantry back out of range of those grenades, *now!*"

With a thought, Bjorn's CASPer detached from the rumbler's umbilical, switching to its own power and comms. With a whine of servos, Left Hook rose from its cradle and trod down the ramp, armored boots clanging. Immediately, the CASPer platoon of Bruin Company formed up, awaiting orders.

The front along the beach was in danger of buckling as squads heavy on green troops tried to fall back in an orderly manner while faced with voracious armored aliens. A few life sign indicators winked out as the leading edge of the crabs' surge contacted infantry too slow to get back. Bjorn didn't need to see the video feeds to know what was happening. Xiq'tal were infamous for dismembering and eating their victims.

"Bruin Command Actual to Polar Alpha." Captain Wirth would be pissed about Bjorn going straight to one of his lieutenants, but there wasn't time for chain-of-command delays. "Do you read, Lieutenant Sanchez?"

"Sanchez here," came the hurried reply after a brief delay. "I am cut off from most of my platoon, I can't raise my sergeants. Position is being overrun by hostiles."

"Bettie, sitrep on those squads?" Bjorn knew Bettie could sort the data faster than he. Since she was privy to his feeds, she knew what units he had been looking at without being told. The updates flashed across his field of view through his pinplants. Sergeants for those platoons showed as out of commission or no life signs. Bjorn cursed Loki; losing all three of those sergeants in the space of minutes was a kick in the nuts that endangered that whole front. As he glanced across the listings of the corporals for each squad, a name caught his eye. Bjorn mentally sent comm orders to Bettie, pushing the half dozen channels he had been monitoring to the back of his mind and isolating a single channel.

"Bruin Command Actual to Polar Alpha Three. Corporal Wicza, do you copy?" Bjorn remembered taking on Charlotte Wicza as a cadre merc-in-training just before starting the garrison assignment. She had been passed over by other merc companies because of her diminutive stature. They would have taken her in logistics; her mental and educational results on her VOWS had been top notch. But she wanted to be in the fighting forces. Even though her size had handicapped her, she still passed the physical portions of the VOWS with flying colors. Bjorn saw a fierceness behind her eyes and had given her a spot in his training cadre. He hoped his intuition was about to pay off.

"Wicza here, Commander. We've lost Sergeant Taylor, falling back to…grid 1-Hotel-5." While her voice sounded urgent, it wasn't panicked, despite the losses her unit had suffered and the enemy forces pushing them back. In the background he could hear the buzzsaw whine of a squad support MAC.

"Bruin Command Actual to Polar Alpha Two and Polar Alpha Four, form up with Three, fall back to 1-Golf-6. Wicza is in charge." Channels switched again to isolate Corporal Wicza's comm. "Wicza, I need you to take those squads and hold that fallback position.

You'll have reinforcements hitting the beach in four minutes. Can you do that?"

"Yes commander! We'll hold those fucking crabs or see you in Valhalla." She punctuated her response with her grenade launcher.

"Praise fucking Thor!" Combined, those units were two squads' worth of troops. If they folded, the crabs would surge through into the city blocks behind them, mostly estates for the well-off. Bjorn switched channels again. "Hawkins, send Bravo to harass the beach flank closest to us, see if they can pull off some of those crabs rushing the promenade." In the battlespace he called up the topographic map and a flight plan implementing program.

"Commander, there are several enemy units equipped with anti-aircraft ordnance in the target formation, especially between here and enemy unit designated QB." Bettie highlighted the projected fire envelopes of the enemy ack-ack. "Operational losses predicted at 25% before you reach your objective."

"That's why we're not going to fly to them." He adjusted the flight plan to adhere as closely to the sand as possible, then let Bettie parse it to the units involved. "Bruin Alpha, who's ready to crack some crab?"

A roar greeted him back over the comms as the flight plans uploaded to the CASPers.

"On my mark…cannonball!" Two dozen CASPers arced upward on jump jets, then rolled forward and torpedoed into the sea. The three-minute dive took ten times as much jump juice as flight; their curving path brought them bursting from the waves among the rear elements of the crabs. Steam rolled off the CASPers' red-hot jump nozzles as they splashed through the knee-deep water.

Xiq'tal troopers were bowled over as the CASPer troopers slammed into them, and the thinner carapaces of their bellies were exposed to armor-piercing magnetic cannon fire. A ripple went through the aliens' formation, accompanied by hisses and clicks as they realized there was a threat within their ranks, and their forward momentum was arrested. On cue, half the CASPers jumped again. The disarray created by Alpha Company's arrival bought them the few extra seconds needed to reach the promenade before the Xiq'tal anti-air weapons could get a lock on them.

Bjorn charged straight for his objective, the king crab. The huge alien was the size of a rumbler and deceptively fast. Kind of like himself, Bjorn mused as he jumped and brought his armored feet down on the crab's back. The dark grey carapace shuddered under the impact and shifted. As he slid off the shell, he grabbed the battle axe in his armor's left hand, the double blade twenty kilograms of monocarbide-edged poly-steel. He swung, the servos in the augmented left arm whining to keep up with the demand. The weapon bit deep into the armor of one of the crab's legs, lodged not quite to the halfway mark.

A squealing hiss sounded as the king crab spun, lashing out with the smaller of its fighting claws. Bjorn rolled back, barely evading the appendage as it flashed by his face. Landing on his feet, Bjorn brought his MAC to bear, unleashing a burst. The larger of the claws came up as a shield, the high-velocity rounds pock-marking the chitin but not punching through. Bjorn tried to target his anti-vehicle missile, a tank-busting shaped-charge round, only to have his laser-guided targeting system flip him off. The same refractive property of the chitin that made lasers less effective also made laser-targeting almost useless.

Bjorn switched to computer-optical targeting, less precise but better than eyeballing it. His onboard computer acquired the target's silhouette and would try to guide the missile based solely on video input. Just as he gave to command to fire, another Xiq'tal tackled him, sending the shot too far astray for the missile's guidance to correct in time. As it streaked over the king crab, the computer picked out another Xiq'tal farther down range. The missile struck it between the optical canopies, the result was overkill as a jet of super-heated metal blew through the alien's upper carapace and out its underside.

Bjorn ripped the new assailant off as it tried to latch onto his right arm. It splashed into the water legs up, exposing its pale underside and constantly-chewing mouth plates. Even as he put a burst into it, another Xiq'tal lunged at him. Bjorn brought his huge armored left fist down in a hammer strike, shattering one of the alien's optical canopies, and driving it into the sand. The exposed triple-eye stalk tried to retreat deeper into the shell. A three-round burst took the fight out of that crab.

Around him, First and Second Squads were laying waste to the Xiq'tal. A quick check of the battlespace showed a fight was raging where he'd ordered Wicza to hold, but it looked like they were holding as Third Squad pushed toward that position. Fourth Squad was holding the promenade, punishing any aliens foolish enough not to fall back to the sea.

A shadow alerted Bjorn, and he dove aside as one of the king crab's fighting claws snapped at his right arm; the crabs knew which of the CASPer's arms had the cannon. A volley from the accelerator cannon brought the shield claw up. Again, no significant damage, but it gave Bjorn the opportunity to dart in and wrest his axe from the injured leg. He fought to keep from falling backwards when the axe finally popped loose, and he activated the magnetic grip in his gauntlet to keep the weapon from flying from his grasp.

The smaller fighting claw snapped in again, only to be batted away. A cannon burst shredded a leg joint too far out for the shield claw to cover, blue blood leaking down the damaged limb. Another intruder in the fray had its shield claw sheared off by the axe. Bjorn pivoted to keep the king crab from capitalizing on the distraction, a volley of cannon shots glanced off its upper carapace while the giant Xiq'tal peppered him with several flechette volleys. More powerful than the weapons used by the smaller aliens, Bjorn felt a stab of pain as one of the spikes punched through the armor at his knee.

Bjorn felt multiple impacts from behind. One of his jump jet indicators flagged red, as did the targeting actuator for his missile launcher. Pain from his hip, accompanied by a servo warning, told him where a third projectile had gotten through. Bjorn's rear camera showed one of the crabs bearing an anti-air weapon kneeling in the sand, tilting its carapace forward so the long biomechanical weapon pointed at him, but another CASPer splashed into view, grabbed the weapon by the barrel and wrenched it loose.

Free to deal with the king crab, Bjorn circled his opponent, ignoring the pain that accompanied each step. A feint with the cannon followed by a swing paid off; the second strike carved enough carapace away that the leg could no longer support the king crab's weight. Another Xiq'tal jumped Bjorn from behind, knocking him forward as it grabbed for his arms with its fighting claws.

Bjorn triggered his remaining jump jets, bowling the pair of them into the king crab. The smaller alien was knocked loose by the impact; the bigger crab listed as both ravaged legs snapped like rotten timber. Bjorn glanced up and saw the grinding plates that formed the king crab's mouth; they looked like an organic wood chipper. Through his pinplants he sent a flurry of commands.

//Magnetic grip off// The battle axe fell into the surf.

//Missile launcher, eject round//

//Magnetic grip on// The jettisoned missile snapped into his open gauntlet.

//Left arm assembly: servo governors disengage//

//Left arm assembly: servos 200% power//

Clutching the round, with a Viking battle cry he punched his armored left fist into the king crab's mouth.

Three more commands.

//Missile warhead arm//

//Self: left arm disengage neural feedback//

//Missile warhead detonate//

The shaped-charge went off inside the alien leader. A gout of hemocyanin blood and chitinous shards erupted from its mouth as one of its optical canopies exploded upwards. A smoking spider web of cracks appeared where the upper carapace bulged outwards then blew open. The king crab slumped backwards, limp.

Alaska, Then

"Come on son, your bionic arm is better, three times stronger than the original."

Bjorn glowered, flexing his new cybernetic hand. "It also disqualifies me from ever playing football."

"Look, it's not like there was a choice. Your arm was too fucked up to save, even with nanites. Having a gimped arm would have flushed your chances of playing ball."

Bjorn glared at him silently.

"What, you think I got that bear to rip your arm to shreds just so you couldn't go to school? Son, this is a shit sandwich, but it's all there is for dinner. Someday you'll see."

Bjorn clenched his new left fist.

Now

Bjorn ripped the stump of his armor's left arm from the corpse, blasting the crab that had jumped him as it tried to regain its footing. Nanites were already staunching the bleeding from the shredded epidermis on his now exposed cyber-hand. He spotted the hilt of his axe and snatched it up in his right hand. The shallows and beach were littered with the handiwork of his company. His squad had pushed up onto the beach while the rest were dealing with the dwindling attackers still in the water. A few crabs made for the cliffs only to be picked off.

"Which of you fucks is surf and turf next?" Bjorn bellowed through his suit speakers. Another ripple passed through the remaining aliens, accompanied by hisses that sounded as much like a steam-powered telegraph as anything else. Beginning with the crabs closest to him, they sank to the sand, folding their legs up in a show of submission and surrender. He turned on the closest capitulator, stomping through the waves towards it, brandishing the axe. "Don't you fucking surrender! I'm good and pissed and ready to chop the fuck out of you blue-blooded pieces of shit!"

Reports rolled in through battlespace and the comms that the crabs were submitting. Bjorn focused past his seething blood, but still kept an eye on the nearby Xiq'tal. It looked like the crabs had done the math, especially with their big boss off the board. "Wicza, sitrep."

There was a pause. Battlespace status showed half her troops were wounded or dead, but the crabs hadn't gotten past the choke-point where she had taken a stand. "Wicza here, commander. Looks like Valhalla will have to wait."

"Damn fine work soldier. Bruin Command Actual to all points. The Xiq'tal have shown their belly. Find their talkers, corral them to holding areas pending ransom proceedings. If a crab so much as looks at you funny, put it down." Per guild rules, the surrendering mercenaries would be ransomed back to their unit, or barring that, their home world. As much as Bjorn wanted to murder every one of the chitinous bastards, that's not how smart mercs conducted war. If you murdered surrendering troops, you could expect no quarter yourself. He reached awkwardly to snap his axe back in its holster.

* * *

Tio Ramon's hadn't been affected by the incursion, as the closest invader had been stopped ten blocks away. Looking out at the street, you couldn't tell a voracious mob of aliens had been unleashed on the planet less than a week ago. When Bjorn first returned, Talita had been waiting for him, jumping up and forcing him to catch her while she kissed him. While Bjorn recovered from his surprise, Talita inspected the replaced left hand, the bio-printed epidermis still soft and pink. It was obvious she'd heard that his hand had been blown off from his troops that frequented the bar. He hadn't been to the bar since the battle, waiting for the replacement hand to be fabricated, installed, and reskinned.

After that, it was back to banter and beer, though it seemed Talita fussed about Bjorn more than usual. Bjorn had plenty of time to spend in the bar; the combat clause of the garrison contract had been activated, meaning that the H'rang were on the hook for material expenditures and a portion of the replacement costs. That meant more paperwork for Bjorn to fill out, even if it was all electronic.

One of Bjorn's slates held the butcher's bill, the personnel and assets lost in the battle with the Xiq'tal. If there was a part of his job he dreaded, it was going through the casualties. He knew it was the same for every mercenary commander, but he felt it more keenly after Moloq. He scanned through the list, 27 dead, another 13 permanently disabled, another 105 still recovering in trauma treatment, most of those from acid burns.

He scanned down the list until he found the name he was looking for, Charlotte Wicza. Injured but expected to make a full recovery within two weeks. He'd have to do something for Corporal Wicza to reward her valor and determination. He made a mental note to talk to Hek and Vek.

"See Papi Bear, you need to stay and protect us!" Talita threw her arms around his neck.

"Princess, I would like nothing better than to sit here and let you bring me cold beer." Bjorn picked up his business slate. "But the H'rang are offering us a fat assault contract to go and kick the Masheen in the balls, all four of them, for sending the crabs here."

"Then I will go with you."

Bjorn chuckled. While camp followers weren't unheard of for merc officers, especially commanders, he would have trouble justifying bringing along a personal cervajadora, especially one that wasn't warming his bunk. For a split second, he considered introducing

Talita to Corporal Wicza. From what he understood, they played for the same team.

"Princess, if I take this contract, we'll be bouncing back to Earth to get ready for the new mission." Bjorn held up the business slate. "As much as I'll miss you, there's no reason for you to follow me back to Terra."

She sat on his lap, her green eyes locked with his. "Of course there is. I have been trying to give you hints for the last year." She leaned forward and whispered in his ear. "I don't like boys, but I do like men."

As she kissed him, Bjorn thumbed the 'accept' box on the contract.

# # # # #

Chris' Introduction to:

Stand On It

by Kevin Ikenberry

When I asked Chuck Gannon if he would consent to doing the foreword for "A Fistful of Credits," little did I realize I would get an author out of it, as well. As we were parting, Chuck said, "You'll want to check out Kevin Ikenberry and grab him now before too many more people find out about him." Trusting Chuck's judgment, I offered him a spot in this anthology, sight unseen, and I'm really happy I did.

Kevin's submission for "A Fistful of Credits" was one of the first ones we received, and I liked his ability to write combat so much that I immediately offered him a contract to write a full length follow-up to "Stand on It." If you want to know more at the end of the story, you won't have to wait long—"Peacemaker" will be out this fall.

"Sleeper Protocol," Kevin's first novel, was hailed by Publisher's Weekly as "an emotionally powerful debut" and was a Finalist for the Colorado Book Award in 2017. He is a retired Army officer, a lifelong space geek, and loves to hike and swim. If you'd like to know more about Kevin, you can find him at http://www.kevinikenberry.com.

STAND ON IT
by Kevin Ikenberry

Unnamed Planet, Praf Region
1700 local

"Hammer down!" Marc called into his headset. "Ghost Leader, you're cleared to LD."

"Ghost Lead, roger," Hex replied. "Crossing the line of departure now. All CASPer systems green and moving."

Marc saw Hex's CASPers light up as mobile infantry icons on the tactical display mounted on the turret wall of his Mark Nine command tank, and proceed west toward the shallow river. The 24 Combat Assault System, Personal mecha were to scout ahead of the main assault. "Driver, move out for overwatch position Bravo."

"Bravo, you got it, sir."

Marc consulted the kneeboard strapped to his left leg. He'd failed to write down the names of the newest Marauders. They'd barely accomplished three days of holotraining before suiting up and wouldn't earn a call sign until after their first mission. *Even after a milk run like this,* Marc thought as he looked up through the external cameras and sighted in on their objective. The ancient Raknar mecha lay curled on its left side in a fetal position. Nested inside a group of low hills, the rusting beast laying under a thick blanket of vegetation was hard to miss.

"Objective marked." He placed an icon on the center of the hills next to the mecha's frame.

"Ghost Lead across the LD into the forest. Tracking a few hundred inbound life forms converging on the objective," Hex said over their private channel. "Gods. I hate Oogars, man."

"With you, Hex," Marc replied. He flipped the radio over to the task force frequency: "All Marauders, weapons free. I say again, you are weapons free."

Marc looked over the breech of the main gun platform at his loader. *Johnson, that's the kid's name, right? Shit.*

"Johnson?"

The lanky blonde kid from Montana turned to look at him. "Yessir?"

Thank Gods.

"Get five RAPS into the autoloader." The rocket assisted projectiles would give them a little more standoff range from the overwatch position if Hex and his team ran into trouble.

"Yessir!" Johnson turned to the rear of the compartment and began pulling the RAP shells from the steel racks. His hands trembled.

Marc glanced at the timer on his display and checked Ghost Team's progress. They were way behind where they needed to be.

"Lucille, get me video from Ghost Lead."

The onboard command and control link was like a second set of eyes. <<Engaged. Screen three.>>

The Tri-V screen above Marc's right knee flickered into a spastic nightmare. Immense feral Oogar poured out of the dense forest, directly at Hex and his six-man team. Only fourteen of Hex's icons were still on the screen. Guns blazing, Hex mowed down a line of purple-furred Oogars and pushed west toward the objective.

"Hammer, Ghost Lead. We're status amber. Committing my reserve and requesting reinforcement forward."

Marc jabbed the radio button on his turret controls. "Roger, all. Hang on, Hex. Marauders, forward on me!"

From the overwatch position, the deep, narrow river lay about three kilometers ahead. Another icon on Hex's team winked out. "Driver. Fast as she goes!"

"I'm standing on the gas pedal, sir!"

The Mark Nine's tracks whined to life as the eighty-ton tank accelerated above 50 miles per hour. Marc initialized the cannon and selected the targeting sequence. "Angel Lead, where are you?"

On cue, the first of the wide-fanned flyers swung over his tank and pushed hard for the river, quad cannons blazing. "Angels are falling, Hammer. Standby for target linkage."

Johnson called. "Five loaded, sir!"

"Got it." Marc watched fresh targeting icons appear on his forward screen. He selected five of them with double-blinks of his eyes. "Firing!"

The tank barely moved as the five RAPs *chuffed* out of the tube, arced through the sky, and impacted along the tree line just south of Hex's position. More rounds descended on the trees from his five tanks. What had been a pristine, quiet forest erupted into a burning cauldron of Hell. Marc grinned as the tank dove down the bank toward the river at 60 miles per hour.

"Hammer, Ghost Lead. Need assistance!"

Marc watched the second to last icon fade out. "Distance to Ghost Lead, Lucille?"

<<400 meters from the far bank. They are 37 percent surrounded by feral Oogar.>> Lucille, his tank's unique command and control interface replied. Without Lucille, he'd need another Human deputy commander—and that was the last thing he wanted.

The tank hit the water and decelerated violently. Marc grabbed the handles on his seat and barely avoided slamming his head into the forward control panel. "Godsdammit, Driver! Tell me when you're going 'feet wet!'"

"Sorry," the kid said. Taking the newbies was supposed to make things easier on the rest of his troops, but more often than not it left him teaching life lessons instead of shooting, moving, and communicating. The Mark Nine crept toward the steeper far bank and gave a satisfying *whump* as the tracks caught their footing and tore up toward the wood line, right into a line of Oogar.

"Holy shit!" the driver called from the hull. The first Oogar bounced off the left forward skirt. Marc selected the quad rocket batteries and raked fire into the crowd of Oogar. A mist of purple blood covered the main exterior camera.

Across the upper turret armor, Marc could hear the Oogar clawing at the sensor arrays and weaponry for any type of purchase.

"Maven!" Marc called into a private frequency. "Clean me off!"

"That's a new one," she chuckled into his ear. He relaxed his grip slightly on the turret controls. Her confidence filled him.

Marc watched the Angel Lead icon swing toward him. A deployment of smoke grenades knocked one of the Oogar off the tank. Three others still clung to the turret. Targeting icons appeared and flashed twice. The Oogars fell away as the tank swerved to avoid a rock outcropping.

"Thanks, Maven."

"Roger, Hammer," she called. As his executive officer and chief pilot, as well as friend and occasional bedmate, she was indispensable. "They're coming in waves. Like a million of them."

Marc nodded. "Yeah, Ch'tek said the Raknar hull was a shrine or something to them. We've got the weapons to keep them away. Keep pushing."

He caught sight of Hex's CASPer moving his way. The infantry commander waved and closed the distance. The familiar *clamping* noise of a CASPer mount made him smile.

I have more guns.

"Hammer, I'm locked on your port quarter. Adjust your sectors of fire."

<<Weapons adjusted.>> Lucille reported. Now Marc wouldn't be able to turn the guns enough to accidentally shoot Hex's CASPer.

"Welcome aboard, Hex. Just in time for another wave," Marc called. "Maven, need you to hit them again."

"On our way, Hammer."

Through the trees, Marc could see thousands of Oogar descending on them. Some of them carried spears. Some had something like slingshots or bows and arrows. Even more carried rocks the size of beach balls. The flyers came in across his nose and a fusillade of rocks went up from the descending mob.

"Pull up! Pull up!" he heard Maven call from her lead flyer as it shuddered violently to the right and pieces of her left, front fan exploded upward. The left, rear fan exploded a heartbeat later. Out of control, the flyer spun into the trees and exploded. In quick succession, two other flyers succumbed to the fusillade of primitive weapons and spun to the ground.

"Maven!" Marc screamed.

Oh Gods no!

"Light the fuckers up!" Hex screamed over the command frequency. "Ghost Two, I need you up here, on the double!"

Marc's vision swam in a mix of rage and tears as he raked the Oogar line with machine gun fire. He glanced at Johnson. "Get me the beehive rounds! As many as we've got!"

"Yessir!"

Marc studied his tactical display and saw a rapidly closing opportunity. "Hex! Get ready to breach their line. All Marauders, on me. Angels, wave off and standby!" Marc selected the main gun and keyed in the sequence for the beehive rounds. Like a massive shotgun shell, each round contained thousands of nail-like projectiles. A long time before, on Earth, the rounds had been outlawed as being inhumane. Intergalactic conflict made them fair game.

"Beehive loaded! Two salvos of four!" Johnson called.

"Marauders ready—eight rounds. Breach on me!"

Marc scanned the line of Oogar and found a bright gold one, a female, and aimed at the large black- and red-skinned male next to it. Targeting reticle centered, he fired the first round. Sixteen Oogar in the line went down along with the two rows behind them. Still more of the snarling, long toothed bear-things pressed forward. Marc fired again and again. Each round rocked the tank from front to rear. Dust billowed up from the ground around them to obscure the view screens and his sighting systems. The tank lurched forward, treads spinning for purchase on what he knew was a pile of maimed corpses, but he kept firing. Abruptly, the tree line opened into a wide clearing near the helmeted carapace of the Raknar.

The Mark Nine pushed past a ring of rock cairns about two hundred meters from the mecha. "Driver, head for the Raknar's knees. Turn left before you get there and take up a position near its waist." He switched frequencies. "Hex, you get gardening duty."

There was no response.

Marc flipped the outer camera on the left side to on and saw the CASPer still in place. Hex was looking behind them.

"Hex? What's going on?"

"The Oogar have stopped, Hammer. They're encircling us but staying behind that ring of rocks. I've got second squad coming in from the northeast before the Oogar close them off."

"Hammer, Angel Four." The incoming transmission was weak and full of static. "Hammer, can you hear me?"

"I've got you Seanan." He locked onto her flyer. All status lights blinked red and she was losing altitude fast.

"Hammer, I'm going down across the river. Too much damage. All Angels down. You've got no air support. I'm sorry."

Marc ran a hand across his stubbly hair. "Seanan, put it down safe and activate your beacons. We'll bring the ship down on your position."

"I'm trying—" The transmission broke up into static.

"Lucille! Where is she?"

<<Angel Four has crashed-landed two point six kilometers to the east. There are no life signs.>>

Dammit. Marc felt the tank slow down, then stop. He blinked away tears and took a sharp, deep breath. *This was supposed to be a milk run!*

<<Commander, I can no longer reach the *Trigger Happy.* The Raknar appears to be leaking fuel and the resulting radiation is blocking all communications but line of sight UHF. There is minimal danger to Humans if exposure is less than three hours.>>

Marc punched the casing of the commander's tactical display with his left hand. *Focus, Marc!*

After two deep breaths he felt better, calmer. There wasn't time for grief or frustration. His forces were safe for the moment, but they couldn't stay. There was only one choice. He fingered the radio transmit button and let the plan form quickly in his mind.

"Marauders, into a coil. CASPers are inbound from the south—let them pass into the center. Defensive posture alpha. If those things come inside that rock circle, nuke 'em with everything you've got." The five remaining tanks circled up and created a perimeter against the Raknar's hull.

"Johnson, you've got command of this vehicle. Lucille, relay a message to Maya. Join me in the middle of the perimeter with Hex." Marc released his five-point harness and stood in his seat. Climbing through the open cupola, he turned and saw the swath of forest they'd destroyed, and thousands of Oogar slowing ringing their position near the Raknar. More lay behind them, dead and dying.

Some of the freakish things shrieked. The sound was unnerving, and then it abruptly cut off. Some of them swayed from side-to-side, a sign of their anxiety he'd learned at the Flight Academy ten years before. Civilized Oogar were very capable warriors; feral ones were downright dangerous. The ring of angry bear-things parted like the sea.

An immense Oogar, so purple it was almost black in the fading light, pushed through the crowd and stood at the rock cairn two hundred meters from the nose of Marc's tank. Draped from both shoulders, crossing in the front, it wore a bandolier heavy with an assortment of stone tools and weapons. The Oogar fell silent. The giant beast stared a hole through him. A shiver ran down Marc's back. Behind him, Hex engaged a flamer to burn back the forest ivy near the hulking Raknar's crumpled midsection.

Marc withdrew an earpiece from his pocket and keyed it with a tug on his left earlobe. "Lucille? Radio check?"

<<Five by five, commander.>>

"Execute pre-task alpha four and transmit current location data."

<<Acknowledged.>>

Marc withdrew a mini-slate from the leg pocket of his coveralls and engaged the device. Acquiring and initializing the slate through his tank's inertial navigation system took precious time. Marc looked again over his shoulder at the ring of Oogar surrounding them. From the south, a fresh burst of machine gun fire signaled the arrival of Ghost Two and four additional CASPers.

Six left.; we started with twelve, Marc sighed. *That lying little shit. Never trust a Zuparti, Marc. Especially ones with big mouths and loose cash.*

"Hammer, Ghost Two reporting," Hex's executive officer called as they approached. Her cameras, though, remained fixed on Hex. Though he was unable to see her face, Marc understood all too well. A familiar pang of loss rose up in Marc's chest. Fists clenched, he closed his eyes and willed himself to breathe. Maven would have wanted him to survive. Not because she loved him, but because their soldiers needed him. Their unlikely relationship violated every rule in Marc's moral handbook, but it worked. That had been all that mattered. Now, he was alone. Again.

"Maya," Marc said, and shook his head. "Ghost Two. Secure the internal space by the Raknar's torso. I'll move in for extraction when you report clear."

"Roger, Hammer." Maya moved swiftly in the eight-foot-tall powered armor. She swung around behind Hex and as gently as a CASPer could, she touched his left arm as he disengaged the flamer. "Second Squad, on me!"

They disappeared into the singed canopy. Marc turned and met the eyes of the waiting Oogar; there was no doubt that he was the leader, given the space and respect shown by the others.

As darkness fell, Marc watched groups of Oogar hustle to the rock cairns with arm loads of wood from the forest. Fires were started with friction bows and loud huffs. Around the Raknar hulk, the forest was alight.

<<Feral Oogar have poor night vision. They are likely setting a watch to ensure you cannot get away.>>

"How many are there, Lucille?"

<<Eleven thousand five hundred. Plus or minus one thousand. They have completely ringed the Raknar at a distance of two hundred and seventy meters.>>

What in the hell do I do now?

Bartertown Starport, Karma
8 days earlier

Above the din of Peepo's Pit, Ch'tek's sleek ears picked up an incoming data transmission from his ship in Bay 12 Charlie. From a small pack at his waist, he removed a slate and tapped a complex password sequence with his long claws. As he read, Ch'tek clicked his tongue excitedly. He glanced up into the somber eyes of his assistant and twisted his maw into an approximation of a grin.

"Why so sad, Gu'chuk?"

The smaller, frailer Zuparti was a lower caste and indentured into the service of this trader. His lips carefully formed the words as he'd not spoken in more than three days. "There must be another way, Honored Ch'tek."

The words caught Ch'tek's complete attention. He pushed the slate to the countertop and leaned back in the high-backed chair. "Why is that, Gu'chuk? Why do you care about them? They are a less-talented species. They've barely tasted war." He smiled again as if daring his servant to speak.

"With respect, Honored Ch'tek," Gu'chuk said, his words almost lost in the constant roar of the mercenary hangout. "Forcing terror upon a frightened species will coalesce fear into resolve. Resolve turns to aggression." Gu'chuk looked away.

Ch'tek roared with laughter. "You quote the Great Scrolls to me!"

Gu'chuk shrank down into his seat. "My apologies, Honored Ch'tek."

"Go back to the ship," Ch'tek sputtered in between his laughs. A message icon blinked on the slate, and he pressed it. As he scanned the message, his laughter stopped. "Our bandit has signed the contract. See to it he has what he needs."

"Yes, Honored Ch'tek." The tiny Zuparti fled as fast as his tiny legs would take him.

Ch'tek wiped at his eyes and tried to relax his quivering abdomen as he watched his servant scamper away. The empty seat slid back, and a wide, flat face slid into view.

"Doontal?" Ch'tek said. "Won't you join me?"

The Buma diplomat bowed its head but did not move to sit. "The Council is much distressed that you have been unable to deliver our diplomatic package to Earth as promised."

Ch'tek nodded solemnly. "I have a team in transit with it now."

"The Council does not trust you. Nor do I," Doontal said. "A simple gift should not have been so ceremoniously delayed."

Ch'tek steepled his claws across his belly. The gift in question financed Hammer's mission. And, it would produce a gift for the citizens of Earth. If successful, the Buma would be partly responsible for destroying the species they'd chosen to bring into the Union. The irony was enough that Ch'tek had to suppress a smile.

"Space flight is not easy, Doontal. I made a choice of using the lowest bidder, and I've paid handsomely for it. My previous courier lost a ship and five crewmen. We have secured the gift and will have it aboard one of my skiffs tonight. We'll get it loaded onto an interstellar vessel and send it immediately. You can meet them at the Sol emergence point, if you'd like. I'm forecasting two weeks, maybe less." Ch'tek shrugged.

Doontal's wide amber eyes blinked slowly. "We will meet our gift. You will inform us of any...adjustments to your plan."

"Then it's settled." Ch'tek made to stand up. "I'll look forward to the news of your presentation to the Council of Earth. You have my apologies for the delay."

Doontal nodded again, an almost complete move of the Buma's torso, and slid from view. Ch'tek did not see the Buma's retreat. On his slate, he keyed his ship's automated system to file a diplomatic flight plan to the Zuparti home world, Baant. He wouldn't go there, of course. Nor could he risk any of his usual hideouts. Tapping the screen with a claw, a smile spread across his features.

Why not hide in view of my greatest achievement? Watching horror appear real-time on the features of the worthless Buma was an event to be cherished, if not celebrated. It had been too long since he'd been to Luna anyway. He froze as a Human female with long red hair tied in an elaborate braid slid onto the stool opposite him.

"Can I help you?"

She smiled. "You've signed Marc Lemieux and his Marauders to a mission."

"My business dealings are confidential—"

"I'll get your package, at half the price," she said.

Ch'tek shook his head. "Until I know who you are, or you show me your bona fides, this conversation goes no further."

She placed her hand on his slate. Flashing circles appeared around her fingertips in rapid succession. Within seconds, the identification software returned a hit from GalNet and Ch'tek clicked his tongue appreciably.

"My dear, I had no idea. Please forgive me. You were responsible for the apprehension of the Buma contingent at D'mack Four and you brought the Boss Ken regime down at Rayu Four? I am impressed, Miss Francis. Very impressed, indeed. But I must ask why a bounty hunter would take on a dangerous mission at such low cost? Something against Mister Lemieux?"

"He has something I want, Honored Ch'tek. That's all you need to know."

Unnamed Planet, Praf Region
2105 local

<<Commander, text only report from Demon One. Message as follows: Drop status is green. I have your coordinates loaded into the pad. Descending through ten thousand meters. Estimated arrival is one three minutes.>> Lucille reported.

Marc looked at his slate and nodded to himself. The autonomous pad would descend under controlled parachutes from ultra-high altitude. The damned things cost more than six million credits a piece and there was only one in the *Trigger Happy's* inventory. If he'd had the presence of mind to get a confirmation on the package's size, he could have purchased a second pad.

Jill would have purchased one anyway.

He shook off the thought and tried to project confidence. He hadn't even considered the gift could be larger than what a man could carry and not a cargo container. All of his eggs were in one basket and descending with only a computer's guidance system. His ex-wife would not have approved.

Marc sighed and glanced at Hex as the younger man dismounted his CASPer. He looked more like his father every day with longish brown hair and bright blue eyes. Hex smirked. "What is it, Hammer?"

I really hate that call-sign. "Nothing."

Hex smirked. "What are you thinking?"

"What we're going to do if that pad doesn't make it into our little circle of Hell."

Hex laughed, "Ye of little faith, boss." He consulted a mini-slate on his wrist and showed the display to Marc. "It's on target with fairly light winds at altitude. I'm going to put it down inside the coil."

Their tanks sat in a wide circle with gun tubes facing out to secure all 360 degrees around the perimeter. Inside, a ring of now-empty CASPers sat waiting as their drivers alternately ate and looked inside the parts of the Raknar's remains they could see.

"Where's Maya?" Marc asked.

"She's down with the package," Hex said, his eyes on his wrist display. "She's got the ration box down there if you want to grab some food."

"Not hungry," Marc said. He climbed up onto the nearest tank and stood atop the turret looking out. The ring of observers was mostly silent and what few Oogars he could see by the light of their fires appeared to stare right back at him.

Creepy shit, man.

Before he could shiver with unease, the exit strategy formed in his head. He climbed gracefully down from the tank and tapped his com link. "Lucille? Link to the other vehicles and have them scan the perimeter. Watch for a fire to start dying."

<<Commander? You are assuming the enemy will fall asleep instead of stoking their fires?>>

Marc snorted. "There's always one soldier that falls asleep, Lucille."

<<Acknowledged. Optics engaged.>>

Hex looked up at him. "Looking for the weak spot?"

"And a way out."

Hex looked at his watch. "Could be a while, boss. Recommend we keep security where it's at and rotate every hour. Keep everyone fresh for when we can make a run for it."

Marc nodded. Hex, like his father before him, could sense Marc's plan before it was even spoken. "Where's the pad?"

"Eight thousand feet." Hex pointed up. "You should be able to see it. Two reds and two whites, northeast."

Marc glanced up and confirmed the pad was there; the blinking lights approximating a rectangular shape gliding toward them. He looked back at Hex. "Bring the pad down to the package. Set security at one hundred percent in case those things try to attack us."

Hex stood. "Yessir."

The night was warm and dry. Burnt vines smoldered in the breeze with a choking smell reminiscent of vehicle exhaust. Other scents wafted through their perimeter: the Oogar fires burning green wood, something like meat cooking, and a strong, dirty, rotten smell that must have been the Oogar themselves. Marc turned from the perimeter as Hex barked orders at his CASPer troops, and took in the monstrosity of the Raknar mecha.

Curled on its side, the width of its hip joints was a good thirty feet, if not more. The upper legs were easily longer than that, maybe forty feet in length. The lower legs would be a little shorter, but if the torso was as large as he thought it was, the mecha had stood about one hundred and fifty feet tall. Marc walked to what he believed was the crest of the mecha's helm and caressed the rusting metal with his left hand.

"Lucille? Have you identified this Raknar?"

<<Negative, commander. Based on the design, there is no matching Raknar in the Union archives on the Dusman. More detailed information may be found inside the control module.>>

I've got a few minutes. Why not?

"Hex?" Marc called. "Keep the perimeter secure. I'm going down to Maya and the package. Let's be ready the minute one of those fires starts to go out."

Hex gave him a thumbs-up and turned back to the CASPer pilots boarding their suits and conducting pre-combat checks. Marc walked away, around the crest of the helm, and into the hollow created by the Raknar's damaged chest plates and drawn in legs. 30 meters down the slope, he reached the pelvic area. The Dusman were a thousand-year-old enigma. Their Raknar had saved the universe, only to be left to rot on godforsaken planets like this.

Marc pulled a rugged flashlight from his belt and flipped it on. Through a large hole in the armor plating, he found Maya studying their package. The cargo container rested on its side and was too large to move without a motorized pad and tow cables. "Any luck with the keypad?"

"Nothing. No power, no nothing." Maya swept back her shoulder-length brown hair. Her tanned skin shined with perspiration. "I tried the manual lift sequencer, too. Can't budge this thing."

Marc tapped on the screen and frowned. "They told me this container had a valid passkey."

"Who told you, sir?"

"Ch'tek."

"The Zuparti trader from Bartertown?" She shook her head. "He signed us up for this?"

"The money was too good to pass up," Marc shrugged. "I figured this was a smash and grab job—we'd be in and out, in half an hour at most."

"Except for the Oogar, their weapons, this container, and no way to lift it, we might have been." She shook her head disgustedly. "Come on, Hammer. You have to trust us on making these plans."

"I had a plan, Maya."

"Maven sure thought you did."

Marc flushed. "If you've got something to say, Maya, say it now!"

Maya chewed on her lower lip. "Brute force only accomplishes so much, Hammer. Prior planning prevents piss poor--"

"I know that!" Marc bit off his rising volume and let the rest of his tirade die in his clenched teeth. "We can focus on my shortcomings when we get off this planet."

"When we get off this planet, I'm out." Maya sighed. "Hex goes with me."

Marc's mind reeled as if he'd been slapped. He shook his head. "Once we get paid, we'll see what you'll do. We're at seven million each right now."

"And what's your cost? Ten million? And every time one of us dies the individual bonuses go up, right? None of us mean anything to you, do we? Not even Maven."

"That's enough."

"Bullshit," Maya said. She looked past him into the darkness. He followed her eyes and saw two headlights searching the depression under the Raknar's torso. "Up here, Hex."

Marc raised a gloved finger and pointed at her. "Use the pad's lifters and get this loaded and ready to move in ten minutes."

"Fine." Maya said. Wiping her hands on her green coveralls, she walked out of the ragged hole toward the approaching pad.

Marc looked up into the twisted torso for a long moment, considering his path to the command module. Raknar sometimes had their modules in the head piece and sometimes in a central chest-mounted section. Maglite in hand, he picked his way toward the central chest as his team worked to get their package out of the Raknar and off planet before the sun rose and twelve thousand Oogar attacked.

Marc found the central control section sealed. The six-foot thick compartment had not ruptured, nor could he find any evidence that the Dusman crew had managed to get out of the Raknar when it fell. Fifteen minutes of crawling through support piping and conduits he could barely fit through left him frustrated. He'd wasted time looking for treasure and left his crew—his unhappy crew—with the package.

What if they take it and run?

Panic coursed through his veins, and he scrambled back toward the torso's storage compartment. The package was there, resting atop the tracked landing pad just outside the ragged hole. He sighed and just as quickly froze.

Concealed behind a torn support beam, he watched a black-suited figure snap a quick-torch to life and lean toward the container's keypad.

Marc slowly let out the breath he'd been holding. Distracted by the task at hand, the intruder would have their guard down. He unholstered his pistol and waited for the torch to bite into the container. *How did they get through our lines?*

Marc knew the answer. The force he'd carefully put together six years before was slowly bleeding to death, and it was no one's fault but his.

Can this possibly get any worse?

The torch snapped on and Marc squatted to take advantage of what little cover lay in the wreckage. He moved slowly, staying low, until he was directly behind the intruder; his gear was heat suppressive and capable of virtual camouflage. Marc raised up and took two quick, light steps forward. He cocked the pistol as he nudged the intruder's head with the barrel.

"Drop the torch."

The intruder's shoulders sagged slightly, and the torch snapped off. He could smell the pungent molten metal from the cuts in the container as he focused on the intruder's torso. He edged back, taking away their ability to sweep his arm away.

"Stand up and turn around," Marc said. "Nice and easy."

The quick torch clattered to the ground. The intruder stood and turned, hands raised, palms up.

Definitely Human. He thought and studied the dark figure in front of him.

"Take off your hood, slowly. Then you're going to tell me who sent you, and what you're trying to do."

Both hands reached for the bottom of the hood and pulled it up and away carefully. Red hair tumbled out of the cowl's opening and Marc felt a pang of dread rise in his stomach. The woman smiled at him, and damned if her green eyes didn't glitter the way they'd always done.

"Jessica? What are you doing here?"

Her smile widened like a feeding shark's jaw. "Hello, Marc. I see you're still dumb as a bag of—"

Marc stepped forward with the pistol at Jessica's face. "I asked you, why are you here?"

"Well, you never signed the divorce papers, for one thing. I had to spend a fortune in legal fees to have our tryst annulled on Earth. It was pretty messy, really. I figure you owe me about six million credits. You can avoid all of that with one simple thing. Give me Elly."

"No."

Jessica grinned. "Then, I'm not telling you a thing."

"You're bounty hunting now? Is that it? Coming after me for a bounty you set on my head?"

She laughed, and he hated the trilling sound of it. "Don't flatter yourself."

"Then what are you doing here trying to jump my mission?" Marc asked. "How did you get past my security?"

"You know, you did tell me a few useful things during our time together. 'There's always a soldier who goes to sleep' has proven very beneficial over the last few years." Jessica said. "I jumped in right behind your adorable little pad over there. Your boys and girls have had a helluva day, I'd say."

Marc clenched his jaw. "Get out of here, Jessica. This is my take."

"Where's Maven? And Hex? Surely they haven't left you already?" She grinned, and it made him sick.

"Maven is dead." Marc said, his voice barely above a whisper.

Jessica's grinning visage cracked. "She's dead?"

Marc nodded. "We took sixty percent casualties on the way in. And unless you want to risk being included in that percentage on our way out, I'd encourage you to leave while you still can."

Jessica shook her head. "Oh, Hammer." In her voice there was more than a little pity and a lifetime worth of resignation.

* * *

The unmistakable sound of an approaching CASPer washed over them. Marc kept his pistol leveled at Jessica's chest. "Again. What are you doing here?"

"I came for Elly."

Marc laughed. "I can't believe you're still throwing a fit over her. Give it up, Jessica, Elly is worthless."

"It's not about money, you idiot. You've never heard of sentimental value?" Jessica lowered her hands to her hips. "Give me Elly, Marc. Once you do, the legal fees and I will be out of your hair forever and ever, amen."

"Your mother said absolutely, under no circumstances were you to get Elly."

"Mother's dead. Her instructions no longer matter, Marc. Hand over Elly. Please."

"Hammer?" Hex's amplified voice came from down the slope. The lights on his tactical-gray CASPer washed over them. "Jessica?" The CASPer bounded forward. "I can't believe you're here."

Jessica smiled and allowed herself to be picked up by the mechanical arms. "Hi, Hex."

Hex's cameras looked at her for a moment, then down to Marc and the gun in Marc's hand. "Is everything okay?"

"It's fine, Hex. I heard you guys could use a hand," Jessica said.

"She's a bounty hunter now, Hex," Marc said. "She's either come for me or our take, but she won't tell me which."

The cameras whirled back to Jessica who was now three feet off the ground, suspended by arms that could crush her in milliseconds. "What's going on?"

"Hammer has something I want. Something personal. Ch'tek wanted an insurance policy, too. He wasn't sure Hammer here could get this package back to the Sol gate on time. Let me guess? Underestimated the enemy response and overcommitted assets on the way in?"

Hex nodded. "Yeah. Something like that." The tone of the younger man's voice made Marc's stomach roil.

Marc holstered his pistol. "Jessica? Leave this site and go home. We can talk about Elly—"

"In six more years?" Jessica asked. "Please put me down, Hex."

Hex lowered her to the ground, and she turned around and marched right up to Marc's chest, like she'd done a lifetime ago when they'd married on the beaches of Kaua'i.

"You're not getting out of here alive, Marc. You've blundered your way into a situation you can't win. Keep the rest of your good people from dying and let me go get my lifter. I can land next to your vehicles and shuttle all of you and your precious package to orbit." Jessica turned to walk away. "Hex? How fast can you muster the CASPers to lift?"

"Hey!" Marc said. "I'm still in charge. Go get your damned lifter and—"

The ground rumbled under their feet and a light shower of dust fell from the Raknar's rusting torso. A second rumble rippled through the artificial cave and there was a howling crescendo from the Oogar outside.

"Lucille, what was that?"

<<Two explosions centered two kilometers to the northwest at the base of a shallow cinder cone volcano. Signature of the explosions indicates the presence of F11.>>

Jessica closed her eyes and shook her head. "They found my lifter." She looked up at him again, her green eyes fierce. "I'm going to help get you and your people out of here, Marc. Then you're going to give me Elly, and I walk away. Is that clear?"

Marc looked at Hex for a long moment. He was far too young to meet the fate of his father on a planet like this or for a package that they didn't even know what was inside. Maven would have told him it was time to get homebound and flying. "Fine. You ride with me on the aux gun."

Jessica looked at Hex. "Get your remaining CASPers mounted on the tops of the tanks with full combat loads. Ensure their magnetic straps are engaged."

"Copy that," Hex said and bounded out of the Raknar wreckage.

Marc looked at her. "You always were better with the infantry."

"I know." She smiled and walked toward their vehicles. All Marc could do was follow her.

* * *

Around them, the Oogar fires burned intensely. They were obviously not going to sleep and, from what he could see, the Oogar appeared to be constructing torches. If they got enough of them, they'd charge.

"Saddle up, Marauders," Marc said on the task force's frequency. "CASPers at the ready. All tanks are weapons-free. Load beehive rounds and prepare to charge on my command."

At the left front skirt of the tank, he climbed aboard and saw Jessica peering down into the loader's hatch, arguing with Johnson.

"Ma'am! You are not authorized to enter this tank!"

Jessica's hands flew to her hips. "Lucille, would you please inform this young man who I am?"

Marc heard Lucille's voice in his headset. <<Johnson, engage the auxiliary gun for Miss Francis. She is authorized to enter this vehicle and more than qualified to operate it.>>

Before Marc could reach the hatches, Jessica dropped inside. He walked to the commander's cupola and did the same. "Lucille, prepare all vehicles for direct penetration. Find the best route and relay to the task force."

Jessica laughed in his ears. "You couldn't see that for yourself? There's a thinner crowd of Oogar at about 060 from our position. That's where we should charge."

<<Bulldog is correct,>> Lucille answered.

He looked at Jessica beaming in the auxiliary gunner's chair. Her cool nickname came from the troopers. She could see tactical advantages in everything and always knew when not to do something. He'd been lucky to have her, but there was no way he could have kept her. She was simply too good.

"Fine." Marc strapped himself to the commander's chair and verified his weapons were charged. "Marauders up. Standby to charge."

<<The enemy is advancing. Fast.>>

"Move out!" Marc called. "Driver, go! Go!"

The Mark Nine roared to life and spun toward what had been the weakest point in the ring of the enemy. The Oogar screamed as one and ran toward them. Each of the beasts carried some type of expedient weapon. The tank rocked from side-to-side with a dozen impacts. Marc fired the first beehive round at point-blank range and, as soon as the auto-loader cycled, he fired again. The auxiliary laser cannon cut swathes through the Oogar, but the empty holes filled just as quickly with more. The tank pitched forward suddenly.

<<Oogar are on the upper surfaces.>>

In a flash, Marc watched his optic relays fail. Unable to see outside, he fired the beehive rounds blindly. "Driver, can you see?"

"No, sir!"

"Lucille, you have movement control."

<<Engaged.>>

The auxiliary cannon whipped to one side and flung Jessica across the main gun assembly. As the tank rocked from side to side, the gun mount and a hefty portion of the vehicle's armor was torn away. The gigantic black-purple Oogar roared and reached a long-clawed hand into the turret. Jessica came up with a pistol and fired six quick shots into the bear-thing's face and, save for a taloned paw clinging to the opening in the hull, it disappeared.

Jessica fumbled for a new clip of ammunition. Her left upper arm was bleeding. "Reload," she said. "Marc! I need your help!"

Marc reached for his pistol as the massive Oogar snarled its way into the jagged opening. Marc fired into the thing's face and chest.

With a roar, it snatched Johnson from his position and tore the young man in two. Marc aimed the pistol again and pulled the trigger.

Click.

Sonuvabitch!

The hand of a CASPer reached in and grabbed the Oogar by the neck. In a flash, the thing was gone. He could see the legs of the CASPer firmly attached to their tank.

"You okay, Hammer?" Hex asked. "Keep pushing! I can see the river!"

<<Commander, combat readiness is at critical status.>>

Marc glanced at the display. Only one tank was still green and moving—his. Another tank reported amber status and was still firing, but not moving. Ghost Two's icon, attached to the trailing tank, winked out. "Maya! Hex we have to get Maya!"

Jessica swung the auxiliary cannon to the left. "She's gone, Marc."

Marc looked back at the still firing tank. Five Oogar, maybe more, clung to its turret and tore at the skin. A chunk of hull flew off and the tank stopped firing.

Dammit.

"Where's the pad?" Jessica yelled at him over the rush of wind through the turret.

Marc looked up and saw it hovering almost directly above them. "It's here. Driver, gun it for the river."

Thirty seconds later, they broke through the line of Oogar and charged into the river. Water pushed through the hull in a dozen places. "We're taking on water," Marc called. "Driver, get out!"

There was no response. Water rushed up through the turret floor. Jessica unbuckled from her seat and tapped on her wrist slate. "Hex! Jump up to the pad and drop a safety line! Come on, Hammer!"

Marc looked up to see the landing pad hovering no more than two feet above his hatch. Slapping his chest, he disengaged his combat harness and stood in his seat. He found the emergency belt and carabiner and held it in one hand as he climbed out of the hatch. Snapping the carabiner onto the pad, he felt water lapping at his boots as the tank sank beneath him. The pad lifted above the surface of the wide river, and he caught Jessica looking at him.

There were tears on her face.

* * *

The pad landed twelve kilometers away from the Raknar shrine on a wide, grassy plain. In near total darkness, they quietly gathered themselves. Hex and his CASPer were badly damaged. The young man's left arm required a hefty dose of liquid tourniquet before he started to stabilize. The kid had never said a thing, just kept fighting.

Marc sat on the pad next to the cargo container and wrapped his arms around his knees. His creditors were going to be livid. A promising mercenary force devastated in combat with a feral species they should have butchered. Jessica slid her back down the container and sat next to him.

"The *Victory Twelve* is on its way down. Should be forty-two minutes."

Marc didn't look up. He stared at an oily spot on the pad's deck. "How's Hex?"

"He'll live." Jessica said. "What's in this container, Marc?"

He shrugged. "I don't know."

"You took a mission where you--"

His head snapped up. "Yes! I took a mission where I didn't know what the package was, okay? This was a 60-million credit mission, and I needed the money to make payroll and pay off my creditors."

"Creditors?" Jessica's eyebrows rose. "How long have you been running in the red?"

"18 months," Marc said. The sinking feeling in his stomach came back with a vengeance. She'd been so much better at the whole business than he had. Since their divorce, things had spiraled almost out of control. "This was going to be what got me back on track. Guess I fucked that up, huh?"

"Yeah," she said. "You did."

"Aren't you a beacon of compassion," Marc chuckled humorlessly.

Jessica stood up. "I'm going to find out what this thing is before I load it in my ship. At this rate, it could be a big damned bomb, and I'm not prepared to take that risk."

"Who says it's going on your ship?" Marc looked up at her. "My ship is—"

"No, it's not. Your ship boosted for Karma about 10 minutes ago. I've reported them for mutiny, if it helps."

Marc shook his head. *Nothing like being a worthless commander and business man. Then...why did Ch'tek come to me?*

He opened his mouth, closed it again, and then looked up at her. "Ch'tek came after me because I needed money and had an expendable force."

"Humans are expendable to the rest of the galaxy. He dangled a lot of credits in your face, and you did what all Humans do. We're expendable for that reason." Jessica said. From the thigh pocket of her outfit, she removed the quick torch. "Are you going to help me or not?"

At the keypad, Jessica cut through and found a manual release that caused one side panel of the container to open with a *whoosh* of stale, pressurized air. An opaque privacy screen shrouded the cargo. Jessica found its edges and shoved it aside. The bottom of the container was filled with partially rotted straw. Jessica knelt down. "This isn't an Earth grass."

Marc looked down. "No. See the red buds on the end? It's all around us. It was packed here. Ch'tek had it waiting for us."

"Makes sense." Jessica played with the controls on the quick torch and snapped on a bright, white light. As she swept it toward the far end of the container, a very large and very black object rested on the straw. It was a long, smooth ovoid and it glittered like obsidian. Below it a small console read 192.54.55, and it was ticking down.

"Oh, Hammer," Jessica said. "You really did it this time."

Marc frowned. "It's just an egg. What's the big deal, Jess?"

"Where are you supposed to take this?"

Marc sighed, "Sol emergence point and then to Luna. I'm to be met by representatives from the Buma. This is a gift for Earth's Council."

She laughed. "I doubt this was the gift. I think Ch'tek stole their shipment, sent the container here, and staged it for you to take *this* back to Earth. Once it got there, the Buma would undoubtedly want a presentation ceremony. By then it would be too late."

"Too late for what?" Marc asked

"Hammer, you idiot, this is a viable Canavar egg." Jessica frowned, and for a long moment she didn't say anything.

"How in the hell do you know that?"

Jessica shrugged and said, "The Besquith Archives."

Marc blinked. "How in the hell did you...forget it. Why would Ch'tek want to give a Canavar egg to the Buma to give to Earth? That doesn't make any sense." Marc sighed, "Unless he wanted to piss off the Buma and kill a few billion Humans."

"Unless that's *exactly* what he intended." Jessica said. "Let's get this ready to load onto *Victory Twelve*."

"We're still taking it with us?" Marc asked.

"Evidence, Marc." Jessica tilted her head to one side and half-smiled at him. "At this point it's all we've got."

"What about the timer?"

Jessica walked over and turned it off and carefully removed two long strips of clear sensor tape. "This would have broken the outer shell open. Once the inner shell senses nitrogen, there is no stopping the Canavar from hatching. Without these, as long as we don't break the outer shell, it will be stable and can be transported back to Earth. Then we'll find Ch'tek and have him meet us; say there's a problem with the package. When he shows up and opens it, we get an explanation or a confession, whichever works best."

Sol Emergence Point, Leonov Station
Eight Days Later

Ch'tek stormed into Hanger 157 at Armstrong Base exactly as Marc thought he would. The little alien saw the scarred, torn container on the deck outside the *Victory Twelve* and immediately launched into a tirade.

"What in the hell have you done to the package?" Ch'tek pointed a claw at Marc and snarled, "I said it was to be undamaged!"

"You also failed to mention twelve thousand feral Oogars who would do anything to defend the Raknar wreckage this was hidden inside," Marc said. "You cost me lives, Ch'tek. Not to mention several million credits worth of equipment."

"Is the internal package unharmed?" Ch'tek asked.

"The panel was damaged, but we couldn't get inside to release the doors to check the contents." Jessica shrugged and held her hand. "Too big."

Ch'tek pushed past them and walked directly to the damaged panel. Reconstructing it had taken very little time, and while Hex damaged the outside with his CASPer, Marc and Jessica closed the hatch and made it so that Ch'tek would be the one to open it. A simple modification to the mechanism meant the internal privacy door would open as well.

"I'll do it," Ch'tek said. "Once the outer door is open, you will leave."

"Once we're paid." Marc said.

Ch'tek tapped his wrist slate. "The transaction is underway."

"I'm not leaving until the credits are in my account."

"Fine." Ch'tek lay down on the deck and paused for a split second before reaching into the small hole with a paw. The outer door slid open with a *whoosh*. Ch'tek rolled away from the container. He stood, wiped his paws in a very Human way, and turned to them. "Now, get..." His small jaw fell open.

Marc turned and saw Jessica holding a very large pistol at Ch'tek's head. "What are you—"

"Ch'tek," Jessica said. "By the laws of the Union, you are under arrest for the unlawful removal and possession of a Canavar egg, deceitful employment of a registered mercenary force, and coercion."

"What are you talking about?" Ch'tek laughed. "That's not what's in—"

Marc pointed at the open container door. The small Zuparti turned and fell silent. The internal privacy door had opened with the outer hatch revealing the Canavar egg. After a moment, Ch'tek turned back to Jessica and grinned. "How much to forget this unfortunate incident? Commander Lemieux? Miss Francis? You're a bounty hunter and cannot arrest—"

Marc watched Jessica pull out a thin black sleeve. On it was a platinum shield with a blue tree. The seal of the Peacemakers. "That's Peacemaker, not bounty hunter. On my authority, Ch'tek, you are under arrest." She raised her voice. "Bay Control? Authorization Zulu Four Zero."

Large hangar doors opened. Marc watched a squad of Peacemakers enter the space with their weapons trained on Ch'tek and the Canavar egg. A dozen other officers of varying species filed past them and surrounded the Zuparti trader. Shackles placed on Ch'tek's arms and legs left the small alien looking defeated as Jessica continued: "By Union Laws, you are under arrest. You will be held until such time as you can be placed before a Peacemaker tribunal. Your rights of redress and citizenship are suspended until released or acquitted. You cannot complete or enter into any contracts with the sole exception of legal representation. You are entitled to obtain said representation, if possible. Credit will be extended to you if you cannot afford said representation. Do you have any questions?"

Ch'tek shook his head and looked away. His eyes narrowed and Marc followed his gaze to a pair of Buma diplomats entering the hangar.

"Peacemaker Francis?" the nearest one said. "Are these allegations true?"

"Of course they're true," Ch'tek snarled. "The Union did not need this pathetic species!"

Jessica looked at two officers standing close by. "Please remove the accused." Ch'tek disappeared behind a group of white-coated scientists rushing to the Canavar egg.

Jessica nodded to the Buma. "Please relay my gratitude to the Besquith, Cael Doontal."

"Well done, Peacemaker." The Buma bowed and retreated from them. Marc looked at her for a moment and smiled, but it froze on his face.

She stared at him for a long moment. "Marc, you are an accessory to this."

"The hell I am!" Marc replied. "My contract was violated. I'm no party to anything. If anyone's an accessory, you are! You took it onboard your ship!"

"I told you that was for evidence, don't you remember?" Jessica smirked. "I'm still trying to decide if I should charge you with anything. I'm sure I could find a few things in your records."

Marc snorted. "Bounty hunter was your cover, right?"

"I never said I was a bounty hunter, Marc. But you're getting there."

"And the egg? You knew it was there, didn't you?"

Jessica shook her head. "Peacemaker business, Marc. It's classified. Give me Elly and you walk away."

"Fine." Marc said. He bent down and carefully unzipped the lower leg pocket of his coveralls and withdrew a small box. "Your mother left explicit instructions—"

"—that I should never get it?" Jessica asked with a chuckle. "I knew she sent it to you. For whatever reason, she went to her grave thinking you were a wonderful man and would try to look out for me. That's code for putting me off to the side and taking me for granted, by the way."

Marc flushed. "That's what you think of our time together?"

"Pretty much." She took the offered box and opened it. Inside was a small, porcelain elephant statuette that easily fit in the palm of her hand. "She's as pretty as I remember."

"I didn't realize it meant that much to you."

"You never realized a lot of things, Marc." She glanced at him with hard, cold eyes. "The guild will pay your fee for this operation on one condition: You are to pay your soldiers and your creditors. With the remaining balance you are to retire, preferably somewhere far from the trade routes. Stop playing mercenary commander; you're simply not fit for it."

The words stung, but he took a long, slow breath of realization. *She's right.*

Marc sighed. "Fine. I'm retired. Are you happy, Jess?"

"Peacemaker pays better than being a merc or a bounty hunter," she said.

"That's not what I meant," Marc replied, his anger building. "You always get what you want! You've taken everything from--"

Marc froze as Jessica dropped the statuette. Elly, supposedly her most prized possession, fell in slow motion. It shattered into a handful of pieces that surrounded something rectangular and black. Jessica bent down and retrieved it quickly. As she stood, she rotated it in her palm and he could see it was a computer chipset with the tiny word "Snowman" printed in bright orange on the dull black surface.

"What the hell is that? Why does it have your father's call sign on it?" Marc asked.

Jessica winked and walked away. "Wouldn't you like to know?"

# # # # #

Mark's Introduction to:

Lost and Found

by Jon Del Arroz

Jon began his writing career in high school, providing book reviews and the occasional article for a local news magazine. From there, he went on to write a weekly web comic, "Flying Sparks," which has been hailed by Comic Book Resources as "the kind of stuff that made me fall in love with early Marvel comics." He has several published short stories and his debut novel, "Star Realms: Rescue Run," went on to become a top-10 bestselling Amazon Space Opera. His latest novel, "For Steam And Country" marks his first foray into steampunk fantasy. Jon himself is a big fan of mecha, which puts him in good company for this book, and he professes his undying love of all things that go "pew, pew."

Jon's contribution, "Lost and Found," delves further into alien societies within the Galactic Union, and conjures up images of shared nightmares. Thousands of years ago a race unleashed monsters called Canavar, and the fear that they might return haunts the dreams of all. When a simple merc contract uncovers the possibility of the monsters' return, terror is on the menu.

Find out more about Jon at http://delarroz.com/.

LOST AND FOUND
by Jon Del Arroz

The *Lilly's* landing shuttle jolted and bounced as it dipped below Threndark's clouds. Thick forests lined the landscape below with their sharp, primal leaf structures. Even strapped into his safety harness, Captain Timothy Rosethorn was just able to see over the front cockpit chair. His height gave him some advantages, but it also had drawbacks. A jolt of turbulence sent his neck whipping backward, causing him to knock his head on the overhead compartment. The sound of skull hitting metal echoed throughout the cabin.

"You all right back there?" asked the pilot, Jebediah Tuoken. He didn't turn back to look, as he was concentrating on finding a suitable landing spot.

"I told you to tighten your straps," said a smirking Grace Montas, his first officer. Her dark eyes sparkled with amusement. A few strands of her onyx hair fell in front of her face from the bumpy ride. She was far too pretty and sensible a woman to be with a minor merc outfit like Rosethorn's Renegades, but for whatever reason, she stayed. They'd talked about it one night over far too many drinks, at which point she shrugged and told him, "I don't know, I like you." It may have been an innocuous comment, but under the haze of alcohol, and combined with Rosethorn's own attraction to her, it had almost led to a far-too-dangerous moment for a captain to have with his subordinate.

Most days, Rosethorn regretted not making a move that evening. He rubbed the top of his head. "I'm fine," he said.

Montas had managed to distract him enough that he didn't notice the final landing. In contrast to the bumpy atmospheric ride, the actual touchdown was smooth. The landing struts had some decent shock absorbers. Jeb parked the shuttle in a small clearing surrounded by looming trees. These trees were strangely proportioned compared to Earth fauna, as their leaves reached for light from both of the twin suns that hung in the sky. Judging from the view outside, it was amazing Jeb managed to fit both the shuttle and its attached cargo pod into the clearing.

The rest of his crew removed their restraints and stood. In addition to Jeb and Montas, he'd brought Jason Palmer and two of his commandos, the hired muscle of his merc outfit. Rosethorn wiggled out of his harness and moved to the exit ramp. Threndark's air was thick in his lungs, but oddly dry. This was not the type of place he wanted to spend much time. The forest obscured any view of the distance.

Jeb already had a scanner out, searching the area for the payload the Cartography Guild had contracted him to find. He'd joined up with Rosethorn over drinks, the alcohol loosening his lips about Threndark. Jeb had been doing consulting work with the guild, mapping star systems that were charted but lost during the ancient Kahraman war. The guild had found evidence that a Kahraman ship had gone missing in this sector, including an ancient distress signal that had never been pursued. That signal had come from Threndark, suggesting the possibility that a remnant of the ancient ship might have survived. Odds were low they'd find anything, but if they could find something about the Kahraman, it would be very lucrative to the Cartography Guild. The guild had been so excited by the prospect they'd guaranteed the fuel expenses up front. A mission right up Rosethorn's alley, risking only time and energy for the possibility of a big reward. He had hired Jeb as navigator on the condition they received the assignment.

The drop team spread out. Their boots sank into the moist ground below, leaving deep tracks in their wakes.

"Huh," Jeb said, his attention on his scanner, even as he walked.

"I don't like that tone of voice," Rosethorn said.

Palmer and his two men forged ahead, cutting branches out of the way with machetes. They wore combat armor and helmets, and had their weaponry strapped to their backs, ready to go into action at a moment's notice.

Jeb lifted his head and squinted. "I'm showing there's a lot of life forms ahead."

"Local creatures?" Montas asked.

He shook his head. "No. Human."

"That can't be right. Humans haven't explored this sector of space," Rosethorn said.

"It's what the scanner says." Jeb shrugged.

Ahead of them, Palmer stopped and did a double take. He turned, scrunching his nose as if encountering a foul odor. "Entropy," he said.

The odor wafted toward Rosethorn and the rest of his crew. The stench of vomit, bad farts, and burned meat mixed in a swirl of awfulness. "What is *that*?" Rosethorn asked, moving toward Palmer.

A large carcass lay on the ground behind some nearby bushes. The beast looked like a cross between a cow and a porcupine, but with a long snout and protruding teeth. Drool dripped from its mouth, and blood caked on the muddy ground. It had released the contents of its intestines, which accounted for the smell. Despite its prickly hide, something had torn into it, ravaged it, and bitten a chunk out of its midsection.

Rosethorn frowned. "Looks like there's a big predator out here; we need to be on the lookout."

"Always am," Palmer said. With that, he motioned to his men, and all three of them pulled their rifles from their backs and readied themselves for combat.

Something ruffled in the forest ahead of them. No, the sound emanated from all around them. Rosethorn's boot slipped in the muddy terrain. A strange predator creature didn't appear, but other Humans did—20 men with guns and spears trained on Rosethorn and his men. These people didn't have combat suits on; it wasn't a group of pirates that followed them to the planet. Judging by the confident way they moved through the forest, they were natives.

"Retreat!" Rosethorn called. He regained his footing, then ran. The others followed. The natives fired a few shots at them, or perhaps near them. For warning? Montas ran beside him, and they hurried toward the shuttle.

A moment later, Montas wasn't there anymore.

Rosethorn looked over his shoulder to see what had happened. Montas had fallen. She squirmed on the ground. The natives had thrown a bolas that had wrapped around her legs. They were fast approaching.

"Go!" Montas screamed.

Leave a member of his crew? The thought appalled him. Even if he didn't have personal reasons for wanting to save her, it violated unwritten merc codes. But there were too many of the natives; the tactical situation was untenable. They hadn't prepared for encountering other people on this planet. He had to keep running, as much as it pained him to do so. Rosethorn led his team back to the shuttle and hurried up the ramp. Jeb, Palmer and the two commandos followed and secured the hatch. Even with their weapons, the natives wouldn't be able to get inside.

Oddly enough, the natives didn't pursue.

Rosethorn huffed, catching his breath after the long run. "What happened?"

Palmer glanced back at the closed ramp door. "Not sure. They got Montas and stopped."

"That's not good," Jeb said.

"No, it's not," Rosethorn agreed. "They weren't trying to kill us, though. They must have wanted to capture Montas—that's why they used a bolas and not their guns or spears. But why?" He frowned, thinking about what they could have wanted with Montas. She was the lone woman in the group. The thought of what they might do to her made him queasy.

"What's the plan?" Jeb asked. His eyes betrayed his nervousness; in his capacity with the Cartography Guild, he'd probably never been in a combat situation.

Rosethorn considered. "We have to try to find her. I've got the entire crew tagged, so your scanner should be able to pinpoint her location. We'll head back to the ship and return with a bigger team, one ready for action."

"We'll take care of it," Palmer said, nodding.

Rosethorn hoped Palmer was right.

* * *

Grace had stopped trying to resist several hours ago. The natives had immediately gagged and bound her once they had incapacitated her in the forest. They'd taken her to their village, which consisted of several wooden cabins and a single larger structure, and had locked her inside one of the cabins. Initially she was fearful; they hadn't taken any of the men, only her. It was one of the potential hazards of being a woman in the merc industry. She'd heard horror stories of men—Human and alien—who took women captive for use as sex slaves. That was why so few women signed up for frontline combat duty.

Grace had never shied away from it, finding that taking more dangerous jobs, ones that required her to have a good head on her shoulders, often led to quicker advancement. Now, the worst scenarios played through her head, and she regretted signing up for not only this assignment, but for the rest of the assignments that had led up to it. She'd spent these last years alone, focused on her career, with no one to love, and no one to love her. Save for that one time with Captain Rosethorn where they almost—

The lock at the front of the cabin turned with a *click*, interrupting her thoughts. The door squeaked open. The men who had taken her didn't come through the door; instead, three women entered. Two heavyset women carried a large wooden container that steamed. The third directed them to set it next to Grace. When they set it down, water swished from the top of it, overflowing onto the floor beside her. Was that a bath?

"Do you speak English?" the third woman asked.

Grace blinked a couple of times.

The woman crossed her arms. "I guess not. This'll be harder then." She made a few motions of scrubbing. "We need to get you cleaned up. Cleaned. Up. Do you understand?"

"I speak English," Grace said, her voice coming out in a soft squeak. Her fear hadn't subsided, and her throat was tight.

"Speak up next time," the woman said. She rolled her eyes.

The other women tugged at Grace's clothes. Still bound, there was little she could do while they pried off her combat armor and stripped her down to her skivvies. When they went for those, she squirmed.

"Stop it," the first woman said. "You have to get clean. If you don't fight us you can have a nice, peaceful bath."

"Who are you?" Grace asked. She did as they asked, despite feeling awkward, and the women unbound her wrists and legs. She had a bit of rope burn from where her ties had been.

"My name is Marianne. They are Laura and Stephanie," she said. She motioned to the steaming water. "It's going to get cold if you don't get in."

Still nervous, Grace removed her undergarments, setting them aside before stepping into the water. She covered her breasts with her arms. Even though she was around women, she didn't know these people, and she was uncomfortable. Why were they bathing her anyway? "Can someone tell me what's going on here? I am Commander Grace Montas, of Rosethorn's Renegades merc unit. We're licensed by the Galactic Union. I don't know the number off the top of my head but I can produce it."

Marianne shook her head. "I have no idea what you're talking about. You need to clean up for the Great Protector. It's part of the ritual."

"Ritual?" Grace was even more confused. Was she being offered as a sex slave as she had feared? Her hair prickled on the back of her neck, and she shivered in the hot water. The two other women brought a brush and soap and began scrubbing her, wetting her hair, then rinsing it. All she could do was sit, helpless. Even if she escaped these women, being alone and nude in a strange settlement did not sound appealing.

"Yes, every year we perform a ritual for the Great Protector. It's an honor to be chosen. The entire town will pray for you and have a ceremony in your honor," Marianne said. As if she sensed Grace's thoughts on escape, she moved over to position herself in front of the door. "My sister was chosen two years ago. She was so blessed."

Creepy. Still, the last thing she wanted to do was offend her captors. People often became touchy if someone criticized their religion, and if this Great Protector was some sort of god to them, as Marianne's reverent tone suggested, she didn't want to rock the boat too much. She didn't know anything about them, and it was confusing enough to be among what appeared to be other Humans here on Threndark. They looked like Humans and spoke English...but what *were* they? "I see," Grace said, keeping her voice neutral. "When's the ceremony supposed to take place?"

"Tomorrow," Marianne said. "We'll bring you before the village council first to make sure you are worthy."

"As an outsider, I'm probably not," Grace said. It'd be better to extricate herself from this situation if she could. The two women behind her finished washing her hair.

Marianne laughed. "When the men saw your ship coming down from the sky, they thought it was a great sign. So often, it's difficult for us to part with one of our own. We are few in numbers. Each loss weighs heavily on our village, blessed or not."

Loss? This didn't sound good at all.

The women held up a big towel. "You're cleansed now. Stand," Stephanie said.

Grace complied.

"You'll be staying here while I inform the council," Marianne said. She motioned to Stephanie as the latter woman wrapped the towel around Grace. "Make sure she dresses in the ceremonial garment. I will return soon."

She had to escape, but even if she managed to overpower the women, could she make it out of the town? Where were the others? They'd run just as she told them to. Still, Grace hoped they would return before this ceremony began. More than anything.

* * *

It took almost a full day for Rosethorn to return to the surface after docking with the *Lilly* and formulating a plan of attack. This time, the shuttle was packed with the power of Palmer's full team— 20 trained men who were ready for action. Even though Jeb had run scans showing there were somewhere around a thousand Humans, or what appeared to be Humans, on Threndark, that numerical advantage would evaporate when facing armored mercs ready for battle. That was the plan, anyway. Even though they didn't have CASPers, they had combat armor beyond anything they had seen on the locals. Palmer also had his men armed with rocket launchers and flame throwers to frighten the villagers into complying, in addition to their usual arsenal of assault rifles, grenades and knives. Hopefully, it would be enough.

Rosethorn still didn't know what the locals wanted with Montas, but he feared the worst. He couldn't imagine a group of off-the-grid men singling out and targeting a woman for anything positive. It would have been nice if his team could have moved faster, but preparation was half the battle. He'd learned early in his career never to rush the plan of attack.

This time they knew where they were headed, too. The shuttle landed in the clearing as it did the day before, with the ramp opening in the same direction to allow Rosethorn and his team to deploy. With a full contingent of commandos in battle armor, they looked much more intimidating and less like a target. The settlers lived in a town with rudimentary buildings made of wood, like the log cabins Rosethorn had read about in history books. In that regard, these people would be like the settlers who came to North America several hundred years earlier, but with slightly more advanced weaponry. It still made him curious about who they were and where they came from. They'd obviously had some time to get established.

He could ask those questions later, once he got Montas back to safety. With the motion of his rifle, his men fanned out and moved toward the village. Palmer found the tracks made by the villagers the day before, allowing for easier passage without having to clear brush.

An ear-piercing sound echoed in the forest. Something nasty, like a combination of nails on a chalkboard and someone screaming.

"What was that?" one of Palmer's men asked, pointing his rifle in the direction the sound had originated.

"You've never been on a planet with wildlife before? Probably just a bird. Relax," another of the men said, then chuckled.

"Jitters," Palmer said, amusement in his voice.

"Keep focused and on target," Rosethorn warned. He was amused, and knew that "jitters" might well be something that stuck as a nickname for the poor soul. That's how these things tended to go. But he had to play captain and keep his crew in line, or no one else would.

The forest thinned as they reached the settlement. Several log cabins appeared through the trees. Rosethorn had waited until many of the men were out working in the fields or hunting, leaving the village more exposed. Several women walked through the square in the middle of town, gathering buckets of water from a well. The buildings were situated on a single main street with a few others on the perimeter. At the end, from Rosethorn's perspective, stood one much larger building that must be their local meeting hall.

The mercs deployed into the town square, and Rosethorn nodded to Palmer.

The commando pointed his rifle into the sky and fired a dozen shots. As intended, the shots drew the attention of the villagers. Eyes went wide, and people screamed. Most of the women in the square hurried to wherever they were headed or ducked behind houses, trying to get out of sight.

Other villagers came out of the cabins, brandishing weapons, and pointed them at Rosethorn and his men. This is why they wore the battle armor; if one of the villagers became trigger happy, they'd find their bullets to be nearly ineffective. Getting hit would still hurt with the armor on, but, unless the locals got really lucky, the worst the mercs would end up with would be a welt. Hopefully, it wouldn't come to that.

Rosethorn lifted his hands, palms facing the villagers, to communicate that he intended peace. His men kept their weapons ready. Several of the natives edged toward the mercs. One was an older man, with a salt and pepper beard and gray hair that fell past his shoulders. He wore a faded suit that looked dated, but he still had an air of respectability to him. "Who do you think you are to shoot up our village?" he asked.

They spoke English. *What?* That did make things easier, though. Rosethorn had assumed there would be a communication barrier they'd have to work around. He flipped up his helmet mask and inclined his head to the gentleman in front of him. "Captain Rosethorn of Rosethorn's Renegades, a licensed and bonded merc outfit. The real question is, who are you? This planet is listed as unsettled."

"Our forefathers came here long ago, after first contact. However, this is our village. You don't have the right to ask questions," the man said, crossing his arms in defiance.

"My colleague's rocket launcher says otherwise," Rosethorn said, pointing his thumb toward one of his men.

The old man cast his eyes to where Rosethorn pointed, and his confidence visibly wavered. "I see your point. I assume you come from Earth as we originally did. I promise you, we have nothing of value that's worth ransacking our village for. We're trying to make a life here, as difficult as it may be."

"You have my first officer. Your men captured her yesterday," Rosethorn said.

The man frowned. "Ah. Her."

"Yes, her." Rosethorn felt himself losing his patience with the man.

The man looked back over his shoulder and then back to Rosethorn. "I'll tell you what. Why don't you come inside the council building and talk with me? I'm afraid we need your woman, but perhaps we could arrange for some compensation."

The way the man said *need your woman* rubbed Rosethorn the wrong way. Not that he could think of a right way for it to be said.

They probably wanted her for breeding. It didn't seem like their population was big enough to maintain a diverse gene pool. From all Rosethorn had read, which admittedly had only been a couple Aethernet articles, it took thousands to be able to guarantee a healthy future for a colony. He wouldn't leave Montas here to that fate, but being agreeable and garnering information as to her location would be helpful. "Okay, I'll talk." He turned back to his men. "Renegades, keep watch. If there's any funny business, handle it. Permanently."

"Aye, sir," Palmer said.

The old man beckoned Rosethorn to follow, then made his way back into the bigger building. Palmer motioned for the other mercs to assume guard positions. A couple of men moved ahead of Rosethorn to flank the building's door, and Rosethorn proceeded inside.

The building was divided into two main rooms. The room they entered was set up as some sort of public gathering place, connected to an office with a closed door in the back. The man proceeded to the door and led Rosethorn through it. In the office was a very dated computer terminal atop a wooden desk that appeared to be built from the same trees as the buildings around them. Two chairs of similar construction were in front of the desk, with another behind. The man moved around the desk and bade Rosethorn to sit.

"I'll stand, thank you," Rosethorn said.

The man nodded. "I suppose I owe you an explanation. I am Meynard Thurmond, chief councilman of this humble settlement." He moved as if to offer his hand, but saw that Rosethorn had no intention of taking it and instead maneuvered to seat himself. "Our forefathers came here to escape the hazards of life on Earth. After first contact, Earth became such a small place compared to the rest of the galaxy. Our forefathers wanted some place to be alone, to have a simpler life like they had in The United States of America back in the old days. It seemed like a good plan."

"I just want you to release our crewman so I can be on my way. No offense, but I don't care about your world, or why you're here," Rosethorn said.

Meynard inclined his head. "I'm getting to that."

Rosethorn motioned for him to continue.

"What they didn't expect was that this world would have predators. It still does. You must be careful in the jungles, Captain. But we have what we call the Great Protector. The creature is huge, reptilian, god-like. It's truly amazing, but it does require sacrifice. In the early days, it would ravage our village. But since those early times—"

Rosethorn turned for the door. "I don't need to listen to this any longer. If I have to bust down every door of every one of your cabins to get Montas back, that's what I'm gonna do."

"Wait," Meynard said. His chair squeaked against the flooring as he stood. "Please. The creature requires a sacrifice, as I said. Every cycle, we give the Great Protector a young girl, a virgin, hoping that will satiate it. If we don't give it one soon, it will destroy all of us."

Rosethorn laughed.

"This is no laughing matter!"

"It is if you think Montas is a virgin, or that we're going to go along with your sick religious ideas for whatever godforsaken creatures are out there. You sound like savages."

Meynard shook his head. "It's not like that. Our population is too small for us to give up any more of the women in the village. My computer model shows our civilization is unsustainable. When you arrived it was like a message from God. It had to be so, don't you know?"

These people were absolutely crazy, of that Rosethorn was certain. They'd been feeding some savage beast one of their own to stave off its appetite? Likely that's what kept it returning to the village. Who would turn down a free lunch? The thought of so many young women being murdered over the years disgusted him. These people deserved to have their village destroyed. He left the office, heading back into the larger room. In the time they had spoken, several of the villagers had gathered inside. Women. Children. A lot of them. How the hell had they gotten past the guards Palmer posted?

"Your men allowed us through," one of the women said. "My name is Marianne. I was on my way to inform the council the sacrifice is ready to be given to the Great Protector."

Meynard followed Rosethorn out of the office and carefully stepped around Rosethorn to join his people. He placed a hand on a young boy's shoulder. "Son," he said solemnly.

Rosethorn huffed. "This whole concept is disgusting. I'm not sure how you live with yourselves." Even as he said the words, he caught sight of Marianne's quivering lips. Her fear was intense and contagious. These were helpless people. But it wasn't his job to save helpless people. It was his job to protect his crew, and earn a profit. "Look, I can't help you. I'm on a mission to find some remnants of an old ship. That's all. You're not my responsibility."

The young boy looked up at his father. "Do you think he means the ruins?"

"It could be," Meynard said. He eyed Rosethorn. "You are a mercenary. Perhaps we can trade information for your assistance."

Rosethorn shook his head. "Ain't no way I'm selling one of my own. That's not how we do things."

"Please. Talk to your men. Consider it." Meynard squeezed his son's shoulder. However, it was his eyes that gripped Rosethorn with what they communicated: *think of the children.*

Rosethorn grumbled to himself. Even though he had a job to do, and even though he'd been hardened by years of intense combat, the damn thought of children getting ripped to shreds by some beast got to him. He hated having morals. It definitely didn't help with the actual mercenary aspects of his job. "I'll tell you what, I'll consider it." Before the man could open his mouth again, Rosethorn held up a hand to halt him. "That's not all. Let me see Montas—I want to talk to her and make sure she's unharmed. Maybe I'll think of something. No promises."

Meynard nodded, his face grim though he seemed less tense. "That can be arranged."

* * *

The door to the cabin creaked open, and Grace's jaw dropped when she saw the group who came through it. Marianne had returned, but with her was an older male settler she didn't recognize, along with Captain Rosethorn and Navigator Jebediah Tuoken.

"Are you okay?" Rosethorn asked as he pushed past the two women handlers to get closer to her.

It was all Grace could do not to reach out and hug him right there. Over the past day, she'd heard a lot more about her intended fate from her handlers. The colony may not have been as backward as she pictured, but she couldn't help but get the sense that she was the subject of something crazy.

Her thoughts proved correct when her handlers told her about what it meant to be the object of the Great Protector. They told her that it wasn't a man or god, but a giant creature that lurked in the forest. They described it as a giant, scaly beast that walked on two legs, with short arms; it was almost like a Tyrannosaurus Rex but with eyes more akin to a fly.

They spoke reverently of the beast, as if it were some immortal being. Having a ritual for a giant lizard didn't bother her. The disturbing thing was that the settlers intended to *feed* her to it. When Grace heard that, she had run for the door, only to be stopped by the two women, who were much stronger than they appeared. Grace realized they had to be, living a life in a harsh colony environment without modern amenities. They had tackled her, bruising her arms and legs in the process.

Through the rest of the night, the handlers stood guard over Grace. They took shifts, just like a well-oiled merc outfit. When Laura and Stephanie returned in the morning, they appeared fresh and energized. Meanwhile, Grace had been worn down from her lack of sleep. Her hopes of getting out of the situation alive had evaporated. After hours of panic through the morning, she'd resigned herself to death. Now, a bright spot of hope returned for the first time since her capture.

"Hi," Grace said to Rosethorn. "I mean, yes. I'm as fine as I can be." She glanced at her captors. "I won't be for long though."

"That's what I've come to talk to you about," Rosethorn said. He had that twinkle in his eye that she had seen when he schemed or planned for the ship's future. He was an ambitious man, and while this merc company was still getting off the ground in a lot of ways, she had faith in where he led. Rosethorn turned to the man next to him. "Mind if I speak with her alone for a moment?"

The man frowned. "If you leave—"

"I won't. I promised you we would cooperate."

The man nodded, and made a motion to the others with them. They all exited the cabin, including Laura and Stephanie. Grace waited to speak until the door closed behind them. "I thought you'd never show up," she said.

"Took a while to put together a force big enough to scare the settlers into listening. The good news is it worked. The bad news is, you're going to have to stay here a little longer," Rosethorn said.

Grace paled. "*What?*"

Navigator Tuoken guarded the door, hands clasped in front of him, remaining quiet while his superiors spoke. Rosethorn paced the room. He was about to tell her something she didn't want to hear. He always got like this when he was about to upset her. That didn't happen with the rest of the crew. Rosethorn's leadership typically was solid. When he spoke, he got to the point, whether stating an ugly truth or not. Grace could only speculate why he did this with her, but she'd have to do that at a later time. One where she weren't in mortal danger from being eaten by some nasty creature in the wilderness.

"You see," Rosethorn said, "I made a deal with the colonists to let them have you."

"What?" Grace balled her fist. He was going to leave her here? That double crossing...

Rosethorn held up his hands. "Hold on. It's just temporary. Let me explain."

"It'd better be a damned good explanation."

"It is." Rosethorn let out a deep breath. "The settlers here know where the old Kahraman ship is that we came to investigate. They call it the ruins and promised to show us the location, but we have to allow them to bring you to their sacrificial altar."

"That's not a good reason at all," Grace said flatly.

"Would you listen for a moment?" Rosethorn's voice became testy. His eyes locked on hers, and they told her a lot more than what his words had so far. He was scared, and more, he loved her.

Truth be told, Grace had suspected that for a while. On more than one occasion, they had come all too close to pushing their relationship beyond what was healthy for a captain and the first officer of a merc outfit. She'd never had the courage to make the first move, and annoyingly, neither had he. And now she was probably going to die. Great. "I'm listening," she said.

Rosethorn glanced over his shoulder toward the door and then back to her. He lowered his voice to just above a whisper. "I have no intention of leaving you here to die. We're going to have the colonists lead us to the source, and then come back around with our full squad to blow that creature off this planet. As much as they call this thing the Great Protector, it's been murdering their people ever since they got here. I know it's not in the contract, but these colonists have kids. I can't let that thing ravage them any more than I can let it kill you."

He had compassion for the villagers. That actually tugged at Grace's heartstrings more than the way he looked at her. Until he mentioned the children, Grace had been ready to let these loonies become giant lizard dinner. But he was right. They were civilians, and they deserved a right to live. Even though they wouldn't get contract money for it, saving these innocents could be used for something positive, maybe public relations. Grace would figure out the marketing aspects if she survived. "I still don't like the idea of being used like this."

"But you'll do it? The villagers won't give us the ship location without your help."

Grace grimaced, but finally nodded. "Yeah. I'll do it. You owe me triple hazard pay though."

"Done."

* * *

Rosethorn trudged through the deep forest with half his drop team and a guide from the village. Sweat dripped down his face and became trapped under his helmet at his neck. His hair had already matted and become drenched. With that monster out there lurking around, he wasn't about to risk removing the armor. Besides, several bugs fluttered around the dense forest environment, and they looked like biters.

He had left the other half of his unit back in the village. That way, if the settlers tried to pull something with Montas, they would be able to react quickly. From what Rosethorn understood, there would be plenty of time for him to get back and then go to their sacrificial altar, constructed atop a nearby mesa. The rest of his men marched with him, keeping their guns at the ready in case the Great Protector or something worse decided it wanted a lunchtime snack.

Jeb walked ahead with the guide, talking about the local planet, and specifically its geography. The conversation had been going on for a while, and Rosethorn had tuned it out until Jeb looked back at him. He must have missed his navigator asking a question.

"Sorry, didn't hear you," Rosethorn said, picking up his pace to get closer to them.

"I was saying that from the sound of this Great Protector, it could very well be a Canavar. I read about them in a galactic history class in preparation for my Cartography Guild license exam. Crazy stuff. Giant beasts that destroyed whole cities. From what I saw though, these things would have left a much bigger footprint. I don't know—maybe the crashed ship we're looking for was a transport of some kind meant to take the Canavar between worlds. This creature may well be their progeny."

Canavar. Rosethorn had heard of them before, but given the amount of time that had passed, he couldn't believe Jeb's theory. "That's impossible. This ship came to the system how long? Twenty thousand years ago? We'll be lucky if the remains have much to offer at all."

"That's where you're wrong. The Kahraman had far more advanced technology than we do. The odds are good that their wreckage is still intact. The aliens used metallic compounds that were far more durable than what we have. The guild has found good, usable data on sites like this before."

They continued ahead, making their way through to a hillside area with some rock formations. The trees cleared in front of them. "If that's the case, why don't we use the same metals in our ships?"

"Haven't figured out how to produce it cheaply, yet," Jeb said, his gaze fixed forward. He turned to the guide. "We're almost there, aren't we?"

The guide pointed ahead. There was a small crack in the hillside, just big enough for a person to squeeze through.

"Ah," Jeb said. He approached the crack, placing his hand on the dirt and rubbed some of it away. Doing so revealed a manmade—or rather alien made—metallic compound. They'd found it. This hill was really an ancient starship. Jeb looked down at his scanner. "No lifeforms inside. Safe for now."

A high-pitched shriek came from the forest behind them.

Rosethorn turned, hearing the echo. Birds quickly took flight from nearby trees, flying away from the sound. "Let's hurry up. I'm not sure how much more time Montas has." He took the lead, squeezing himself through the crack and into the ship. The lights on his helmet turned on automatically, illuminating a small space in front of him, allowing him to see the ship's interior. Dust covered everything. It made him thankful for his suit's internal filtration system. The crack opened into a larger hallway with strange alien markings.

Jeb and the guide squeezed into the ship while the rest of the guards kept watch outside. Jeb didn't seem to be in awe of his surroundings, the ancient construction, or the markings on the walls. Instead, he stayed focused on his scanner. "We're looking for a computer core, a backup, something like the black boxes we use for our dropships to figure out what happened after a wreck."

"Think it's still here after all these years?" Rosethorn asked, continuing ahead. An open door led into a much larger room. Dirt was caked everywhere on the walls and platforms. The passages had been dug out by the settlers to some extent, but there was still a lot of alien ship left unexplored.

"Don't know. That's the gamble. If it is, our payout from the Cartography Guild is going to be huge," Jeb said. He waved his scanner around. "According my readings, there should be a bulkhead to your right. I've got the ship's dimensions now, and I can confirm it isn't a Canavar the villagers are dealing with. The layout is in line with their standard troop transports. They would have needed a much larger cargo compartment to carry one of those beasts."

"I told you it wasn't one of those things," Rosethorn said. "They aren't the type to take a bite of some animal or young girl and leave a place alone. The Canavar rampaged through whole cities and caused massive destruction. There wouldn't be a village left if that's what we were dealing with." He produced a knife from his belt and scraped the wall where Jeb had pointed. Hard dirt flaked off where he ran his blade. He could feel the wall behind it, something his knife couldn't penetrate. Over the years of working as a merc, he'd learned patience in situations like these. A younger man might have gotten frustrated with having to wiggle a knife back and forth to loosen ancient dirt, but to Rosethorn, it felt good to do something so simple. He saw the results of his labor as he unveiled strips of the wall. Taking joy in little victories kept him sane after doing dirty work for years.

His knife nearly slipped from his hands as it pushed into a groove near the top of the wall. He'd found the compartment. Now to loosen it up a little. After sawing back and forth, Rosethorn pushed on the hilt of the blade, and the wall creaked open. This was the bulkhead all right. He pushed upward on the hilt, allowing his leverage on the blade and gravity to do the rest. The panel in front of him fell, and Rosethorn hopped backward to avoid getting his toes smashed. Inside was a bunch of strange tubes, wiring, and electronics. "This what you're looking for?" he asked.

Jeb's eyes went wide at the sight. He crouched down in front of the open panel and whistled. "Pay day." His scanner dropped from his hands as he eagerly went to work trying to remove some of the components inside.

A voice came through Rosethorn's suit comm. It was Palmer. "Creature…firing…no effect…getting Montas…need backup!"

"Shit," Rosethorn said. The alien metal must have blocked some of the comm signal. It should have been hours yet until the creature arrived at the village's sacrificial altar. What happened? "Jeb, how much longer do you need?"

Jeb looked up. "I just started and need to be careful. Twenty minutes?"

Rosethorn grimaced. He looked to the guide. "Lead me back to the village. Jeb, I'm gonna leave a couple of men with you. When you're done, get back to the ship and prepare for takeoff. The rest of us are going to see what the hell happened and get our people to safety." Before Jeb could respond, Rosethorn jogged down the hall and slipped back through the crack. The guide came with him.

"We can't interrupt the ritual. The Great Protector—" the guide said.

Rosethorn glowered at him. "I'll tell you where you can shove your Great Protector. What you're going to do is lead us back to your little altar before I decide to get trigger happy. Now move."

The guide didn't stop to think. He nodded and ran toward the repeating gunfire.

* * *

Grace screamed, but the sound was dampened by the gag in her mouth. Bullets ricocheted off the hide of the giant lizard-beast in front of her—far too close to her for her own comfort. The thing had a scaly, silver hide and eyes like multiple shiny black bulbs. It looked vaguely like the dinosaur her captors had described, though with longer arms ending in devastating claws. Those claws, about as long as one of Grace's arms, ripped through one of Palmer's commandos, body armor and all. The shredded man spun to the ground, his blood pooling in front of her.

When the creature stood erect, it nearly blocked out one of Threndark's suns. The shadow cast by its fifteen-foot height spread over Grace and the altar.

One of the commandoes fired a rocket launcher at the creature. The projectile exploded, booming in the air, and shrapnel flew everywhere. The blast forced Grace to cringe and shield her eyes. A fragment clipped her shoulder. It stung, but there was little she could do for the wound. When she looked up again, the creature was still rampaging toward her.

She was stuck on the altar. Her guards had not only gagged her, but had also bound her hands behind her back, anchoring the bonds with weights to keep her immobilized. Although Meynard had made an agreement with Captain Rosethorn, the local had double-crossed him. Rosethorn had underestimated the settlers; they had been smart enough to split the force that had invaded their village, and had taken an unguarded route from the back door of her cell directly to the mesa.

Fortunately, some of the crew was scouting the altar, and they had ambushed the settlers when they arrived, but when they did, they found the creature already lurked there, and all hell broke loose.

Jason Palmer crouched behind her, using his machete to snap her rope. Grace didn't have time to thank him as the creature came bounding toward her, swiping at the altar with its claws. She rolled off the platform, and the creature's claws narrowly missed turning her into diced Human. Palmer distracted the creature by opening fire with his assault rifle, its bullets just as ineffective as everything else the mercs had tried. All they had managed to do was piss it off.

The creature speared one of the other commandos, piercing him through the chest with its claw and lifting him off the ground. The commando flailed, kicking helplessly as he tried to find footing, before the creature opened its gaping maw and ripped the merc's head off with its sharp teeth. It swallowed the head whole and tossed the body aside. Then, the creature let out one of its ear-piercing screams.

"We have to get the hell out of here," Grace said. With all the gunfire, it was likely no one heard her. She backpedaled toward the trail but lost her footing on some rubble. Before she could fall off the mesa and tumble down to the forest below, a hand gripped her by the arm. It steadied her. Grace turned back.

Behind her stood Captain Rosethorn, eyes set on the monster in front of them. "Status?" he asked her.

"I'm okay. But we won't be for long if we don't figure out a way to deal with this thing," Grace said. Seeing Captain Rosethorn, her heart felt as though it would leap out of her chest.

Rosethorn nodded, quickly surveying the situation. "Two down already? Entropy. Where are our rocket launchers?"

"Palmer's already fired one. It didn't faze the thing," Grace said.

Not much broke Rosethorn's usually stoic composure, but a small twitch on the left side of his mouth betrayed his stress. Grace had seen it on a few occasions, and each time it had been a portent of ill tidings for the crew. The last time had been when they nearly ran out of fuel before returning to the Trentiri starport. This time it meant he didn't know what to do about the creature any more than she did.

One of Palmer's men fired another rocket at the creature. Rosethorn covered Grace to protect her, even as he recoiled from the blast. "You'd think they'd warn us when they're about to do that!"

The creature stumbled, then screamed for a third time, sounding angrier than before. It charged the man who fired the rocket.

Palmer and several of the others used the opportunity to retreat, heading straight for Grace, Rosethorn, and the trail behind them. "Run!" Palmer yelled, his voice muffled by his helmet. Rosethorn's men looked around, confused.

"You heard him!" Rosethorn shouted. He still had Grace by the arm, and he tugged her along. They hurried down the trail, the steep slope and gravelly surface making it difficult to gain any traction. Grace didn't dare look back or slow her pace. The pounding footsteps of the beast were enough to keep her moving full speed ahead. Rosethorn dropped back behind the rest of his team, ever protective of his crew. Grace wanted to curse him; if the captain died, they'd all be screwed. They needed him more than the others.

Out of breath and running as fast as she could, she didn't have the time or ability to harass him. She only prayed he could come up with a way to deal with this thing before the creature slaughtered them all.

* * *

Rosethorn chased the rest of his crew down the trail, back to the village. Without some way to kill the thing, there was no other option but to retreat toward their ship. All their weapons had proven ineffective against it. He understood the terror the cities must have felt when they faced actual Canavar all those years ago.

In the village ahead, settlers pointed and screamed. Many ran in circles, haphazard and panicked. So much for their 'Great Protector.' Rosethorn felt guilty for bringing it back where it could rain destruction on so many innocent lives, but by the same token, the villagers had betrayed him. His agreement with Meynard was that the locals were supposed to wait until Rosethorn returned before bringing Montas to the altar. Happily, he'd had the foresight to leave some of his men behind; otherwise, Montas would be dead. As much as the loss of a couple people bothered him, he wasn't sure if he could have lived with himself if he had been responsible for her death.

His whole plan was idiotic in hindsight; it had been pure hubris to think he could handle this situation, despite not having an accurate assessment of the creature. If he made it out alive, he silently vowed to never order such a harebrained scheme ever again.

The creature came barreling after them, far too quick for its size. It knocked over several trees at the edge of the village, which crashed with a *crack* to the ground.

"Keep running," Rosethorn commanded. "Move, move, move!"

His people did just that, and there were enough of them that the creature, although still gaining on them, hadn't decided on a target. It was more than just hungry; it was enraged, and that was likely Rosethorn's fault, too. The mercs came to the center of town. A nearby village woman scooped her children into her arms and took off toward the forest.

Meynard rushed out of the council building. His face was bright red, incensed. "My village! My people! I should have had my hunters shoot you all on sight. You brought down the Great Protector's wrath!" He maneuvered himself into the path of the mercs, forcing them to slow in the square.

The creature arrived soon afterward. It jerked its giant head to the side, its bug-like eyes vibrating as it howled. One of Palmer's men stopped too close to it, and he barely managed to dive out of the way when the creature swung its claws at him.

Palmer spun around, leveling a rocket at the monster. "Fire in the hole!" he yelled.

The rocket blasted out of its chamber. A moment later, it exploded—a direct hit on the giant creature's torso. The force of the blast pushed the creature back into a nearby cabin, and the wooden wall collapsed under its weight. The roof crashed down on the creature, and dust spread out into the square.

"Out of the way," Rosethorn said, not wanting to waste a second of the diversion Palmer had created.

"You'll have to go through me," Meynard said, crossing his arms defiantly.

"Gladly," one of the commandos said, leveling his gun at Meynard.

Rosethorn reached out and forced the merc to lower his weapon. "No shooting civilians. We can go around him."

"Captain," Meynard said, desperation apparent in his voice and facial expression. "You can't leave my people like this. The Great Protector will destroy us all!"

Behind them, the creature writhed under the rubble of the house, trying to escape, but was pinned down. For now.

Rosethorn clenched his jaw, once again cursing his own sense of ethics. He had agreed to keep the children of this village safe, even if he hadn't verbalized it to them. By the same token, he didn't want to waste another breath on this nut job. Wait. *Breath.* Something clicked in his mind. Even if this creature could fend off all the weapons they had, it still needed air to breathe. He had an idea. "Palmer," Rosethorn said. "Keep pissing that thing off. Make sure it follows us. We're going to lead it back to the shuttle."

"Why?"

"Just do it," Rosethorn said. He stepped forward and clasped Meynard on the shoulder. "I'm going to help you, despite the fact that you tried to kill my first officer. Let us do our jobs. Get the civilians out of the way."

Meynard looked confused, but he nodded. "People of Threndark," he yelled. "Run for the council chambers. Let these men handle the Great Protector!" The remaining villagers in the square followed his orders, and Meynard jogged off after them.

That was enough time for the creature to get free. One of Palmer's men fired another rocket into the rubble, managing to collapse one of the side walls onto it. The wood caught fire.

Rosethorn motioned his men forward, and they ran across the square toward the opposite edge of the village and the shuttle. Rosethorn tapped his comm. "Jeb, come in. You back at the shuttle?"

"Ready and accounted for," Jeb replied.

"That equipment; you didn't use the cargo pod, did you?"

"Nope. What we needed to retrieve was a lot smaller than we anticipated. I would like to excavate that ship more—"

"We don't have time now. Maybe on the next drop. Get the ship ready. We're taking off immediately. Keep the back ramp open. We're going to be bringing a very large visitor with us."

"What?"

"Captain out." Rosethorn ran as hard as he could, guiding his men to their destination. The creature let out its loudest shriek yet, the sound drowned out by continuous gunfire from several assault rifles. With a glance back over his shoulder, he saw the creature was back on its feet and on a rampage. It trapped another one of Palmer's men between its jaws, and paused to rip the man to shreds.

"Filthy Phil!" Palmer cried. It was one of his best men. Palmer fired on the beast again.

The rest of the unit ran back into the forest to where the ship waited. The creature followed in hot pursuit, just as Rosethorn had hoped. "Palmer. I need you on the cargo pod ramp. The rest of you, cease fire and get into the shuttle. We're going to lure this thing into our rear cargo pod and take off. Palmer and I will draw its attention."

"Aye, sir," Palmer said. His voice relayed his feelings; he didn't like the plan in the least.

Rosethorn wasn't about to let his men bear the brunt of the danger. He raced up the cargo pod ramp, scanning to make sure that Montas, in particular, made it to safety. He turned and opened fire on the creature, and it charged toward him. "Jeb, get ready on the ramp and take off."

"Aye, sir," Jeb said.

Rosethorn and Palmer fired simultaneously, directing everything they had at the creature. Rosethorn fired until he ran out of ammunition, then removed the sling from his shoulders and threw the rifle at it. The creature dove for him and extended its claws to impale him, but Rosethorn jumped off the side of the ramp. The creature fell off balance and stumbled on the ramp, falling into the pod.

Palmer leapt off his side of the platform, landing much more gracefully than Rosethorn had, as the ramp ticked closed. The beast turned around in an attempt to escape, but flailed helplessly against the ramp as it trapped him inside. It attacked the ramp, biting furiously, but it couldn't escape.

The shuttle rocked. There was no telling how well, or even if, the cargo pod would hold the monster. It wasn't rated for the stress of a giant creature ramming against its walls.

Rosethorn scrambled toward the crew hatch, with Palmer behind him, and both men threw themselves into the shuttle. "Go, Jeb!" Rosethorn shouted.

Jeb fired the shuttle's thrusters. The rear monitor provided a view of the creature, angered beyond belief, as it threw its entire weight against the ramp wall. The shuttle lifted, and the creature stumbled and fell deeper into the pod. Rosethorn braced himself against Montas' harness, unable to make it to his own seat.

The creature turned its attention to the opposite wall, as if knowing where the Humans were. Though it should have been impossible, the creature seemed to sense its prey, and it pounded on the bulkhead as the shuttle continued to ascend.

And then the bulkhead began to give. It started with a little divot, right under where the cargo pod viewing monitor had been mounted. Then, after several more hits, it became a full-fledged dent in the shape of the creature's skull.

Montas wrapped her arms around Rosethorn's waist. Though it was an act of fear, Rosethorn couldn't help but enjoy the sensation. The respite was brief as bile rose in his throat from the acceleration and his own fear of what would happen if the creature made it through. "Jeb," Rosethorn warned.

"Almost out of the atmosphere," Jeb said.

The creature crashed once more against the wall. If it broke a hole through, they wouldn't be able to open the rear ramp in vacuum. He didn't want to risk dropping the thing back onto Threndark and having it somehow survive the fall; if rockets couldn't kill the creature, there was no telling what would. "Hurry!"

"We're clear!" Jeb shouted.

"Vent the cargo pod," Rosethorn said.

His co-pilot hit the control that opened the ramp, and Rosethorn could see the paper and debris being sucked out into the vacuum of space on the monitor. After a couple of seconds, the creature, despite its enormity, was pulled toward the nothingness, and it went overboard as its body imploded.

Rosethorn's knuckles had turned white from holding onto Montas' harness for dear life. Montas relaxed her grip, but kept her arms around his waist. She cocked her head up toward him. "That was gutsy. It could have torn us all apart."

Rosethorn let out a deep sigh of relief. "I had to trust my gut."

Palmer laughed and shook his head, having managed to squeeze into his seat and harness somehow, sandwiched between two other mercs. "That was too close for comfort, Captain."

"What's important is we made it, and we're going to get a nice bonus from the Cartography Guild," Rosethorn said.

"What about those people down there?" Montas asked. "They've lost their Great Protector." She rested her head against his hip, and it didn't seem like she intended to let him go any time soon. None of the other mercs appeared to notice, or they were at least too polite to stare.

"They'll need more protection from the influx of colonists and tourists once word spreads about this planet. I may even come back some day when I retire," Rosethorn said wryly. The monitor changed to a view of Threndark from the rear of the shuttle.

"Seriously?" Montas asked, her arms tightening around him once more.

Rosethorn laughed. "Yeah right. I intend to be running this company until the day I die. Let's hope it's not soon." His body felt as if it were about to float away, but he couldn't determine whether that was from the lack of gravity or from Montas' touch.

# # # # #

Mark's Introduction to:

Gilded Cage

by Kacey Ezell

Kacey is rather new to the writing game, but I believe you'll be hearing a lot more from her, which is why she's in this anthology. Her addition, "Gilded Cage," is interesting in that it introduces a quite unique race to the Four Horsemen universe, and touches on the seedy underbelly of our libertarian Galactic Union; assassination for hire.

Kacey has been part of a number of anthologies, including "Sha'Daa: Inked," and wrote the cover story to the greatly-acclaimed zombie apocalypse anthology "Black Tide Rising," in the universe of the same name created by Baen superstar John Ringo.

Find out more about Kacey at

http://amazon.com/author/kaceyezell.

GILDED CAGE
by Kacey Ezell

Huh. That's odd.

I scrubbed my hands over my face, feeling the fading effects of the *Malluma Songo* trickle through my skin. That had been a good hit. I'd lucked into that score. Prasser Ghat was an asshole of the highest caliber, but at least he got good drugs. Painful as his party had been, I'd probably do it again.

Not right away, though. I hurt too badly, and I'd lost a lot of blood there at the end, when things had gotten really wild. A quick nanite spray would have fixed me right up, but it was either nanites or the *Songo*, and there was never a question which I'd choose.

Not these days, anyway.

These days my hands shook like tree branches in a heavy wind. They looked about like that, too. Skeletally thin (because I rarely remembered to eat) and covered in scabs (from when the itching got really bad), they didn't look much like the precision instruments I'd once trained them to be. Plus, they were dirty and covered in a crust of sweat and station dirt and filth, just like the rest of me.

I crossed my arms over my chest, tucking my wasted hands underneath my armpits, letting them hide in the nest of rags that was all Ghat's party guests had left of my clothing. My forehead drooped to rest on my knees. Maybe I'd sleep for a while, here in this forgotten corridor. It probably wasn't safe, right outside of Ghat's place, but I didn't care.

A soft, heavy tread. Like that of someone big trying not to be noticed. Not claws or hooves, soft-soled boots. Probably Human, then?

Despite the lullaby of my diminishing high, my occasional sense of self-preservation kicked in, and I lifted my head enough to peek out through the lank, greasy strands of my hair.

Two men, then two more. Dressed like partygoers, but they didn't look like partygoers. One carried a large instrument case...a cello. My mind supplied the word, pulled from memories long forgotten. Musicians? Someone to play for Ghat's pleasure? He liked to hire fellow Humans for his club, it was true, but classical instrumental music from Earth didn't seem quite like his style. He was more of an old school thrash metal kind of guy from what I'd seen.

One of the other men turned to look down my corridor. I ducked my head back down again, feeling my heart rocket into thudding overdrive. Great. Now I'm paranoid and anxious as well. What the hell had Ghat cut the *Songo* with? Maybe it wasn't such good shit after all.

"You going down there?" I heard.

"Nah," he said. "It's closed off. Prass said we's to expect a threat coming in from outside. Not already here. Can't get in that way."

I tried to make myself look as small and garbage-pile-esque as possible without moving.

"It's clean," another voice said. "Well, it ain't *clean*, exactly. But from the smell, if there's anything there, it's long dead. Let's head back inside and make ourselves inconspicuous. Remember, nobody makes a move until the threat shows itself. Got it? Prass wants this 'contract' issue settled quickly."

A chorus of vaguely affirmative grunts, and again, the soft sound of big men moving quietly and swiftly. Then I was, once again, blessedly alone in my fetid sanctuary.

Or so I thought.

A *frisson* ran down my spine. Not unpleasant, it felt like an arpeggio played out in fur over the surface of my skin. I lifted my head once more and noticed the faintest shimmer in the air, like a heat mirage under the desert sun. Though it'd been years? Decades? Since I'd seen either desert or sun.

A small figure appeared to coalesce out of the shadow of the piles of refuse by the entrance to the little alcove. With pointed ears and a sinuous, furred body, I had a moment to wonder if I was hallucinating about the cats I'd had as a kid. But then the cat stood up, and I could see its front paws featured a prehensile digit, and its pelvis tilted back well enough to allow it to walk bipedally. Memory flooded my brain with a shock like top grade *Songo*.

The visitor seemed completely disinterested in me. In fact, if I didn't know better, I would have said that it never even knew I was there. But of course it knew. Because this was more than some furry cuddlemonster like my childhood pets had been. This was a Depik assassin. Once, long ago, I would have given my very life to see one so close. How ironic that it should happen now, when I had no life left to give.

Before I realized what I planned to do, I called out. The sound I made was even reminiscent of the greetings I used to give my cats when I'd come home from school. Deeper, though. With more emphasis to the 'R' sound, which was the best approximation available with my Human vocal cords. I called out a single word in the Depik's native language. A word of warning.

The Depik froze, then turned slowly to me. A thrill skittered down my abused nerves as I unexpectedly, suddenly, achieved what had once been a life goal.

"Why do you know this word?" the Depik asked, through the translator I could see clipped to a vest-like garment. "Though you speak it like a lisping kitten with a damaged brain."

"I...I have studied for many years to learn your language," I said, my words rusty and hoarse.

"You?" the Depik asked, derision dripping from the word. Despite my awe, despite my self-loathing, the disdain of the creature I'd waited so long to meet stung my long-forgotten pride. I straightened my spine and raised my chin.

"Yes, I," I said in Depik, and then I quoted something I'd read in the few Depik writings I'd been able to get my hands on. "'What is, is not always what was.'"

"Though lives may pass, nine times nine times ninety and nine," the Depik responded, and its eyes blinked slowly in that species' version of a smile.

"Hunter," I said, using the Depik form of address, but switched back to English and let my trusty translator do its work, "I must warn you, all is not as it seems. You are expected within."

"Am I?" the Depik asked. "That is of no consequence."

"I do not doubt you," I said. And I didn't. Depik assassins had a well-deserved reputation for lethality. "But it is a foolish kitten who does not gather what information presents itself."

The Depik's mouth dropped open in an expression I assumed was either surprise or amusement. Had it been otherwise, I would probably have died in that moment.

"You speak words of truth and wisdom, but you have the look and scent of someone with no wisdom. How is this?"

"Yeah, well," I said, feeling my sudden attack of pride deflate. "What is, is not always what was."

The Depik looked at me for a long moment, then dropped to its quadruped gait and stalked slowly toward me.

"Perhaps not," it said, speaking slowly. I could hear the burrs and rolls of its native language under the translator's voice. "Tell me why you think I am expected."

"I just saw a squad of mercs casing the place. They didn't see me, but they checked the area out and talked about surprising an expected threat. They mentioned a contract issue, which, now that I think about it, could be referring to your contract."

The Depik made a deep, thoughtful, rumbling sound. I waited for a moment to see if it had anything else to say and then went on.

"They were all dressed as partygoers—no visible armor or anything. One of the men was carrying a large instrument case. Big enough to hold rifles."

"Ambush," the Depik said, drawing the word out as it blinked another slow smile. "How delightful." It focused its eyes on me and stalked closer, sniffing the air around me.

"I smell *Malluma Songo* on you," it said. "Would you like more?"

Longing punched me in the gut, twisting my insides with need. I nodded, mutely. The Depik stood up and reached into its vest. "Come inside the club with me," it said, "and I will give you more, and of better quality, than you've yet experienced."

"Wha—? Why?" I wanted it. Oh, how I wanted to say yes. But…come into the club? What could I do there? Despite the worthless misery of my life, I wasn't ready to die.

"You will provide a distraction. The mercs will be focused on you, and I will fulfill my contract. Do you want it? I will not offer again," the Depik said, and I caught a note of impatience in its voice.

"Yes," I breathed, before I realized I had done so. The Depik slow-blinked again, and withdrew its paw/hand from inside the vest. Light from the sign on the club glinted off the tiny metal of a hypodermic needle. I raised my shaking arm. The Depik made a face as it grabbed my wrist, which was streaked and smeared with dirt and old blood...and possibly other things. Who knew?

I felt the pinch as the Depik inserted the needle into the vein in my elbow. Then the blissful burn of the drug entering my bloodstream. I exhaled slowly, feeling the hit take hold of my mind.

Damn. The Depik hadn't lied. This was *really* good shit. Euphoria soaked through me, sloughing away layers of pain and fear and self-loathing. Joy bubbled up into my brain, and I tilted my head back and closed my eyes, letting the pleasure rain down on me from nowhere and everywhere at once.

"Come," the Depik said, and I *felt* it push at me, all over me. Though the Depik only held me by the wrist, I could feel the soft, prickly sensation of fur all along my skin. It tugged at me, urged me to my unsteady feet, pulled me along until I found myself walking, alone, through the front doors of the club.

A man I didn't know stepped in front of me, so that my face impacted his chest. I felt the hardness of the body armor hidden under his shirt bruise my forehead, but thanks to this amazing *Songo*, I didn't care.

"The fuck are you doing in here, junkie?" the man growled. I recognized his voice from outside. "Phaugh, but you stink!"

Once again, I felt the susurration of fur sliding along my skin, and I knew that I was not, in fact, alone.

"It's here," I whispered, unaware that I had done so. Adrenaline sang through the pleasure centers of my brain. Delicious entropy swirled around me, drowning me in bliss.

"What's here?" the man said, suspicious. His hand went to his hip. A corner of my mind registered my peril as he pulled his weapon free, but it didn't matter. Nothing mattered except the sensations enflaming my brain.

A soft wave of fur pulsed through me, and the man holding me crumpled, blood fountaining from a stab wound that appeared at the base of his neck. A bright, metallic scent wrapped itself around me as I felt his dead weight drag me to the floor, and a hot rain of iron-red liquid pattered onto my skin.

I heard a distant scream that swooped and merged into the driving beat of the night club's dance music. Bodies, mostly Human, but a few alien forms, gyrated in time with the sound.

It was all I could do to push away from the dead merc and the sticky coolness of the dance floor. My awareness skipped, and something sour reached up and wrapped itself around my throat. I'd found my feet, but I fell back to my knees as my insides tried to crawl out of my mouth and nose. Through the tears and smoke, I could see the merc's body in front of me. Black smoke had started to issue from the wound that had killed him, and it was this putrid stench that was causing my heaves.

Once again, I felt the invisible fur pushing through my skin, comforting me like an old blanket. Somehow I managed to climb back to my feet, because when my awareness skipped again, I tottered on gelatin legs toward the back of the club, where Prasser Ghat usually sat with his women and flunkies.

The furred wind that pushed me on seemed to reach out with an invisible hand of death. I passed another merc, who looked at me and then tried to cry out, only to find his windpipe constricted by a garrote. I turned to look at him, but the purple of his face bled out into the air around me and merged with the pulsing lights. His fall to the ground looked choreographed. He must have been a hell of a dancer.

The other mercs had their weapons out, and they'd backed up against Prasser's table. Apparently they'd abandoned the secret ambush plan. There were four, or maybe five. I couldn't really tell, between the shifting lights, the pounding music, and the swimming shadows that wrapped around anything my eyes touched.

I shivered and watched as one of the mercs fell heavily to one knee, blood pouring from the back of his boot. For just a moment, I could see the Depik make a fantastic twisting handspring-type leap from the floor up to land on the forearm that held the man's rifle. A glittering line of metal flashed red and blue in the club light at me, and then the merc's fingers sprang open as the hand separated from the wrist. He must have screamed. I would have screamed, but the music swept the sound away like water flooding a decades-dry gully.

I must have skipped again, because the next thing I knew, I was looking across the table at Prasser. The broken, wasted bodies of the merc security squad lay radiating out from us like the rays of a star.

I'd never seen the gangster look the way he looked right then. He was the perennial big shot, but now he stared at me, pale-faced and hollow-eyed with fear. I smiled slowly and shook my head.

"It's not me," I said, or tried to say. "It isn't me you have to fear."

"How did you—?" he asked. I shook my head again, and that movement nearly made me fall. The music lifted me up though, the music, and the feeling of fur running along the inside of my skin.

"Good evening Prasser Ghat," the Depik said. I blinked, and the felinoid alien sat on the table, looking calm and unmoved by either the music, or the lights, or the iron-hot scent of blood that curled around us all.

"A Depik?" Prasser breathed. "Who—?"

"That is not your business," the Depik replied. "What is your business is that you still breathe. I am under contract, so that is, unfortunately, a temporary condition. However, you have information that may be useful to me; therefore, you are in a position to choose whether you will die painfully, or instantly."

"What—? I don't...I don't know anything!" Prasser said, sliding slowly away from the Depik along the curved seat of the booth. The music changed up, and the beat dropped down, bumping along the floor and pulsing in the colored darkness. I may have skipped again, or perhaps the Depik was just that fast, because all of a sudden it was standing on the booth seat, next to the terrified Prasser. I could taste the sudden tang of sweat in the air.

"Untrue. You knew that someone was coming for you, though not, perhaps, that they would send me. Was this a lucky guess on your part? Or did you know of the contract?"

"I...I knew that...someone...I had enemies..."

"How did you know the threat would come tonight?"

"Rumors...and... "

"And?" The Depik asked. It leaned close, and Prasser Ghat folded into himself. I could see his fear, like a living thing, winding around and around in time with the music of the club.

"Movetskin," Prasser said, naming another drug kingpin, from a neighboring system. I forget which. "I got a message from him telling me that I'd be sorry for double-crossing him, that I had no chance of escaping. That before the next lunar cycle, I'd be dead. Tonight's the last night of this cycle."

"Ah," the Depik said, nodding. "And so the client breaches his own confidentiality. Well. His choice. I thank you for being so forthcoming."

Prasser Ghat opened his mouth to say something, but all that came out was a little cough and a spray of red that splattered over the table. I'd never even seen the Depik move. It leaped upon my shoulder, and I felt wrapped in that delicious, safe, comfortable fur inside and out.

"Come," the Depik said in my ear. I couldn't see it, but I could feel its weight on my shoulder. "You interest me. I claim you as my own. Let us go home."

I tried to acquiesce. I tried to ask where 'home' was. I tried to say that I had no 'home,' that I hadn't had one for many, many years. I could do none of those things.

My last conscious thought was that the red light in the club made the bloodstains appear black, and almost none of the club goers had even noticed we'd been there.

* * *

I woke in completely unfamiliar surroundings. The room was small and dimly lit, the grey walls curved in such a manner that I guessed we were on the grav-ring of a ship. I felt...unaccountably good. Better than I had remembered I could feel, actually. I tried to sit up, and only then realized I'd been lying in an actual bed. I didn't know the last time I'd slept in a bed.

Time to take stock, I thought, and looked down at myself. My rags were gone, replaced by the light blanket that had fallen to my waist. Under that, nothing. I looked down and saw that someone had obviously bathed me and given me medical treatment. All the wounds from Prasser Ghat's last party were gone, as were the constellations of track marks I'd acquired over the years. I was still thin enough to count my ribs, but I'd obviously been fed intravenously, because I wasn't hungry.

I looked around the small space and noticed something that looked like a cupboard. I swung my feet experimentally to the floor and found it steady enough, if a mite cold. I took one tentative step toward the cupboard and pulled it open.

Shelves of folded clothing waited within. I blinked in surprise and wondered if I was to take one, then shrugged and figured that clothed was better than naked. I pulled out a one-piece coverall that would cover my feet and zip from my crotch to just below my chin. It had long sleeves and felt delightfully soft and slightly fuzzy. I almost couldn't wait to put it on. The feeling of the fabric against my fingers reminded me of the delicious furry high of...

Oh.

Flashes of memory returned in rapid-fire confusion. I sat down on the floor with a thump, the coverall still in my hands. To my right, a door I hadn't known existed slid open with a *whirr*ing sound.

"You have awakened," the Depik said. "How do you feel?"

"Good," I said, startled into answering. "Really good. Better than...what did you do?"

The Depik long-blinked its smile at me and walked fully into the room on all four legs. It padded over to sit, cat-style, directly across from me.

"I fulfilled my contract, then I directed you back to my ship, where I gave you a lengthy nanite treatment…and a bath. You were quite filthy."

"Why?" I asked.

"I imagine because you'd been indigent for some time."

"No, I mean, why did you do all that…for me?"

"Oh. I have claimed you. You are mine now. I am quite pleased about it, actually. I have the feeling you will make an excellent companion. And I've recently birthed a litter of kits. They will be very excited." It…*she* slow blinked again, and I could hear a deep rumbling sound coming from somewhere within her chest. Was she purring? I never knew Depik *could* purr!

The part of my brain that used to be a xenobiologist thrilled at the chance to get to spend more time with her…and to see her young! How fascinating! What a coup! Dr. Black would have been so proud.

But another part of my brain surged to the forefront of my consciousness and spilled out of my mouth.

"Wait, what? I'm not…you can't! I'm not a *slave*. You can't just *claim* me!"

The Depik stared at me for a long moment, and then she slow blinked again. The tip of her tail twitched back and forth, and I abruptly had the feeling she was laughing at me.

"Are you not?" she asked, her tone nonchalant. "It seemed like you had done a rather thorough job of enslaving yourself when I found you."

I rocked back, stung by the naked truth of her words. Shame flooded me, and I dropped my gaze to watch my hands twisting in the soft coverall fabric.

"But if that is how you prefer it, I will respect your wishes. I am prepared to offer you a painless death...no charge," she added, with a hint of humor in her tone.

"Wait, what?" I asked again, looking up.

She raised one hand/paw in an elegant gesture that seemed to equate to a shrug.

"You know our language. You observed me fulfill a contract. You cannot be allowed to run free."

"I know too much," I said, unable to keep from letting out a half-hysterical kind of laugh.

"You know too much," she agreed. "So I must eliminate you. I can offer you a painless death...or a place as my companion and that of my kits. You would live in my home. I would care for you. You would never want for anything ever again. But you would be mine."

"Why?" I asked, unable to stop my once-professional curiosity. "What benefit do you gain from an arrangement like that? Why keep me as a...a pet?"

She blinked another smile and got to her feet. She padded toward me and rubbed her furred body along my naked arm, which caused me to shiver all over. Then she sat down beside me again.

"Your species keeps 'pets,' yes? For the same reasons, I imagine. For companionship, for affection. My kits will find you fascinating and will adore you. I, myself, find you interesting, and I bear you some gratitude for your timely warning the other day. The contract would have been more difficult to fulfill without it. I would like to keep you alive for these reasons alone."

"What is so interesting about a strung out, half-dead *Songo* junkie?" I asked, feeling the words drop bitterly from my lips.

"The fact she knows my language, for one," the Depik replied. "The fact that she *is* a *Songo* junkie, and thus felt it when I shifted the light around me."

"The *Songo* did that?" I asked. "I could tell…it felt…furry-warm, and oddly safe. I didn't know what it was, but I started to associate it with you."

She blinked at me, and yawned a silent laugh.

"I am not often associated with safety," she said, and again I could hear her dry humor in her tone. "But yes, that is an effect of the *Malluma Songo*, it allows your baryonic nervous system to sense my quintessence field, which is what shifts the proton paths as I direct."

"Quintessence field…you mean…"

"I believe you call it 'dark energy,' she said gently, as one speaking to a not particularly bright child in the midst of making a discovery. "An impossibly quaint name."

I blinked several times as the world shifted around me. Depik could manipulate *dark energy*? That was incredible…impossible! It was completely unheard of! No other species could…

But then, no other species could shift light the way the Depik could. Nor could they move as quickly, nor…

"Your nervous system," I breathed. "*That's* why nerve agents don't work on your species! Somehow, instead of chemical-electrical interactions, your nervous system employs *dark energy* interactions!"

"Both, actually," the Depik said. "Otherwise, how could I be seeing you in this light? My matter is as baryonic as yours, it is just configured slightly differently, so that we can access the quintessence around us. Just as you did, with the help of the *Malluma Songo*. And now that you have discovered this deadliest of facts, I really must insist on an answer to my proposition. For unless you are completely mine, within my control, you cannot be allowed to live with this knowledge."

I blinked, and the researcher in the back of my head howled in frustration.

"Do you know why I became a junkie?" I asked, courting danger by answering her question with a question.

"I am interested to learn," she said, though her tone said she would only indulge me for so long before becoming more insistent on her answer.

"My name is Susan Aloh. *Doctor* Susan Aloh, actually. Former Professor of Xenobiology at the University of Texas. I used to be one of Earth's foremost experts in the field. I was hand-selected by Dr. Adelaide Black to accompany her team of researchers and study the Galactic Union. It was fascinating work, and I loved it...but I became intrigued by one race in particular...yours."

"Mine?" she asked, amusement threading through her tone.

"Yes. We'd discovered so little about your species. You were such a mystery. A handful of writings, a catalogue of legends. That was it. Your system appeared to have only two exports. Death, and..."

"*Malluma Songo*," she said slowly.

"Yes," I breathed. "I first tried it because I wanted to analyze it, but I couldn't get it through any kind of reputable source. So I had to buy it from a low-dealer, and he insisted I do my first hit in front of him...and from then I was lost.

"Oh, I kept working for a while. Another Earth year or two. But I craved it; I had to have it. Eventually, I missed meeting up with my team and got left behind. And after that...I don't remember. It all runs together in my head. There was only the now, and the need for more."

"Yes," she said. "It was designed that way."

"Why?" I asked, anguish flooding my tone. "Why would you put something out into the universe like that?"

"Because the demand is there," she responded. "Why else?"

"But it destroyed me!" I sobbed, and only then realized I was crying. Had been for some time, if the hot tracks down my cheeks were any indication.

"It did not appear in your veins by magic," the Depik replied, mercilessly. "You made a choice to put yourself under its spell. As I said, you enslaved yourself. Do not blame the chain-maker when you locked the manacles willingly about your own wrists."

I lost it. Great, wracking sobs shook my whole body. I bent double, head in my lap, my tears soaking the fuzzy fabric of the coverall I had yet to put on. I screamed and howled for my lost life, for all the pain I'd inflicted upon myself, for the shame that I'd sunk so low...and all by my own hands. All because of my damned ambition to know *more*.

A warm slide of fur against my side. I wasn't high, so it couldn't be the quintessence interaction again, but it had that same feeling of safety and comfort about it. The Depik had rubbed the length of her body against me. I could feel the deep rumbling sound of her purring throb through my skin.

"And yet you live," she said softly. "And you may live still, if you stay with me. Or you may die in comfort now. Once again, the choice is yours to make."

"I don't want to die," I whispered, not knowing this was true until I said the words.

"Then you choose to stay with me, be my companion?"

"Yes," I whispered.

Another warm slide of fur, the feel of her paw/hand stroking my hair.

"I do not think you will regret this choice, my Human. I think you will be very happy with me."

But I will never again be free, a tiny corner of my mind whispered. I ignored it. The Depik was right. I hadn't been free for a very long time.

* * *

My Depik mistress had a name, of course. I couldn't pronounce it. I settled for calling her Reow, for that was about as close as I could get to the actual sound of her name. According to her translator, the English version of her name was Deadly Night Wind. Reow just seemed an easier (and slightly less unsettling) choice.

Reow was, it turned out, quite wealthy. The ship we travelled on belonged to her. It was fast but small, barely big enough to justify having a grav-ring. The fact that it had one at all spoke elegantly of the level of luxury she expected…and got, if my eyes were to be believed.

The crew, though small, was clearly very well trained, both in the operation of the ship and in Reow's personal preferences. Though they represented a mix of several species, it was obvious they'd worked together for quite a while, for they were very good at what they did.

It took surprisingly little time to reach the Depik home system, though whether that spoke to the speed of the ship and skill of the crew, or to our proximity to begin with, I had no idea. I didn't really know, nor did I care, where that last station had been. It didn't matter, for it was very much in the past, along with the rest of my old life.

As Reow made very clear to me.

"I will not provide you with more of the *Malluma Songo*," she said, apropos of nothing, as we took a meal together shortly after I'd awakened. Somehow, the crew had known to provide me with bread and salad, and a little cooked meat that tasted like beef. Reow dined daintily on some kind of raw, shredded meat of her own.

I looked up at her, careful to keep my face blank. She slow-blinked a knowing smile at me. She really was beautiful, now that I could see her in full light…well, as full as the light on the ship ever got, anyway. Depik eyes were adapted to darkness, so the ship seemed to exist in a kind of perpetual twilight. But at least she was no longer cloaking herself in shadow all the time.

The majority of her body was covered in black fur, but it lightened to a grey on her face and throat. Black stripes accentuated her huge green eyes, and ran up her forehead between her triangular, pointed ears. Her nose was less pointed than an Earth cat's, but her small, quick bites showed very clearly her pointed predator's teeth. She tended to wear very little, and that only if it had some kind of purpose, like her utility vest, or her weapon harnesses. I suspected that when we arrived at her home, she would wear nothing but her silky fur.

"You have noticed, I am sure," she went on after I said nothing, "that the physical manifestations of your addiction were healed with the nanite treatment. Any further withdrawal passed while we kept you sedated, afterward. All that is left is the emotional attachment you may have for the euphoria and false escape of the high. I cannot remove this from you so easily. However, I can ensure that you do not get more, and time, I am told, will do the rest."

"That makes sense," I said, as she seemed to expect an answer. I could hear the raggedness in my voice. Whether it was because I missed the high, or because of this stark reminder that I was no longer free, I cannot say.

"Also, I cannot have you impaired around my offspring," she said. As Reow spoke, she reached out and stroked the back of my wrist with her fingerpads, claws retracted. She liked to touch me, whether for her comfort or mine, I didn't know. But I was starting to associate her little caresses with safety and affection, and I didn't mind them at all.

"I understand," I said.

"Good," she said, and held out a small box to me. I blinked in surprise and then put down my eating utensils to take the box. It opened on a tiny hinge, and inside lay a pendant on dully metallic chain.

"Titanium?" I guessed,

"Do you like it?" she asked. "I selected the metal for its lightness. I don't want the sigil to be cumbersome and uncomfortable to wear, but I thought it was attractive to the eye, even so."

"It's beautiful," I said, lifting the pendant out. It was a sinuous shape that I didn't recognize. It looked something like one of the letters of the Depik alphabet, but slightly different.

"It is my sigil," Reow said. "It is the mark of my clan. When you wear it, all who see you will know that you belong to us and are not to be harmed."

I ran my thumb over the shape, let the titanium chain slide through my fingers.

"Do you like it?" she asked again.

What could I say? It was both beautiful and thoughtful, but that didn't change the fact that it was, at the end of the day, a collar. Another chain of my own choosing. A symbol of the way I'd abdicated my freedom in the name of ambition, then pleasure, then survival.

"I love it," I whispered, because it really was beautiful, and she seemed so hopeful that I would. "Will you help me put it on?"

"Of course, my Human," she said, and pushed up to her back feet.

I handed her the necklace, and ducked my head while she fastened it under my hair. I'd kept it cut close for longer than I could remember, but Reow liked it long, so I was letting it grow.

I felt her fingerpads trace the line of my cheekbone. Without knowing why, I leaned into her touch.

"You're such a pretty kita," she said. "You're going to be so happy at home. I'll take good care of you, sweetling. You'll see."

* * *

Not long after that, we arrived on the Depik home world of Khastash.

Before we started our re-entry, I got a look at the planet's surface. It looked *impossibly* green. With the exception of some rather small polar ice caps and three relatively large oceans, every bit of landmass was deeply, violently green. As we sped toward our re-entry point, we crossed over the spine of a mountain range, and even the tallest of peaks stood cloaked in viridian up to the snow line.

"Your world is so green!" I said to Reow, who twitched her tail in a laugh at me and rubbed her body along my shoulder as we stood looking out of the ship's viewport.

"It is," she said. "90 percent of the landmass is covered in triple-canopy jungle. That is why you cannot see any of our cities from orbit. They're all concealed."

"Fitting," I said, and she twitched her tail again with a purr.

Beautiful as it was, I didn't get to see much of it up close, because Reow told me I had to travel from the spaceport to her home in a capsule-like container. I'd never had much of a problem with small spaces (hard to do so, when one is homeless, living hand-to-mouth on some backwater space station somewhere), but I didn't like the capsule thing at all. It felt too much like sensory deprivation once I'd piled myself inside, and it had closed around me.

I felt the capsule moving, and after what felt like an eternity (but was probably no more than an hour), we arrived somewhere. A hissing sound heralded the opening of my capsule, and the twilight dimness that passed for Depik light poured in. I blinked, slowly, and tentatively stepped forth out of the capsule into a long, low room furnished in brightly-colored furniture of various heights. I looked around in curiosity, wondering what this room could be.

I was immediately attacked by four small, fierce, carnivorous assassins bent on my destruction. One leapt down from somewhere above me and landed on my shoulder, tangling claws painfully in my hair. One twisted through my feet, causing me to overextend and lose my balance. A third sprang from the ground to bury 20 tiny, sharp needles into my side, and the last waited until I had fallen, and then immediately stalked toward my face.

Before I could do more than raise my hands to try and protect my eyes, I heard Reow's commanding yowl, and all movement stopped.

"Kits!" she said, her voice cracking like a whip, "Your speed and aggression was commendable, but you failed the most important test! Do you not see the sigil around this Human's neck?"

I risked peeking through my fingers as the last kit, the one who'd attacked my face, sniffed and pawed delicately at the titanium chain around my neck. The sigil fell free from where it had lodged under my chin when I hit, and I heard the tiny Depik draw in a sharp breath.

"Our sigil, Dama?" he asked in a tiny, piping voice. He wasn't wearing a translator, of course, but enough of the language had come back to me that I understood him.

"Indeed, Cunning Blade. That is our sigil. I have brought this Human home to be a companion for you and your brother-kit and your sister-kitas."

Sharp, interested meeps of excitement followed, and I slowly lowered my hands and pushed up to a seated position, legs crossed in front of me.

"Greetings, small hunters," I said as best I could.

"It talks!" one of the other kits said, a female, judging from what I could see. I thought she might have been the one who tangled in my hair, but I wasn't sure.

"Yes, kita, *she* does, insofar as her Human mouthparts allow. Humans are quite intelligent. So how do we greet a member of an alien species politely?" Reow asked.

The tip of the kita's tail twitched slightly, and she rose up to her hind legs and reached out a paw.

"I, Death From Above, greet you, Human. Welcome to our negotiation." She said the words as if they'd been memorized by rote.

"That would do for a wild Human encountered outworld, my kita. Very good," Reow said, a rumble of approval in her voice. "But what about one who wears a clan sigil?"

All four of the kits sat abruptly on their rumps as they considered this new problem. I glanced over at Reow, to find that her ears and her expression indicated both great pride and not a little amusement at the antics of her offspring. Happily, the wounds the kits had caused me were small, and I didn't have to worry about them, much, while we waited.

"The stories do not tell of other sigiled Humans," Cunning Blade said slowly, as if puzzling it out. "Dama, have you brought us the first?"

"I have," Reow said. The kits leapt up in celebration and once again became a roiling mass of fur and energy as they attacked first Reow and then me. The difference was that this time, the intent was exuberance and love, not assassination.

"Her name is Susa, and she is the first sigiled Human any of our kind have claimed," Reow said, tail twitching in laughter as she spoke out loud over her litter's tight *mews* of excitement. "The Humans are a mercenary species, but their skins are fragile. You must take care not to hurt her as you play. However, she has been all across the galaxy and has seen many things. I think she will be a good addition to your education as you grow into true hunters."

"Susa, Susa!" the little ones started to yell, and I found myself laughing as I reached out my hands in welcome to them. Sure enough, they started to climb all over me. Somehow, in the raucous deluge of sound and play that ensued, I managed to learn all of their names.

Cunning Blade was the eldest of the four and most often assumed the position of leader. He apparently was becoming quite a tactical thinker, and he began asking me about the Human merc companies, particularly the famous "Four Horsemen," before his littermates had even been introduced. He looked like a smaller, male version of his dama, down to the stripes around his eyes.

Death From Above had introduced herself, of course, and I tried to thank her for that. Her entire body was striped in shades of grey and brown. She was clearly the best climber of the litter, and before long, she'd claimed the perch on my right shoulder for her own. I supposed that would work well enough for now, though I wasn't sure what we were going to do when she grew much bigger.

Silent Flame was the second kita, the most striking of the bunch. Her fur was all black, and her eyes a bright, vivid blue. She took the longest to warm up to me physically and seemed content to sit beside me, not touching, while her littermates explored their new pet.

Choking Deluge, on the other hand, was the largest kit in the litter, and he knew it. He'd been the one to trip me, using his mass applied at the right moment to bring me down. Unlike his brother-kit, he was about as subtle as the rainstorm for which he was named. Boisterous, charming, and a bright, rusty orange in color, he instantly began begging me to play-wrestle with him.

I looked to Reow for permission, only to see that she'd gone and the door had closed behind her. Clearly, I was to entertain the kits until she returned.

So we played. We played chase and climb and wrestle and tag. And when the kits (and I!) started to tire, I sat and let them crawl over me while I told them stories of Earth, our legends and histories. Eventually, all four of them were yawning wide, sleepy yawns, and I could feel fatigue dragging at the edges of my own mind when the door slid open, and Reow returned.

"Dama!" Deluge said, but even the boisterous kit was too sleepy to do more than lift his head from where he lay with his littermates in my lap.

"Are they sleeping?" Reow asked me, slow blinking.

"All but this one," I said.

"Put them in their beds, then," she said, pointing to a ledge high on the wall, "and come with me. I will show you where you may sleep."

"Reow…" I said, tentative.

"What is it, my Human?"

"I…" I broke off, unsure what I even wanted to say. She stared at me and then padded toward me with the deadly, liquescent grace of her species.

"I…thank you," I whispered. "For letting me play…for trusting me with your kits."

Reow slow blinked again and then rubbed her face against the back of my hand where it cupped Flame and kept her from falling off of my lap. Little Death, next to her, seemed poised to shove her sister-kit off, simply by virtue of sprawling everywhere in her sleep.

"You are a part of the clan, Susa," Reow said softly. "They love you, as I knew they would. I know you find it hard, but this is a new life for you. Can you accept it? Can you accept their love, and mine?"

I looked down at the kits in my lap, then up at their deadly dama. Her eyes blinked slower than usual, in an extended gesture of love and affection, before she rubbed her cheek against my hand again.

Even before my addiction, even before all of that, emotions had never been comfortable for me. I had buried myself in my work, because that was safer than feeling something for someone who could turn around and hurt me. That had led me to the research trip with Dr. Black and eventually to the stinking blocked corridor outside of Prasser Ghat's club on a forgotten space station. In all that time, I'd never cared about anyone, nor had anyone care for me. It had seemed better.

But now, as I gazed at the pile of sleepy kits, I felt as if my heart might explode in my chest. A feeling of fierce protectiveness washed over me, and I knew that for the rest of my life, I would die before letting harm come to these four most precious beings. They'd drowned me in their love, and like the addict that I was, I let it wash over me and hungered for more.

"Yes, dama," I said, using the Depik word for mother and queen. "And I give you my love in return."

# # # # #

Mark's Introduction to:

Legends

by Christopher Woods

Christopher falls into the category, much like myself, of authors who are battling away in the indie/small press publishing world, working hard to make a name for themselves. Although his first book, "Soulguard," was only published in 2014, he's already released seven books. His preferred genre is usually more of a fantasy bend, so his journey into Mil-SF is a bit of a divergence for him, but the story shows it was a really good one.

In "Legends," you're introduced to a merc who didn't set out to be anything special—he didn't even want to be a merc—and turned out to be anything but. His escapades are, well, legendary. Any war story told over beers is automatically going to be a fun tale, and since this is the only one told here that takes place before the current 'present day' of the Four Horsemen universe, we get a glimpse back at how things got to be where we are today. Have a drink and enjoy the story, at a cool 100 credits a can; this one's on me.

Find out more about Christopher at
https://www.amazon.com/Christopher-Woods/e/B00PEAG6WM/.

LEGENDS
by Christopher Woods

Chapter 1

The parade ground looked almost the same as it had looked ten years before. The same, yet it was infinitely different as I strode in with my fellow Legionnaires. This would be my last time walking these grounds. My final day as a resident of the Legion Compound in Wichita, Kansas.

Ten years ago, I entered this very compound a scared kid, barely out of my teens. The same raised platform stood at the north end of the huge square. Today that platform held the Four Generals of the Legion, and the man who changed my life forever, Jerrod Lancer.

Actually, I would have to say he was part of the change. It takes a hammer and an anvil to create a weapon. And it takes a lot of heat. I would say Jerrod Lancer and his Legion were the anvil. The hammer was another man who gave me a choice. And the heat? Every contract I took with the Legion provided that.

It all started in a restaurant, because of a girl.

I sat in a booth, enjoying my dinner. I hardly ever got to buy dinner in a restaurant, much less a restaurant like Puertos. Puertos served cuisine that originated in Mexico and had become prominent in the United States long ago. It was still a favorite of many, including me. I really couldn't afford to eat at *any* restaurant, but I was celebrating my raise at the factory.

At Binning, I had been promoted from probationary to official, and I had received my first paycheck at the new wage. Binnig had

257

plants all over the world and kept a great deal of people employed. We created combat suits for the Mercs; sometimes it was difficult to build them as fast as they destroyed them.

I used the tortilla to sop up the cheese sauce and glanced up to see a girl staring at me. Her whole face seemed to light up as she smiled, briefly.

I smiled back as a form walked by. He was a big guy, at least four inches taller than my modest five feet, eight inches. As he moved by and I could see the girl again, the smile had disappeared.

"What was that?" I heard him snarl at her.

"What?" she asked.

"Saw you looking at that guy," he said. "Is that what you like?"

"What are you talking about, Glenn?"

"How would you like it if I stomped his face in?"

"You're being an asshole," she said. "I want to go home."

They left the restaurant. She never glanced in my direction, but he stared at me as they exited. If looks could kill, I would certainly have been vaporized.

I shook my head after the pair left and gave it no more thought.

As I passed my Yack across the sensor to pay for the meal, the fellow behind the counter motioned toward the door.

"Be careful of that one," he said. "That's Glenn Moverti. His father owns Moverti's Monsters. He's a bastard, but he's a connected bastard."

"Thanks," I said. "There wasn't anything going on. I see no reason for him to be upset."

"Reason is rare when dealing with unreasonable people," he said. "Just watch yourself."

"I will."

I should have paid more attention to the man's advice. Perhaps things would have been different for me. The door to my car unlocked at my approach, and I had reached to pull it open when something slammed into the small of my back. Pain lanced through me, and I tumbled to the ground.

Rolling to my left I saw the Moverti kid closing in with a bat. That must have been what hit me. As my vision blurred from the pain, and the kid approached, I felt fear for the first time. Oh I've been scared before, but this was the kind of fear that grips your mind in a vice. It washed over me and pushed me down into the wailing darkness of my consciousness.

When I crawled out of that darkness, I stood with the bat in my hand and Glenn Moverti at my feet. The windows of my car and the one next to it were smashed in. 20 feet away stood the girl that had smiled at me. The look on her face was pure horror.

"Put down the bat, son," a voice came from behind me.

Turning, I found a small man standing about ten feet away. The weapon in his hand was enough for me to recognize the Wichita Police. It was an Enforcer model used by most law enforcement departments. He didn't have on the uniform but I still wasn't about to do other than what he ordered.

"Y-Yes sir," I stammered as I dropped the bat. Looking down at the bloody form of Glenn Moverti, I gasped. His breath gurgled through his shattered teeth.

"Now place your hands on the rear of the vehicle."

I followed his orders in a daze, and before it began to lift I found myself in the Wichita Detention Unit.

What the hell had happened?

It was less than four hours before I was taken from my cell, and I followed the guards down the hall to an interrogation room. I sat in the room for another hour. The table in front of me was metal and bolted to the floor, and my hands, which were attached to the table, could reach just far enough to allow me to rest my elbows on the edge of it.

The door opened, and a large man strode in. He was bigger than the boy, but I could see the resemblance immediately. This was Moverti, owner of the Monsters. I could feel the hollow pit open in my stomach. This was the father of the one who had attacked me.

"Don't look like much," he said. "I don't know if you had any clue who that boy you put in the hospital was. It wouldn't make much difference. Your life is over, boy. You just destroyed any future you ever dreamed of when you beat my son with that bat."

"He attacked me," I started.

"Doesn't matter," he said. "You hospitalized the son of the leader of one of the premiere mercenary outfits in this town. What did you expect?"

He stood and shook his head, "It's a shame, boy. You'd have made a decent merc with a little training."

Max Moverti walked out of the room leaving me to my own misery.

One of the guards unhooked my chains. "Follow me."

"Where are we going?" I asked.

"Processing and sentencing," he answered. "There's not much that can be done for you, kid. What I can do is put you in front of Judge Heidell, who at least is fair. There are limits as to what can be done in a situation like this."

"How can he do this?" I asked. "I defended myself."

"There are seven witnesses who are willing to testify you instigated the fight."

"They're lying."

"I know, kid," he said. "But the Movertis have a lot of money, and you're a factory worker. Tell the judge the truth. Don't lie to him, and he'll do what he can."

I nodded, and the guard led me down another hall into a chamber with an ornate desk and several chairs. Behind the desk hung the robe anyone would recognize as a judge's. The chair behind the desk held a middle-aged man with black hair, who was going gray at the temples.

"It seems you are in a bit of a predicament Mr. Quincy," he said, motioning toward a chair. "Have a seat, and let's see what we have here."

He looked into a folder on his desk, "With VOWS like these, how come you didn't get picked up by a merc?"

"I have no interest in killing anyone, sir."

"Not according to this file," he said. "You beat Glenn Moverti badly enough for him to need nano treatments."

"He attacked me, sir," I said.

"Not according to the testimony of seven people."

"They lied, sir."

"I know they did," he said. "Their stories matched in every way. Never in my life have I heard seven eye witnesses' testimony match exactly. I've never even seen two that match this completely. At least true testimonies, anyway. They were rehearsed, and they didn't even bother to hide it. Moverti is arrogant, but he's connected. He has left you with, he believes, no choices. I beg to differ, young man. I offer you another choice. The only person in this town that can protect you from Moverti is quite a bit like him. The man is also an arrogant bastard, but he is married to my sister."

"You have two choices in front of you, boy," he continued, placing two forms on the table. "Number one, you will be sentenced to no less than ten years detention."

The pit in my stomach was back.

"Or number two." He pushed a form toward me. "Fill this out and report to the Lancer's Legion compound, immediately. This form is a contract to work for Lancer's Legion for that ten years instead of wasting away in a prison cell. Moverti was right on one account, your life is over. This life you have right now. That's over. Choose the future."

And thus I met the Hammer to the Lancers' anvil.

Chapter 2

Fourteen of us stood in the front row of the formation, our red and silver uniforms immaculate. We were the ones whose contracts were up this year. Most mercs only signed a two- or a four-year contract when joining a merc group; I was the only one who had signed a 10-year. It was part of my sentence, so it had to match the time I would have served. Ten of those who stood with me were two years in and looked like kids. Two had been there four years and looked like bigger kids. Then there was Kal. He was on his fifth two-year contract. He was there the first year I came to the compound. He was there on that first drop.

"Was wonderin' if I'd ever see you at one of these, Marty," he muttered from beside me. "How long was that damn contract?"

"Ten."

"Son of a bitch, Marty," he answered. "Bet he'll have to make a hell of an offer to keep you."

"Not stayin'," I said.

"What are you gonna do? Make shoes?"

"I don't know, Kal," I said. "Maybe I will."

"Like that'll be enough for the Legend."

"Don't you start callin' me that," I muttered. "You were there."

"Yeah," he said. "Yeah, I was."

The first drop was the one we were talking about. Both of us were there, fresh from training.

I lost my breath during emergence. The transition from hyperspace affects people differently. My system shut down for that first second, and I staggered against the safety straps. As this was the first translation for many of us, we were harnessed into our racks on our dropships in case hyper caused any unexpected effects. We were tasked with taking a base. It was a regular land assault, nothing spectacular. The brass thought it would be a good place for the rookies to get some experience.

I checked my gear as the ship closed with the planet, which hadn't even been named in the contract. It was an outpost. We were tasked to take it. They expected minimal resistance so it should have been a cakewalk.

"Alright, men!" Commander Jessop barked. "This is the plan. We land and deploy our force here."

He was pointing at a spot on the Tri-V.

"This we will call the Borana Trench," he continued. "Named thusly because Captain Borana has decided we will approach through the trench to hit the outpost. The trench should keep us hidden long enough to get through any defenses they have."

"Trevos, your squad will be on point."

Lieutenant Trevos, my squad leader nodded, "Yes, sir."

"Everyone will form up on Lieutenant Trevos and his squad."

Our squad numbered 14. Lieutenant Trevos, Sergeant Goros and three fire teams of four. Each fire team was led by a corporal and the three others were privates. There were nods along the lines as my squad mates acknowledged our orders.

"Now we suit up and prepare. Less than two hours until separation. Then we get to go for a hell of a ride. You've never lived until you've ridden a dropship down."

Commander Jessop was grinning widely, "Don't worry boys and girls! The wings hardly ever fall off these birds!"

My stomach felt jittery again.

"That's not true, is it, Corporal?" Bailey asked. "The wings won't fall off the dropship, will they?"

Trevos grinned and cinched the straps across his chest. "Hardly ever, Private."

She gulped and cinched her straps, as well.

The dropship was eerily quiet over those few hours. Except for the snoring of Sergeant Goros.

"How does he sleep like that?" Bailey asked. "I would give half my pay to sleep like that. I didn't get to sleep much at all last night."

"A few drops and you'll sleep like a baby, Private," Trevos answered. "The sergeant's been with the Legion close to ten years, now. This is just another day."

Trevos cocked his head to the side as he heard a message through his comms, "Separation in...Three...Two...Now!"

The hull shuddered as the dropship separated from the cruiser.

"Here we go kiddies!"

Sergeant Goros opened his eyes and looked around the bay to see if everyone was settled. He grinned at me as his eyes crossed mine. Then the dropship hit the atmosphere.

It's hard to describe the ride in a dropship. The whole ship shakes, and you can hear the metal groan. It feels like the whole thing could disintegrate around you.

"We have a winner!" Corporal DeLacroix yelled as Private Hearney threw up. "Hearney buys the drinks at Carvel's!"

We had been warned. You puke in the dropship, you buy a round for the squad. You get puke on a mate, you owe him a bottle. Hearney would be buying bottles for a week.

My hands gripped my weapon with white knuckles, and I swallowed to keep my stomach from the same sort of reaction. I looked at the sergeant again, and he was chewing on a ration bar. How could this become so normal you could have a snack? I was terrified.

Then the drop jets ignited, and it felt like a horse had just settled his hindquarters on my chest. The ship slammed to the ground with a bone-jarring thud.

"Unhook! Out you go!"

My straps fell to my sides, and I lowered the visor on my helmet. Gripping my weapon tightly, I followed Sullivan, my fire team leader, out of the ship, and I stepped onto my first alien planet.

The trench was just ahead, and we moved forward.

"Something's wrong," Goros said.

Then everything went completely off the rails.

Laser fire erupted from ahead of us.

"...under fire!"

The dropship opened up with her guns. Moments later there was a massive explosion behind us, and I glanced back to see the fireball that had been our ship.

A laser ripped across our position and Lieutenant Trevos went down. Some of the enemy used flechette weapons. I tasted copper as the pink mist that had been Private Bailey sprayed across me.

The trench ahead of us erupted with forms. That mind numbing fear settled over me again, but this time I didn't black out. It was like something else was in control, and I was only a passenger. I could see what I was doing, but as if it were someone else. I ran.

I ran straight into the charging enemy, my weapon firing, screaming at the top of my lungs. I ran into that mob of aliens. They had superior weapons, but they couldn't use them because I was in their midst. The laser is a magnificent weapon at a distance, but up close you are just as likely to hit your own.

I didn't even know what race these mercs were. They were about five and a half feet tall with rodent-like features. Bipedal, they held the lasers in hands that appeared to have two large fingers and an opposable digit of the same length. They wore a shiny sort of combat armor that seemed to be designed as a defense from lasers. It wasn't as good at blocking bullets.

My weapon ran out of ammo so it became a very expensive club. It was designed for hitting, with a reinforced butt and a bayonet attachment. Searing pain lanced through my left leg, as one of the Rats shot at me with his laser. It grazed the back of my leg and burned one of his fellow troopers. Then my bayonet slammed into his chest.

Out of that mob strode a figure that was at least seven feet tall and had dog-like features. He snatched the weapon right out of my hands and grabbed my harness. It lifted into the air like a toy; I was pulled from the mob. His fetid breath filled my nostrils as he pulled me close to rip into me with his fangs, but I slammed my combat knife to the hilt in the side of his neck, and thick blood spewed from his throat into my face.

There was a loud shriek from the Rats around me as the giant toppled. They charged in, trying to get me, as I landed on my back with the giant on top of me. The huge form was the only protection I had. I jerked the knife from its neck, and slashed at anything that got near me.

Then everything seemed to go silent. The Rats stopped trying to get to me. My helmet was gone, and I felt blood running down my face, though I wasn't sure if it was mine or the Dog's. I felt a tug at the big form on top of me, and it slowly flipped over sideways. I lashed out with my knife, but my wrist was caught in a solid grip.

"It's over, Private," Sergeant Goros said.

I sat up, my whole body shaking with adrenaline. The trench was littered with the bodies of Rats and Humans. There were a couple of Dogs in there, as well.

"Someone leaked our mission," Goros said into his comms, "but the job is done." Goros dragged me to my feet, "There's a medivac incoming, Private. Be on it."

He turned to the remaining Legionnaires, "Round up the prisoners! We have incoming forces to take care of the cleanup."

I joined the rest of the wounded awaiting the Medivac.

"That was some legendary shit, man."

I turned to find another private behind me.

"Kalvin Turner," he said with an outstretched hand. The other arm was wrapped in a field bandage. "Friends call me Kal."

Chapter 3

"Who does that kid remind you of?" Kal whispered.

I chuckled. "Looks a lot like Jonesy."

"Yep," he returned. "Has that same farm boy look."

"Was a sad day when we lost him."

"Hardly ever had a drop when we didn't lose someone," Kal muttered. "Now we're losing the Legend because his contract is running out."

"Seriously? Quit with that 'Legend' shit."

"I can't," he grinned. "You earned the name, fair and square, with that mad charge into the Peterii Mercs."

The Peterii were the "Rats" on the outpost world where we landed with the 230 men and women in Obsidian Company. They were a race that due to their overpopulation were about as cheap as a merc company could hire. Life is cheap on a world where they used to kill an allotted amount per year to control the population. A lot of rogue mercs hired them as cannon fodder. The commanders had been several Zuul. We landed with 230, we left that world with 80.

"Whatever," I muttered.

"Come on, Marty," he continued. "It wasn't just that one. Who was it that got both action *and* injury bonuses on that training op?"

"I have no idea what you're talking about."

"It was a little place in the Crapti Region. Te'Warri, if I remember correctly. I'm sure you remember it."

He was grinning from ear to ear as I was shaking my head.

Te'Warri was a company-sized mission working with the new police force in the capital city. We were part of a training cadre that would help get the Torvasi Enforcers up to the standards of an official police force. The Torvasi were one of the three major races that inhabited the world. They were humanoids averaging about five and a half feet in height, with a dense bone structure and a wide stance. The average Torvasi was at least four feet wide at the shoulders. They were squat and powerful, but they had little experience with the whole idea of squad movements. They were brawlers who tended to think in singular paths.

The second race was the Sirra'Kan, which looked like six-foot-tall bipedal cats. While they had many cat-like features—soft thin fur covering their bodies, prehensile tails and pointed ears—they were surprisingly similar to Humans. They were the "Royalty" on Te'Warri, which had been established by a Sirra'Kan mining company. They brought in the Torvasi as a police force and the Zeewie, a small race with rodent-like features, as the mining workforce.

The mines produced well and the capital city of Sinn'Ra created wealth for the company. The city also attracted other races who filled the city as entertainers, barkeeps, and any other thing you could think of that would help a thriving workforce part with their credits.

Thus we were hired to train the Enforcers to work more closely as units. These training opportunities usually lasted six months to a year, depending on the contract. Our initial contract was for six months.

The training cadre didn't fill out the company-sized force required by the contract, so quite a few of us were sent along to work directly with the patrols on the streets. My squad drew that straw. Lieutenant Sammon and Sergeant Goros were our squad leaders. I was a Corporal by then and headed Fire Team Delta, Third Squad, Obsidian Company.

"Damn you, Marty," Kal mumbled.

"What was that, Private?" I returned.

"Nothin' Boss."

"I can't help it if you drank too much last night," I said with a chuckle.

"You hoomans can't take the Looda," Orto laughed.

Orto, Solarsi, and Trebo were our Torvasi unit. We were working with them as they patrolled their assigned blocks.

"Hoomans need to leave the heavy drink to us," said Solarsi, joining in the laughter. "Not fault of Martee for the change in schedule."

"I don't care whose fault it is." Kal groaned. "He's the one who woke me up so he's the one gettin' blamed."

"I'll try to live with the guilt." I laughed.

"I still can't figure why we have to carry these things," Rillen said. She held up the stun baton.

"Cause that's what we're allowed to carry," Portes answered. "Didn't you listen to the briefing back when this started? You've been bitchin' about the damn things for a month."

"If they let you carry a real weapon, you'd probably shoot your foot off," Kal added.

"Screw you, Kal," she answered. "It was just once, and I didn't hit anyone, much less my foot."

Kal turned to the Torvasi, "You really don't want to give that one a gun. There's no telling what she'd hit with it."

Zaapppp!

Kal yelled.

"Keep it up, and I'll turn the juice up on this thing!"

Kal limped forward with his hand rubbing his left buttock.

"Damn vicious chicks," he muttered.

"What was that?" the stun baton whined as the charge was turned up.

"Nothin'."

"I thought so."

Glancing back, I saw the three Torvasi grinning.

Smiling, I turned back to look ahead of us, down the street where three black Sirra'Kan transports wheeled toward us. My peripheral vision caught movement on a fourth level balcony as someone leaned against the railing.

"Incoming!" I screamed and dove for the cover of a parked transport. My team was quick to find cover, but the Torvasi reacted more slowly.

Solarsi was still in the open when the hand-held rocket slammed into the side of the lead Sirra'Kan transport. The explosion shook the street and a piece of the transport ripped her nearly in two.

"Frak me," Kal muttered, eyeing the stun baton in his hand.

I stared at the mess that had been our friend and felt the fear clawing its way out again. This time there was another emotion accompanying it. The rage was as potent as the fear, and I slipped into that state where I was watching my body do its thing.

"Orto, Trebo," I barked. "Call in backup. Delta, break in four directions and get across the street. We need to get inside that building."

"Sir!"

"On my mark! I'll lead to draw fire. Three…Two…Mark!"

I launched myself from the cover of the transport just as the third Sirra'Kan transport went up in a fireball. I heard the bullets whine as they passed through the space I had just been occupying. It took seconds to get across the street.

"Tell me again why we're carrying these things," Rillen said as she joined me under the cover of the door stoop.

"Character building," Kal answered as he slipped into the stoop.

"Well, my character is just fine," she said. "Give me a rifle!"

"You'd just shoot yourself," Portes said as he entered the stoop.

"Why, you…"

"He's got a point," I said. I grinned and pushed the door open.

Kal dove through the door and rolled left coming up with his baton.

"Clear!"

We charged into the foyer of the apartments. The stairs were directly in front of us so I sprinted up the first flight. We didn't have guns so we had to get close to them as quickly as possible. There was no resistance until the platform leading to the fourth floor. I threw the baton at a startled Blevin, who ducked to the side. He straightened back up to bring his gun to bear, only to be slammed to the ground as I hit him at full speed.

My foot crunched down on his throat with finality, then I retrieved my baton and charged through the door. I would love to have grabbed the Blevin's gun but, after seeing men lose hands to booby-trapped weapons, I chose not to risk it. The hallway was clear. My team joined me.

"This one?" I asked, indicating a door.

"Hell if I know," Kal answered.

"Shit," I muttered trying to remember what the building looked like from the outside.

"Hell with it," I grumbled and kicked in the door. There were two Zeewie huddled in the corner so I charged across the floor to the balcony, only to find it empty.

"Damnit, man!" Kal yelled. The balcony to our left held a tripod-mounted machine gun and another Blevin.

The gun began to swing toward us. I charged the edge of the balcony and hit the rail with my right foot, then I was sailing across the ten-foot gap between the balconies. Landing just as the first burst ripped past me, I rolled forward to slam into the Blevin and the gun.

He blocked my first punch, but the baton slammed into his chin with a loud zap. As he tumbled backwards, I grabbed his shirt front and threw him off the balcony. Bullets whizzed past my head as I charged forward to launch myself across the gap to the next balcony.

"Son of a bitch!" I heard from behind me as Kal reached the balcony I had just vacated.

As I slammed into the Blevin on the next balcony, he dropped his weapon. Tumbling back, he drew an ugly dagger that looked a lot like a Kukri knife used by the old Gurkhas. I hoped he wasn't as deadly with the damn thing as the Gurkhas had been.

He wasn't. The knife fell to the floor as I slammed him against the masonry then spun and threw him over the edge. The scream was short-lived and ended with a crash as the Blevin slammed into a parked transport.

There was one more manned balcony, so I hit the rail and jumped again.

"Shit," I said in mid-air as I saw what waited on the other balcony.

A frakkin' Oogar. What the hell was an Oogar doing here?

I was already regretting my actions, before the eight-foot-tall purple behemoth rose up on its hind feet, its clawed arms outstretched. Still, I was 200 pounds of muscle and bone with another

50 pounds of combat armor. I hit his chest, barely missing the clawed hands as they struck at me.

His immense roar was cut short with a thud and a gasp as my weight slammed into his chest, and my baton impacted his throat with a strong zap. He jerked a little as he staggered from the impact, but his hand slammed into my back. I felt his grip on my armor and lost my baton as he jerked me backwards.

His breath was horrible as he roared in my face. Then three batons hit him at the base of the skull. He staggered, and I dropped to the floor. I pushed myself up, hit him in the chest with my shoulder, and the Oogar toppled over the rail and plummeted to the ground. Glancing over the edge, I winced. One of the pickets from the iron fence below protruded from the top of his skull.

"What took you so long?" I asked.

"What?" Kal answered.

"You're supposed to follow my lead."

"Only safe way to follow your lead is from a distance, Boss."

"Hmph."

I staggered a little as I stepped into the apartment. "Clear it."

We spread out and entered different rooms. The bedroom I entered had an occupant. A female Sirra'Kan lay bound to the bed. The ropes were tight, and the girl couldn't move anything but her tail which was twitching rapidly. There was fear in her gaze.

"You're okay now," I said.

"There…is…Oogar," she said in halting English.

"Not anymore," I said with a grin.

I worked loose the knots. As soon as her arms were free, she grabbed me and pulled me to her chest in a crushing hug.

"Tank you so much, Hooman." She felt a great deal like a Human woman as her body was against mine. Her tongue, raspy like a cat's, trailed from my neck to my cheek.

I was almost disappointed when she let go of me. "My father?" she asked.

"I have no idea," I answered as I continued removing knotted rope. "Who's your father?"

"I am," a deep voice said from the door in much more practiced English.

Turning, I found myself staring at, perhaps, the only Sirra'Kan I would recognize on sight.

"Prime," I said and eased into the common bow we were taught to give the royals of Te'Warri.

"It seems I am further in your unit's debt than our contract could have foreseen, Human."

"Just doing our job, sir."

"You have done much more than your job today, Human," he said. "This was an assassination attempt. If you had not intervened, my transport would have been next. Then my daughter would have been killed, as well. There will be a sizeable bonus for your company."

I grinned as the memory of that drop was relived.

"That was an interesting drop," I said.

"No shit," Kal answered. "I remember a certain corporal disappeared for two days of downtime, only to come back with gashes on his back. No one asked how he got injured. They just patched him up and entered the injuries in the log."

"Those ceremonial claws aren't ceremonial," I answered.

"I think it's safe to say you're the only man in this outfit to sleep with a Sirra'Kan," he said. "A princess, at that."

"She just wanted to show her gratitude."

"To top it off," he said, "the injury bonus meant you got paid to do it."

His hand slapped my back. "And that, my friend, is frakkin' legendary."

Chapter 4

"This is the final payout for your contract, Sergeant," General Tarpin said as he placed the envelope in my hand. "But I would like you to wait a moment."

I nodded.

He turned to the men lining the square, "We came here today to honor those that have completed their contracts in an honorable fashion. Sometimes these men and women complete their contracts in a fashion that goes above and beyond honorable."

"In front of you stands a man who came to us ten years ago through the court system. I know the courts tend to send us 'less than desirable' members, but sometimes, there is a diamond in the rough. Sergeant Martin Quincy is just such a man. I could speak of his first deployment, or his third, or any one of many. He has served honorably in all of them, but he is now being recognized for a deployment where he and his squad truly did go above and beyond...."

We all knew what deployment he was speaking of.

Emergence didn't even draw a reaction from me anymore; I was strapped into the rack on the dropship, half asleep. One thing Sergeant Goros had instilled in me was a readiness to sleep or eat at every opportunity. There may come a time when you just couldn't do either.

The half-sleep was a great tool to allow rest yet still be semi-aware.

"Look at the sarge," DeLamont said. "How does he do that?"

Corporal Kal Turner laughed aloud, "Practice, Private."

"Detach in Three…two…Now!" Lieutenant Pim announced.

There was a familiar thud as the docking clamps released. We'd all had the mission brief and knew our job. Pekoni was a mining colony under the control of the corporation listed as the Pekoni Initiative. There were three races combined in the Initiative, the Metial, Rantofa, and Meedin'Tal. Many of the Metial were planet-side, as they were the workforce.

There had been threats from a rival group, and we were tasked with delivering a sizeable shipment of weapons and ammo. Our company would train the Metial in the use of the weapons so they could protect themselves. Our dropship held a single squad of Legionnaires and ten thousand semi-modern ballistic weapons.

They weren't quite as good as the weapons we were equipped with, since they were older stock that was being replaced with newer models, but we had spent the last ten years using said weapons in a multitude of contracts.

The rest of the company was in the other dropship.

Just as we hit the atmosphere, and the dropship began to shake like a toy in a dog's mouth, the comms went crazy.

"Under fire! We are under fire!"

The ship jerked around much harder than the typical drop.

"Oh Frak! We lost the frakkin' *Zephyr!*"

The lieutenant gasped, "That's the whole company…"

"Hold on tight, kids," I said.

The dropship wasn't made to dodge and weave but I had to give it to the guys in the cockpit. Whoever was flying this brick was a genius. He wasn't doing my intestines any favors, but we were still flying.

I was beginning to think we had made it when the ship slammed to the side, and a huge hole ripped in the ceiling above us.

"Frak me," Kal said as one of the crates of guns broke free and exploded out of the hole.

"Masks on!" I yelled and closed the faceplate on my helmet.

The ship spun around, putting us under the strain of some serious G's. The hole that had been bright darkened as we hit clouds. Dark clouds.

"Really!?" Kal asked. "Crashing isn't enough?"

Flashes of lightning illuminated the interior.

"Might just save our asses," I grunted into the comms. "Depends on the weapons they're using."

"Can't do anything about the spin," a woman's voice came from the comms. "If I stop the spin I can't stop the drop, too."

Pim was slumped in his rack, and his mask was open.

"Damnit, Boss!"

There wasn't anything I could do for him without unstrapping. The spin would toss me around like a rag doll if I did, and I still wouldn't be able to help him. The way his head lolled, I was pretty sure he was gone.

"Do what you have to, pilot!"

"I'll do my best," she answered.

Watching my troops, I could see Tarkle, Simms, and Dorn were unconscious. My own vision blurred and I could feel unconsciousness coming for me.

Then I was kicked in the gut as the drop jets fired. The spin eased but the G's were from straight below this time. We slammed to the ground with a large crunch.

The ship was still spinning as it slid along the ground. I could see limbs and tree tops exploding upward as we skidded through the stormy forest. My vision dimmed for a moment.

"Sarge!" my eyes popped open.

"I know you can sleep through almost anything but this is ridiculous," Kal said.

"Just takin' a break." I groaned as my muscles screamed at me from the tension they had just endured.

"SitRep?"

"About to take stock, Boss."

I slapped the release on my straps and staggered forward.

"Check the kids," I said and looked into the helmet at Lieutenant Pim. His face was an unhealthy shade of blue.

Shaking my head, I climbed toward the cockpit. There were three pilots, and I dearly wanted to find those flying geniuses alive.

I was lucky enough to find the single female pilot still breathing. Unfortunately the other two pilots were gone. One was a grisly mess with a tree limb impaling him to the seat. The other was just gone. There was blood where he had impacted the viewport and shattered a hole in it big enough to get sucked out. The living pilot's leg was obviously broken; it was probably a good thing she was unconscious, as she would have to be removed from the ship.

"Kal!" I yelled back into the bay. "How is it?"

"Surprisingly good, Boss!" he returned. The lieutenant is the only fatality."

"Get everyone off the ship, and send two to get the pilot," I said. "She just saved all our asses. It would be rude of us to leave her behind, even if she is a navy puke."

I could hear Kal chuckle as he entered the cockpit behind me.

"That'll leave a mark," he muttered as he passed the other pilot. "Aren't there supposed to be three?"

I pointed to the bloody viewport.

"Shit."

I popped the straps and pulled the woman from her seat. She was lighter than I expected. Dead weight was always heavier, but this girl was tiny. She was no more than five feet tall and probably weighed 95 pounds.

"Careful," I warned as I passed her down to Kal. "Leg's broke. I'll bring the kit out with me."

"Got it, Boss."

Private Tripper was right outside the cockpit.

"Trip," I said. "Dig out the medkits from the back. I'll get the two from the cockpit. She's light, Kal can handle her."

"Yes, sir."

I scavenged both kits, and headed toward the back. The others were off the ship, and Trip was at the door with three kits. I nodded to him, and followed the private out of the ship.

We moved a short distance from the ship.

"What now, Boss?"

I was quiet for a moment, looking back toward the dropship through the dark rain.

"That was a straight-up ambush. I'm assuming our clients were hit and lost the base."

"I would say that's a safe bet," Kal said.

"We need to remove any trace of our survival to get some breathing room," I said. "But first I want the cargo off that ship."

"Yes, sir."

Kal turned to his fire team, "You heard the man, let's get that cargo."

I placed a poncho over the unconscious pilot and felt along her leg. It seemed like a clean break.

"Glad you aren't awake for this," I muttered and gripped the leg.

There was a crunch as the bone slid back into place and her body twitched. Reaching into the kit, I pulled out the painkiller and the hardset. I shot the painkillers directly into the affected area and pulled a clear plastic boot from the kit. I held the tube of hardset to the thin plastic as I slid it up and over her leg. When I pulled the trigger, the hardset filled the boot in seconds. Less than thirty seconds later, I peeled the boot off and her leg was encased.

Pulling the poncho down to cover her leg as well, I joined my squad. It took three hours to unload the dropship and get the weapons far enough away from the ship for the next part of the plan.

The explosion rocked the whole valley when the dropship self-destructed.

Kal and I stood, staring down into the valley at the ruined ship.

"They'll not be searching for survivors after that," I said. "Which is a two-edged sword. Our folks won't know we are alive either."

"So what's the plan?"

"If I remember the brief correctly, there are two major mining operations."

"Yeah."

"There were four minor operations, as well, and several closed mines."

"We get to one of the closed mines and see if we can't get a signal out," he said with a nod. "Sounds like an excellent plan."

"There are problems," I said.

"Of course there are," he replied.

"If it was easy, we'd let children do it."

"True enough." He grinned.

"It's close to a hundred miles, filled with the hostile indigenous life forms."

"Is that all?"

"That's not enough?"

"Not for a Legend…"

"Bite me."

He laughed. "I'll get the kids ready to move out."

"Has the pilot come to?"

"She's still out," he said. "She took a knock to the head in addition to breaking that leg, and somebody put enough painkillers in her to put Horton to sleep."

Horton, part of Kal's Fire Team Delta, was the size of a horse. Close to seven feet tall and as wide as a damn Torvasi.

"Had to guess." I shrugged.

"That's not a good thing, Boss," he said as he turned to get the others ready. "Last time you guessed you had to fight an Oogar."

"Fun times," I answered. "I hope we don't run into any of those bastards again."

The plan was risky, but I could see no other way out. Our starship was still in the sky, at least I hoped it was. We would need to cover some ground to reach the closest mine. I pulled my slate from my pack and checked the maps I had downloaded. If we could just find a powerful enough transmitter, the slate would do for communication. The comm system on the ship was toast.

Placing the camo nets and plenty of living camouflage over the weapons, we moved out to the west. Even with the unconscious pilot, we covered close to twelve miles through the dense forest before nightfall.

Two guards were placed when we bedded down, and I thoroughly enjoyed the fact that I could sleep anywhere.

"Boss!" Corporal Rillen shook me. "We got trouble."

My eyes shot open, and my mind came instantly awake. I rose to my feet to find the camp completely surrounded by indigs.

"Shit," I muttered.

The indigs of Pekoni were a centaur-type race. They had long bodies with six legs. At the front of those legs the torso turned upwards, and two arms with usable hands met shoulders much like ours. The heads were elongated with wide mouths, but I could see intelligence in the eyes of the one I stared at.

The indig spoke into a translator, "You our prisoners."

I was surprised he would even have one of them.

"I don't think I'm going to be a prisoner today," I answered. "I suggest you leave while you can."

"Challenge?" he asked, incredulously looking at my tiny form. He was literally a thousand pounds heavier than me.

"Challenge," I returned.

"Accept," he rumbled, and he pulled out the spear he had carried in the harness across his back.

He smiled—well I think it was a smile—and stepped toward me.

I drew the fifty caliber handgun holstered on my chest and shot him in the head.

There was silence for nearly a full minute as the indig toppled to the ground. Then the whole horde let out all sorts of yells and such. I glanced back at my squad and shook my head as weapons were raised.

The pilot groaned and woke up. She sat up on the stretcher she was carried on, looking at the centaurs running in circles around us, yelling madly.

"Frak me," she said.

Another of the indigs approached with a huge grin and retrieved the other's translator.

"Challenge victory," I stated.

He nodded, "Come. Join."

"What now, Boss?" Corporal Portes asked.

I looked at the howling indigs and back the way we came, and a slow smile crossed my face. "I have an idea."

My mind snapped back to the present.

"The initiative Sergeant Quincy showed in recruiting the Andori of Pekoni to join them in the assault on the mining hubs was far beyond our contract, but we were contracted to provide weapons to them so that they could defend themselves.

"When the Pekoni Initiative members asked what they were to do about the Andori, Sergeant Quincy gave them a simple solution that more than fulfilled our contract. It garnered us another contract with the same group.

"He suggested that they bring the Andori into their Initiative as a partner. They held ten thousand weapons and a force that was more than willing to use those weapons for their defense.

"Our new contract starts tomorrow as we launch Phoenix Company for a training mission of six months to help the Andori become a modern force, along with a shipment of fifty thousand guns to arm them.

"For this effort by a lowly squad sergeant, we award the highest-level bonus to his final disbursement."

There was applause, and the general placed a second envelope in my hand.

Chapter 5

Raising the beer to my lips, I smiled at the Legionnaires as they celebrated after the latest contract. I sat in the back, watching from the shadows. The lights were dim back in the corner, and it was good for a private vantage.

Six months had passed since my retirement. I'd traveled to various places I thought I wanted to see only to find them drab and unappealing. I had tried to lose myself in women and wine when the boredom had set in, to no avail. Two days with a Sirra'Kar princess was damn hard to match.

Watching the Legionnaires brought it all back to the forefront of my mind. There was only one thing I was great at. I hated them for that. I had avoided the mercs because I didn't feel the need to kill anyone. They showed me it was the only thing I was truly good at.

It hurt to think that my greatest skill was destruction.

I watched the Legionnaires and loved them as much as I hated them. The brotherhood in arms was something I missed greatly.

I almost stood up and joined them.

The door opened, and a stranger to the bar walked in. He cast his gaze around the room, and Tommy, the barkeep, nodded and twitched his head in my direction.

My hand fell below the table to grasp the hilt of the pistol I still carried. Then my mouth dropped as the man turned completely, and I could see his features.

Jim frakkin' Cartwright of the Four Horsemen made his way across the bar to sit right in front of me.

Tommy placed a cold bottle of Coke in front of him as Mr. Cartwright stared at me for a moment, then asked, "You ready to play in the big league, Quincy?"

As I walked from the bar with Jim Cartwright, still somewhat dazed, Kal Turner walked from the shadows to smile at Tommy.

"That, my friend, was frakkin' legendary."

# # # # #

Chris' Introduction to:

With the Eagles

by Doug Dandridge

Doug likes to say that no area of the fantastic is outside his scope, as he has completed works in both near and far future Science Fiction, Urban and High Fantasy, Horror, and Alternate History. That isn't surprising to me, as he has led a very diverse life. For example, he studied biology, geology, physics, and chemistry as an undergrad, but then ended up with an advanced degree in Clinical Psychology. He was also an infantryman and squad leader in the Army, and was the trooper chosen to hump the M60 as the leader of the machine gun squad, which is about as far as you can get from clinical psychology. Or maybe it's not, as having someone fire an M60 at you will do wonders for getting you to change your mind about what you were just about to do.

One of the first commercially successful indie writers I met when I was just starting out, I've known Doug for almost as long as I've been writing. We've met a number of times, but it's always been in passing—we've never really had time to sit down and talk. I hear he's a great guy, and I'm looking forward to rectifying that issue soon.

One thing's for certain, though; his readers love him, and I think you're going to like "With the Eagles." If you'd like to know more about Doug and the books he's published, take a look here: https://www.amazon.com/Doug-Dandridge/e/B006S69CTU/.

WITH THE EAGLES
by Doug Dandridge

Crap, thought Jonah White Eagle as he looked at the climb ahead. Another 500 meters. He refused to look back at the 2,000 meters below. *Why the hell did I let Charley talk me into this contract?* He wasn't afraid of heights, normally. He had always loved climbing, when the cliffs were 200 meters or less. And when the multi-thousand meter cliff was not on a super-Earth with more than one and a half times Earth's gravity. The extra weight tired him out faster, and the thought of the gravity-assisted acceleration on the way down was enough to make his hands shake.

Charley didn't seem to have a problem with the cliff. Jonah had always thought the Gurkha, his partner from the first day they started the Fierce Eagle Company, was just a bit crazy. But he seemed to know how to pick the best contracts for the company, at least until this one.

Jonah was of Apache ancestry and had grown up around some tall mountains, but not like these. And he had been a jungle warfare junkie since reaching the age of majority. Jungles had mountains, but they also had lots of trees and bushes to grab onto.

His partner placed another of the special pitons they had obtained. The flat surface of each hook eye was coated with nanites that bonded to the rock face, alleviating the need to hammer them in or use explosive anchoring that could give them away.

Jonah pulled himself up the thin cable a couple of meters then looked back, against his better judgment, to see how the rest of the team was doing. Four other operatives followed him up the cord, and none seemed to be having problems. There was no risk in this climb if Jonah stopped to think about it. Each team member had a parachute that would lower them gently to the ground if needed. But then they wouldn't be available at the top.

Sandra had suggested they come in by ducted-fan vehicle, using firepower to overwhelm their opponents, but Jonah had nixed that idea. They might have been able to overwhelm the opposition, but not before the enemy killed the hostage, and that would reduce the payoff.

Charley gave a hand signal, indicating he had seen something. Jonah pulled in a quick breath and went still, depending on the diamonoid nanobubbles to keep his blood oxygenated. They couldn't be seen ascending the cliff; if they were, one enemy with a laser could wipe them off the cliff like a maintenance worker sweeping ants out of the kitchen.

Charley gave another hand signal, then started back up. Jonah followed suit, pulling himself up another couple of meters and setting a foot on a piton. With the sound of crumbling stone the shale facing broke off, tumbling down as the piton fell before coming to a stop on the cord.

I'm going to have a word with that little SOB, he thought, glaring up at his partner. Charley was in charge of the company for this mission, since mountaineering was his specialty. He thought the mountaineer would know more about geology than to use surface contact climbing gear on a metamorphic rock face.

The climb went on for another hour, with Charley finally disappearing as he went over the lip and into the small sheltered gorge they had located on the satellite view. The Gurkha's hand came back into sight and waved. The way was clear. It took five minutes for

Jonah to make it up to the spot where they would rest and prepare. He lay on the rock panting after Charley helped him up, getting his breath back. Charley helped Sandra up next, then Zack and his brother Ezekiel. Motambe, another mountaineer who was responsible for making sure everyone ahead of him made it, was the last up.

"How's it look?" he asked Sandra, who was scouting the plateau with a fiber optic camera.

"All clear so far, boss. No movement. And I see the cavern entrance."

"How do you know it's the right cavern?" asked Zack, wiping sweat off his face with the back of his hand.

"Because there's a Besquith with a large rifle standing by the entrance, you idiot," she said, handing the viewer to Zack.

There was some under-breath cussing. Jonah held up a hand, silencing everyone.

"We knew there might be some of them up here," he said.

"So what do we do?" asked Ezekiel, fingering the small medallion hanging under his shirt.

"We do our job," said Charley, glaring at the merc. "We take out any of those sons-of-bitches we run into, kill everything else with them, and rescue our target." He looked at Sandra. "It's up to you to keep them off us."

"Right," she acknowledged, snapping the scope onto her magnetic accelerator rifle, a magrail like they all carried. "Anything that shows its ugly head will be sporting a new cranial orifice."

"We go this way," said Charley after nodding to their sniper. "Everyone stay low and quiet."

Jonah smiled at the worried tone of his partner. Everyone in their company was stealthy; that's why he'd hired them. If they were the kind of troop that stumbled around and made noise, they would be working in CASPers. Charley started off, crouching, his rifle at the ready, with Zack following right behind. Jonah was last this time, watching the others and making sure they didn't show above the lip of rock they were hiding under.

They never did find out what gave them away. Besquith had better hearing than Humans and a much better sense of smell. The team had done everything they could do to mask their scents, but sweating Humans still gave off a distinctive odor. And as quietly as they could move, it might not have been enough. The first they knew they had been spotted was when a magrail round cracked overhead. The rifle made no sound when it fired, but rounds traveling over the speed of sound still carried a tiny sonic boom.

"Zack, Ezekiel," called out Charley. "Stay here. Lay down a base of fire."

Zack nodded for the both. They held their weapons up over the rock wall, the image of what they were aiming at on their HUDs, and started firing. The three remaining soldiers hurried on in their crouches, heading for the high ground. The rock path sloped upward, while the protective wall decreased in height. Jonah expected them to come under fire at any moment. Instead the incoming fire stopped.

"Sandra got the bastard," said Zack over their now-activated comm.

"It took long enough," said the woman. "He stayed concealed, but then he got greedy and came out to take a clear shot at our boys."

Jonah acknowledged, then followed Charley and Motambe up and over the steep lip, rifle at the ready. They had to hurry, no matter the risk to themselves. The kidnappers knew they were here, and it was only a matter of time before they killed the hostage. They would still get partial fulfillment of the contract if they killed the kidnappers. But Jonah didn't want a partial payment; that wouldn't pay the outstanding bills.

They reached the overlook just as a trio of small, furry aliens, almost like large Flatar, came out of the cave, lasers at the ready. *Shit*, thought Jonah as he saw the weapons. He hated light amp weapons. The beam was invisible in most cases, only noticeable when there was enough particulate matter in the air to reflect the light. The first one knew they were being fired at was when the beam struck. Jonah knelt and aimed in one motion, putting a burst of rounds through the body of the alien who was turning toward them the fastest. Charley put a burst of rounds into another. The third didn't aim so much as sweep his beam toward them; it hit rock on the way and revealed the path of its beam with the glow of heated stone.

"Down," yelled Jonah, trying to reach out and push Motambe down before the beam swept through him. He was able to reach the man and started to shove him out of the way when the beam struck. A sleeve on Motambe's jacket burst into flame, and the merc yelled out in pain as it sliced into his arm. Jonah threw himself back and out of the way as the fabric of his jacket scorched at the shoulder, thanking the gods above that he had opted for the heavier material that could resist the heat for a second.

Charley sighted in and fired another burst, and the laser wielder went down with pinkish blood splashed over his chest fur. Five more erupted from the cave and immediately sought cover, bringing their strange-looking rifles to their shoulders.

"How bad is it?" asked Motambe as Jonah landed beside him and gave the burn a look.

"You'll live," said Jonah, showing a quick smile. "At least that burn won't kill you, anyway," he continued as a beam shone through the dust and smoke that was now in the air.

"Bring them in," shouted Charley over the comm, radio silence no longer needed.

"Roger," said a familiar voice in Jonah's ear bud. The sound of ducted fans filled the air, and the noses of two gunships poked over the edge of the escarpment. The air was filled with the crack of hypervelocity rounds spurting from the cannon on the gunships' noses as mercenaries in heavy CASPer combat suits leapt out of the large cargo compartments.

"Shit," cursed Jonah under his breath. The gunships and the heavily-armored mercs were only supposed to be used if things went in the crapper. The plan had called for them to come in quietly, take out the kidnappers, and free the hostage. He doubted they would get him out alive after all of this noise. *Couldn't be helped,* he thought. They would still get half the contract money for taking out the assholes who had kidnapped the local factor of the Caroon-run company. But he didn't want half the money.

"Clear," yelled the chief pilot. Jonah jumped up and ran for the cave entrance, a pair of armored mercs on either side. Charley waved their medic over to look at Motambe, then followed him. Zack and Ezekiel were immediately over the lip of their cover and running the short distance. The entrance was too narrow for the suited mercs, leaving his original team with the task of clearing the cave.

It wasn't much of a fight. There was only one alien remaining in the large cavern inside the small entrance...and the being they had come to rescue, lying on the floor with a large burn hole in his head.

"I surrender," said the small furry creature. Jonah had never seen his species before, but there were so damned many in just this arm of the Galaxy. Not knowing their capabilities could be trouble.

"Secure him," said Jonah, looking at Zack. He looked back at the alien, who had a translator box hanging around his neck. "My employers will be interested in talking to you."

"I'm asking for asylum," said the alien. "This is a political fight between my people and those who paid you to take this pig back."

"And where did the Besquith come in?"

"He was a merc we hired," said the being after a moment's hesitation.

"And I don't believe you," replied Charley as Zack pulled the small being's hands behind his back and secured them with plastic cuffs. "The people who hired us will get the truth out of you."

The alien started to protest, but Jonah pulled the translator off his neck. As far as he was concerned, the creature had cost him a lot of money, and that was all that mattered.

The flight back to the spaceport was a combination of celebration and depression. The employees had made their money. They had fulfilled their contracts to the company and would get paid the full amount, though without bonuses. He and Charley would go without, anything they made going back into the company. Some bills would be paid, but not all, and Jonah could already hear the complaints of their creditors. They needed a successful contract, and they needed it now. But from where?

"We have a comm from the company," called the copilot. "Looks like they have another contract for us."

* * *

"Well, this is different," complained Charley in a soft voice, wiping the sweat from his face with a hand cloth.

Jonah nodded, feeling the sweat drip down his face. While the last job was on a heavy gravity planet, this one only had point seven that of Earth, so the loads they carried would have been lighter—if it hadn't been for the fact that they had added more on. Where the last had been cold, this planet was very hot, over forty degrees Celsius, or one hundred and six Fahrenheit. And the humidity was so high Jonah was surprised they didn't have to swim. All things considered, though, he preferred the jungle to the mountains. This was his specialty. He could move through this kind of foliage with a full load on his back and make less noise than the wind. Their active camouflage would blend them in with the weird red and orange vegetation like they were invisible. The only thing that worried him, besides those they would be fighting when they got to the target, was his unfamiliarity with the local flora and fauna.

He didn't know the signals here. What was harmless, and what was deadly? What displays did the deadly ones have to warn him away? At least his inner clothing was proof against most punctures, unless the creature happened to have some sort of super-hardened fangs and claws. Not likely, but not unheard of.

He did know there was nothing edible in this jungle, at least not by his species. It went both ways. He wasn't edible by the local carnivores. That didn't mean they wouldn't try to take a bite out of him if they could—they would only learn their lesson after they had done the damage.

The alien who was their guide, a local native wearing only a necklace of animal teeth, fur sandals, and a loin cloth of some reptilian hide, turned and pointed something out, his translator box squeaking out hushed English.

"Our guide says to avoid those flowers over there," said Charley, standing closer to the alien than Jonah. "He says they're dangerous."

That was enough for Jonah. He didn't need to know if they would eject poisonous pollen if he trod on their roots, or if the actual flowers were carnivorous, or even if he needed to eat one to experience the threat. He knew they were dangerous, which meant they needed to be avoided.

The acting colonel cursed and swatted at something that bit his cheek. He missed, and the creature, this world's analogue of the mosquito, flew off, six wings buzzing while it brought its eight legs up to tuck under its body. It wobbled in flight, then fell limply out of the air. *Eaten something you didn't like?* Jonah thought as he scratched the small wound which itched fiercely. If not for the nanites in his system, he too might be wobbling prior to falling down, thanks to the incompatible proteins the bite had injected. It was a bad match, blood-sucking insect and blood from another world, but the bug didn't know that. It was genetically programed to attack animals, without a thought that they might not be to its digestive system's liking.

There was a cloying odor to the place, a mixture of old rot and the scents given off by plants that had organs resembling flowers. It was sort of familiar, but nothing like the rainforest he had worked in on the Amazon River. His olfactory glands didn't know how to react to it, and he wondered how many odors there were he couldn't detect.

"This place sucks," complained one of the mercs, pushing up the multi-spectrum visor on his helmet. "I can't make out shit in this damned shithole."

Jonah grinned. They had been warned about this jungle, but many of the people had ignored the briefing. Mostly the newer people. The old hands had learned enough by surviving to realize that any information presented might be used to survive in the future.

The trees of this jungle were exogenous, producing heat with their metabolism, much like animals. Many of the plants had muscle-like fibers that allowed limited movement. Leaves could turn on branches to seek the best angle to catch the rays of the sun. Or take other, less savory actions. The important fact was they gave off heat, which made infrared sensors almost useless. The larger specimens also had working circulatory systems, the muscle-like fibers forming pumping chambers to move nutrients and wastes through them. That caused the incessant murmuring sound of liquids being pumped, which made it difficult to pick out other sounds. Jonah had hoped all of this would be to their advantage, since they would be harder to see in infrared, and they would have to make a lot of noise to be heard, but it was turning out to be as much of a detriment as an asset.

There were bird analogues in the jungle, their cries audible though muted by the background murmur and the rustling of large animals. One especially loud noise caught his attention, and he looked on in fascination as a large creature that reminded him of an armored, trunkless elephant chomped down on a branch while the tree tried to pull away. Jonah wondered what kind of animal preyed on that beast, if any. He had seen videos about the local predators and didn't want to run into any on this mission.

"Our guide just informed me it will be night soon," said Charley, moving to Jonah's side and taking a look at the battle between herb and herbivore going on, something they were unlikely to see on any other world.

"He knows we're going on through the night, doesn't he?"

"He knows. He doesn't like it, but he knows. And he thinks we're damned fools for trying."

Jonah nodded. Of course the jungle would be more alive at night—most were—but they planned to strike the enemy compound in the late hours of the night, just a couple of time units before dawn, when their foes weren't at their most alert.

Really being here, in the nightmare of a landscape, he was re-thinking his plan. Unfortunately, they had as far to walk to get out as they had to move forward, and calling in an airlift was a non-starter. Anything coming in over the canopy would be seen, especially when they were hovering while pulling the mercs out of the jungle. They were committed. Still, he could understand why some of his people had spoken of preferring garrison duty, where they would be warm, safe, and dry for the most part. And some would rather be in CAS-Pers. Seeing the herbivorous beast, he wouldn't mind being in the armor as well, though he wasn't sure even it was a match for a creature like that—at least not without weaponry.

The two score and three mercenaries continued on through the heat and buzzing insectoids. There was low cursing as people stumbled over branches or vines lying along the ground. One woman yelled out as her hand went through a rotting trunk she had attempted to push herself over, and numerous worm-like creatures swarmed over her hand. She jumped back and batted the creatures away, not one of which tried to bite through her gloves. It wouldn't have done them any good, but it showed they weren't carnivores and had probably been feasting on the rotting wood of the log.

"Quiet down," hissed Jonah. "There's no telling what's listening to us." He didn't think there were surveillance devices this far out, and their passive electronic sensors had shown nothing, but Jonah wanted to live to a ripe old age and ignoring possible threats just because they were unlikely was not the way to do that.

Their guide led, pointing out hazards along the way. One looked like some kind of bog, except for the skeletal remains of animals that looked like they had been trying to get out and couldn't. Another was a bunch of flowering vines descending from branches above; several bodies of small furry flying creatures stuck to them, a viscous purplish substance flowing over their forms.

Jonah knew that this would be a complete nightmare without the guide. He was considering the extra bonus he would give the native, something that would help his people considerably, when a scream from behind drove all thought from his head.

Like most of his people, Jonah was on the ground in a heartbeat, rifle coming up to his shoulder as a head motion flipped his visor down. Most had dropped to face the direction of the scream, but he was satisfied to note that enough were looking in other directions to give complete coverage. His people were thinking and not just reacting.

The guide ran toward the sound, stopping a meter way from the thing that had grabbed one of the mercs, and jabbed his spear into its flesh. The thing jerked immediately, then stopped moving. *So that's how they survive in this hellhole,* thought Jonah. Some kind of poison, probably lethal to anything in the jungle.

"Doc," he called out in a low voice.

Doc Salsbury came running up, medical bag over his shoulder to look at Cameron. He hadn't paid attention to the guide, or maybe the signal hadn't been relayed back, but Cameron was half into the maw of some horrible-looking thing, something that looked like a plant, but had multiple rows of teeth like an animal. Cameron was still alive, his mouth working in a soundless scream of pain.

Doc pushed an airgun into the neck of the man after pulling aside his protective scarf. The drug went to work, and Cameron calmed as the pain signals were damped. Next came a shot of nanites, while a pair of mercs cut into the creature with lasers, careful to not get the beams near their comrade.

"The guide said this is an ambush hunter," said Charley, walking up beside the mission leader. "It doesn't move very fast, but that maw can move like lightning."

Jonah nodded and looked into the fearsome mouth. The creature appeared to be all mouth. As the people cut away parts from it, the small lower body was revealed, and the commander had to wonder how it had gotten around at all with the pitiful worm-like legs underneath.

"How's he gonna be, Doc?" asked Willard, their heavy weapons man.

"Looks like there were no punctures, thank God," answered the medic. "His body armor kept those teeth from digging in. But I think he has internal injuries from the crushing force."

"Can he move?"

"Not on his own, and I would hate to leave him here. Something's sure to come along and try to take a bite out of him." That would be death to the attacker, but Cameron would still be dead, too.

"Rig a stretcher. We'll carry him along. One trooper can watch him while we go in to the base."

That would remove two people from his order of battle. He didn't like that, but he also didn't like losing people. He considered himself a good leader, and good leaders didn't let people die without reason. They would have to make do. It wasn't like any other fighting force in history hadn't had to make do after sustaining casualties.

It grew dark while they got Cameron free and rigged up a stretcher. The guide had shown them what branches to use, though the mercs had acted like the dead wood was going to come back to life and attack them. Jonah couldn't blame them. This jungle made his skin crawl, and he was sure they hadn't seen everything it could throw at them yet. He wondered how the enemy's snatch and grab crew was handling it, and he could only hope they were losing people at every turn.

Everyone had their visors down now, using the light gathering function to see in the dark. The jungle looked like a nightmare in night-vision mode, despite the clarity of modern equipment. The colors shown on their visors might have been accurate, but they wouldn't be able to tell until they saw them in the daylight.

"We need to start moving," said Charley, pointing ahead. "We've fallen behind schedule."

"Right." Jonah hated the thought of hurrying through this jungle. He hated even more the idea of spending an extra day out here, waiting for night to fall again. Even worse, the longer they took, the more at risk the hostage was.

Jonah cursed again and pulled the hatchet from his belt. His men joked about him carrying the small weapon, but he was good with it, and having a lot of backups was always a good thing. He looked at the razor-sharp edge, then secured it back in its harness. He doubted he would use it on this operation; if he did, the shit would really have hit the fan.

* * *

"Have we heard anything from the boss yet?" asked the leader of the small furry aliens that were the majority of the group.

"No, Niplo. We have not," growled the Besquith who was the overall leader. He really hated working with the little aliens. They were weak and stupid; they were the worst soldiers he had ever seen. He would have preferred to have more of his kind, even if he was just a lowly soldier among his own. Here he was the commander, even if his command was pitiful.

The little alien looked down at his feet, then up at the larger Besquith. "I am worried. I don't like this place. Another of my males is missing from a patrol, and I suspect a party will be coming to rescue our hostage before long."

The Besquith growled deep in his throat at the cowardly creature. There was no way the company whose factor they had kidnapped would know where they were. He thought about that for a moment and remembered they had believed the same of the other operation, the one that the damned Human mercenaries had attacked. Sure, they hadn't recovered the hostage, but the group hadn't gotten their ransom either. So the boss had decided they would try again, as if that wouldn't lead to the same result.

"We need you to keep sending out patrols," said the Besquith to his minion.

"But you said the Humans will not find us here."

"And so they won't. But it shows a lack of discipline to not keep up our guard."

"My people are starting to grumble. Some may refuse."

"And any who refuse will be grumbling in my stomach," said the Besquith, leaning over and glaring at the small creature, showing as many of his carnivore's teeth as he could. The little alien shivered in fear, but didn't dare run away from the larger monster that could run it down. "Make sure your people continue to patrol the jungle surrounding this place. If I find out otherwise, you will pay with your life."

The alien gave its version of a head nod, then ran out, the stink of its fear staying behind. The Besquith growled again, then cursed the uselessness of the race. If he had his way, they would all become rations before they left this planet. And then he wouldn't have to share the reward with the weaklings.

* * *

Thankfully, the planet, even though a backwater world, still had an orbital navigation system. Jonah hated to think what it would have been like trying to navigate with the age-old tools of map and compass. He had the training, as did most of his people, though the maps were projected onto the visors as heads-up displays, and the compass was projected beside it. But trying to find the way through the jungle, even with the directions of the compass, could still be the ultimate confusing experience. The orbital system allowed them to get an exact fix on their location.

"We should be there in an hour," he told Charley after checking the three dimensional representation of their position. There were some hills ahead, and with them a change in the biome, going from jungle to dense forest. From what he had read, it was a much less dangerous area. There were regions of exposed rock, and from the intelligence they had, the hostage was located in a fortified area within those rocks. Orbital photos had given them a probable location, and the sighting of a Besquith from a high-flying drone had confirmed it.

"The guide is concerned about our night attack," said Charley, squatting down for a moment.

"What's his problem?"

"He says it's better to move during the day, since the jungle plants will come alive."

"And what the hell does he mean by that?" asked Jonah. He looked down at the ground and spat on a small worm-like creature that was crawling along. The worm curled up and started to thrash, then stopped, curling into a circle. *What the hell. It couldn't handle the enzymes in my saliva?*

"The trees will awake at dawn," said the guide, appearing like magic behind the team leader. His voice was high-pitched, almost beyond the range of Human hearing, but the translator box he was wearing converted it to English in the normal audible range of the mercs.

"I think he means the vegetation around here starts its business when they can get energy from the sun," said Charley.

"Noise increase," said the guide, eyes blinking in what they recognized as his race's version of a nod. "Plants pump, sound fills the forest."

"But we'll be easier to see," replied Jonah, not sure he liked the idea of changing plans.

"See for little bit," said the guide. "Can hear for much further."

"He's right, you know," agreed Charley. "And we'll have to push it to make it to the jump off point before dawn."

"Okay. We'll do it your way," he told the guide, almost reaching out to pat him on the shoulder, then thinking better of it. He didn't know the mores of these people, and didn't want to offend the one person they were depending on.

20 minutes later the jungle threw the next assault their way.

* * *

"We have intelligence the Humans will be assaulting your position within a couple of days," said the Besquith that the group leader only knew as The Boss.

"What do you want me to do?"

"Be ready to move to the secondary location, today, and make sure the hostage is safe. We can't afford to lose another one, since his company has increased security on their other high rankers."

The group leader acknowledged. They were in this for the ransom; kidnapping vital operatives of an Interstellar conglomerate to have them killed was not attaining their objective. The only problem he could see with their plan was that the company didn't seem to want to play along.

"I could use more of our people," he told The Boss. "These little, furry insects don't fill my heart with confidence."

"They're all we have for now. After we buy our way back into the good graces of the leaders of the guild, we will be able to recruit all of our own kind we need. But for now, these are the instruments we have, and we will use them."

And after they are of no further use, they will make fine meals, thought the group leader.

"Get your people ready," barked the group leader over the local comm. "We will be moving in three hours. Full security, and I don't want anything showing to the air assets of our enemy. Now, get to it."

* * *

The people were grumbling under their breaths as the column made its way through the jungle. The night was filled with the continuous buzzing of insectoids, and all the Humans had their scarves up, protecting their flesh from painful bites. The insectoids would die, but that was small consolation for the itching that resulted from the foreign anticoagulants entering their systems. And of course fully-covered faces led to more sweat rolling down faces and onto torsos. And more cursing.

Jonah was alerted to the attack by a loud noise, followed quickly by more shouts and the muted sounds of magrail rifles. Jonah was pissed at the shouts; his people should know better.

When he saw the creature, he understood the noise. Even the best-disciplined soldier would have a hard time not shouting when a multi-ton mass of bone and muscle erupted claws-first from the jungle. It had collided with Jess, one of the smallest of the mercenaries, and the one who must have looked to be the easiest target. Its mouth had closed on her helmet, crunching it inward despite the toughness of its alloys. Claws had raked her chest, ripping through the cammo cover, but had been unable to penetrate the body armor. Still, it looked like Jess was gone; her neck had to be broken the way her body flopped around as the creature swung her.

Rounds hit the creature, penetrating its thick fur and the leathery-looking skin underneath. Jonah raised his own weapon and fired a burst. He aimed at the head of the beast, but hit Jess instead, not that she noticed. The guide ran toward the predator, spear at the ready. The beast must have noticed the alien, and must have had some experience with the natives and their weapons. With a tensing of its hind legs, the predator became a blur of red fur and disappeared into the jungle.

"We have to get her back," shouted Zack, starting after the beast.

"Stand down," shouted Jonah. "She's dead. We don't have time to chase that damned thing around in the rain forest."

As he spoke, the first drops of a heavy rain started falling, almost as if he had called it down.

"She needs to be avenged," shouted Zack, storming over to his leader.

Jonah shook his head. He was sure the beast would find a way to get enough of her flesh to fill its belly, and then it would sicken and die in agony, poisoned by her incompatible proteins. It would have to be revenge enough.

"How many more of those things are there around here?" asked Charley of the guide.

"Should be only one. They are very territorial. Not to say there won't be other predators around, but none that large."

Great, thought Jonah, turning to walk toward their objective. He waved everyone else on. They wouldn't have to worry about any more of those big bastards, but that didn't mean they wouldn't run into any ambush predators, or packs of smaller, swarming beasts. His experience in jungles hadn't prepared him for this. Nothing here was familiar, and there was so much that could kill them without warning. Right now, all he wanted to do was get this mission over with and get out of here.

The rain started coming down harder, hitting the thick canopy and pounding down on them with heavy drops. All they could hear was the rain, and visibility was less than 20 meters. In one respect it was an aid to their mission, as no patrol could see them. One the other hand, they could walk by a patrol waiting in ambush and not have a clue.

Minutes later the rain stopped. The Humans were still mostly dry in their combat suits, whose fibers repelled water. The air started to steam up as the rays of the morning sun penetrated the canopy in places, and the incessant murmuring of the plants rose in volume until it almost drowned out any other sounds.

"We are near," said the guide, pointing the way with his spear.

He would know, thought the team leader. The natives had been the first to notice the aliens, intruders on their territory that had come and set up camp without asking permission. The natives had not attacked, which was good sense on their part, since they would have been slaughtered. Instead they had reported it, and word had gotten back to the company, which led to the second contract. They needed to fulfill this one, or the bills would again go unpaid, and Jonah and Charley might find themselves working for someone else.

"No damned way," said Jonah under his breath. He and his partner had worked too hard to start up their specialty company. They were small, but the contracts they pulled in were lucrative, since few other companies could do what they did.

The point man, Ivan, knelt 30 meters down the trail, at the edge of visibility in the thick foliage, raising a hand to stop the column. It would have been nice to use the comms, but it was too much of a risk this close to their target. Instead, Jonah jogged forward at a crouch, his anxiety rising as he thought about what might be in front of them. He knelt beside the man and followed his pointing finger, to see movement further out in the jungle.

"See them?" whispered Ivan.

"Yeah." Small gray forms moved through the jungle up ahead. They were the same creatures they had run into on the last op. The same aliens of unknown origin. Someone probably knew where they came from, and what their world was like, but no one that Jonah knew. All Jonah cared about was that they were known associates of the Besquith that seemed to be leading this operation, and they needed to be killed so they could accomplish their own mission.

The merc leader waved more people forward, and the well-trained mercenaries knew who he wanted—the stealthiest of the group and the best at the silent kill. The rest stayed low, weapons at the ready. Jonah waved the three that came up to the right, while he and Ivan went to the left. There appeared to be seven of the creatures, a squad-level patrol, but he wasn't sure if there were any more. He doubted it. The creatures were small and stealthy themselves, but obviously not at home in this jungle.

Jonah and Ivan cut along the brush at an angle, reached the path the aliens were taking, and set up 30 meters ahead of them. They waited for the few seconds it took the creatures to get to them, then came out of the foliage in a rush, cutting blades in one hand, and pistols in the other.

Jonah buried his hatchet in the exposed throat of one creature as it turned his way, mouth open in shock. He ripped the hatchet out, killing it instantly. He aimed his pistol at the head of the next in line, squeezing the trigger and putting the round straight between its eyes where he figured the brain was most likely to be.

Ivan had taken out another one, and there was only a squeak from further up the trail where the trio of followers had killed their victims. Jonah looked over the dead, hoping they didn't get off an alert. He couldn't see how, but it never hurt to be cautious.

As he was thinking, the rain started coming down again. It hadn't rained much the day before, but now the jungle was living up to the name 'rain forest.'

"We need to move, now," he told the others. "Wave the rest of the company forward."

They were within a kilometer of the target, and it would be difficult for the enemy to pick them up in the rain. But there was no telling if they had electronic surveillance out here. Nothing was showing on their passive sensors; then again, it wouldn't until they got very close.

The company moved forward in crouching steps, passive sensors on the lookout. They found some sensors, worked their way around them, and continued on.

"Maybe we shouldn't have taken out their patrol," Jonah told Charley as they moved forward.

"They were in our way," said Charley, a cold smile on his face. "We would either have had to kill them there or kill them at the target. And if they hadn't moved we would have been out of luck, so don't second guess yourself."

Jonah nodded, then turned his attention forward again. They were almost to the small clearing in front of the rocks. Contact could occur at any moment. He just hoped it didn't occur until they could get to the hostage.

* * *

"We're ready to move, Boss," said the group leader over the comm to his superior Besquith.

"The transport will be waiting for you at the river," came the reply. "Make sure you stay near the banks on the way out."

The Besquith growled his acknowledgement. The banks along the river were overhung with the branches of trees, and if they kept the boats under there, they wouldn't be spotted from the air.

"And make sure the factor makes it out alive. It does us no good to have another dead Caroon on our hands."

The Besquith growled lightly at that. He wasn't sure they would ever get a ransom from that damned company; it seemed more willing to pay a higher amount for mercenaries than it would for ransom. He knew what they were thinking—if they paid once they could expect to have to pay again—so they were taking the hard line, and his group was taking the risk they would cave. He didn't think so, but his superior didn't care what he thought. If he had a way to reenter the society of his people on his own, he would have taken it. But he didn't, so this was it.

"Are we ready to move?" he asked the senior of the little aliens.

"We are ready. We're just waiting for our patrol to return. They are running late."

The fur on the Besquith's back stood up. "What did you say?" He stalked over to the little alien, towering over it, frightening teeth showing in its snarl.

"I said they were late reporting back," stammered the alien.

The Besquith backhanded the creature across the room, slamming it against the wall. "Why didn't you tell me?" he screamed.

The creature didn't answer, nor would it; its spine had been crushed against the stone wall of the chamber. The Besquith cursed the foolish creature and his temper that had killed it, just when he needed it to command the others.

"Sound the alarm," he shouted as he left the chamber. "We are under attack."

* * *

"What the hell is that?" whispered Ivan, once again on point with Jonah, who prided himself on being the stealthiest of the bunch. In the background, a faint buzzing sounded.

"We've been made," said Jonah, standing and waving everyone toward him. "Turn on your comms," he said in a carrying voice. Moments later they were all on the net, even the pilots in the gunships with the supporting squads.

"They know we're here," said the leader over the net. "I doubt they know exactly where we are, but knowing we're near is bad enough. So we go with plan Delta. Get into your assault groups and move to the target."

"Sandra," he said, turning toward his sniper. "I want you on some high ground covering the area. Any sign of that Besquith, put a round through his head. And try to keep the hostage alive."

"I'm kind of leery about getting into any of those trees," answered the woman. She looked at the guide. "Any suggestions?"

The guide pointed and started off, the woman right behind him, configuring her rifle for long range, precision fire.

"We need to take this one alive," said Charley, releasing a small disc shaped drone into the air to weave its way through the canopy. Now that they were no longer worried about the enemy knowing they were here, they could deploy their electronic assets, giving them eyes and ears in the sky and a complete comm net.

"We don't need to lose most of our people doing it," cautioned Jonah. "I want the full payoff as much as you, but we have a responsibility to our people."

Charley nodded, a frown on his face, then ran off to lead the left hand squad, while Jonah waited for his squad to gather around him. He looked into the visors of the 20 men and women who would follow him, sending information into their HUDs.

"Let's move."

The first fire team ran forward, weapons at close carry, while the second knelt and aimed, providing overwatch. As soon as the first team got fifty meters ahead, they knelt, and the second team ran past and into the clearing, this time looking for cover, since concealment was no longer the priority. Jonah came down behind a log, his head and rifle pointed around the side so he didn't present as much of a target. As soon as they were set, first team started forward. The sound of an explosion to the north, on their left flank, stopped everyone in their tracks for a moment, but all knew that to stand still in the open was to ask for death, and in an instant they were going forward again.

A laser struck the log Jonah was sheltering behind, the pop of wet wood exploding the only warning that a light amp weapon was in use. The rain had stopped, but there was still a fine mist in the air, and he spotted another beam going overhead. Fortunately, the other mercs saw it as well and started directing automatic fire at the enemy shooter. Rounds cracked through the air, hitting rock, and a smattering of stone chips flew through the air.

More lasers entered the fray, and the life signs of a merc spiked for a moment, then faded. Another shouted out, and Jonah's HUD showed he had lost another man. He raised his weapon and took a reading on the position of the enemy. The merc leader fired a grenade, and the 30-millimeter projectile flew toward the enemy and detonated, taking out the shooter. He fired again and cursed as his grenade exploded in midair halfway there. The enemy was using a radar-aimed laser system that, while it wouldn't do much to the solid rounds of the rifles, would detonate any explosive devices that came their way. It took away one of their most potent weapons.

Damn, we're pinned down, thought the leader as another life sign fell off his HUD. He hated losing people, and he hated even more getting his ass kicked by a bunch of wussy aliens. If they were Besquith it would be one thing, but these little furry bastards? No way.

One of the little aliens screamed, a high-pitched blast of sound that went silent in an instant. It was soon followed by another, and it looked as if the fight was not going all their way. There were more of the enemy, though, and fire superiority was still on the enemy's side.

"We're getting slaughtered here," yelled Charley over the comm.

"Great," replied Jonah. "So I guess you're not going to come to our rescue, huh?"

"Not likely. I've got three down."

"Doing better than me," said Jonah as the life signs from another member of his team blinked out. *I guess it's lucky we aren't facing a bunch of Besquith,* he thought, though he couldn't see how it could be any worse.

A shot cracked overhead, and another of the aliens screamed just before it died. Sandra had entered the fight, though her first shot hadn't been her best as the alien had time to scream. Her next shot hit the mark, and a laser rifle fell from the rocks without a sound from the wielder.

A pair of lasers flew out from the enemy position, aimed at the sniper.

"I'm hit," yelled Sandra.

"How bad?"

"I'll live. But I've got a bad burn on my left arm, so I won't be a steady shot for the rest of this mission."

"Take cover. We'll handle it from here." Jonah wasn't sure how they were going to handle it, but he was determined they would.

The rains started again. This was a real downpour, double the volume of the ones that had come before. Lightning flashed in the sky, followed seconds later by the rumble of thunder.

Lasers flashed through the rain, vaporizing liquid droplets, and losing their focus as they were dispersed by the tiny prisms that filled the air.

"Yes," shouted Jonah, raising his rifle and sending a stream of grenades into the rock outcropping. Small flashes burst through the rocks, the sounds of their explosions drowned out by the rain. "Don't just lie there," he yelled over the comm. "Let's get them while we have the advantage."

Battle cries sounded over the comm as the mercenaries got to their feet and charged the rocks, weapons firing at their maximum cyclic rate. There were a few magazine changes along the way, since the two hundred round pellet stores emptied quickly on full auto. The little aliens were braver than Jonah would have thought. They stood their ground while the larger Humans charged them, even though their weapons weren't working. The rain stopped suddenly, but the Humans were already in among the enemy, and it was close combat, something the mercenaries excelled at.

Jonah checked his unit on his HUD and cursed under his breath. Five dead, six wounded, leaving him with only three quarters of his group still combat effective. And they still hadn't found the target, if he was alive.

They quickly searched the cavern, finding nothing except some evidence that the factor had been there.

"Dammit," shouted Jonah, throwing a glass to the floor. This was a disaster. Since some of the kidnappers had gotten away with their victim, there would be no payment, and it had cost him people for no gain.

"One of the drones picked them up," called Charley. "I'm about to head after them."

"I'm coming with you," growled Jonah. "I want the scalp of that Besquith."

"Something your ancestors were into, I guess," said Charley, whose Gurkha ancestors were more into taking the entire head.

Jonah was happy to settle for the revenge his Apache ancestors preferred.

* * *

The Besquith pushed the factor along, growing angry that the being was not able to move faster. He would have ordered his last soldier to carry the being, but the little alien was incapable. And he was not about to lower his guard with only one soldier at his back.

"Move," he growled at the factor. "Unless you want to end up as tonight's main course."

The factor shouted as the big paw hit his shoulder.

"Quiet," hissed the Besquith. "I will not allow you to be taken alive. So you had best hope they don't find us. Now move, you worthless sack of meat."

* * *

Jonah hadn't grown up in the jungle, but in the American Southwest, while Charley had been raised within driving distance of the Southeast Asian rain forest. Although Charley might have seemed better-suited for this job, Jonah had worked in the Amazon rain forest for years, and, even though this was a different jungle, the rules of tracking were still the same. He was also pursuing creatures which either weren't as good as he was, like the Besquith, or who had no interest in covering his tracks, like the factor. There were footprints along the path and broken twigs along the side; there was plenty of evidence for even a blind man to follow, much less someone of Jonah's abilities.

He cautioned himself to patience, even though there was the risk they would get away, but running into an ambush would not get him what he wanted. There were several mercenaries behind him, and they were not able to keep up with their leader. The smart thing to do would be to wait for them, but the smart thing might lead to the quarry escaping.

Jonah heard voices ahead, including a growling snarl that could only be the Besquith. *I need to take that bastard out fast*, he thought. He didn't relish the prospect of fighting one of the creatures hand to hand. His attention was so focused on the Besquith, he didn't notice the smaller one until it jumped out of the brush and tackled him.

His rifle went flying away, and Jonah cursed himself for not having the strap around his neck. The little alien tried to bring a knife into play, but Jonah was able to overpower it. He needed to finish it quickly, before the Besquith got into the action. A quick grab and a wrench of the neck, and the creature was dead.

A roar of anger foretold the charge of the Besquith. Its kind thought of Humans as helpless prey, and this one displayed the same attitude as it came at him with its claws extended. It was more than a match for most Humans, but Jonah had been a warrior all his life. He ducked under the claws and pushed his knife into the thigh of the Besquith, pulling on the handle to set the barbs, then moved away, leaving the blade in the muscle of the alien.

"I will destroy you, puny creature," roared the Besquith, hand going to his thigh. He tried to pull the blade out, but the barbs caught and ripped through more of his muscle until he stopped. "I will rip your head off," the creature screamed, stumbling forward, claws reaching for Jonah.

Jonah glanced at his rifle, quickly deciding that he would be caught before he got to it, and instead ran backward, hand pulling his hatchet from its harness. The Besquith laughed when it saw the weapon and lurched after him.

"Laugh at this," Jonah roared as he swung the hatchet at the left paw of the Besquith, slicing deep between the digits. The creature jerked its hand back, and Jonah struck again like lightning, slicing into the Besquith's other forearm. He pulled the hatchet out and hit again, then ran backward to get out of reach of the creature.

The Besquith came forward, claws ready, but held its arms close to its body, unwilling to take a hit if it could help it. Jonah swung again at the injured paw, trying to disable it completely. The hatchet head hit, slicing in, and almost severed a digit. The Besquith roared again, closed its fingers around the head of the hatchet and jerked its hand back, pulling it out of Jonah's grasp.

The mercenary tried to pull his pistol, his last weapon, and the one he should have been using. His arm was still coming up as the Besquith struck; its heavy paw hit his forearm, and one claw actually penetrated his armor. The pistol flew away, and a sharp pain shot through his forearm. Before he could think, another paw came down on his shoulder and knocked him to his knees.

The Besquith looked down at his victim, and Jonah looked up at death. The creature reached up with it paw, readying the killing stroke, and Jonah voiced a silent prayer that his afterlife would be pleasant, though he doubted that would be his reward. The paw was still coming down when the forehead of the creature blew outward, splattering the Human with brains and blood. The paw hit, but all it had behind it now was weight and no strength. Jonah still fell forward, and the heavy body of the Besquith fell on top of him.

"You okay, partner?" Charley asked, working with the other mercs to pull the Besquith off Jonah.

"I thought I was dead."

"Hell, I couldn't let you die," said a smiling Charley. "I don't know how to cook the books like you do."

"And how's the hostage?"

"He looks mad as hell," said Charley, looking over at the factor, who was busy kicking the body of the Besquith while screaming at it. "But I think he'll be good, and we have a payday coming."

"I think my forearm's broken," said Jonah through gritted teeth. "Get Doc over here. And I need to take care of something. Can you lend me your knife? I need to take a scalp."

It felt to Jonah like his collarbone was also broken, but it would heal, and having money in the bank would help. Now, if only they could figure out a way to get around the taxes Earth was going to levy on their bounty.

# # # # #

Chris' Introduction to:

Dead or Alive

by PP Corcoran

Like Doug Dandridge, I'm still looking forward to sitting down with Paul Corcoran over a beer. Unfortunately, he keeps telling me that it's supposed to be a warm one, which is a continuing point of contention.

I've known Paul several years, though, and we have had fairly similar careers, having gone from the military to becoming authors to expanding into the publishing business. Neither of us know which was the bigger surprise—surviving a career in the military or unexpectedly becoming an Amazon bestselling author, like he did with his Saiph series of novels.

I'm happy I reached out to him for a cross-promotional deal several years ago—it worked well at the time and introduced me to a great guy—and I have been able to keep up with his career ever since, including appearing with him in the anthology "Explorations: First Contact."

Some time, we're going to have that beer (and I greatly hope it'll be a cold one.)

Paul is a great guy and an outstanding author, and I'm excited to bring you his story, "Dead or Alive." Want to know more about PP Corcoran? You can find him here: http://www.ppcorcoran.com.

DEAD OR ALIVE
by PP Corcoran

Chapter 1

It was supposed to have been a simple smash and grab. The Zuparti crew had no idea that Ulah and his fellow Besquith had secreted themselves aboard the luxury yacht. Ulah and his two compatriots had hidden among the crates in the cargo bay as the yacht prepared to leave on its maiden voyage from the construction yards around Tora IV bound for Soland and its new owners.

For four hours, they bode their time, as the yacht boosted toward the stargate. Once the ship entered hyper, the second stage of Ulah's plan began. The part which he, Pukil, and Kalaz had looked forward to. The killing!

According to the information Ulah purchased from a sniveling Jeha at the construction yard's offices, the yacht was sailing with a skeleton crew. Ulah had no doubt the three Besquith could overpower a few Zuparti. Those paranoid weasels were traders who hired mercenaries to do their fighting for them, so taking control of the yacht should be easy. Ulah had imagined selling the yacht for a tidy profit.

How was he to know the wife of the new owner would decide to deliver the yacht, a present for her husband, personally?

When Ulah reached the cockpit entrance, instead of the expected confrontation with two Pendal pilots, he ran slap bang into the owner's wife and her Lumar bodyguard.

Close combat in a weightless environment was never pretty.

The Lumar, seven feet tall with four arms, were known throughout the galaxy as great brawlers, especially in close quarters. Fortunately for Ulah, he reacted first and got the drop on the Lumar. Razor-sharp teeth and claws disemboweled the Lumar before he could get his laser pistol free of its holster. Then things started to go south.

The bodyguard's dying brain sent an order to his muscles; they complied and pulled the trigger of his pistol. The single shot missed Ulah by a mile. However, in the confined space of the corridor, the owner's wife was not so lucky. The shot speared through her neck, neatly removing her head from the rest of her body. She was dead before she knew she was hit.

Ulah raced along the once spotless corridor, now splattered with the bodyguard's blood and entrails, and burst into the cockpit. The Pendal pilots' four arms were a blur of motion. Ulah grabbed the pilot's upper left hand, braced his feet against the back of the now squealing pilot's seat, and pulled with all his considerable strength. The squealing rose in pitch to an ear-shredding scream as the arm separated from the shoulder socket. Bone, muscle, tendon, and skin ripped asunder and arterial blood sprayed the victim's fellow pilot and the interior of the cockpit.

"Stop what you are doing immediately!" Ulah ordered. He whipped the separated appendage like a club, and he struck the screaming, mortally-wounded Pendal, knocking him unconscious. A blessing, perhaps, as his life blood spurted from the ragged wound to the beat of his ever-weakening heart. A final shudder indicated the pilot's death. "I told you to stop..." Ulah's words died in his throat; the cockpit control panel went dark as the second Pendal pilot's hands stopped their feverish movement. The yacht's controls were locked out. Whatever the ship's destination, the computer would ensure the yacht reached it, with or without input from the pilots.

Ulah let out a mighty rage-filled roar, grasped the remaining pilot by the throat, and pulled his face close to his own salivating mouth. Teeth bared, the blood of the bodyguard and the first pilot combined to mat the fur around his snout.

The foul, iron-tinged smell of his breath filled the squirming pilot's nose.

"Tell me the access codes, Pendal, and I will make your death quick. Refuse and I will ensure it lasts an eternity." The pitiful whimper that escaped the lips of the Pendal did nothing to salve Ulah's rage.

Behind him, the familiar deep voice of Pukil came from the cockpit entrance. "Ulah, my brother. If the cursed Pendal has indeed locked the controls, the possible combinations run in the hundreds of millions. We could spend the rest of our lives trying to enter the correct combination into the computer and never get it." A wicked-looking claw extended from its sheath, glinting in the overhead lighting. Pukil's voice came out low and steady. "Perhaps I can persuade him to share it with us."

Ulah released his stranglehold on the Pendal who floated above his seat. A short, barking laugh filled the cramped cockpit. "He's all yours, brother. Where is Kalaz?"

"Searching the rest of the yacht in case we missed any of the crew" replied Pukil as he floated over to place a heavy, furred hand on the pilot's shoulder. His extended claw touched the Pendal's skin, causing an involuntary shiver to run the length of his body.

"I'm going to enjoy our time together, Pendal. Somehow, I don't think you will, though."

Ulah let out another, more prolonged, laugh as he left the cockpit in search of Kalaz. He pushed past the headless corpse of the wife. Too bad she was dead; she would probably have been worth a small fortune in ransom money. Well, they had 170 hours to find and strip everything of value from the yacht before they emerged from hyper, and a ship like this would fetch them a pretty penny on the black market.

Ulah, Pukil, and Kalaz had no idea the chain of events they had set in motion.

Chapter 2

Nikki tuned out the animated Wathayat freighter captain that filled the Tri-V. The Wathayat freighter was crewed by Cochkala, and this specimen of the badger-like species whipped his long prehensile tail around so much that Nikki saw the other Cochkala avoiding being near their obviously-irritated captain. Not for the first time in the 170-hour trip from Karma to Hano, she wished that another, *any* other ship, had been heading for Hano.

Deciding enough was enough, she interrupted the captain mid-flow. "Again, you have my thanks for allowing me to piggy back on your hull, Captain. You have my gratitude, and I will be sure to mention to my employers your invaluable assistance in helping me complete my mission." The Cochkala captain uttered something which the translation pendant hanging around Nikki's neck struggled to find a fitting English word for. Nikki cut the link and his image vanished from the display.

Nikki ran both hands through her long auburn hair, held back from her face in a ponytail that only served to emphasize her classical bone structure and striking emerald green eyes. "Sculpted by an artisan of ancient Greece," one suitor had described her; many others had done their utmost to woo her over the years, only to have their advances dashed like a matchwood ship upon a reef. Nikki Sinclair had neither the time nor the inclination to become any man's trophy wife. Her father, Alastair Sinclair, commanded the Sinclair's Scorpions mercenary company and was somewhat over-protective of his only daughter, which also tended to dissuade suitors' advances. Nikki would probably die of sheer boredom if, God forbid, she had to play the part of a genteel housewife and host. Hence, Nikki's current chosen profession, and her presence in the Crapti region of the Jesc arm, which was about as far from Earth as she could get.

Nikki adjusted the four-point harness hugging her to the seat so it didn't press on her pistol. The vintage M1911, a present from her father on her sixteenth birthday, sat in its shoulder holster on her left side.

Coming from a merc family, she was brought up around weapons and could not remember a single day when either her father or one or two of her two elder brothers had not been on the range, practicing with the latest hand-held laser rifle or one of the state-of-the-art CASPer Mk 7s. Nikki remembered vividly how, on first receiving the pistol, she felt deflated and even a little annoyed because her brothers got to play with lasers and armored combat suits while she got an antique pistol from the beginning of the twentieth century. Disappointment had turned to pride, though, as her father explained the pistol had been passed down the generations from her great-great-grandfather to him; now, he was entrusting it to her, so she could continue the tradition. From that day, the pistol was never more than an arm's length from her side.

Nikki reached out and grasped the thin lead that floated free in the zero-g environment of the cockpit. Cocking her head to one side, she clicked the lead onto the pinplant behind her left ear. With a rush that almost took her breath away, her brain connected directly with the flight computer of her ship, the *Anat*. Closing her eyes momentarily, Nikki controlled the flow of information, slowing it to a more manageable stream. Satisfied, Nikki commanded the computer to disconnect the magnetic grapple which held the *Anat* firmly to the Wathayat freighter, then she applied power and set course for Hano's starport. A familiar tingling ran down Nikki's spine. It had been a long hunt, but now...her quarry was near.

* * *

The *Anat* was well into atmosphere, and closing on the starport rapidly, when a tickle from her pinplant alerted Nikki to an incoming call. A half-thought command activated the Tri-V, and Nikki was confronted by a pair of yellow eyes with black, unblinking, slit-like irises set in a green-scaled bulbous head. A pink forked tongue flicked out from a lip-less central mouth. *Why is it the Hano reminds me of Vassily?* Nikki had mixed feelings about the pet lizard she owned in middle school.

"Unknown vessel, this is Hano Traffic Control. State your business and intentions." The Hano's tone of voice did nothing to disguise his obvious irritation at being distracted from something of far greater importance.

Nikki ordered the ship's computer to transmit its identification and her credentials. The traffic controller scrolled down the information on his display until, finally, he reached the seal at the end of the transmission. A blue tree. The seal of the Peacemakers.

The reptile's body went very still, and Nikki swore his scales took on a sickly blue tinge. The corners of Nikki's lips twitched as she fought to suppress a full, cocky smile. She watched silently as the Hano wrapped his arms around his chest, dipping his chin as he assumed the position of supplication. His voice, when it came, was free of all previous signs of irritation.

"Please accept my apologies, Peacemaker. How may I be of service to you?"

"I require a landing pad cleared for my imminent arrival at the outer edge of the starport."

Six green, claw-tipped fingers flew across a control panel. "It is done, Peacemaker. Landing Pad 17 is at your disposal for the duration of your stay. Is there anything else you require?"

"Yes, you will immediately erase any record of my arrival from the planetary database..." Nikki's voice dropped an octave and her face hardened. "You will inform no one that a Peacemaker is on the planet. If it comes to my attention that my presence is known then there will be..." Nikki locked eyes with the traffic controller, ensuring her words left no room for misunderstanding. "Consequences."

A pink tongue flicked out to wet suddenly dry scales, accompanied by rapid blinking. Yeah, he got the message. Nikki cut the link and busied herself with preparations for landing.

* * *

Nikki stood before an open locker in the cramped personnel bay of the *Anat*. Reaching inside, she retrieved a utility belt complete with thigh holster. Buckling on the belt, Nikki bent to secure the holster to her right leg before slipping in a sleek, custom-made laser pistol. Shrugging on a battered leather flying jacket, she slipped a pair of mirrored aviator sunglasses from her pocket and put them on. She brushed her left hand behind her ear, making sure the arm of the glasses had an unobstructed connection with her pinplant. Slamming the door closed, Nikki headed for the aft loading ramp, and her booted footsteps echoed around the bay. Ready or not...

Walking into the bright sunlight, Nikki stopped at the top of the ramp and drank in her surroundings for the first time. To say the starport was rundown was a disservice to the word. Shithole was a much more fitting descriptor. The pad upon which her ship sat was nothing more than an engine-scorched circle of concrete. Off to one side were a couple of locals standing beside a motorized bowser. A bored-looking third local, with a laser rifle slung over his shoulder, stood a few feet away. Nikki made an educated guess the bowser contained F11. Why else have an armed guard unless they protected something valuable? F11, the element which made space travel possible, had caused a number of wars and was certainly worth protecting. After hitching a lift on the Wathayat freighter, though, her ship's F11 bunker was still topped off, so Nikki threw a dismissive wave at the crew, and they jumped aboard the bowser with the armed guard in tow. The bowser's engine burst into life, and the vehicle chugged off in the direction of a cluster of buildings partially hidden by a line of low trees.

Setting off down the ramp, Nikki moved out of the protective lined hull of the *Anat*. Like all spacefaring vessels, the ship was designed to protect its occupants from deadly solar radiation; as a result, it hindered the passage of normal radio frequencies. Nikki's glasses, while admittedly shit hot, were not just for appearances; a micro transmit and receive chip was embedded in the frame. This chip activated as it detected the signals from a planetary GalNet node, and, after a brief electronic handshake identifying Nikki as an authorized Peacemaker, the entire data store of the node was at her disposal.

If I were a Besquith with credits to burn, where would I be? pondered Nikki. Accessing the GalNet node via her pinplant, Nikki ran a quick search for any active Universal Account Access Cards, or Yacks as they were commonly known, belonging to Besquiths. The answer jumped out at her immediately. A Yack, with a balance that had too many zeros and belonged to a Besquith, was regularly used at a place called Walars. Per the local directory, Walars was a multi-species bar in a rather disreputable part of the starport. A soft ping alerted Nikki that the Yack had just been used at...surprise, surprise, Walars.

"Time for a drink, I think," Nikki said to no one in particular as she headed toward a line of flyers waiting to whisk disembarking passengers and crew off to destinations throughout the sprawling starport.

Chapter 3

Walars was exactly as Nikki imagined. A dive. The first thing to hit her as she walked through the door was the stench of too many species in close proximity eating 100 types of diverse food.

In the dim lighting, Nikki saw the bar was divided into seating areas, each surrounded by a low privacy wall. Green-scaled Hano waitresses weaved between the tables with practiced ease, carrying unrecognizable liquid concoctions. A bubbling azure-colored beverage caught her eye; there was a large worm-like thing doing the backstroke in it. Alien Tequila? Nikki wondered.

Stepping to one side to avoid being highlighted in the doorway, Nikki scanned the booths. It took one pass of her glasses' biometric recognition software to ping Kalaz. Slipping the aviators off, she placed them into her jacket pocket. The same hand continued its downward motion to rest lightly on the grip of her laser pistol.

Strolling to the bar on the far side of the room, she squeezed between two Caroons who, despite the low lighting, both had darkened goggles over their eyes. The Caroons were more adapted for life underground than above. Nikki supposed a mining corporation must have imported them rather than using locals. A slate was attached to the bar's counter top, and Nikki scrolled through the alien drink menu until she found a drink she recognized. Gosh Berry juice. Tapping her Yack against the slate, she placed her order. Turning her back to the bar and resting against it, she got her first proper look at the booth containing Kalaz from her new vantage point. Shit, he wasn't alone!

On either side of the large Besquith were a pair of Flatar. No wonder she hadn't seen them at first. The raised wall around the booth had easily been tall enough to hide the one-foot-tall aliens who looked like overgrown chipmunks. The crossed bandoliers and the ugly-looking compact pistols they carried made them well-armed chipmunks, and where there was a Flatar, there was most likely to be a Tortantula. Nikki now had an inkling that going into the bar without back up was a bad idea. Besquith were one thing. Tortantula were a decidedly different kettle of fish. Taking the glass of Gosh Berry juice that had magically appeared behind her, she took a sip and scanned the crowded bar with fresh eyes. No sign of any Tortantula; at 10 feet long, they would have been hard to hide.

Nikki downed the remainder of the juice and casually walked over to the booth containing Kalaz and the Flatar. It took a moment for the three aliens to notice her; their animated conversation centered on a slate propped up on the table in front of them stuttered to a halt. The Flatar on the left was the first to speak, and the pendant around Nikki's neck converted the Flatar's squeaks and yowls into standard English.

"Get lost..." The Flatar eyed Nikki up and down. "Whatever you are! This is a private conversation."

"It's a Human," the second Flatar said helpfully.

"You heard my friend," growled Kalaz, baring his teeth.

Nikki looked from one Flatar to the other, before her hard, emerald eyes focused on Kalaz like high-intensity lasers. With her left hand, she lifted the collar of her battered leather jacket and revealed the glowing blue tree secreted there. Conversation in the bar ceased, as if someone had flipped a switch.

"Kalaz of the Besquith. I have a warrant for your arrest." Nikki's voice held not a shred of emotion as it carried across the entire bar. On either side of Kalaz, the Flatar slowly slid away, pointedly keeping their hands in plain sight and as far from their weapons as possible.

"The charges are: murder, piracy, theft..." With a roar, Kalaz surged to his feet, and his powerful arms flung the table in Nikki's direction. Well, it would have been in her direction if she had still been standing there. With the grace of a gymnast Nikki rolled to the side and came up on one knee, laser pistol in her right hand, M1911 in her left. Kalaz moved with frightening speed, bearing down on Nikki, teeth and claws intent on ripping her to bloody pieces. The high-pitched whine of the laser pistol firing was overshadowed by the deafening blast of a .45. Being a near-light-speed weapon the shot from the laser pistol struck Kalaz first; it pierced his chest, cut his heart neatly in two and killed him instantly. The arrival of the heavy .45 round, a fraction of a second later may have been unnecessary, but it didn't detract from its spectacular nature. The round hit Kalaz square between the eyes and blew the back of the Besquith's head off. Bar patrons directly behind the charging Besquith were covered in a mix of Kalaz' remains.

Regaining her feet, Nikki took three steps and stood over the dead Besquith. Around her, the bar quickly emptied, its clientele deciding their interests were best served by not being around when the local law arrived. Ignoring them, Nikki bent down and retrieved the slate from underneath Kalaz's lifeless hand, then she wiped its face on Kalaz's fur to clean off the blood splatter. Activating the slate, she read the information it displayed, and a single eyebrow cocked up in wry amusement. Displayed on the slate, for the world to see, were the details of the three, correction, two, gang members' next job. If this information was correct, they had used a significant amount of their ill-gotten gains from the sale of the yacht to buy weapons, and the location of the warehouse where the weapons were stored was on the slate.

Nobody ever said the Besquith were smart.

Nikki looked around; the Flatars had fled. Although they were probably guilty of any number of crimes, none of them involved her. Nikki turned and walked out of the bar.

Chapter 4

"Well?" Ulah asked as Pukil entered the warehouse on the edge of the starport.

The second Besquith held up his hands in a placating motion. "The deal is done, brother." Pukil calmed Ulah, momentarily, before continuing. "Although...the news of Kalaz's..." He stopped while searching for the appropriate word. "Demise, at the hands of the Peacemaker. Well, the news reached the cursed Cochkala...before the sale was finalized." Pukil's carefully chosen words and hesitation in delivering them allowed Ulah to guess the likely outcome of the negotiations.

Ulah responded in a low and unusually calm tone. "How much?" When his compadres' response didn't come quickly enough, Ulah moved to stand in front of Pukil, his face just an inch away, and repeated, "How much?"

Pukil was unable to look Ulah in the eye as he said, "They lowered their offer by twenty percent."

Ulah's pent up anger exploded like a volcano. "I will kill them all! I will kill their families and feast on their bones!"

Pukil stood his ground in the face of Ulah's wrath. The Besquith were not known for their calm demeanor. As Ulah's anger subsided, Pukil finally judged it safe to speak once more.

"Listen, Ulah, as part of the deal, I have secured passage for us on a Wathayat freighter. It is due to leave within the hour...bound for Karma. Once we reach the planet, it will be a simple matter of joining one of the Besquith merc companies, and we will be two more Besquith among hundreds. Not even a Peacekeeper would dare hunt us among our own."

The simple logic of Pukil's plan appealed to Ulah. Still...the burning desire to gorge his murderous appetite on the Peacemaker who had killed Kalaz tore at his innards. Pukil sensed his brother's indecision and decided to force the issue.

"Time is short, brother. I have already converted our profits from the sale of the weapons into precious stones. We can change them back into credits at a time of our choosing. The Peacemaker will not be able to track us. But we must leave now!"

With a curt nod, Ulah signaled his agreement. Taking one last look around the warehouse, and its stacked crates of weapons that now belonged to the Cochkala, he swore a silent oath.

This is not over, Peacemaker. I will see Kalaz revenged!

* * *

Seeing the Cochkala busily swarming over the contents of the warehouse, Nikki realized her quarry had made good their escape. One of the bipedal badgers was standing off to the side, watching the rest work. You'll be the boss then, thought Nikki, as she wandered casually over to him.

"A recent acquisition?"

The Cochkala glared at the questioning Human, seeing only his own reflected face in the mirrored sunglasses the being wore. How dare the Human approach a trader of his eminence without permission? He could never tell which were male and which female; they were all equally ugly. If this one was a potential buyer, though, perhaps he could make an exception, just this once.

"Yes, my most recent," he said. "A shipment of weapons. All the highest quality, I can assure you. Are you interested in procuring a few items?"

Before Nikki could stop him, the Cochkala beckoned a hauler loaded with crates. Unsealing a crate, he stepped aside to allow Nikki a view of the contents. Nikki's eyes opened wide, and her jaw dropped; it was a row of neatly packaged MACs. Magnetic Accelerator Cannon were common on powered armor; the cannon in the crate were in their original packaging and must have been worth a good number of credits. Exactly the sort of thing two Besquith looking to make a profit would invest in.

Nikki fixed her most innocent look upon her face before asking, "Were the previous owners two Besquith, by any chance?"

The Cochkala, an experienced trader, recognized a loaded question when he heard one. "I'm afraid my business dealings are confidential, Human."

Nikki raised the collar of her jacket exposing the blue tree symbol. As the Cochkala's eyes fell upon it, his tail twitched wildly—a sure sign of his unease. "No dealings are confidential when they pertain to Peacemaker business. Answer my question."

"This is most unusual," the Cochkala spluttered. "I purchased these weapons in good faith. I must protest..."

Nikki's ice-cold voice cut him off mid-sentence. "Need I remind you that failure to cooperate with a Peacemaker has the direst consequences? Your loss of status within the Wathayat. The revoking of your trading license by the Merchant Guild. Refusal of stargate travel by the Cartography Guild. Imagine..." Nikki indicated the run-down warehouse and the ramshackle buildings. "Being stranded on this backwater planet for the rest of your natural life."

If someone had ever wanted to see a Cochkala turned into a blubbering wreck, the Cochkala standing in front of Nikki would have been a perfect example.

"That will not be necessary, Peacemaker. You shall, of course, have my complete cooperation. These items were indeed purchased from two Besquith."

"And where might I find these Besquith now?" Pressed Nikki.

"Ah... Part of the agreement of sale was passage to Karma. I believe I overheard one of the Besquith mention something about joining a merc company..."

"Shit!" Nikki exclaimed. She turned and ran for her waiting flyer, accessing the GalNet node via her pinplant as she did so. By the time she flopped into her seat she had brought up traffic control's outbound log for the day. Only one Wathayat ship, the *Kacha*, was due to leave for Karma today, and it had passed through the stargate half an hour ago. The next scheduled departure was not until early tomorrow morning, a freighter called *Forger*.

Nikki banged on the glass separating her from the driver. "Can't this heap of crap go any faster?" The flyer's driver gave a very Human shrug, although the flyer increased its speed.

Via her pinplant, Nikki sent a message to the captain of the *Forger* requesting they grant Nikki and the *Anat* travel aboard his vessel, the answer was a forgone conclusion. No ship's captain was likely to refuse a Peacemaker's request.

Forcing herself to relax, Nikki considered her next problem. If what the Cochkala had told her was correct, and Ulah and Pukil intended to join up with a Besquith merc company, the most likely place for them to do that was Karma. The whole planet was merc-controlled which meant every individual and its dog was armed to the teeth. If she was going to separate Ulah and Pukil from a bunch of shaggy-furred, fang-faced killers, she was going to need help. The question was from whom?

Chapter 5

The usual flip-flopping of her stomach indicated the transition from hyperspace back to normal space. Aboard the *Anat*, Nikki released the magnetic grapple that secured her to the freighter which had carried her small ship from Hano. A burst from the maneuvering thrusters pushed her away from the vast bulk of the million-ton freighter as the *Anat's* systems sprang into life at her pinplant command to the ship's computer. The main engine came to life, pushing her back into her seat as *Anat* powered away from the stargate and headed in-system.

During the 170-hour journey, Nikki'd had plenty of time to ponder her next move. If Ulah and Pukil did indeed intend to join up with a Besquith merc company, they only had two choices of destination. Karma's capital city of Bartertown or, and Nikki thought this option more likely, the massive, spinning orbital transfer station which hung like a miniature moon above Karma VI. The orbital transfer station was the de facto merc guild headquarters for this entire arm of the galaxy, and held numerous 'merc pits,' places where various merc companies bid for contracts. Nikki had heard endless stories from her father and his friends about one particular merc pit, Peepo's; if there was a lucrative contract to be had, it was advertised at Peepo's, and merc companies would be looking to recruit fresh meat there.

There was only one tiny, minuscule, infinitesimal problem with Nikki's plan. Only mercs and ex-mercs acting as brokers were welcome in Peepo's Pit. Shit...If I'm called out...I'll worry about it then.

* * *

The *Anat* looked tiny in comparison to the XenSha frigate it sat beside in the enormous hangar. Nikki gave the frigate an admiring look as she floated past, heading for the first glideway to take her to the gravity ring. Nikki lifted her legs as she entered it, allowing the air pressure to blow her along. The increasing gravity, as she neared the main gravity ring, forced Nikki to first break into a bouncy walk, then to a more normal one.

The closer she got to the main ring, the busier the corridor became. Most of the beings she saw belonged to one of the thirty-seven merc races; most were big, powerful creatures like the Jivool, with their retractable wrist claws or the ten-legged Tortantulas. These species' sheer size and physique meant they were virtually built for combat, whereas Humans were forced to rely on the Combat Assault System Personal, or CASPer for short, to level the playing field.

In her time as a Peacemaker, Nikki had come across a lot of mercs and knew how dangerous they could be; however, this was the first time she had been in such close confines with so many of them. She was reassured by the weight of her M1911, safely secured in its shoulder holster beneath her leather flying jacket, and the gentle bumping of the laser pistol's grip against her right thigh. The temptation to reach down and touch the grip was almost unbearable; only the nagging memory of a lesson on mercenary etiquette from her Peacemaker training restrained her. Mercs frequently interpreted the actions of other mercs as challenges, and these often led to duels. The resulting attention from a duel would ruin any chance Nikki had of moving around the station unnoticed.

A tingle from her pinplant let Nikki know she had reached her destination. She gave the door an incredulous look. The plain door looked no different than the 100 other doors she had passed. "Nothing gained by procrastination," Nikki said out loud, quoting her father. She took a step forward and entered the establishment.

A tidal wave of noise hit her and almost caused her to miss a step. The sounds of hundreds of voices in hundreds of languages washed over her. The floor space was jammed with tables surrounded by chairs, filled with more species than she could count. Nikki methodically moved her head from left to right; the slow glance allowing her aviators to identify each species by name and type. Arrayed above each table and along the walls were large Tri-V screens upon which scrolled numerous languages. Her glasses identified and instantaneously translated the text into standard English.

Nikki made her way to the large central bar, managing to avoid the robotic serving machines as they maneuvered back and forth from bar to table. It took but a moment or two to locate a seat that was suitable for a Human at the bar. She had barely sat down, when a distinctly alien voice carried over the general hubbub.

"I believe you may have wandered into the wrong establishment; Peepo's Pit is not a tourist destination."

Nikki turned her head and was confronted by her own reflection in the dark goggles worn by a female Veetanho. The Veetanho stood as tall as Nikki but had far shorter arms and an elongated body that ended in equally short legs. Nikki had come across Veetanho before in her travels. They were tactical masters and controlled the mercenary guild. In an odd twist of evolution, they were usually albinos. Sensitive to normal light, they usually preferred to protect their eyes behind dark goggles.

"Oh, I think I'm in the right place. Am I correct in assuming you are Madam Peepo? Proprietor of this fine establishment?"

If Nikki's knowledge of the Veetanho's name came as a surprise to Peepo, she showed no reaction. "I have that honor...and may I know your name in return?"

Nikki paused for a moment. If she revealed her identity as a Peacemaker to Peepo then, even with the best intentions, that information could reach the wrong ears. Information was a prized commodity, prized as highly as a lucrative contract among mercs. On the other hand, if anyone knew of a Besquith merc company open to new hires and why, it was Peepo. The choice was taken out of her hands, though, as a loud Scottish accent reverberated across the bar.

"Och, there you are lass. I thought we'd lost you there. And it being yooor round tooo, ya wee scallywag."

Nikki's head snapped around and her eyes came level with the barrel chest of a man-mountain. Her eyes followed the seal of his tan uniform upwards, to the high collar, adorned with twin silver bars and a red scorpion emblem, to a neck, as thick as a tree stump, upon which sat a head the size of a pumpkin, and settled on the huge, toothy smile plastered across its face. Nikki's arms moved a couple of inches involuntarily, as if to hug the newcomer, before she remembered where she was.

"Ahem... Captain Buchanan there you are..." Nikki managed to get out through gritted teeth.

"You know this female, Captain Buchanan?" Peepo asked pointedly.

"Know her?" Buchanan laughed loudly as he slapped Nikki's back so hard she thought her spine would come out her chest. "Know her? I practically raised her." Buchanan placed a meaty hand on Nikki's shoulder spinning her chair so she fully faced Peepo. "May I introduce Ms. Nikki Sinclair? She is the daughter of Colonel

Alastair Sinclair, commander of Sinclair's Scorpions." Buchanan leaned in towards Peepo and stage-whispered conspiratorially, "Be nice, Peepo, she's my boss's daughter, and I could get in trouble if he finds out I brought her into a merc pit."

Peepo let out a small chuckle of her own before replying in the same conspiratorial tone. "Your secret is safe with me, Captain Buchanan."

"Yerr a damn fine woman, Peepo. Come lass, we're sitting over here." Buchanan locked a hand firmly around Nikki's elbow, practically lifting her from her seat, and he guided her through the thronging crowd which parted before him as if the large Scotsman was the bow of a ship.

"Not a word till we get to the table, lass. You never know who is listening here," Buchanan said out of the side of his mouth. Nikki obeyed his instructions as he led her to a secluded corner table about as far from the bar as possible. Already at the table were two men in the same tan Sinclair's Scorpions uniform as Buchanan. On seeing who was with Buchanan, both men sprang to their feet.

"Sit down, ya eejits," ordered Buchanan. As they regained their seats, Buchanan dealt with the introductions. "That useless lump on the left is Corporal Jonny Vega..." Vega nodded a curt welcome to Nikki. "And this is First Sergeant Ethan Croll. Your father brought him on board after we lost Anders during the Olas Three contract." Croll's cool blue eyes appraised Nikki as though she were a tactical problem. Nikki removed her aviators and held his gaze. Neither blinked or averted their eyes until Buchanan intervened.

"Enough of the mind games, the pair of yees, for the love of God. Y'd think yees were a couple of bairns." A serving robot rolled up to the table and Vega ordered drinks for the four of them. As the robot headed for the bar, Buchanan hunched his shoulders, lowering his head to the height of the other three. All trace of his thick Scottish accent evaporated. Over the years, Buchanan had learned that acting and speaking like a thick highlander led many an unwary opponent to underestimate the cold, calculating brain hidden behind his jovial exterior. Usually to their undoing.

"What the hell are you doing in a place like Peepo's, Nikki? Are you trying to get your pretty little head blown off your shoulders?"

"I'm working. What about you?"

Buchanan's cheeks flushed red. "Now, don't you be the smartarse with me, young lady. You'll never be too old or too big for me to put over my knee and thrash you. So, answer the bloody question!"

The return of the robot with their drinks gave Nikki a pause in which to consider her options. Buchanan was right, coming to Peepo's had not been her best move. Mercs recognized mercs and she was not a merc. But, what other option had she had? She needed to locate Ulah and Pukil before they disappeared among the ranks of a Besquith merc company.

With a resigned sigh, she filled in the three Sinclair's Scorpions troopers, sparing no detail of the Besquiths' crimes or her hunt. After fifteen minutes of talking, her story was finished. The four drinks on the table remained untouched. Vega pushed himself back from the table and reached for his drink.

"Mother fu..."

Buchanan cut him off. "Language, Vega! There are ladies present."

"My apologies, Miss Sinclair..." mumbled Vega.

"Call me Nikki," Nikki said, gracing the corporal with a blinding smile which Buchanan did not fail to see.

"It's Miss Sinclair to you, Corporal Vega. Understood?" Buchanan's rumble was accompanied by a warning finger aimed squarely at the man's chest. "OK, here's how we play it. Vega, you're with me. We'll do the rounds here. Somebody is bound to know what Besquith outfits are on the station, and when they're due to ship out on contracts." The toothy grin was back on the Scotsman's face. "Besides, old Peepo owes me a favor or two."

Nikki was dying to ask why the Veetanho would owe Buchanan a favor, but held her tongue. Instead, she decided to ask another question. "And what am I supposed to do while you two are doing my job for me?"

Buchanan's fat finger now zeroed in on her. "You, young lady, are going back to your ship and hunkering down until I tell you different. Croll, you're on escort duty."

Nikki launched from her seat like a missile, her face stopping mere inches from Buchanan's. "Now you listen to me, Captain Buchanan." Nikki emphasized the rank. "I'm the..." Nikki faltered as she caught sight of a few heads at the closest tables turn in her direction.

Buchanan took advantage of her enforced pause keeping his voice low enough that only those at his table could make out what he said. "You're what? Are you going to broadcast to the entire pit that you're a Peacemaker and blow your only chance of catching these vermin? Or, are you going to play the part of my boss' spoiled, little rich kid daughter who's spending daddy's money on a visit to see how his employees earn their pay?"

Nikki felt the urge to punch the man-mountain between the eyes but she couldn't fault his logic, damn him! Closing her eyes, she took a deep breath, letting it out slowly between thin lips, and resigned herself to her fate. "So be it," she said in her most petulant tone, spinning on her heel, head held high as she strutted towards the exit with Croll in her wake. From various tables came the sound of unsuppressed laughter in a hundred dialects.

Chapter 6

Leaving Peepo's, Nikki turned left and stalked up the corridor. Croll was taller, but he still had to pick up his pace to catch up with her. After about 100 yards, they came to a fork in the corridor; Nikki stopped without warning in the middle of the busy corridor, forcing Croll to swerve into a gaggle of elSha. The three-foot-tall reptilians scattered as Croll tried to avoid tripping over them.

"What the hell did you do that for?" Croll asked. When she didn't reply, he turned and saw Nikki standing stock-still. Like a bird of prey tracking its quarry, her head scanned slowly, then froze. Croll followed her line of sight until he spotted a group of four enormous aliens. Each was over six feet tall and had long, shaggy-furred arms ending in needle sharp claws—Besquith!

"The one on the right...that's Pukil," whispered Nikki. "Biometrics confirm it."

Croll stepped directly in front of Nikki and blocked her view. "Well, I strongly suggest you stop staring at him. We're no match for four of those damn werewolves. We need to find the captain and Vega and come up with a plan to..."

"You go fetch Buchanan and Vega." Nikki said in a rush. The group of Besquith were about to disappear out of sight around the curve of the corridor. "I'll follow Pukil, and we'll rendezvous back at the *Anat*. Docking Bay 4C." Slipping past Croll, Nikki hurried after Pukil before Croll had the chance to stop her. Croll broke into a jog and headed toward Peepo's.

* * *

Nikki gazed through the toughened glass of the observation gantry high above the steel reinforced deck of Docking Bay 4D. For a fleeting moment, the irony of her quarry sitting in the bay next door, blissfully unaware of her, brought a wry smile to her lips. A smile that faded as the sound of magnetic boots on steel announced the arrival of the three Sinclair's Scorpions' troopers. Buchanan skidded to a halt beside her and, from the angry frown creasing his forehead, he was not in the best of moods. Nikki spared a glance towards Croll. The First Sergeant shrugged his shoulders and rolled his eyes.

"Ah, I see you got my message, nice of you to join me," said Nikki in her best dulcet tone.

Buchanan took a deep breath, obviously prepared to berate Nikki; however, she turned her back on him and returned her focus to the docking bay. Behind her, Buchanan's half-opened mouth closed with an audible click as he realized the futility of his planned tongue-lashing. Taking a step forward he leaned heavily on the rail running below the glass and cast his eyes over the bay's contents. There was a single ship residing in the bay—a Besquith assault ship. Its four drop ships, two on each side of the ship's main body, were the focus of a flurry of activity as at least a dozen of the furry aliens fussed over and around them. A wide loading ramp at the rear of the assault ship was open and a steady stream of boxy missile launchers was being ferried aboard. If he was not mistaken, the oblong crates stacked nearby were the component parts of a Particle Accelerator Artillery Battery. The Besquith ship was loaded with some pretty serious hardware.

"Vega. Access the station's main frame. Find out what outfit these Besquith are with and get me a solid read on their numbers..."

Nikki held up a hand staying Vega's movement towards the gantry's computer terminal. "No need, Corporal. The ship belongs to a merc company called the 'Blood Drinkers.' As for numbers, not counting the ship's crew, they have 37 on the payroll here."

Croll let out a low whistle. "I suppose going down there and talking to them is out of the question. You never know, they may come peacefully." The comment generated a nervous laugh among the four Humans before they lapsed into a heavy silence. Eventually, Nikki spoke.

"Captain, what was it you were doing on the station?"

Buchanan had been busy trying to figure out a way to get into the bay and approach the Besquith ship without alerting them. He hadn't yet solved the problem, and Nikki's question rescued him.

"Eh? Oh, right. We were on our way back to Earth after fulfilling an apprehend contract with the Duplato out in the Jesc arm. A band of rogue Zuul had seen them as an easy touch so we gave them a bit of a bloody nose before handing them over to the local law. We got here, but then were held over by the station's administration. A camera spotted a couple of unidentified aliens coming off our ship and the administration said they were somehow linked with something that came off a Cartwright's Cavaliers' ship. Anyway, the search never found them, and we were finally cleared." He shrugged. "Alien politics, maybe."

The germ of an idea began to form in Nikki's mind. "Wait, so you were on a mission with all your normal gear?"

"Sure. It's all in secure storage until our ride arrives next week. Why?"

Buchanan did not like the mischievous glint that appeared in Nikki's eye. "Including your CASPers?"

"Three brand spanking new MK 8s," Vega acknowledged.

"Outstanding!" said Nikki, her delight evident.

Buchanan didn't like the direction of the conversation, so he decided to put on the brakes. "Woo-ah! Hold onto your horses there, Nikki. No way are they going to allow us to deploy CASPers within the boundaries of the station. If we try, we'll be the ones behind bars not the Besquith!"

"Oh, I don't think that's going to happen." Nikki said with a sly smile.

"And why the hell not?"

"As a Peacemaker, I can deputize anyone I choose to act as I need them to..."

Buchanan backed away, wagging a finger at her. "Oh, no you don't! Don't you pull that shit with me, Nikki Sinclair!"

The sly smile morphed into a wide, flashing smile. "Saddle up boys! Consider yourself deputized."

Vega had been watching the exchange between Nikki and Buchanan with growing amusement. He had never seen his captain back down from anyone or anything before, yet here he was, backing down from a five-foot-two-inch woman who was half his age and weighed about 119 pounds. A woman who had just deputized them and was about to order them to use CASPers on board an alien station against a bunch of bloodthirsty mercs. There was only one word to describe this, and Vega said it aloud. "Cool."

Chapter 7

20 minutes later, the crew of the XenSha frigate could hardly believe their eyes as three CASPers zipped past their cockpit windows to land in perfect triangular formation adjacent to the sealed bulkhead that separated Docking Bay 4C from 4D.

"Well, we're here. Where is our intrepid leader?" growled Buchanan over the radio link, obviously still smarting from being railroaded.

"Check your twelve o'clock high, sir," answered Vega.

Buchanan shifted his Tri-V heads-up display and caught sight of a fast-moving object close to the bay's roof. The object, with a glowing blue tree symbol on the front breast plate and rear spinal armor, flipped in midair, activated its jump jets to brake, and executed a perfect landing, its magnetic boots locking the suit to the deck next to them.

"Nicely done, Nikki. I see you're keeping up your skills."

"You were the one who said skills are perishable commodities, which are lost if not constantly practiced."

Buchanan let out a grunt of agreement as he cast a critical, appraising eye over her CASPer. It looked like his own MK 8: an over-the-shoulder 20-millimeter anti-personnel/material cannon, an eight-millimeter gun-pod on the left arm, and a high-cyclic-rate laser on the right.

"I see the Peacemakers ensure you are well-equipped."

Inside her CASPer, Nikki shrugged her shoulders, a move mimicked perfectly by the armored suit encasing her. "You know how it is, Captain. A girl just never knows who she's likely to run into out here."

"So how do you want to do this?" Croll asked.

Through her pinplant Nikki tapped into Bay 4D's surveillance cameras and brought the image up on her display. She scanned the group of Besquith, and in a matter of seconds, the biometric scanners identified Ulah and Pukil; both were roughly in the middle of the group. Nikki pushed the images over to the other three Humans.

Vega was the first to give his opinion. "Looks like they all have sidearms and a couple have laser rifles."

"That's my take," agreed Croll.

Nikki knew these men were professionals, and it would be stupid not to utilize their knowledge. "Suggestions?"

Buchanan had kept his peace, letting Nikki take the lead, but he was grateful she was willing to listen to experience. "OK, here's how it's going to go. As soon as the bulkhead opens, Croll, you go high right. Vega, high left. You pair are overwatch. Kill anything that twitches. Understood?"

"Understood." Both men answered in unison.

"Nikki. You and I will go up the middle on the ground. I don't see any deployable laser shields on that fancy suit of yours, so stick close to me."

"Yes, boss."

Buchanan decided to let the sarcastic reply slide. "Doors, if you please, Nikki."

Nikki sent the correct command, and the heavy bulkhead doors split neatly down the middle and smoothly retracted into the side walls. The gap was barely large enough for a CASPer when Croll activated his jump jets and raced through the widening gap, with Vega hot on his heels. Buchanan counted slowly to three before following, time enough for them to reach their overwatch position and come to a hover in the low gravity. At his side, Nikki activated her external speakers, turned on her suit's recording system, and transmitted in Besquith to avoid any misunderstanding of her job and intentions, "Ulah and Pukil of the Besquith. Surrender yourselves in the name of the Peacemakers."

If the Besquith had not noticed the arrival of Croll and Vega, the booming voice of Nikki grabbed their attention. Lips curled back to reveal rows of snarling canine teeth, and ears went back flat against their skulls, instinctive reactions to a threat. Hands reached for laser pistols and rifles slipped from shoulders.

Still, Nikki tried to stop the inevitable. "Peacemaker! Stand down, and you will not be..." In the blink of an eye the first laser shot flashed from somewhere among the group. Buchanan activated his laser shield, leaning into it as the second shield also sprang into operation, interposing a barrier between the Besquith and them.

The heavy, ripping, tearing sound of chain guns filled the bay, the noise so loud that Nikki cut her external microphones. In the Tri-V of her heads-up display, she witnessed what she could only describe as wholesale slaughter as Croll and Vega used their jump jets to carry out an intricate dance of destruction. Fire a burst. Move. Fire a burst. Move. Fire a burst. Move.

When the firing ceased, the bay floor looked like the inside of an abattoir. Pieces of chewed and mangled Besquith were everywhere; identifying each of the Besquith would only be possible by individually sampling the pieces still big enough to be called remains.

Descending through the cloud of pale blue gun smoke like two avenging angels, Croll and Vega settled on the deck, the exhaust from their jump jets throwing up a mist of red blood. Nikki popped the top cover of her CASPer, and the rich stink of death and cordite permeated her nose and lungs. Beside her Buchanan followed suit. He ensured his radio link was deactivated before he spoke so Croll and Vega couldn't overhear him.

"You OK, Nikki?"

Nikki slowly nodded her head. "Yeah. Sure. The warrant states dead or alive. Looks like they chose the former, besides..." Nikki gave Buchanan a weak smile. "There's less paperwork this way."

Buchanan gave a deep, rumbling laugh. Yeah, she'll be fine; she's definitely her father's daughter.

Epilogue

"What are we supposed to do about all this?" the station administrator asked, his pointer claw gesturing at the bloody carnage.

"Not my job," Nikki replied. "As far as the ship and all the equipment goes, I've seized them for attacking a peacemaker. The equipment goes to Sinclair's Scorpions for their assistance in bringing the Besquith to justice. The ship will be going to the Peacemaker Guild."

She walked away, leaving the administrator sputtering. The case had gone to shit, but at least she'd gotten the bad guys and turned a profit for the guild. Nikki smiled as she took out her slate to see her next case. Ooh, that should be interesting.

# # # # #

Chris' Introduction to:

Hide and Seek

by Christopher Nuttall

Many readers will already be familiar with Christopher Nuttall's works, and it will only be the fastest of readers who are able to keep up with the master of prolific-ness. I asked him for a 7-10k story, and wasn't surprised when he had it ready for me by noon the next day. The man can write.

How much? He is currently in the double digits of stories in both his "Schooled in Magic" fantasy series as well his "The Empire's Corps" military scifi series, and he has a number of other series, as well. With over 50 published stories to his credit, I don't think a month goes by without something new from Chris, which is great for his readers because it's all outstanding. Chris has a number of bestsellers, and he is truly deserving of them. You can find out more about Chris at http://www.chrishanger.net.

For all of his ability to write, he is great guy who is very unassuming in person, and I am happy to call him a friend. Chris' contribution to the anthology takes a look at the clash of company vs. governmental rights in the Four Horsemen universe, especially as it affects two different planets, with a spy thrown in, to boot. Chris' story, like many others in this anthology, is going to leave you wanting more...

HIDE AND SEEK
by Christopher Nuttall

Paperwork, Security Officer Allen Jermaine considered, was the bane of his existence, closely followed by company bureaucrats who seemed to believe that nothing, not even a terminal threat to EPS *Capricorn* herself, was a suitable excuse for not filling in the goddamned forms in triplicate. It wasn't as if much had happened during the four-week trip from Bonjour to Talus that deserved to be logged. The upper-class passengers weren't the sort to cause serious trouble—and minor trouble would be quietly ignored, even if it was reported—while the lower-class passengers knew better than to start anything. Indeed, it had been a reasonably peaceful cruise for Allen and his staff.

But that wouldn't mean anything to the bureaucrats.

He rubbed his forehead in frustration as he looked down at the slate. A list of incident reports, a demand for statements from witnesses and liability assessments from people who hadn't been anywhere near an event that had never—officially—happened. But he knew better than to decline filling in the details. The bureaucrats would pass the word and Allen, along with his subordinates, would never get another post again.

"Bastards," he muttered.

The intercom bleeped. "Mr. Jermaine?"

Allen grimaced, despite himself. "Yes, Captain?"

"There's a shuttle *en route* from Talus, ETA twenty-one minutes," Captain Richardson said, flatly. "She's broadcasting a local government security ID. Her passenger insists you meet him at the airlock."

"Understood, Captain," Allen said.

His eyes narrowed as he glanced at the live feed from the bridge. There *was* a shuttle heading directly for *Capricorn*. That *was* a surprise. The giant liner was due to enter orbit in less than seven hours. She was currently decelerating, riding her fusion torch as she fell towards orbit. The local government agent—either intelligence or counter-intelligence, under the circumstances—could have boarded the liner then, without fuss. Coming out in a high-speed shuttle was a considerable expense, one that smacked of trouble. No wonder Captain Richardson, a man wedded to routine, was playing messenger boy. Allen had no doubt the captain was already trying to figure out a way to separate himself from the affair before it blew up in his face.

Or to claim credit for it, if it works out in the company's favor, Allen thought.

Allen rose in the half-gravity. "I'm on my way," he said, trying to keep his voice level. Cloak and dagger affairs never boded well, particularly given Talus's...*delicate*...relationship with the rest of humanity, let alone aliens. "I'll meet him at the airlock."

He scooped up his equipment belt and hurried out the hatch. It wouldn't take twenty-one minutes to reach the ventral airlock, but it *would* give him time to think. The company wouldn't thank him for doing something—anything—that would make ITC, Interstellar Travel and Communications, look bad, particularly if a despotic regime like Talus's First Minister was involved. The Earth government was already unhappy with how this, the largest of their colonies, was turning into a soup sandwich. But they wouldn't thank him, either, for starting a diplomatic incident that might get the company into hot water. He had no doubt that he, not Captain Richardson, would be the scapegoat if things went south.

Maybe you don't need to worry, he told himself. *This might just be a simple issue.*

Sure, his own thoughts mocked him. *And you're in line to be the master of the Merchant Guild.*

* * *

The super-rich, as Jeanne had discovered over the past few months, were uncomplicated souls. Most of them, the women as well as the men, were only interested in wiling away the long voyage by enjoying as much fine dining, dancing, and sex as they could stand, all three of which were easily obtained on *Capricorn.* It was amazing just how attractive an overweight and balding man became when he considered a thousand credits to be small change. The cynical side of her knew that she would have no trouble taking most of them for a ride and sucking them dry, if she felt like it. Trust fund babies had very little conception of the real world.

She made her slow way through the crowd, keeping a warm expression firmly fixed on her face as she looked for potential targets. Many were a bit ungainly in the light gravity. It was hard to imagine that these beautiful people—each one rich enough to afford the finest cosmetic surgery and nanotreatments—were people of influence, but Talus *was* opening its doors to outside investment. The prospect of opening whole new markets had attracted far too many potential investors, most of whom didn't have any real prospects back home. It made them easy to seduce, easy to influence...she'd need that, when her mission began. Contacts among the outside investors would come in handy.

Eyes followed her as she moved, lingering on her low-cut black dress and long legs. The light gravity gave her bust line considerable gravitas. She concealed her contempt behind her smile, knowing that it was better that most of them thought of her as nothing more than another courtesan. People who'd inherited their money rarely thought of other people as their equals, particularly if they had less than a million in their trust funds. The idea that she might be more than a particularly attractive young woman was foreign to them. They wouldn't notice her manipulations until it was far too late.

Her pinplants pinged. The computer and connections in her brain that allowed her to connect with computers and store information were nearly invisible, hidden under the hair behind her ear. She frowned, surprised. She'd hacked the starship's main computer when she'd first boarded, of course; she'd installed a handful of subroutines and backdoors just in case something went badly wrong.

She smiled at a potential mark as she checked the message. The subroutine that watched for approaching ships had notified her that a shuttle was approaching, broadcasting priority signals. Her blood ran cold as she realised the implications. Talus wouldn't have sent the shuttle unless they had a reason to intercept *Capricorn* outside of orbit. And that meant...

They want me, she thought. There wasn't anyone else on the ship, as far as she knew, who demanded such attention. Talus would want to remove her quietly, rather than risk spooking the investors or outside powers. And that meant her mission had been exposed before it had fairly begun. *Damn it!*

She forced herself to walk normally, a part of her mind watching through the computer network as the shuttle came into dock. Richard Ambrose, the youngest scion of a fantastically wealthy family, had been eying her with a hungry expression ever since she entered the ballroom. No one would think anything of it if she let him take her back to his cabin. And once they were alone...

Richard smiled at her. She smiled back.

* * *

Allen was not surprised, somehow, that the captain had failed to materialise by the time the airlock started to hiss open. The captain *would* want to put everything in Allen's hands, wouldn't he? Allen made a mental note of it for later consideration—perhaps he could quietly ensure the right people knew the captain had neglected his duty—and then stood to attention as the security officer stepped onto the ship. It probably wouldn't hurt to pretend he was showing respect.

"I have a warrant from my government to search this ship for a particular passenger," the officer said. He didn't offer his name, let alone salute the company's flag. "If this person is found, I have authority to place her under arrest and remove her to Talus..."

He held out his UAAC, Universal Account Access Card, commonly referred to as a Yack, and a computer chip with red and yellow markings that said, "OFFICIAL." Allen took both and swiped the Yack past his slate. IVAN DRAYAN, Talus Internal Security Agency. The man's photograph was surprisingly accurate—he looked like a thug. His snappy uniform couldn't disguise the brutality under the surface. Allen suspected he wasn't really trying. Talus's Internal Security Agency had a reputation to uphold.

Allen inserted the chip and read the contents on his slate carefully, cursing the captain under his breath. If they allowed the ISA to take someone, with or without a warrant, it would make the company look bad; if they refused to allow the ISA to arrest someone, it would damage the line's relations and throw the company's long-term position into doubt. There would be a diplomatic incident, one that would probably cast a long shadow over the company—and his career. Galactic Union law wasn't too specific on these matters, or many other for that point. But if you were in someone's star system, you were subject to local rules.

"We can take her into custody," he said. Jeanne D'Arcy didn't ring a bell. His pinplants informed him that she was a second-class passenger, a tourist who was probably hoping to snag a rich husband. A glorified whore, in other words. "However, we cannot hand her over to you."

"I have a warrant," Ivan insisted. "It was issued..."

"It doesn't say *why* you want her," Allen said. On Talus, he had no doubt that an ISA warrant was reason enough to do anything. That wouldn't fly with the media on Earth. "I need a reason."

He skimmed the passenger files as quickly as he could, stalling for time. Jeanne D'Arcy hadn't tripped any red flags, according to his staff. She'd never travelled off-world before. Nor was she related to any of the investors... There was no logical reason for Talus to arrest her in the first place. And even if they did have a reason, why not grab her when she went down to the planet?

"My government demands your cooperation," Ivan said, flatly.

"And *my* government will be very unhappy if we arrest an Earth citizen and give her to you without following proper procedure," Allen countered. "I can take her into custody and hold her until the diplomats sort it out, but I cannot simply surrender her to you."

"I can have your ship boarded," Ivan threatened.

"Of course, you can," Allen countered. He'd been in space too long to be threatened so easily. "And *your* government will not be pleased when ITC hires a merc company to come and take it back."

Ivan looked displeased. Allen didn't really blame him. His superiors would be furious if he failed to bring Jeanne D'Arcy to them, but—on the other hand—they would be equally furious if he caused a major incident and mercs got involved. Or worse, a Peacemaker. Talus was trying to turn over a new leaf and attract investment from Earth. Their prospects would crash and burn if wealthy investors saw stormtroopers smashing through an unarmed passenger ship. Ivan's superiors would turn him into the scapegoat and throw him to the wolves.

"Take her into custody," he said, finally. "As long as you have her in the brig, I'm sure my government will be pleased."

"Very good," Allen said. He turned. "If you'll come with me..."

He frowned as he used his pinplants to scan the rest of Jeanne D'Arcy's file. It was odd. The more he looked at it, the more he wondered if it was fake. Jeanne D'Arcy's life seemed to be nothing more than a basic framework, a list of names and dates rather than anything more detailed. Jeanne D'Arcy's file was unusually sparse.

It proves nothing, he told himself. *And her ID passed muster...*

He froze, just for a second. Forging a Yack was incredibly difficult. The card was Union technology that was largely considered unbreakable. He knew better than that. It was possible, he knew from experience, but staggeringly expensive. But if the Yack had been issued by the government...was Jeanne D'Arcy a secret agent? No secret agent had 'secret agent' written in their file. And if *that* was the case, where did his duty lie?

Ivan cleared his throat loudly. "Yes?"

"I was just arranging for my staff to find and hold your person of interest," Allen lied. Talus wasn't *that* advanced, not compared to the rest of the Union or Earth. It was unlikely Ivan had pinplants of his own, let alone fully knew what they could do. "Hopefully, we can pick her out of the crowd without trouble."

"Good," Ivan said. "I'm glad you've decided to cooperate."

* * *

"Get your panties down," Richard ordered, as they stumbled into his cabin. "And bend over the chair."

Jeanne barely heard him. His fumblings were clumsy—it was clear he wasn't used to giving his partners pleasure—but she found it hard to care. Two more notifications from her hacked subroutines had just gone off in quick succession, both on her passenger file. And that meant the newcomer had asked for her by name. Her cover was thoroughly blown.

She briefly considered surrender. If she went to the captain with her other Yack, the one identifying her superiors, the captain would probably decline to hand her over. It would be embarrassing—Talus would make a diplomatic stink and her career would probably be over—but she'd survive. And yet, the ship was far too close to Talus for safety. The local government might be sane enough to realise that boarding the ship in space would be bad politics...or it might not.

Richard's fingers slipped into her panties, tugging them down. "Bend over," he ordered. "I want to..."

Jeanne hit him. Richard staggered in the low gravity, then collapsed slowly to the deck. Jeanne was tempted to kick him a few times—she was pretty sure he'd been unpleasant to the other girls he'd bedded—but she didn't have time. Instead, she used her pinplants to hack the internal security network as she tried to think of a plan. Getting down to the planet, preferably without a small army on her tail, was the only way to continue the mission. There was no way she could hide on the ship indefinitely.

They'll think we're in the ballroom, enjoying a last dance before orbit and freefall, she thought, as she inserted false readings into the network. *That should keep them guessing for a while.*

She opened the hatch into the bedroom and glanced inside. It was incredibly luxurious and completely empty. Jeanne wasn't surprised. Richard would have servants, of course, but he wouldn't let them bed down with him. Not that the servants probably considered that a bad thing...she smiled at the thought, then searched the bags. There were no weapons, unsurprisingly, but enough clothes to outfit a dozen or so people. She tore off her dress, swapped it for a suit that was surprisingly muted and checked her appearance in the mirror. Richard wasn't an overly large man. The image wasn't perfect, but it would have to do.

They know they're looking for a woman, she thought, as she bound up her hair and donned a hat. There was no time to cut it short. She grabbed a scarf and wrapped it around her breasts, making them unlikely to flop around in the low gravity. *And if they think they see a man, they won't look any closer.*

Her feelings darkened as her pinplants reported more warnings floating through the starship's network. The security officers were already being ordered to arrest her. And that meant...

She walked back into the main room, kicked Richard in the head to make sure he stayed unconscious, then opened the door. The corridor outside was empty.

Hurry, she told herself. *You need to find a way off this ship.*

* * *

"She's not here, sir."

Allen blinked. "What do you mean, she's not here?"

"I mean we searched the entire ballroom," Officer Combs said. "She's not here."

Allen felt a trickle of ice running down his spine. The internal security network monitored the location of everyone on the ship, from the captain himself to the lowliest fourth-class steerage passenger. No one should have been able to evade it. His officers shouldn't have had any trouble locating their target using the signal from her Yack, then quietly ushering her out of the ballroom...

"Right," he said. He had faith in his officers. They might be corporate security rather than ex-merc, but they knew their jobs. "Ask the staff if they saw her leave."

Ivan looked up. "Trouble?"

"Yeah," Allen said.

He forced himself to think. *Capricorn* was 800 feet from bow to stern. Even assuming their target had remained within the passenger section—something he knew he didn't dare assume—they still had a vast area to search in less than two hours. Once *Capricorn* arrived at Talus, their room for manoeuvre would grow considerably more limited as the passengers clamoured to disembark, and gravity ceased. A couple hundred civilians in freefall was bad enough, without a manhunt!

"She's a very dangerous woman," Ivan said. "You have to be careful."

"It's starting to look that way," Allen agreed. He checked the records, then shrugged. "We'll inspect her cabin."

"Carefully," Ivan said.

Allen's pinplants pinged—again—as they hurried down the corridor to second-class accommodation. "Sir, the bartender says she left with Richard Ambrose," Officer Combs said. "Apparently, Ambrose was all over her."

"Understood," Allen said. Richard Ambrose...that could be a problem. Ambrose *did* have a security file, one that would have ensured he spent the rest of the trip in the brig if his family hadn't been incredibly wealthy and well-connected. Allen pitied anyone unfortunate enough to draw Ambrose's interest. "Go to his cabin—if she's there, arrest her."

"Yes, sir."

Jeanne D'Arcy's cabin was identical to the 200 other second-class cabins; a small bedroom, a smaller washroom and very little else. Allen opened the door carefully and peered inside, keeping a wary eye out for unpleasant surprises. Jeanne D'Arcy shouldn't have had time to rig a booby trap, he thought, but he might be wrong. The room was certainly messy enough to conceal something nasty. Ideally, he would have sealed off the whole area before conducting a search...

"Clean," Ivan said.

Allen glanced at him. "How can you be sure?"

Ivan waved a hand. "She wouldn't be sloppy unless she knew there was nothing to hide."

Allen had to admit that Ivan had a point. Jeanne D'Arcy's cabin was definitely messy. A swift check of her drawers revealed nothing more interesting than a small collection of fancy underwear, a couple of very revealing dresses, and a small slate. Allen dropped the latter in an evidence bag—it might hold secure files, only accessible with the right codes—and took one final look at the cabin. There was nothing, nothing at all, to suggest that the occupant was anything more than a young woman taking an interstellar voyage for the first time.

We might have to put the ship on lockdown, he thought. *And that won't please the captain.*

* * *

Jeanne tensed as she saw the two security officers heading towards her, readying herself to fight. She didn't *think* they were ex-merc, judging by the way they held themselves, but that didn't mean they didn't have any training. Her training was probably superior, yet she knew better than to take that for granted. The guns at their belts likely only carried taser bullets, but would even the odds, if she gave the officers time to draw them.

They showed no reaction as they walked past her, not even the quick once-over that told her they'd noted her femininity. Either they were incredibly professional or they hadn't noticed the slight swell of her chest. She smiled to herself, then forced herself to walk faster as the officers vanished around a corner. She'd code-locked Richard's door, but it wouldn't take a trained officer long to override it. And then they'd start thinking about people they might have seen on the way.

I have to change clothes again, she thought. *And I need an excuse to be outside the passenger decks.*

She briefly considered her possible options, then changed course. If she was lucky, she might even reach her destination before they sent out a general alert...

* * *

"Richard Ambrose has been knocked out, sir," Officer Combs said. "It was a professional blow."

Allen swore. "Get a medic in there," he ordered. Ambrose might be a bastard, but the company could be sure of some pretty bad publicity if he died on the liner. "And have a look around; see if there's anything out of place."

"Yes, sir," Combs said. There was a long pause. "There's an indecent little black dress here—and a pair of thong panties. The dress matches the bartender's description."

"She changed clothes," Ivan said.

Allen nodded in agreement. Jeanne D'Arcy was still one step ahead of them. Worse, she might well have access to the main computer. He didn't *think* she could tamper with anything really important—the life support systems, engineering, or the helm control—but he knew he could be wrong. And there was no way he could simply deactivate the whole system. The captain would throw a fit.

"See if you can determine if anything is missing," he ordered. "I'll speak to the captain."

He linked to his commander through his pinplants. "Captain, I'd like permission to take the main computer network offline," he said. "All command and control functions need to be switched to manual."

"Impossible," the captain said. "We're due to arrive in orbit in ninety minutes."

"Jeanne D'Arcy has subverted at least part of the network," Allen said. "At the very least, we need to put the ship into lockdown."

There was a long pause. Allen could imagine, easily, what the captain was thinking. A lockdown would be inconvenient for the passengers, particularly the ones who'd been looking forward to watching from the observation lounge as the liner entered orbit. But if he *didn't* put the ship into lockdown, and their quarry escaped, it would look very bad. Leaving the main computer network up and running was bad enough.

"Very well," the captain said, finally. "Put the ship into lockdown. But the systems remain in normal function."

"Yes, sir," Allen said.

* * *

Jeanne cursed under her breath as she heard the lockdown announcement. It was a smart move, even though it would annoy the passengers. Anyone who was outside their cabin in ten minutes, but wasn't in uniform could be stunned first and interrogated later. It would take some time for the first-class passengers to be shoed back to their staterooms—second-class and below wouldn't be given any consideration at all—but after that, the crew would have plenty of time to search the ship.

She kept her expression blank as she prowled down the corridor, approaching one of the crew's sleeping compartments. *Capricorn* had one thing in common with a Human military ship, if nothing else; crew sleeping compartments were slotted in everywhere, as if they'd been afterthoughts when the designers were finalising the plans. The hatch was sealed, but a touch of her pinplants opened it. Inside, three crewwomen were dressing hastily.

"Who are...?"

Jeanne threw herself at the first crewwoman, slamming a fist into her throat. The woman gagged and fell to the deck, but Jeanne was already lunging at the second. She felt a flicker of sympathy as she shoved her victim into the bunk, cracking her head against the solid metal, then turned to the third. The third crewwoman was clearly a more experienced fighter—weaklings didn't last long on starship crews—but she was no match for Jeanne's training. Jeanne caught her by the throat and hoisted her up in the half gravity, shoving her against the bulkhead.

"Answer my questions," she snarled. "Are there any weapons on this deck?"

The woman shook her head, frantically. Jeanne believed her. *Capricorn* wasn't a military ship. The crew wouldn't go around armed, even if there was a prospect of being boarded. No, any real weapons would be locked in the ship's armory, next to the bridge. She banged the woman's head against the bulkhead, knocking her out, then scooped up a spare uniform, slate and ID badge. Posing as a junior officer was too risky—there were too few such officers on the ship for one of them to be unknown—but there were dozens of crewwomen. As soon as she was dressed, she hurried out of the cabin, checking the main computer as she moved. The shuttlebay was the logical destination...

But they'll know that too, she thought. *And that gives me a chance to go elsewhere.*

* * *

"I demand to speak to your superior," a woman snapped. "I paid good money and..."

Allen tuned her out. The woman *had* to be wealthy, if only because she was both ugly and strikingly fat. Only a person who didn't have to care about outside opinions *wouldn't* have taken advantage of cosmetic surgery. And the dress she wore was both gaudy and incredibly expensive. It looked like a slug had vomited on a Picasso. Allen found it hard to believe that *anyone* would want to wear it.

He raised his voice. "Return to your cabins," he called. "Anyone not in their cabins within the next five minutes will be arrested."

The woman gave him a nasty look, then stomped off. Ivan elbowed him. "You let her talk to you like that?"

"She's got enough clout to get us both fired," Allen said. He was starting to suspect that his career was at an end. There were 127 first-class passengers on *Capricorn*, all of whom had considerable influence. People had been clamouring to visit Talus for years. The rich and influential wouldn't miss this first mass chance. It would only take one of them complaining to get him in deep shit. "We have to be careful."

He sighed, inwardly, as he watched the casino emptying, patrons complaining about losing sure things as the dealers closed up shop. Allen rather doubted that *all* the gamblers had been on the verge of winning big, but there was no way to *prove* that wasn't true. The lawyers were going to have fun, afterwards.

"You Earthers are so undisciplined," Ivan said. "On Talus, people do as they are told."

"And your government invited these people here," Allen said, curtly. He glanced at his watch. 70 minutes to orbit. "Are you sure you want them to stay?"

Ivan scowled, and Allen smirked. He had guessed the secret police wouldn't be happy with the decision to open up to outsiders.

Allen tried to ignore him, thinking hard. Jeanne D'Arcy had committed at least one crime now, assaulting Richard Ambrose. It was clear she had no intention of surrendering and trusting the captain to keep her safe when Talus started upping the pressure. And that meant she had to get off the ship *before* the full-scale search began. Where would *he* go, if he wanted to escape?

We don't even know she left the passenger decks, he thought. *She might have...*

He scowled. Whoever—whatever—Jeanne D'Arcy actually was, it was clear she was no amateur. She'd want to go for the shuttles, but she'd also anticipate that *he'd* deduce her most logical course of action. And that meant...

"Put additional guards on the shuttles," he ordered. He already had security officers stationed at the exits to the passenger decks, making sure that no one could enter or leave without the right authorisation, but it was possible that their target had already left. "And then start to muster all non-essential crewmen."

"Aye, sir."

Ivan turned to glare at him. "My government will not be pleased if you do not find our target," he said. "She must not get down to the planet."

"So you said," Allen said. "Who is she, anyway?"

"It doesn't matter," Ivan said. *"Find her!"*

* * *

Jeanne forced herself to walk calmly and professionally as she strode towards the shuttlebay entrance. She'd never been anywhere near it before, but—unless she was very much mistaken—there would be at least one guard, probably two. If *she* was hunting someone, *she* would have made damn sure to block all the possible exits.

She smiled, inwardly, as the giant hatch came into view. Two men were standing there, both appearing as though they were trying to look watchful. Their superiors couldn't be very far away, then. Jeanne smiled at them as she approached, trying to look like just another crewwoman who'd been ordered to report to the shuttlebay. She hoped—prayed—that the officers didn't know the names and faces of everyone who might have a legitimate reason to walk past them.

"Halt," the officer ordered. "Keep your hands where I can see them."

"The shuttlebay has been sealed," his partner added. "Who are you?"

Jeanne held up her stolen ID card, bracing herself. The photograph *might* pass muster—the poor crewwoman shared the same sex, race, and hair color—but she'd be sunk the moment they tried to check her against the database. She'd tested the system, only to discover that someone had been setting up flags of their own. They might not have shut down the whole system—it was what *she* would have done—but they had taken care to limit how much damage she could do. There could be traps in the computer just waiting for her to meddle in the wrong places.

"I have orders to report to the shuttlebay," she said, trying to sound nervous. Men were always more relaxed when they felt they had the upper hand. "My supervisor..."

The leader's hand dropped to his sidearm. Fast, but not fast enough. Jeanne lurched the last two steps and struck him in the throat, then slammed a punch into the side of his head, sending him falling to the deck. She twisted around and thrust at his partner, only to have him jump backwards. Jeanne cursed and threw herself forward. The lighter gravity made these kinds of fights iffy, at best. If he sounded the alert or even zapped her with his stunner, she was dead. She'd just added a possible murder to her list of crimes.

There was no time to think about it. Her jump had been timed to meet him when he landed. The security officer abandoned all hope of drawing his stunner and lunged at her. She crashed into him hard enough to send them tumbling over; she yanked up her knee, catching him in the groin an instant before she hit the deck. The officer convulsed, gasping in pain; she shoved off him, then smacked him in the head. He slumped, out for the count. Considering how hard she'd nailed him in the balls, it was probably something of a relief.

Damn it, Jeanne thought. The first guard was alive, thankfully. She scooped up both guns. She popped the magazine and confirmed, taser rounds. She took both their magazine pouches, which easily fit on her belt. Then, holding one gun and attaching the other to her belt, she looked around to be sure no one had seen. *They'll know where I am now...*

She opened the hatch and peered into the shuttlebay. Three shuttles were clearly visible; all were of alien design and looked new. She knew they'd be fueled and ready this close to the planet. A shuttle could take her to the surface, but...

"Hey," someone shouted.

Jeanne turned. Three security officers were running towards her, weapons drawn. Jeanne switched the gun in her hand to burst, then opened fire. Two of them took hits, face-planting in the low gravity—the third, better trained or simply luckier, managed to get out of the way in time. She heard him calling for assistance and swore under her breath as she swapped mags. Even if she got him, his reinforcements would catch her sooner rather than later. And that meant...

She fired a handful of shots down the corridor, more to force him to keep his head down than anything else, then drew the other gun. Firing both weapons, alternating first one, then the other, she keyed the shuttlebay hatch to close—if she was lucky, they'd assume she was in the shuttlebay—and then hurried down the corridor. Hopefully, they'd be slow about coming after her.

And if they are faster than I thought, she told herself, *surrender is no longer an option.*

* * *

"She's in the shuttlebay," a voice snapped. "Two men down, she's armed!"

Rich or poor, no one boarded *Capricorn* without having their luggage put through a series of security sweeps. She had to have taken a gun from a crewman, which meant taser rounds only. No one could have spoofed the scanners without more tech than Jeanne D'Arcy had...

Unless she really is a government agent, his thoughts pointed out.

It didn't seem likely. *Capricorn* had carried diplomatic pouches before. Allen had *always* been told about them, even though he'd never been told what was actually *in* them. They might have been scanned and opened otherwise. No, there was no way that Jeanne D'Arcy had smuggled something through the security gates. And that meant she was unarmed, save for whatever she could improvise...

"Wait for reinforcements, then move in," he ordered. The shuttles had all been powered down and locked. Assuming Jeanne D'Arcy could crack their locks, it would still take her at least ten minutes to power up the shuttles and open the shuttlebay doors. "I'm on my way."

He jogged down the corridor, Ivan at his side. It didn't feel right. Jeanne D'Arcy hadn't made any real mistakes so far, save for whatever had tipped Talus off in the first place. She knew she was being chased, so why walk into a trap? The shuttlebay only had two entrances and both were sealed. Unless, of course, she wasn't in the shuttlebay...

His pinplants bleeped. "Sir, this is Montagu," a voice said. "Crewwoman Dixie just sent in an emergency call. Three of her bunkmates were attacked and knocked out."

Allen sucked in his breath. If Jeanne D'Arcy had attacked a trio of crewwomen, that meant... she was probably *dressed* as a crewwoman. It was a smart move. *Capricorn* had over 500 crewmen and at least a third of them were female. Someone who saw a lone crewwoman probably wouldn't think anything of it, while a passenger outside the passenger zone would probably draw attention. And that meant...

"Order all crew not on essential duties to return to their cabins," he said. Their target might be able to pose as a man. Reducing the number of potential suspects was only logical. "And get the three of them to the medics."

"Aye, sir."

They reached the shuttlebay just as the security officers opened the door and flooded inside, weapons at the ready. All three shuttles were there. The compartment looked to be empty of anyone; perhaps it *was* empty. And that meant...what?

"Search the compartment, carefully," Allen ordered. He was fairly sure it would be pointless, but he had to try. "And then deploy search teams to..."

Ivan caught his arm. "This is useless," he said. "I demand to bring my own personnel onto the ship."

"Ask the captain," Allen said. "Until then..."

He closed his eyes, recalling the deck plan. Logically, Jeanne D'Arcy couldn't have gone very far...especially if she thought they hadn't realised she was dressed as a crewman. And yet, there were no shortages of places to hide. Anything more drastic than sweeping the entire ship—like venting the hull—would be vetoed by the captain.

Once we dock, the locals will insist on searching the ship, he thought. *And that will be unfortunate.*

* * *

Jeanne checked her link to the computer network and swore, under her breath, when she saw the order for all non-essential personnel to return to their cabins. Someone had discovered the crewwomen, then. They had to have *some* reason to issue an order that would cause massive inconvenience over the next few hours, even if they caught her at once. This wasn't a merc ship. The disruption of their routines would probably drive them mad.

And they're blocking all my lines of escape, she thought.

Jeanne gritted her teeth. She was sure she could beat two or three guards in hand-to-hand combat—and she still had one of the guns with an extra mag—but they had her measure now. The guard posts would be in constant contact with their fellows, allowing them to tighten the noose. She could get into the tubes, she figured, but they'd anticipate that, too. There was no way she could avoid them indefinitely.

I need to think out of the box, she thought. *And that means being clever.*

Shaking her head, she turned and hurried towards the nearest airlock. There probably wouldn't be a guard, but if there was she could deal with him...

It wasn't ideal, she admitted freely. But options were growing more and more limited.

* * *

"The guard posts are reporting to me every five minutes," Allen said, as he organised the remainder of his team. "She's somewhere within the sealed zone—and she can't get out without crossing the line."

"Good," Ivan growled. "And when you catch her, you will give her to me."

Allen shrugged. "Ask the captain," he said. "He'll handle all such affairs."

* * *

Jeanne peeked around the corner—and cursed as she pulled her head back. A single guard...he looked alert, too alert. And she knew the others were closing in. They might not have seen her, but given time, they could probably use the internal sensors to track her down.

She pulled off her top, allowing her breasts to bounce freely, then started to walk down the corridor, hips flowing in a natural seductive rhythm. The guard stared, just for a second, then grabbed for his gun. Jeanne brought her own gun up from where she held it behind her back and put two taser rounds into his chest. Her feminine charms had bought her the edge. Men were so easily caught off guard by a C-cup.

The airlock hissed open an instant before the next set of guards arrived. Jeanne darted inside, closing and sealing the airlock behind her. They'd be careful about opening it as the system was designed to ensure only one set of hatches was open at once. Cutting through the hatch would risk depressurising the entire section. She had no idea if the security officers had spacesuits. Even if they did, cutting through the hatch wasn't worth the risk as the ship's passengers were all civilians.

She plucked a suit from the hanger, checked the life support system, and started to open the hatch.

* * *

"She's opening the exterior hatch," the bridge officer said. "She's launched herself into space."

Allen frowned. The spacesuit was rocketing into space, propelled by gas jets and what little atmosphere had been left in the airlock. It was a stupid move. *Capricorn* was a great deal closer to the planet now, but there was little hope of her finding safe harbour before she ran out of air or was caught by the locals. And yet, it was hard to see what *else* she'd done...

"Then I'll go after her," Ivan snapped. "Take me back to my shuttle."

"Very well," Allen said. If nothing else, he would be glad to be rid of Ivan. The man was a thug, a thug and a bully. "Combs, escort him back to his shuttle."

"Aye, sir."

Allen watched them go, then turned to look back at the airlock. It was cycling open now, revealing an empty compartment. There was nowhere to hide. Nor were there any missing suits, save the one they'd seen flying off into space. Perhaps she *had* tried a desperate leap after all...

Or perhaps...

He stopped. He knew, suddenly, *precisely* what she'd done.

* * *

As she moved along the hull, Jeanne silently promised herself that she would thank the man who'd given her this assignment by killing him. Technically, she *could* survive in space for a brief period. She had let her eyes tear up and narrowed them to tiny slits. The water froze, making a narrow viewing port of frozen water which protected her eyes. She'd emptied her lungs of air, and clamped her mouth closed. One hand pulled her along the holds on the outside of the hull while the other held her nose closed.

As she moved, her pinplants kept up a running toll of how quickly she was expending the nanites in her subcutaneous booster. Fast was the answer. Fucking fast. Too fucking fast. She hurried more, climbing up the ship's exterior against gravity. With her terrible vision, she risked missing a handhold and dying the loneliest death ever. Or she'd be instantly incinerated by the hellfire of the *Capricorn's* fusion torch. So, she moved on and didn't think about permanent damage or the radiation she was soaking up.

She reached the airlock and burned more precious seconds with her slate before opening the hatch and diving inside. The hatch *had* to be operable from the outside—that was a basic safety requirement dating back hundreds of years—but normally it would have set off an alarm on the bridge. The outer door closed silently, and the lock screamed as air flooded in. Sweet, fresh, life-giving air!

Jeanne got to unsteady feet and stumbled to the door. She had almost no feeling in her limbs and she reached up and pealed the ice, and the contacts which had concealed her identity, away from her thankfully intact eyes. As she opened the inner hatch, she hoped she'd successfully prevented the alarm from sounding; right now, she was in no state for a fight. The booster—billions of nanites released into her bloodstream to repair damage from being exposed to direct vacuum—was 90% expended.

It didn't *sound* as though an alert had gone off, she noted as she accessed the computer once again. Indeed, it looked as though the locals believed she'd thrown herself into space to die. She smiled at the thought; they really had no idea! She hurried down to the nearest lifepod. A little reprogramming, and she'd be on her way to the surface before anyone realised what she'd done...

"Stop," a voice ordered. "Now."

She looked up and froze. A man was standing there, his gun aimed at her. He was *just* out of reach...she knew from his pose he understood *precisely* how dangerous she was. If she moved—and failed—she'd be stunned, time and time again. And that would be the end.

"You're some kind of secret agent," the man said. A security officer, then. Probably ex-merc. "You have nanite boosters, or you wouldn't have survived to climb up two decks. I guess you probably work for the Earth government."

"Yes," Jeanne said. There was no point in trying to deny it. The boosters were well beyond what anyone but a high-level operator could afford. Even mercs didn't use them. Her little stunt in space had probably burned half a million credits' worth of nanites. The way she felt, she wished she had another loaded booster. But the devices had their limits. "I *suggest* you let me go."

The man kept his weapon trained on her. "Why?"

Jeanne shrugged, suddenly feeling very tired. "My superiors believe Talus needs a new government," she said. "It doesn't do humanity any good the way it is. My job was to get the ball rolling. As for who betrayed me..." She shrugged. There *had* been a leak, a very high-level leak. They'd known precisely who they were looking for, and what ship she was arriving on. But there was nothing she could do about that now.

"One escape pod will never make it down to the surface without being tracked," the man pointed out.

"It will if dozens more are launched at the same time," Jeanne said. She met his eyes. "Let me go or stun me now. Time is not on our side."

The man eyed her for a long moment, then motioned to the lifepod. "Go."

Jeanne didn't hesitate. She climbed into the lifepod and closed the hatch. A moment later, the boosters fired...

* * *

"The lifepods are launching," Captain Richardson said over his pinplants. "All of them!"

Clever, Allen thought. He wondered, absently, if anyone would realise he'd spoken to Jeanne before she left. She'd done enough damage to the network to make it hard for anyone to say anything with certainty. *They won't dare shoot them down.*

"She must have left a booby trap in the system," he said, out loud. Ivan was wasting his time with the spacesuit, but there was no need to call him back too early. "I dare say we will have to check the entire network carefully."

The captain snorted. "Once we dock," he said. "We will go over the whole affair very carefully."

So you can find a way to cover your ass, Allen thought. *And explain your refusal to shut down the computer network. My recommendations are recorded in the computer.* He smiled. *I might just come out of this smelling of roses!*

He shrugged as he returned to his office. Had he done the right thing?

He had a feeling he'd never know.

* * *

Jeanne allowed herself a giggle as the lifepod fell through the atmosphere and landed in a field 50 miles from the nearest city. The other lifepods were targeted to land closer, much closer, to the city center...if she understood the locals properly, they'd be so interested in those pods, she might be able to slip into the city before she was caught. It would give her time to hide before they found the final lifepod.

She clambered out of the pod as soon as it landed, then hurried into the forest. She'd hide for a while, listening to the local transmissions and preparing for her insertion into the city proper. And then...

Her smile widened and took on a predatory edge. And then the *real* work could begin.

# # # # #

Chris' Introduction to:

Information Overload

by Charity Ayres

I first met Charity at an event at the Suffolk (VA) library. The library was a lot further off the beaten path than I thought it was going to be, and the number of people who came by that day could generously be labeled as "sparse." Since there weren't many people interested in the ten or so authors sitting around at tables in the lobby, we had plenty of time to walk around and meet each other, and I realized there was only one other serious author beside myself there—Charity Ayres.

Since then, I've watched as she continued to write and expand her following, while working as a high school teacher during the day. Anyone who knows teachers (my mom taught high school for over 40 years) knows they have more homework than the kids, so I find her struggle to work, write, and still be mom for her family (and dad, too, when her husband is deployed with the navy) to be incredibly admirable. She once told me her most note-worthy accomplishment was completing four novel-length works and still remaining sane. I might qualify the 'sane' with a 'mostly,' but that's just because of the way our relationship works. If you'd like to know more about her, you can find it at http://www.authorcharityayres.com.

In all seriousness, though, Charity is a hard-worker, and I'm happy to have her in this book. Her story expands the Four Horsemen universe by taking a look inside one of the other guilds, and the value of information in the future...

INFORMATION OVERLOAD
by Charity Ayres

"Are you ignoring my instructions, Major Stephens?"

The "again" was implied, even if it went unspoken as Commander Janna McCloud continued to type at the console. The grunted response came a few heartbeats later than she expected but was cut-off as though someone had slapped a hand down to stop the sound.

"No, Commander."

So much in those two words caught McCloud's attention. Her hands froze over the keyboard as she inspected the tired, droopy-eyed man to her right. His dirty-blond hair was sticking out at odd nap-matted angles. McCloud had woken him when the computer systems went offline.

McCloud swatted her braid away as it floated in front of her, more through misdirected anger than annoyance. Stephens yawned into the back of his hand as he gripped her seat and leaned over her to see the screen scroll through her typed commands. She wanted to raise her voice or bark a directive at the major but managed to restrain herself. Experience with the younger man had shown that neither would do anything to improve the tense dynamic.

Damn south colony recruits. The men that came from that quadrant were always so cocky, and the women tried too damn hard to find shortcuts through the ranks. Neither seemed to last long.

McCloud lifted her eyes to the roughly-welded patch several feet above her head in the control room. She traced the lines in her mind to keep from snapping at him, but the mantra never completely quieted her thoughts.

"I'm a bit confused as to why you're still here," she finally gritted out, her fingers once again flying across the keyboard.

"They didn't have any other recruits available for your crew," Stephens said as he raked his hands through his hair in what she assumed was an attempt to de-snarl it. "To be honest, I think some say this ship is cursed."

McCloud rolled her eyes. "That's not what I meant." Line after line continued to scroll across the screen. "What are you still doing in the cockpit?"

Stephens blinked slowly.

"Right. You need it spelled out. Get down to engineering and see what's taking the CHENG so long." Her quiet words came out without inflection. McCloud was proud of how calm and emotionless she sounded, despite the desire to let the words roar out of her. At least she knew Chief Engineer Diggs would tell her what the hell was going on without hesitation or attitude…beyond what was reasonable for him, anyway.

Stephens said nothing before launching himself away from her seat and floating across to the cubbies on the other side. He opened one of the four re-worked metal doors and pulled out a pair of gravity boots. A moment later, she heard the cymbal-clash of boots on the wire-grate floor as Stephens finally did as he was told. The sound was so loud, she half-imagined the young man was stomping away like an angry toddler. She grinned and wondered if a pacifier would solve her problems.

The continuing sound of gravity boot treads banging down to the next level was a symphony to her overwrought nerves. McCloud refocused on the screen in front of her and kept typing in different commands, hoping to fix the garbage of mismatched letters and symbols that rolled across the primitive green face. Voice commands had stopped working first, then they had begun displaying garbled text, and now they had an almost complete loss of sensors and communication links. Life support and basic shielding sputtered along on emergency power and were the only reasons she hadn't activated a full system hard reboot...but she couldn't wait much longer. If she did reboot, she ran the risk the system would not come back up before their oxygen ran out; there also wouldn't be any insulation from the cold of space. Not wanting either of these outcomes, she continued to try manual patch after manual patch, while hoping Diggs would be able to find a fixable equipment malfunction.

If thoughts could conjure a person, McCloud's thoughts just had; curses and grunts preceded the individual who carried her hopes for a quick resolution.

"Hell's fire, Cloud," Chief Engineer Diggs said. "I can't find a fracking thing wrong with this giant piece of shit they call a ship."

McCloud lifted her gaze from the rolling script on the screen to face the demon-bear of a man. Digg's hair stuck out in curly tufts of black and gray over a broad face with a flat nose. His beard looked as though he had been using it to clean the passageways. Blue eyes that ordinarily peered out from under bushy brows with mischief now held the cold morass of space ice. There was likely to be some equipment that had gotten a good kick; either that or the major she had sent, which would have been far more preferable.

"Well, it isn't like we can dock at a spaceport and get help," McCloud stated coolly. "We can't even dial in to ask right now."

They grumbled back and forth as they sorted their efforts; her voice was cold, and his snarling. Were it anyone else, their discussion would have become an all-out brawl.

"Did you find any shorts?" She knew he had checked even before the words left her mouth.

"Could only check physical links and circuits in the dungeon," he said as he shook his head. "None of the computers are responding to commands."

She tapped her fingers. The CHENG was the next best thing to having another systems tech onboard; if he said the backup systems in the engineering department weren't responding, he wasn't blowing smoke. Just the same, the Merc Guild was going to be more pissy than usual if they showed up late; she'd been told the information they carried was perishable.

"Okay. Stephens can..." she began. She realized that the major had not come up with Diggs. "Where's Stephens?"

"He veered off partway back, saying he was going to check some of the physical pathways aft." Diggs shrugged, but his blue eyes indicated he knew she wouldn't like the newbie messing with anything without her approval.

"Of course he did." Her words were a bare whisper of ice.

Diggs's white teeth shined through his whiskers like tiny pinpricks of light, and his eyes flickered again. McCloud knew Diggs's nose had been broken in a few fights, and she was sure it could take further damage. She barely managed to convince herself not to test the theory; the bastard enjoyed getting her temper up way too much.

"Find him and send him up, CHENG. Encourage him not to get lost along the way." Each word came out as though she were spelling them instead of speaking. "I need him in here to keep entering code to help the system reconnect," she added as she turned back to the screen. "I'll meet you in the dungeon, afterward. We can check the physical connections in the belly after that."

Diggs zipped through the circular access hatch in the floor and down the ladder like the space monkey he was.

Her fingers flew across the keyboard, sounding like surface weapons fire. One line of code after another pulsed on the tiny green screen. It was the only one not filled with garble and was only there as a back-up. The builders had never really imagined anyone having to use the ancient bit of technology; it was likely older than she and Diggs combined.

After what seemed like an endless amount of coding later, steps sounded behind McCloud.

"Stephens, keep typing so I can check the relays." She neither looked up nor paused to give the command.

"Yes, ma'am."

The assent was quiet and slow, but she didn't have time to address his sullen attitude. McCloud slid out from the station and hurried to meet Diggs. She grabbed her braided hair as it drifted out behind her, curled the strands around her fingers, and worked it into a knot looped to the back of her head. If she was going to crawl around in the ship's belly, she didn't need her hair getting tangled in gears or around lines. One of the first times she had gone in to do repairs, her hair had gotten caught and had shorted out several of the systems when she tried to jerk it free. Lesson learned.

She went aft, entered the belly of the ship, and started pulling out the gear she needed. With the systems offline, it would only be so long before they began to have serious issues besides their tardiness. It would likely start with life support, assuming no one showed up to take pot-shots at them; they were adrift and what little shielding they had operational wouldn't take much damage before it failed. If it weren't a death sentence to do so, McCloud would have shifted some power to amplify the homing beacon.

And of course, it had to happen just after the scheduled communications check.

She shook her head at the timing. With that sort of bad luck, most of the life support would be gone before anyone even wondered if there were a problem. She half-hoped that Diggs, who had been monitoring communications just before everything went down, had forgotten to check in. She knew it was unlikely but had never asked in the chaos.

"Diggs, I'm going to gear up and climb into the rigging," she called as she entered engineering, or 'the dungeon' as they called it. The vertical piping and crossing of different systems made it look like an oversized jail. The grid-like pattern even blocked most of the lighting, enhancing the feeling. She never understood how someone as massive as the CHENG could be comfortable in such a space. At least on the bridge, she could see the stars on a monitor if she so chose.

McCloud pulled on shock-proof coveralls and a tool belt. Despite being the commander, it wasn't unusual for her to take the job, because she was the only one small enough to fit through the insignificant spaces between some of the relays. For a crew this size, it wasn't unusual for her to do anything that needed doing.

Before Stephens had been assigned to *Black Relay*, it had been her, Diggs, and Lieutenant Garrous running information. Garrous had been built as much like a gorilla as Diggs was a bear. Thankfully, the man had been excellent in the control room and in monitoring the helm. The ship practically jumped to do whatever the man wanted without prompting. Unfortunately, he had been so good that someone had noticed, and Garrous had been promoted and trans-ferred to a cushy desk job where fewer people would try to kill him, not that she would call that job safe by any means. Since Garrous had left, they had run through a string of south colony recruits, but none of them had worked out.

"Diggs, I need you to monitor the lead and tighten the harness for me. Get your ass out here," she called, with more than a little annoyance in her tone. Her voice echoed within the cavernous space, and she paused and listened. No response came, nor did she hear the sound of his boot treads approaching.

Any other day, she would have assumed he was going to pull something, but even Diggs knew the situation was serious. She took off the tool belt that connected to the harness, clipped it around a handrail to keep it in place, and tied the coveralls around it. She wove in and out of the piping and relays, heading in the direction of the CHENG's 'office,' which was where the back-up systems were.

No movement or sound greeted her from the darkened space. The only light was from the monitors that continued to scroll gar-bled text. She shook her head. None of what was happening made sense. Were they docked, she would have assumed someone had hacked into them. But en route?

McCloud watched one of the monitors, looking for tell-tale cod-ing that showed someone had hacked the system. She was momen-tarily mesmerized by the text; it was hypnotic, and she couldn't help but look for patterns. Then the screens went black for a moment, and her brain staggered to a stop.

Nothing.

McCloud remembered an old space rat who had talked about having "gremlins" in the tech that caused it to go into this rampant state of disorder. It had been like a virus to the system, but less malevolent because it just happened on certain routes or going through magnetic fields. She knew they weren't far from a known mag field, but found it unlikely they would have stopped in the center of one. The shielding on the vessel would have kept the interference at bay in any event. It didn't seem possible, but she wasn't ready to rule anything out, especially when the alternative was sabotage.

"Diggs, this really isn't the time," McCloud whispered.

She called his name a few times, but knew it was pointless. She knew Diggs wouldn't abandon her. Her heart knocked against her sternum loudly enough to block any other noise.

It had to be that jackass newbie, Stephens. He was probably a plant from one of the other guilds that wanted the information they carried. At least Diggs would still be alive, wherever he was— whomever Stephens worked for wouldn't be able to get the information implanted in his brain if he weren't.

The Information Guild had been experimenting with Human information transport. Each member of every transport crew had a small chip implanted in his or her brain. The information nanites it held were wrapped in live-cell membranes that would prevent them from degrading in the cerebral fluid. The tech required a constant electrical charge, which the brain supplied. The information was uploaded anonymously at regular docking checks they were all required to have; like a checkup with lots of noise and sharp pain. It meant the information could be carried by any one of them.

McCloud turned around in the dark underbelly, the lack of light now ominous. The monitor that served as a repeater for the backup system flickered back to green and drew her attention. The face of the monitor showed a blinking cursor where the last code had been typed.

/end.

Shitshitshit.

There was no telling what had been added to the code before that final execute command. She knew she hadn't typed "/end" before handing the job to Stephens, and as the systems still seemed to be on emergency power, it must not have been to run the systems. No, someone had typed a command that, if it had been allowed to run, would likely have wiped the system and killed the crew.

Thankfully, Stephens likely didn't realize the system was only coded for her, instead of all the crewmembers, and it would take her DNA to wipe the logs. Only commanders had the ability to completely wipe a system, though any crewmember could activate a wipe that would, on the surface, clear both buffer and codes. The added precaution included an additional nanite in her brain that transmitted a secure code every few hours.

Her gravity boots made more noise than she would have liked, but she didn't want to take them off as they were the only thing keeping her upright in the lack of gravity. However, even with the lightest tread she could manage, her boots sounded like a machine's gears scraping together. A shiver ran up her spine; she would have to remove the boots if she wanted to be able to maneuver without announcing her every step.

She unlatched them, left them with the gear she had tied around the rail, and pushed off with as much speed as she could muster to get to the cockpit of the ship. The amplified effect of the noise of her movement made the trip seem longer. When she pulled herself through the airlock, the main control room was empty. The tiny green screen blinked at her as though surprised by her presence.

It was petty to be annoyed at the machinery for something so silly. McCloud shook it off and flew across the floor to the panel beneath it. It popped open from a quick tap on the metal cover. She knew it opened if you hit it in the right spot, but still, it seemed too easy.

Then, she saw why—cables hung out as though they were the dead tentacles of the now-dismantled circuit. The wire from the touch board to the system hung loose with mauled edges; although the other wire allowed inputs to go to the screen, the commands went no further.

She had to reconnect it.

McCloud shifted under the navigation station, hooked her legs around the seat, and leaned back against the cabinet. The flat panels pressed the sweat that had begun to crawl down her spine against her back. She tapped her head back against the cabinetry behind her in time with her thoughts. Where could she get the cabling needed?

McCloud froze. She had it—the circuits from the cockpit ran through the cabinets and flooring; she could use the cabling from the main control terminal to operate the back-up console.

She eyed the open hatch she had used moments earlier. It would be difficult to be quiet once she started taking apart panels and flooring. McCloud needed to find the other two crewmembers, but knew they were all living on borrowed time if she didn't get the system operational.

With a quick jerk of her chin and a snarl at nothing, McCloud crawled forward, braced herself, and shut the hatch. The old hinges screamed, and she wondered if anyone had ever closed the door before. The primary control center could be jettisoned as an escape module in a last-ditch effort for survival. It only had a limited oxygen supply—less now that the ship's airflow systems had been running at minimum capacity since the malfunction.

Fuck it. Since the sabotage.

Admitting it pissed her off. McCloud slid her feet beneath the anchoring clips and strained as she pushed the lever until it sealed. Sweat dripped off her and floated around her head like raindrops frozen in time. She shifted away from the door, shut the circular access hatch in the floor that led to the level below, and spun the locking wheel. Nothing short of a massive explosion was going to crack that seal. She'd be dead if that happened and doubted she'd be concerned with lack of air at that point.

McCloud crawled back under the interface and pulled a tiny blade out of the sensor board casing. Diggs had taken most of the tools from the tool kit into the dungeon when the ones there had worn out.

McCloud set about dismantling the cover on the primary console. Within the console, she found the wire she needed and popped the panels necessary to trace it. It took longer than she had hoped, but eventually, the cable led her to a large relay box.

She sighed a bit too much carbon dioxide in relief and reminded herself to take slow, even breaths. She disconnected the wire at the relay box and began taking the box apart. By the time she was done dismantling the relay so she could get to where the wire needed to be inserted, there were bits of wires, casings, and various paneling parts floating around her and wedged in the gridded flooring; she had removed everything she considered non-essential.

Rewiring the backup should be fairly easy now, though, as most of the panels were already open. McCloud reinserted the primary wire and ran it over to the backup system. Removing the severed link, she made the final connection and almost cried when the board lit up.

McCloud pulled herself up to the keyboard, punched in a command, and then sighed as the auxiliary systems finally kicked on and filtered air pumped through the primary ventilation system. She could feel it humming to life under her.

She wrapped the core system in insulation and paneling, then removed a high-voltage wire from the flooring with the help of the gloves in the kit. Removing the insulation from the wire, McCloud wound it around the outside of the cabinet, grinning at the image of Stephens grabbing it. That would serve him. It was an old-tech trap, but it would have to do.

She grabbed the small knife as her only weapon and steeled herself to open the hatch. She needed to find the treasonous bastard who had taken down her ship and crewmate. Before she could turn the wheel more than once, the system beeped, and she turned to see a number of alerts in angry red letting. They had unidentified vessels incoming.

Of course they did.

McCloud had to hope their full shields would be back up before the other ships arrived, but it took a while for the system to reload after a full drop. No matter the outcome, she still needed to take back her goddamn ship, and she wasn't going to wait any longer.

She spun open the lock on the circular access hatch, but it slammed into her before she could grab it, and her pitiful blade slipped through her fingers and floated up toward the ceiling.

McCloud bounced off the bulkhead, stunned, then found herself being pulled down the ladder with an arm wrapped around her chest, squeezing her lungs so no air was left. Reaching the next deck, a hand went over her mouth while the other arm continued to pin her arms to her side.

"Don't scream." Stephens' voice was a sharp hiss, and she tried to bite his hand or bash his face with her head, but he had her at an angle where she couldn't.

"You can't scream, because if you do, he'll find us." Stephens's voice was more a growl than words, but his words gave her pause. He took it as assent, but didn't uncover her mouth. Instead, he drew her into an open storage area, releasing her mouth to pull the door shut behind them. This one, of course, didn't make a sound on its well-oiled hinges.

Stephens pushed her across the room ahead of him and, with a shove, let her go. Lacking her gravity boots, she floated across the space until she hit the back wall and latched onto a pipe. He started to turn away but thought better of it.

"Commander, it isn't what you're thinking," Stephens said as he raised a hand. Though his hand was palm out, she caught a glimpse of bloody knuckles. "The CHENG has information he's planning to sell to a mercenary group or one of the other guilds. He jumped me when I went to check the systems."

"Why the hell should I believe you?" she hissed. "I've known Diggs for years." She didn't buy his story. If she could stay calm, maybe she could get him talking. If he dropped his guard, she would cold-cock his arrogant ass, assuming she could find something with which to do so. When she struck, she'd make sure he didn't get up anytime soon.

"Look," Stephens said, ducking his head to the side to peek into the corridor, "I know you hate me for some reason. Maybe it's that mercenary man-hater bullshit the guilds train women in, I don't know or care. Just don't screw us over by letting that monster kill us both."

"You seem to think I'm an idiot and betrayer. Diggs has been the best CHENG I could have hoped for, not to mention the reason I'm alive today. He's saved me from scavengers, attacks, and my own stupidity more times than you can count. You, on the other hand—you're just another damned southern recruit foisted on us by the guild. Not one working brain between the lot of you hicks. I'd be better off with a Selroth; at least it would be cleaner. Gods know I'm sick of scraping you bastards off my ship!" She hissed the words at him. So much for her plan to stay calm.

"Scraping us off? What the hell is that supposed to mean? I'm busy trying to keep us both alive."

"Then look to yourself because it always seems to be asshats like you that come here to cause problems and die. I don't need to weld another hole closed or send another casualty report because you can't secure your damn tether. I think they must teach you all to have death wishes."

She spared a thought for the last two crewmen before Stephens. Roberts had drifted off into space trying to repair some loose shielding. Mirra had been the idiot who had tried to kill herself in the command center and shot a hole in the cockpit's ceiling. Southern idiots, both of them.

"Are you telling me the last couple of recruits died, and you didn't find it odd?"

McCloud stared at him. Her upper lip lifted into a curl, and her eyes narrowed.

"Not after the first one, Jim Macky, tried to kill me. His dumb ass vented the bridge, and he ejected with our one life pod. Diggs shot it down, and we never got a new one."

"Wow," Stephens sighed. "Either you don't see the connection or you're just too stubborn to. Either way, it doesn't matter; I just need to keep you alive and get the information to port."

Not for the first time, she bemoaned the policy of not allowing weaponry inside the ship. It would have been nice to blast a hole through the pity that seemed to envelop Stephens' face.

It was common knowledge that laser weapons weren't allowed, not just because of the suicidal recruit, but to prevent mutinies. It was pointless to worry about it, though—mutinies were uncommon because of the strict screening process for recruits and the secretive way their cargo was transferred. The information *couldn't* be hijacked.

"Commander, I am a highly-trained agent put on this ship specifically for this mission. The CHENG has been seen associating with outliers and has made a deal with them. I'm here to stop him."

"Do you have any proof? You're asking me to trust your word, and I don't know you, Newbie. I know Diggs."

McCloud fought her hammering heart and tried to slow her breathing. Her anger stiffened her spine until it could have withstood a missile strike without bending. She looked at Stephens and estimated the time it would take her to cross the room and slam his head into the bulkhead.

A sound in the passageway drew Stephens's attention, and McCloud grabbed a multi-tool from the holster on the bulkhead. It didn't carry a large charge, but it might be enough to knock Stephens out. It fit perfectly inside her hand. Before she could maneuver, though, the door swung open and, with a clash of metal and a bestial roar, Diggs raged his way in and dove at Stephens.

The men hit the wall in a mass of snarls and flailing limbs. Diggs's meaty fists grabbed the younger man and wrapped a huge arm around his neck like some of the snakes she had seen in the wilder areas of Earth. Bone snapped, and McCloud watched Stephens flail until the smaller man passed out. His boots held him in place once Diggs let go. He looked like he was sleeping standing up near the wall, but there was no further movement. Red dripped from a cut near his mouth and red droplets floated in the air around him.

"Cloud, you good?" Diggs panted as he took a step back from the unconscious major. He started rummaging in the gear locker and pulled out an old harness.

"Yeah," She fought the urge to yell at the big man and clap him on the shoulder. "Off taking a nap, were ya?"

Diggs grinned at her, and she saw bloody teeth and several purple bruises around his ears and eyes.

"You could say that," He rubbed his hand under his nose, and it came away bloody. "You couldn't say it was by choice, though. Little bastard snuck up on me and hit me with a grav-boot."

McCloud nodded. That would explain how Stephens was able to overcome him.

"Well, truss him up. We've got incoming," she indicated the unconscious major with her chin.

"I amped the distress beacon to max when the system dropped so it would scream as soon as we got things back up," Diggs said with a shrug. "Why don't you go up and make sure they can dock while I take care of the traitor? We can give them Stephens to take with 'em."

"Sounds like a plan," she said, nodding to Diggs, but what Stephens had said nagged at her as if she were missing something important.

Diggs nodded back and reached for some extension lines. As he moved, she saw his nails and fingers were blackened more than normal from the work he did below-decks. The skin on his neck was flushed as though sunburnt.

McCloud used the doorframe to propel herself from the room toward the cockpit. Sweat drifted off her despite the steady flow of air around her. She reached the ladder and launched herself into the cockpit like a rocket. Footsteps on the grating sounded behind her.

Her heart was racing but not from exertion. Diggs had been shocked by electricity. Badly. She recognized the blackened marks and flush.

The cockpit was more of a mess than she had left it. She swatted a bit of floating debris away and took stock: the panel was slightly out of place, but the wire was still attached and there were obvious scorch marks on the metal.

She pushed away from the access hatch and over toward the lockers. She needed gravity boots, but the lockers were empty. Her heart hammered in her ears, and she fought the panic that sought to unfocus her.

"Looks like you have a choice to make, Cloud."

Diggs had followed behind her a lot faster than she would have given him credit for. She turned to face him; his top half poked up through the access hatch, and he held the rim of the opening as he watched her.

"You let those ships send people onboard, or I knock you out and do it anyways," he threatened, scratching his beard with his charred fingers. "I would prefer if you let this go smoothly. You can say Stephens overcame you. No one would have a hard time believing it, and then we can go on as we always have."

As we always have, he said. McCloud heard the conversation with Stephens again in her head. She had bought every lie Diggs fed her. He told her about the attempted murder by venting. She saw Roberts float away; she had found the unlatched harness and had made assumptions based on the recruit's inexperience. Diggs had saved her; she hadn't lied about that to Stephens—he'd pulled her from a merchant ship that was taking her to sell to one of the less-savory outfits who liked to deal in Human flesh. Credits could buy anything in this galaxy, from all appearances…including a formerly-loyal Chief Engineer.

Maybe she *was* blind or stupid. Maybe she had always been.

McCloud looked at the stranger wearing the face of her friend and wondered how any of it was possible. It was so crazy, she expected to wake up at the console or sick in her rack; she didn't want to believe what her senses told her. She didn't reply; she just stood looking at him, her mouth agape, but no words came out.

"Well, almost the way we've always done it, anyway," Diggs added when her silence continued. "We'll have to train another recruit when the guild takes Stephens' head." Diggs jutted his chin in the general direction of where they had left Stephens. "I strung him up in case he comes to, though I think I broke his collarbone. Pain should keep him out for a good while."

"Why, Diggs?"

He sighed. She didn't know if it was her lack of acceptance or because he had planned to kill her all along, but his face changed into a sad look she had never seen before. There was less regret than she would have hoped for.

"During transfer a few trips back, I caught some of the information we've been passing, though they tried to hide it after it happened. They said I was just tired or imagining it, but I found out that what I was carrying was going to the highest bidder—the guild had double-crossed the buyer. The buyer also found out I had seen the information, and his guild found me. They offered me a choice—death or a new life working for them. I didn't have much of a choice."

"What you're saying isn't what we do," McCloud started, but Diggs was shaking his head. "No, Diggs. I don't know what you got caught up in, but we carry information this way to stop the random killing between guilds. You should have told our Information Guild liaison. It isn't about the credits, Diggs; our contracts are clear. We regulate the information, so people don't kill each other over it."

"All lies, Cloud," Diggs said, shaking his head. "They've been lying to us from the beginning."

Like you? She wondered. She bit back the words but only just. McCloud thought back to the meetings and the changes in security. She knew Diggs was wrong, but knew there was no way to prove it to him. Diggs might have been the one who got her into the guild for training, but she believed in what she was doing.

"I can't support you, Diggs. As much of an annoying ass as Stephens is, you're talking about handing him over to die so you can profit."

Diggs nodded at her and reached into his pocket. He had a knife that slid out of a sheath when he clicked it.

"Sorry, Cloud."

He didn't look sorry, though. He looked resolved as he started to climb over the rim and into the cockpit. The space appeared to have shrunk in the last thirty minutes.

Diggs got one leg above the rim before his body slammed to a stop. Diggs frowned, then he grabbed the rim and pushed down on it hard, thrusting himself all the way into the cockpit. McCloud saw copper wiring wrapped around his leg as he flew toward the ceiling, pulling Stephens in behind him.

McCloud had found a children's book once. Though she hadn't been able to read the story, there had been an anthropomorphic primate wandering around a city with a Human pet and a floating ball on a string. At that moment, it seemed as though she was reliving the story in a way she never would have imagined—Stephens was the primate and Diggs was the ball on a string.

Diggs grabbed hold of one of the exposed pipes on the ceiling and used it to brace himself so he could remove his gravity boots. McCloud wedged a foot into the open grating on the floor, grabbed the wire from Stephens, and pinched it onto the live wire running around the console. Light flashed, and a burning smell assailed her.

* * *

Janna McCloud found herself staring at a bubbled section of the cockpit, her mouth tasting as if she had tried to eat a space ration without removing it from the packaging. She floated just above the pilot's chair and main control panel.

"Shit that stinks," a voice said.

McCloud was pulled down by Stephens, who floated over to her. Diggs continued to sizzle on the other side of the cockpit, the blackened husk of what had once been a man. The skin flickered and sparked as the current burned through the remaining bodily fluids.

"Do you need a cold pack? You aren't going to faint again, are you?" Stephens inched over to McCloud, who fought the urge to shove him into the line that had ended her CHENG's life.

Stephens reached for her head, and she swatted his hand.

"I think you forget yourself, Major."

Cold slid through her body as she tried to process everything that had just happened. It wasn't easy to look away from the body. Stephens knocked the wire loose from the console with a wooden pole, making the grate and metalworks of the cockpit safe to touch. The smell was truly horrendous and reminded her of the aroma surrounding the black-market food vendors.

"It's Lieutenant Commander," Stephens grinned. "Might even be commander, after this."

"Bully for you. We still have incoming ships."

She stretched her abused muscles and shifted up to read the alerts on the screen as the communications speakers clicked on, and a ship identified itself with a military call sign and code. McCloud blinked a few times, but otherwise limited her surprise to a few perfunctory swear words under her breath.

"They've been tracking us since we left," Stephens said with a broad grin. "Even though they knew I could handle it."

McCloud frowned and looked back to where the young man floated. He had blood all over his face, bruising around the eyes, and a torn uniform. One of his shoulders was lop-sided, an ear was caked with dried blood, and he had a nasty red welt around his neck. She wondered if the blood on his ear marked the frying of any brains he had been in possession of.

"*Right.*"

He continued as if she hadn't spoken.

"You'll need to come with us, Commander McCloud, for a debriefing while they download the information from my nanite." He stood and dusted himself off.

"What information?" she asked arching an eyebrow at him.

"The stuff Diggs was looking for," Stephens said, grinning.

"How would they get that from you?"

"What do you mean? Are you telling me that it was in Diggs?" Stephens grimaced as he looked at the blackened husk.

"No."

"Well, like I was saying, then—"

"I have the information, and it won't be downloaded anywhere until I get my orders from command, Major Stephens." She entered her code to allow boarding.

"How the hell—"

"When I reset the system, the nanite surged and the system sent a signal through it," She dropped her eyes to the wire, thankful for the nearly endless power the fusion core gave. "Clear away the wiring and put the body in a capsule so they can extract his chips. I'll let you know when to come in for the debrief after I speak to the unit leader. I expect you to standby until I'm ready, is that clear?"

"Commander—"

"I don't think I stuttered. Hop to, *Major,*" McCloud looked down her nose at the younger man and turned back to the console to send a transmission report. The information would continue to flow, as the guild intended. Hopefully, next time they would send her someone who wasn't from the southern region. She wasn't sure she could take another one.

# # # # #

Mark's Introduction to:

Enough

by Chris Kennedy

I simply cannot say enough about the professionality and skill of Chris, both as a writer and a publisher. When he heard about my concept for "Cartwright's Cavaliers," he not only agreed to publish it, but suggested I had the makings of much, much more than just a single novel. And thus, I was both rescued from obscurity and catapulted onto the Amazon bestsellers list. Thanks to his help, ingenuity, and boundless patience with what I try to call writing, the Four Horsemen universe is a rich tapestry of tales which has already thrilled thousands of readers. Chris comes from a background in Naval Aviation, where he had a successful career before retiring to be a school principal, and then onto publishing, where he's already had multiple bestselling books, with many more to come.

His story in this anthology, "Enough," deals with what every military man dreads: a no-win scenario. It also touches on alien merc codes of honor and brings us back to humanity's first adversary in the Four Horsemen universe, the MinSha. Pay close attention, because if you are a fan of the Four Horsemen universe, you'll want to remember Walker. He's someone who doesn't go gentle into that good night.

Find out more about Chris at http://chriskennedypublishing.com/.

ENOUGH
by Chris Kennedy

Chapter 1

"Sorry to—," Colonel Roger Applewhite broke off, coughing, and Captain Dan Walker turned his head to keep from getting splattered by the blood the colonel was coughing up. When Applewhite continued, his voice was much weaker. "You're in...in charge," he gasped. "Get them home. Roughnecks...yours." His head rolled to the side, and the slate he'd been holding slipped from his fingers.

Walker looked up for someone to share the moment with, but the rest of the company had pulled back to give him some privacy while he talked with the colonel.

There was a moment of utter silence, then everything came crashing in on him. The crackle of fire from the dropship as it burned. The CASPers on the front line as they fired at their lowest rate, trying to conserve rounds. Even the radio intercept chatter they picked up from the MinSha as the enemy worked to surround his company.

He sighed as he surveyed what was left. Applewhite had once told him that if he was in the mercenary business long enough, he would eventually take a contract that went bad. Whether it was because the intel was off...or the enemy did something unpredictable...hell, maybe the gods just decided you had lived long enough. Who knows? At some point, you'd end up on the wrong side of a contract that went bad. As Captain Walker reached forward to close his colonel's eyes, he realized that he'd never really had one go bad on him before.

Until now.

As a captain, though, he'd been in the business long enough to know they were screwed. The enemy had shown up in force, with enough troops to bag their dropships and prevent any more from coming.

And now, this.

Colonel Applewhite's suit had died, and he'd only taken two steps outside his CASPer when he hit the damned mine. Even though it was a relic of a previous war, it was still capable of claiming both his legs, and it was way more than they could fix with their medkits alone...even if the damned MinSha hadn't been breathing down their necks.

Walker picked up the slate, his eyes focused somewhere beyond it. The bloody thumbprint was just a red smear in the center, and the text on it nothing more than a blur. "Congrats, sir," Sergeant First Class (SFC) David Wethington said, looking over his shoulder. "Looks like the colonel just left you the Roughnecks."

When Walker didn't say anything, the platoon sergeant pointed to the top of the screen. "Transfer of Ownership of a Mercenary Company," he added.

Walker still didn't react as he listened to Colonel Applewhite's voice inside his head, giving him advice about how to run his platoon...'Take care of your troops, and they'll take care of you'...and later how to be the best company commander he could...'Quality training builds confidence and cohesion in your soldiers. Make it as hard as you can, so when you get into a real conflict, it's nothing they haven't seen before.'

Wethington took the slate from the officer as he reminisced, tapped it several times, then put his thumb to it. "Now it's notarized," he said. "So, Colonel Walker, the company's yours. What are your orders?"

"Orders..." Walker asked, finally hearing him. "Wait...colonel?"

"Yes sir, Colonel Applewhite transferred ownership of the Roughnecks to you before he died. I saw it and witnessed the bequest. You're the boss now; you're the colonel. I need to know your orders, sir, because we're in a real world of shit."

A MAC fired, and several MinSha weapons fired in reply. The enemy was a lot closer than he remembered them being.

"Sorry, Top, I was kind of out of it," Walker finally said. "What's our situation?"

"Our situation? It's bad enough that I'd almost rather be with General Custer at Little Big Horn than here." He shrugged. "All they had to worry about was Indians killing and scalping them. They didn't have big-ass bugs with lasers and magnetic accelerator cannon chasing them."

"You do know all of Custer's men died, right, Top?"

"Yeah, I know," Wethington replied. "I'd still rather be there than here. If I'm gonna die, I'd rather do it on Earth. Preferably in bed."

"Well, how about if we don't die then? What would you say to that?"

"Sounds great, sir. So, how exactly do you propose we go about doing that?"

"Well, we're going to have to write off the contract, at least for now."

"I think it's pretty safe to say we'll have to write off the contract," Wethington said, sarcasm heavy in his voice, "especially since our company is down to less than a platoon, and there's a lot more of the bugs than there are of us."

The Roughnecks had been contracted to hold a mining facility in the midst of a civil war, but as they flew in on their dropships, they found the mine already invested by the rebel forces...and the MinSha *they* had hired to guard it from the Roughnecks. Two of their four dropships had been bagged on the initial salvo, and a third right after. The ramps had been down for the assault, and some of the CASPers had made it out, but not many.

Walker's dropship had almost made it clear...but the last missile got it. The pilot had held the craft steady long enough for the CASPers to jump out, but had crashed it at the edge of the jungle when he had attempted to put it down. Already on fire, the fuselage of the craft had tumbled several hundred yards before hitting a tree large enough to stop it. Along the way, it had left a trail of devastation as pieces had separated, making the recovery of anything of value problematic, at best.

Wethington used an open hand to indicate the wreckage of the dropship. "That was the last of our dropships; without it, we don't even have a means of getting off this crappy planet. What do you suggest?"

"Top, here's what we're going to do. First, we're going to get back into our suits so we can control this goat fuck, then we're going to salvage what we can quickly, including the fuel cells from the colonel's suit, and any others that are available, then we're going to walk through 100 miles of suck-ass jungle to get to Clifford, the capital city of our employers, so I can have a little talk with them. And when I say 'talk,' I mean I'm going to kick their asses for not warning us about the MinSha."

"Well, shit," Wethington muttered.

"What?"

"Sir, you just gave me a reason to live, because I surely do want to see that. Okay, let's make this happen." He turned and jogged off to where he'd left his CASPer. After a second, Walker sprinted toward his.

Chapter 2

"One, two, *three!*" The CASPer made a giant splash in the center of the river, and the other two CASPers turned and walked back to the bank.

"Well, shit," Private Chan said, "there goes my ride. Guess I'm walking from here."

"We'll all be walking soon," Wethington noted as he sharpened one of his kukris. "Even with all the fuel we siphoned from the rest, the two we're keeping won't last us the entire way to Clifford. The colonel wants to keep the two with missiles as long as we can, so that we can at least keep their air support away from us."

"I get that," Private Chan said, "but why are we throwing the CASPers in the river?"

"Because the colonel has this crazy idea that we'll be back, and he doesn't want the bugs to get our CASPers. If we can bring some fuel back, we'll be able to reactivate them."

"Works for me," Private Chan said.

Wethington walked over to Walker, who was inputting data into his slate. Walker nodded at the kukri as Wethington slid it into its scabbard; the senior enlisted had one on each hip. "If it comes to those," Walker said, "we're screwed."

"No doubt," Wethington replied; "still, I like to keep them handy in case I have a close encounter of the giant bug kind. They've got enough weight to cut through MinSha chitin." He motioned toward the CASPers. "We scavenged what we could of the fuel, sir. We've got enough to run the two we're keeping a while yet."

"Good, we'll want to get going as soon as we can; we opened up some separation on the MinSha, but they'll be faster than us now that most of us are on foot. I want one of the CASPers at the point and one in trail."

"Faster than us, sir?"

"Yeah, the damn bugs can fly, so obstacles like that river aren't obstacles for them. That's why I had you pitch the CASPers into the river; they'll probably fly right across and won't see them. That's also why we're going through the jungle, not around it. They'd be on our asses immediately if we were out in the open."

"Well, can we set some traps for them?" Wethington asked. "Maybe do something to slow them down?"

"Not right now—I'd like to cover as much ground as we can while it's still light. Besides, how do you set traps for a race that flies and can go right over them?"

"Tie lines across the trees and hope they run into them?" Wethington asked.

"Hope isn't an operational strategy, Top; besides, it would take too long to have the troopers climb trees and run the wires across. Hell, we don't even know what altitude they'll be flying at. As thick as this jungle is, maybe they will be walking. What I do know is, at this time, we can see where we're going, so let's make the most of it."

The platoon moved out, led by one of the CASPers, but it wasn't long before Walker lost comms with it.

"Hey, Top, do you have comms with the CASPer in the lead?"

"No sir, I don't," Wethington replied.

The platoon moved up warily, only to find Corporal Amos getting out of the CASPer, an annoyed look on his face.

"What happened?" Wethington asked.

"Damn thing just shut down on me, Top. I've seen it before in these Mark 7's; the darn fuel cells are just stupid on how picky they are. I got a fuel warning light, but before I could do anything about it, it shut down. We must have somehow polluted the hydrogen when we swapped the fuel, and it's gone and wrecked the fuel cell."

"What do you want to do, sir?" Wethington asked. "If the fuel cell is shot, we'll need a new fuel cell, and the only other ones are at the bottom of the last river we crossed."

"Yeah, and unfortunately we just contaminated half of the fuel we had," Walker added. "Damn it! Well, that one is down, and there's no recovering it. Leave it and continue. We'll just have to do this the old fashioned way."

"Scouts out!" Wethington shouted. "Everyone else, move out slow."

Walker shook his head as he walked past the non-functional CASPer, successfully fighting off the urge to kick its metal leg. He had needed two of them for his plan to work, so that plan was trashed. He'd have to come up with something new, and fast. He just didn't know what that was...yet.

Chapter 3

"I've got movement back here," Corporal Joseph Reynolds radioed. The trooper was driving their remaining CASPer, and was at the trail position of their formation.

"How much movement?" Walker asked.

"It's hard to get a good scan, because the damn bugs don't show up on thermal as well as people," Reynolds replied. *"Also, the damn jungle makes getting a good reading difficult, as do all of the damn creepy crawly jungle creatures moving around. That said, I have to imagine there's at least a company of MinSha in pursuit, if not more. The bad thing is, I think they're moving faster than we are, so they're catching up."*

Walker looked at Wethington. "What do you think? Is it worth trying to ambush them?"

"We could…and the CASPer would help balance the odds, but if we don't really squash them, we're going to be in some serious shit, especially since we don't have any sort of transport to get us out. Also, there's no telling what they have in reserve that they may hit us with if they can pin us down."

"Hey, Colonel, I've got some bad news," Reynolds called. *"I need to revise my estimate. There are at least two companies out here, and there's at least one flier, although I can't tell if it's a fighter or a transport. I can try to take it out, but it's a ways behind their line, and I'll probably expose myself to their fire if I do."*

"No, I don't want to lose you," Walker said. *"Catch back up with us."* Walker looked at Wethington. "What did we do to them?" he asked. "Does this seem normal to you?"

"You mean, what did we do to make them all come out from defending the mine to chase us through the jungle?"

"Yeah. If there's two companies chasing us, they're leaving the mine pretty open to attack, unless they really have a lot of troops here."

"I don't know," Wethington said. "Maybe they have a really nice combat bonus, or they get paid extra for every body they bring back."

"Have you ever heard of that?" Walker asked.

"A combat bonus? Yes, absolutely—"

"I know that," Walker interrupted. "Hell, we have…had…a combat bonus for this job. I was asking if you'd ever heard of a contract where you get paid a bonus for every enemy you kill."

"No sir," Wethington replied. "Never. Slaughter contracts are bad for business."

"Well, we've already had combat, so they would get the bonus. I don't understand why they're still chasing us. There's no business case for wiping us out, unless that's what their contract says, and I can't understand why the locals would write that in."

"Maybe they didn't. Maybe the MinSha did."

"That doesn't make any sense, though. Why risk trapping us and having us fight like cornered animals? They have to know that, even without our suits, we're still going to kill a bunch of them."

"So what do you want to do?"

"I don't know. I feel like if we knew why they were chasing us, maybe we could make a deal with them."

"Well, why don't you ask them?"

"Because any time they've seen one of our people, they've shot first and asked questions…never."

"Call them on the radio," Wethington suggested.

"I've tried. Either their radios aren't compatible with ours, or they don't want to talk to us."

"Well, aside from grabbing one of them and bringing it to us," Wethington said as the CASPer strode into camp, "I don't see how you're going to do that."

"Top, that's it!" Walker exclaimed. "You're a genius!"

"So I've been told," Wethington agreed. He paused and then asked, "Care to tell me what for, this time?"

Chapter 4

The CASPer's antenna rose slowly from the waters of the river, sampling the electromagnetic spectrum for any signs of activity. Finding none, the trooper cautiously emerged from the river and walked to the shore. The darkness didn't bother Corporal Reynolds inside the suit; he had a variety of low-light and thermal cameras to help him find his way in the dark.

He walked as slowly as possible, placing his feet where they would make the least noise. He knew there was no way he could be 'silent,' so he instead settled on 'as stealthy as possible.'

He saw the MinSha camp after about an hour of walking and was concentrating so hard on not making any nose that he nearly walked into it before he realized he had arrived. If the MinSha had been hard to track by day, they were even harder when bedded down for the night. Only the residual heat from the dropship, sitting in the middle of a small open area, gave it away.

He tweaked some of his filters and the camp came into focus. The majority of the MinSha were on the ground, presumably sleeping, or whatever they did at night, and their body temperatures had cooled to within a few degrees of the ambient temperature, making them hard to differentiate. Additionally, as he looked closer, he saw their outside chitin was transparent at the infrared wavelength he was using, so he could look through them and see their internal organs, with a backdrop of the ground beneath them.

He found himself staring at one of the MinSha, almost as if looking at a science experiment, and had to force himself to look away. It was gross, but at the same time, strangely fascinating.

Now that he knew what to look for, he was able to pick up the rest of the MinSha camp. Sentries were out on the opposite side of camp, facing west toward where the rest of the Humans would be, and there were a couple of roving patrols to the north and south. He showed the computer the signature of the MinSha and asked it to calculate the number of targets. 127. Not only were there two full companies that he could see fairly easily by the dropship, the computer also determined there was another company to the south.

He had been toying with attacking the camp, but with the numbers that far against him, he decided discretion was the better part of valor. He would instead focus on his mission…and maybe just cause a little mayhem along the way.

Reynolds surveyed the bugs where they were sleeping, looking for one that might be a leader among the group. Most of the MinSha had a tarp or other piece of material strung between the trees above them; he would have to watch that his sensors didn't get tangled in them as he rushed through the camp. He was looking for…there! Almost all the MinSha were sleeping in pairs, but there was one sleeping by itself. The good news was it was alone; the bad news was it was sleeping near the center of the camp.

Having made up his mind, the rest was easy, and he plotted it out so the suit's computer could assist him. As he made the final calculations, Reynolds realized it was time to go; one of the roving patrols was headed straight for him.

The trooper took three steps to get some momentum and jumped about 40 feet. One thousand pounds of steel and Human crashed down through one of the tarps, ripping it from the trees, and landed on a pair of sleeping MinSha. A massive titanium-alloy boot came down on each, and the MinSha bodies exploded outwards in all directions. Reynolds leaned forward and jumped again, the rocket motors in his jump jets flash-boiling the remains of the two aliens.

He landed again, and the remains of two more aliens painted the ground in blue Rorschach test patterns. His target now only 15 feet in front of him, he took three big strides and reached the alien as it was starting to rise. Scooping it up in his left arm, he removed two K bombs from his belt, armed them, and threw them toward the center of camp. The first laser bolt from one of the patrols snapped past him as he planted his left foot and pivoted, tapping his jump jets to fly into the air about 30 feet. As the dropship came into view, he locked three missiles onto it and fired.

Reynolds tapped his right jumpjet to break the spin, and then both of the jets together as he crashed down onto one of the sentries. The blade on his right arm extended, and Reynolds chopped the head off the other sentry. Taking three more steps, he jumped again, a major jump this time, using up nearly the remainder of his jump juice in the launch and subsequent landing.

The MinSha under his arm struggled to free itself and emitted a high-pitched keening as the trooper landed and began running away from the MinSha camp. With his free hand, he tapped it as gently as he could on the head. Reynolds didn't know whether he had killed the MinSha, or if it was just unconscious or pretending to be, but it stopped struggling, and that was all he cared about.

Chapter 5

A hand shook Walker from sleep. "I'm awake," he said.

It was Wethington. "Hi sir," he said. "It's almost dawn. I thought you'd like to know Reynolds made it back with one of the MinSha."

"Alive?"

"Mostly. He had to whack it on the head once to get it to settle down, and he cracked its carapace. We sprayed it with a medkit, and that sealed it back up again. It didn't look like it lost any blood or had any major exterior damage, but if they get concussions, it's probably got one."

"Is it awake?"

"Yeah, it just woke up. C'mon, sir, and I'll show her to you."

"Her?"

"Yeah, the damned MinSha says she's a 'she.' Not that I can tell or give a shit about it. Her name's Proptayl."

Walker followed Wethington over to where the alien stood under guard. The alien's hands were zip-tied, its legs shackled, and there was a black band wrapped around its thorax. "What's that?" Walker asked, indicating the band.

"Ordnance tape," Wethington said. "As soon as Reynolds let her go, she tried to fly off. She wouldn't give us her word not to try it again, so…"

"Ordnance tape."

"Yes, sir," Wethington confirmed.

Walker inspected the MinSha; he'd never been this close to one. Like most Humans, he had a natural aversion to them after what they'd done to Iran at first contact. It wasn't that a response hadn't been deserved—and had probably been warranted for some time—it was the over-the-top nature of the attack that made humankind in general tend to be wary of the MinSha; people in New Persia, though, tended to be a little more…extreme…in their outlook.

Up close, Walker was struck by how much the MinSha looked like oversized versions of Earth's praying mantises. They walked on four legs and used two more as hands, and they could fly as this one had already tried to demonstrate; hell, they even had triangular heads with beady eyes that stared back at you when you looked at them. While sort of creepy in a four-inch insect, it was tremendously disconcerting to have it done by a six-foot-tall alien. The only two things he could find different, besides the size, were that their captive was a light blue in color and had a somewhat funky smell.

Walker stepped forward to address the alien. "Hi, I'm Colonel Walker," he said as a half-smile crossed his face. "Sorry about the ordnance tape; it's going to be a bitch to get that off. You'd have been better off giving your word that you wouldn't try to escape."

"If our positions were reversed, would you have given *your* word?" the alien asked, the translator putting a harsh tone on her words.

Walker considered a moment. "No," he finally said. "Probably not." The smile went full. "Still, that tape is going to suck to get off you."

The MinSha continued to stare at Walker. "Is there a reason you abducted me?" Proptayl asked after a long pause. "Am I to be tortured by you Humanssss?"

"Straight to business, eh?" Walker asked. "Of course there is a reason we grabbed you, but I hope to avoid any unpleasantness between us. That will depend on you, though, of course."

"And what would your reason be?"

"I'm looking for information," Walker said.

"I'm sorry, but I am a private on my first tour of duty. There isn't much I know, even if you do decide to torture me."

"I'm not looking for secret information or anything that might be proprietary or privileged; I'm just trying to figure out what we did to you."

"What do you mean?"

"I'm trying to figure out what it is we did to you to cause you to continue pursuing and attacking us. If your mission was solely to guard the mine, you wouldn't have companies of troops out here trying to run down our platoon of soldiers. I've gone over this hundreds of times in my mind, and I just can't figure out the business case for why you'd want to risk loss or damage to your personnel and equipment."

"Really? I would think that it would be pretty apparent, even to you," the MinSha replied.

"Why is that?"

"Because there are always repercussions when you do things that are generally accepted as impermissible."

"Impermissible? What things are we talking about?"

"Wiping out orphanages, of course," Proptayl spat, "as well as the factories that produce the food to feed the children there."

"I agree with you," Walker said; "we'd never do anything like that."

"*Liar!*" the alien exclaimed. "I have already seen the Tri-V photos. The locals showed them to our leaders, and our leaders showed them to us!"

"What photos are you talking about?"

"The photos that convinced my leaders to wipe your disease off this planet. What you did to the younglings was horrible. They looked just like baby MinSha; to see their broken bodies was ghastly. And to think you have come here and done that repeatedly...Although the locals offered us a small stipend, we probably would have taken the contract for free."

Walker jerked back. "*What?*"

Wethington was more to the point. "That's fucking bullshit!"

The MinSha cocked its head. "I suppose you are going to say that's not true?"

"There is *nothing* that could be further from the truth," Walker said. "I've never even *been* on this planet before this week, nor has anyone else in the company that I'm aware of."

"I certainly haven't," Wethington added.

"The only reason we're here now is that we were hired by the local government to guard the mine from the rebels in the civil war they're having."

"Interesting," Proptayl said. "Really? When were you hired?"

"About 30 days ago," Walker replied. "Why?"

The MinSha ignored the question. "And how much were you paid to guard the mine?"

"We haven't been paid anything yet; we were supposed to collect our first installment on arrival. It was a fairly big contract, though. We stood to make 40 million credits over the next year."

"Let me guess," the MinSha said; "the locals didn't have an exit clause to get out of the contract, did they?"

"No, they didn't," Walker confirmed. "The contract was pretty iron-clad. It was the only way we'd do it without at least a partial advance payment." His eyebrows knit. "Why are you asking all these questions?"

Proptayl's voice, when she answered, was much quieter than before. "The civil war ended two weeks ago. A week ago, we were hired by the new government to defend the mine from *you*, and to terminate you...all of you...on sight. No questions or communications with you. We accepted payment of five million credits to cover our expenses while we performed the job, plus a modest retainer to make it worth our while."

It all clicked into place for Walker. "Those sons of bitches! They hired you, at a minimal salary, to kill us so they wouldn't have to pay us! *Those bastards!*"

"Sir," Wethington said, "we've got to stop the MinSha. This is all bullshit. None of us need to die...on either side."

"Unfortunately, that is not entirely the case now, though." The alien finally broke the stare and focused on something on the ground. "The locals here, while somewhat backwoods in nature, are very quick learners. They took your iron-clad contract and used it to make one that is similarly iron-clad for us. I heard some of our leaders talking and, if we fail to wipe you out, we are responsible for paying them a large sum...40 million, I believe...plus we forfeit our initial retainer."

"That's bullshit!" Wethington exploded.

"What about if we cover your fees and payments?" Walker asked. "Do you suppose we could buy our freedom, if we were to explain what actually happened?"

"Unlikely," the MinSha said. "Our commander gave her word, and that is something we do not back down on. That is why people hire us—once we give our word on something, we either do it, or we die trying."

Chapter 6

"Colonel Walker!" a voice said, shaking him. It seemed like he had just laid down—maybe he fell down?—and his eyes were all gummy as he tried to focus.

"Uh. Yeah?" he finally asked.

"Top Wethington is gone, sir!" Staff Sergeant Rapp exclaimed.

"Gone?" Walker asked, instantly awake. "Where did he go? Did the MinSha capture him?"

"No, sir, he just vanished. I might not even have noticed he was gone, but one of the men found his kukris and a note to you." He held out a small piece of paper.

Walker flipped on his mini-light and looked at the note. "Colonel Walker, this whole situation sucks; someone had to ask the MinSha for quarter. I know you couldn't order anyone to do it, so I volunteered. I couldn't live with myself, otherwise. Sorry, sir, but I had to try. Sergeant First Class David Wethington."

Under the signature was a postscript that said, "Watch out for my kukris for me while I'm gone. If I don't make it back, kill a MinSha or two with them for me."

Walker looked at Rapp. "Who's in the CASPer?"

"Corporal Reynolds, sir."

Walker switched to his radio. *"Reynolds, Colonel Walker. Have you seen Top Wethington?"*

"Yes sir, I have. He went by here about 15 minutes ago. He said he was going to go scout their positions and to hold where I was."

"Do you still see him on any of your monitors?"

"No sir. I saw him get to about where their lines are, but then his heat signature laid down. I thought he was trying to sneak up on them, but it has kind of faded away now. I'm afraid they got him sir. Want me to go take a look and see if I can recover him?"

"No, hold your position for now." Walker's shoulders slumped. "Damn. He was a damned good trooper. It's a damn shame to lose someone for something as stupid as this mission." He shook his head and looked at Rapp. "You're Top, now," Walker said. "Don't do anything foolish; I can't afford to lose you too."

"Colonel, this is Reynolds again. It looks like the whole damn MinSha force is coming!"

"Copy that, Reynolds. We'll get everyone up and moving, but I need you to do what you can to hold them off as long as you're able. Most of the troops are asleep; we're going to need some time."

"Will do, sir. Reynolds, out."

Chapter 7

"Reynolds, out." The trooper did another scan of the CASPer's systems, but he was already intimately familiar with what he'd find. The suit was low on power, low on ammo, and badly in need of some heavy-duty maintenance. There were more red lights than green, with most of the systems showing at least a little yellow. Worst of all, he

was out of jump juice and wouldn't be able to go three dimensional anymore. Even the suit's occupant wasn't fully functional; he was so tired he could barely see straight, and had already caught himself nodding off twice. The only thing that was still fully functional was...he laughed; the suit was one of the early Mark 7s that was equipped with a climbing mode. That was the only fully mission capable system; not that climbing would be especially helpful against the forces his sensors indicated were coming his way.

He tried to think back to the early CASPer training classes, but couldn't remember a lesson titled, 'How to Stop a Battalion of MinSha with One Broke-Ass CASPer.' He chuckled. They needed to put that into the syllabus. If he made it back, he was going to become a teacher; that would be the first lesson he taught.

Taking the MinSha head–on seemed a bit of a waste, though. He'd get dead fast, and then the bugs would roll on by him. He looked up the large proto-tree he was standing next to and reconsidered his earlier assessment. The suit still had enough power to let him climb, and the cedar-analogues were big enough. Hmm...it was going to make him a huge target if seen, but the platoon needed time, and he was going to give them that time.

Reynolds made the motion for climbing mode, and small spikes snapped out from the toes and insteps of his boots, as well as the palms of his hands. He wasn't as quick as a cat going up the tree, but he was fast enough. He climbed up 20 feet, jammed the spikes in as far as they would go, and put the suit into low-power mode.

He didn't have long to wait; one of the MinSha flew past his position five minutes later, followed 30 seconds later by two he could see on the ground. He waited until they were past, brought the spikes back in, and dropped to the ground.

Although he bent his knees before he slammed into the ground, and the suit absorbed some of the impact, he still hit much harder than he was used to, and it took him a second before he could spin around toward the MinSha. Having heard the half ton suit hit the ground, they were already starting to turn as his MAC began firing. He killed two, then triggered his jump jets to avoid the return fire.

The "No Juice" light flashed in his display, and the suit went nowhere. He was too tired from lack of sleep; his ingrained reflexes were working against him. A laser bolt hit him but didn't penetrate the suit, and he dove forward to avoid additional fire, turning the fall into a roll. Coming up on one knee he fired the MAC again, killing another MinSha. A MinSha MAC round hit his CASPer shoulder. More lights illuminated and several turned from amber to red.

He turned to return fire, but the MAC was mounted to his right arm…and the entire arm went dead.

Reynolds turned and ran, going deeper behind the MinSha lines. If he could just lead them away from the rest of the Roughnecks, his mission would be complete.

The suit lasted another hundred yards before he got the red light indicating it had 10 seconds of fuel remaining. He barely had time to dodge behind a tree before the systems began shutting down. The canopy only opened about six inches; he wasn't getting through that. He blew the emergency jettison, and the canopy dropped away from the suit.

Free, he climbed down, grabbing the items he could, and turned to run. Suddenly, he was thrown forward, and he got a mouthful of the detritus on the jungle floor as he face-planted. He spit it out and tried to lift himself up, but his right arm wasn't working. He glanced down and saw that his arm had been removed at the shoulder and was laying several feet away; the blood was already pooling next to him…so much blood.

The light in the forest, already dim, began to get darker. He brought his left hand up to his mouth before he could forget, pulled, and then spat out the tiny piece of metal. Movement caught his eye as a chitinous leg stepped into the pool of blood still trickling from his body. How…disrespectful.

The device rolled free from his nerveless fingers and stopped next to the squad leader. The MinSha had just enough time to recognize it before the grenade exploded.

Chapter 8

"*Fire and retreat!*" Walker ordered. He took a shot at a MinSha, but the alien ducked back behind a tree. He didn't know what Reynolds had done the night before, but his sacrifice had given them another day of freedom. The MinSha force had finally caught them, though, and the aliens were pushing hard to eradicate the remaining Humans. If the Roughnecks didn't make it to the city soon, they were going to be overwhelmed. He could see flashes of blue to his right as the MinSha scouts tried to flank them; if that happened, it was game over. They had to retreat faster; they had to break contact with the enemy and avoid encirclement, but he didn't see how that would be possible. Time was rapidly running out for the Humans.

"Colonel Walker, you better get up here to the point, right now!"

Walker ran to the front, conscious of the MinSha rounds whipping past him. As he ran by Corporal Jennings, the soldier slumped, a large hole in her chest.

He sprinted to where Staff Sergeant Rapp waited…at the edge of the forest! He was standing at the last tree, and beyond it, a large open space beckoned. "We made it!" Walker exclaimed. "How close to the city are we?"

Rapp pointed to the left, and Walker could see the spires of the capital city in the distance. "It's only about seven miles that way, sir. Or…about five miles beyond the battalion of MinSha that's dug in out there."

"What?"

"Yes, sir. There's a battalion of troops, with heavy weapons, waiting for us out there. In addition to the ones chasing us. There's no way we're getting past them. Pickett had a better chance of getting to the Union at Gettysburg than we do at making it past them."

"So…we're screwed."

"Yes, sir, we well and truly are. We'd be better off trying to get past the ones behind us than trying to get across that cleared area."

"Hey, sir!" Corporal Stevens called. "The MinSha wants to talk to you. She says she has a way out of this."

Walker strode over to where the trooper guarded their prisoner. "What's that?" he asked. "If you have a way out of this, I'd love to hear it."

"I will tell you how to get out of this trap if you promise to let me go," the MinSha said. "Certainly, even you must know by now that you are trapped; the plan all along was to drive you here, where you could be surrounded and easily destroyed. There is no way out for you; you are doomed."

"You just want us to let you go?" Walker asked. "You're not going to ask for money? What kind of a mercenary are you?"

"I am a practical one," Proptayl said. "I might as well ask a stone to give me water. Telling you how to beat our commander is not the same as actually having you do it. You would have to win in order for me to get paid, which is highly unlikely. But even if you did win, it would not look good for you to send me money. My egg-mates might get the wrong idea if I were to receive money from someone who defeated my unit while I was his captive...they might think I told you how to do it, when in fact I only advised you of the possibility."

"So, are you going to tell me, or what?"

"Are you going to let me go?"

"Are you sure you want to do that, Colonel?" Staff Sergeant Rapp asked. "She's probably the only thing keeping them from hitting us. If we use her as a hostage, maybe they'll let us pass."

"They won't," Proptayl said. "Our orders were to keep you from getting to the city. Even if my life had any value, which it does not, they would kill me in order to complete the contract and keep you away from the city."

"I think we're about out of options, Staff Sergeant," Walker said. "If this is my last card before doing something that is going to get a lot of us killed, I'm going to play it." He turned to the MinSha and said, "Yes, if you tell me how I can get out of this trap, or at least get my unit to safety, I give you my word as the commander of the Roughnecks that I will let you go."

"Then I give you my word that if you let me go, I promise I will tell you how you can get out of the trap."

"If I let you go, do you promise not to shoot at us or harm myself or my troops?"

"I do."

"Cut her loose."

Staff Sergeant Rapp pulled out a knife and sliced through the zip ties, then he cut through the tape holding her wings closed. "Sorry," he grunted, "we don't have any of the solvent needed to take the tape off your carapace."

"That feels better," the MinSha said, spreading her wings.

"Okay, Proptayl, you're free," Walker said. "How do we get out of this trap?"

"The only way I foresee you getting out of this alive is to challenge the leader of our force to a one-on-one duel. If she decides to fight you, you can ask for free passage to the city as your reward for winning."

"And what if I lose?"

"I suspect she'll kill all your troops…but that's what's going to happen in any event." Propayl cocked her head and looked up. "There are two of our fighters circling above us. If you take one step outside the jungle, they're going to attack you. Without your suits, you have a very limited chance of shooting them down, at best. Meanwhile, the rest of our troops are going to assault this position and kill all of you."

Walker risked a glance up. He could see two specks in the sky, but couldn't tell what they were. As the Roughnecks were out of aerial assets, though, it was unlikely the aircraft were friendly.

"Regardless of how this turns out," Walker said, "I'm glad we had a chance to talk. It was interesting getting to meet you. You aren't as bad as your civilization is made out to be."

"It was…interesting getting to meet you, as well. I could say the same thing about your civilization." She looked around. "Am I free to go?" she asked. "If so, I can fly to my unit and tell them you released me so that I could bring the challenge to my leader, since you were afraid any of your people would get shot if they stepped outside the jungle."

Walker nodded. "You are free to go."

Proptayl spread her wings, but Walker waved at her. "Yes?" she asked.

"Thanks," Walker said.

"You're welcome," Proptayl replied. She launched into the air and was gone.

Chapter 9

After an hour of tense waiting while the MinSha forces continued to press in on them, killing two more troopers, the assault finally ceased. After a few minutes more, a MinSha flew across the intervening no-man's land beyond the forest, bearing the parley flag. "I don't see any weapons," Staff Sergeant Rapp noted. "Still, everyone stay alert and keep her covered. It wouldn't be the first time someone attacked under a parley flag."

The MinSha landed at the edge of the woods and dropped the flag. "I am here to speak to Colonel Walker," it announced.

"I'm Colonel Walker."

The MinSha waved him over away from the rest of the platoon. When they had a limited amount of privacy, the alien said, "I have a message from our commander. She says that she accepts your challenge with the following provisos. If you win, your force will be allowed to pass freely through our lines to the city. If she wins, all your force will be taken to our home world of Chitaa where you will be slaves."

"Unacceptable. I—"

"She expected you would try to caveat her terms, and I am to tell you that no modifications will be allowed. She said to let you know that, although what the locals did was wrong, she cannot rectify it. Therefore, if you have not thrown down all your powered weapons and left the forest by 10 minutes after I return to my force, our assault will re-commence, and will not stop until all of you are dead. I am authorized to tell you, since you can't do anything to stop it, that this section of the jungle will be firebombed 10 minutes after that, which will most likely terminate any resistance. Your choices are to either duel our commander or die. That is all."

The MinSha nodded once, turned, and flew off toward the waiting mass of MinSha.

"*Everyone, here's the deal,*" Walker radioed. "*We were just given an ultimatum. I can either duel their leader, or they will firebomb us until we're dead. If I win, we will be allowed to pass through their lines; if I lose, everyone will be taken back to their home world as slaves. There is no way we are going to be victorious here, so I am going forward with the duel. If you are with me, leave your powered weapons in the forest and come out with me. If you don't come out, I suspect you will be killed...probably badly.*" Walker paused a few seconds, then he added, "*No matter how it works out, it has been an honor serving with you.*"

Walker set his rifle down, nodded to Staff Sergeant Rapp, and stepped out onto the hard-packed ground that surrounded the forest. After a couple of minutes, Rapp joined him.

"Are you it?" Walker asked.

"They're still deciding," Rapp said, "but you're my colonel. I'm with you, regardless."

After a few more minutes, nine other troopers filed out of the forest. A MAC fired once from within the forest. "Corporal Jones chose the third option," Sergeant Booth said. "Sorry, sir, I tried to talk him out of it."

"Now what?" Rapp asked.

"Well, I'm not wearing myself out walking to them," Walker said. "I'm tired enough as it is; they can come to us."

"They already have," someone muttered.

Walker looked back at the forest; at least a battalion of MinSha ringed the edge of it. How many freaking MinSha *were* there, anyway?

When Walker glanced back to the other force, he could see they were in motion. Although some drove vehicles, the majority flew. Within a few minutes, the group of Humans was completely ringed by more MinSha than Walker had ever wanted to see, and all of them pointed weapons at the tiny, outmatched group.

At some unknown signal, the entire force shouldered their arms, then relaxed in place. A single MinSha approached the group.

Walker did a double take as he looked at the MinSha. Although he had often thought they all looked alike, this one was the *exact* twin of the one they had held captive. Including the line around her middle, where dirt clung to the glue from the tape they had used to keep her from flying. Proptayl. He nodded once. "Well done."

"Are you referring to the ease with which I tricked you into believing I was just a minion, and used that knowledge to get you to release me?"

"Yes, that."

"You will notice I never gave my word to anything, besides the fact that I wouldn't shoot you or do anything else to cause you direct harm. Since I gave you that oath, I have held to it."

"You haven't ordered your troops to kill us?"

"Not since I gave you my word, no."

"So, was this whole challenge thing made up, too, or are you actually going to duel me for our freedom?"

"Oh, it is very much real," the MinSha said. "After I kill you, I look forward to taking one of your people as my slave. You will, of course, have to free me from my promise not to do you any harm first."

"Of course," Walker said. "Can I ask you one—no two—questions before we begin?"

"Certainly. You are in no danger of escaping, and I am feeling somewhat magnanimous, having beaten you. Ask your questions."

"I'll let the outcome of our duel determine whether you have beaten me. As for my questions, first, I'd like to know how I can be sure your troops will honor your promise to let us go once I kill you."

Proptayl's red compound eyes didn't flinch. "They will do so, because I have given my word, as leader of our clan, that they will do so. To do any less would be to bring dishonor on the clan."

"Won't that violate your contract?"

"Our contract says to kill you. When I win, you will all die. The contract doesn't specify whether that is by weapon on this planet or a life of servitude on Chitaa."

"I see. Well, thanks for that," Walker said, sarcasm heavy in his voice.

"It has been my pleasure. Truly, I do not see why there is such a mystique about you Humans. All you have proven here, as warriors, is that you can run and die. I will enjoy parading my new slave around to show how worthless your society is."

"I don't know about 'worthless;' I would say you had a sizable advantage over us the entire time. If we had all of our gear, we could have killed you a long time ago."

"The measure of a warrior is not what she does when everything is in her favor, but in what the warrior does when everything goes against her. So far, I have found humanity to be…lacking."

"The jury is still out on that," Walker said.

"I don't know what that means, but I grow weary of this conversation. What is your second question?"

"My second question is simple," Walker said. "I just want to know why."

"Do you Humans always have to be so obtuse?" Proptayl asked. "Why what?"

"Why did you tell me to challenge you? Why are you giving us the opportunity to escape?"

"That's two questions, although I'll admit they are somewhat linked. The answer, however, is quite simple. I wanted to kill you."

"What?"

"I lost my honor by being tricked and captured by you. The only way I could regain it was to out-trick you, then prove my dominance over you by killing you. A duel was the only way to accomplish that. There was a danger you would get killed before you could challenge me, but I was forced to accept that risk." She paused and then asked, "Are you finished? Can I kill you now?"

"You can try. What are the rules?"

"The rules are simple. One of us must die. You are not allowed powered weapons. Beyond that, there are no rules. You may have a ceremonial spear if you'd like." She raised her voice. "Lieutenant Colonel Crostayl!"

Another MinSha trotted forward with a box that was nearly seven feet long. It set the box in front of Proptayl, turned, and retreated back to the ring, drawing its laser rifle. Proptayl opened the box and drew out two six-foot-long spears. The last eight inches were a metal point with a bleeder insert. The point was attached to the shaft of the spear with a crossbar, a metal piece that extended to both sides of the spearhead to keep someone stabbed with the spear from drawing it through the wound.

Proptayl extended one, butt first, to Walker. Walker took it, looked at it, then gave Proptayl an annoyed look. "Is there a problem?" the alien asked.

"Yes," Walker said. "I don't know anything about MinSha physiology, but it would seem to me that this crossbar would keep you from being injured if your important organs aren't close to the surface, while all of mine are. Also, your arms are longer than mine, so you have an advantage with these."

"No one said you have to use it," Proptayl said, "but you challenged me, so I get to choose the weapons."

"Fine," Walker said. He drew one of the kukris to go with the spear.

"Are you done delaying?"

"I am."

"Very well then, begin."

The two combatants began circling each other, making small thrusts to feel each other out. Proptayl thrust and then swung the spear like a club, and Walker had to dive backward as the point flashed in front of his nose. Proptayl charged forward, but Walker rolled and came up with the spear facing the alien, and grounded it like a pike; she had to claw herself to a quick halt to keep from impaling herself.

Walker jumped back to his feet as she tried to skewer him again, and he leaped out of the way, although he picked up a nick on his upper arm.

The alien raised the spear over her head, stepped forward, and slammed it down like a sledgehammer. Walker blocked it off to the side and spun around, thrusting with his spear toward the alien's thorax. Proptayl saw the thrust coming, though, and she reared back on her hind legs and grabbed Walker's spear by the crossbar with her middle legs. As she slammed back down, she pulled on the crossbar, trying to draw him closer. Walker had to release the spear as she brought down her own and stabbed at him; the spear glanced off his ribs, opening a cut in his side.

Walker drew his other kukri and defended himself by crossing them and using them to block her strikes. With the bends in their middles, they weren't the perfect tools for blocking, but he could sometimes use one to block while using the other to counterstrike against her. Still, she could outreach him by several feet, and he picked up another few nicks in no time.

Walker could feel himself wearing down from lack of sleep and blood loss. He searched for a way to get inside the arc of the MinSha's weapon, but every time he thought there was an opening, it closed before he could take advantage of it. His reflexes were slowing down.

Proptayl was on the attack now, driving him back to the circle of the watching MinSha. He backed into them and several clawed hands pushed him back forward. He saw the alien pull back to strike, and he feinted right and then dodged to the left. Proptayl didn't fall for the feint, though, and the spearhead went through the flesh of his right leg, all the way to the crossbar. The crowd drew a collective gasp; they knew the fight was close to its end.

Before Proptayl could exploit her advantage, Walker dropped the kukri in his right hand and grabbed the spear point protruding from the back of his leg. Wincing as the blade cut into the palm of his hand, he held it steady and chopped down on the spear's shaft with the other kukri, slicing it off just below the crossbar.

Without the weight of the Human at the end of the spear, Proptayl overbalanced, falling forward toward Walker. Realizing her mistake, she gathered herself and reared back onto her back two legs to get away. Walker dove forward and swung the kukri, hacking off the last two feet of her right leg, then he dove to his right while she tried to regain her balance.

Proptayl tried to stomp the Human, but without her fourth leg, she missed, landing awkwardly, and her three remaining legs flexed, bringing her thorax almost down to where Walker lay beneath her. He rolled onto his back and stabbed upward, and then a second time as she tried to lift a leg to stomp him. The second stroke hit something vital, for blue blood jetted from the wound, and she stumbled. She took a step, trying to get away, and collapsed on Walker's legs.

Walker screamed as the spear point was slammed back into his leg and driven into the hard ground, and all he could see was the white light of pain for a few seconds. As it cleared, he realized she hadn't moved; she was still laying on his legs. He did a sit up and stabbed her several more times.

Proptayl's last breath escaped from her in a small sigh, matched by the collective release of breath from all the onlookers, especially the Humans. Walker pushed her body off him and pulled the spear point out of the ground. He left it in his leg as it partially blocked the wound, even though blood drained out both the front and back.

Walker tried to stand, but his leg wouldn't support him. Things started to get gray around the edges of his vision, and he knew he didn't have much conscious time left before he went down from blood loss. He stripped off his shirt and tied it around his leg as Lieutenant Colonel Crostayl walked up to him.

"Congratulations, Human," the MinSha said. "Proptayl was the victor in over 100 previous duels, so defeating her is something of note. You and your troops are free to go. None of our soldiers will hinder your passage; in fact, we will be returning to the mine, so you can do as you please."

"Is letting us go going to cause you problems?" Walker asked.

"Perhaps, but nothing we can't handle. There was a clause in our contract that voided the contract if our honor was at stake." She cocked her head and looked at Walker the same way Proptayl had. "So, what are you going to do, now that you have been given back your life?"

"What am I going to do? I'm going to get some medical attention, then I'm going to find our employers and express my dissatisfaction with how they cancelled our contract."

"That's not much of a goal in life."

"No, it's not much of a life-goal," Walker agreed, a look of grim determination on his face, "but as long as I get a chance to see them face-to-face before I die, it will be enough."

# # # # #

Mark's Introduction to:

CASPer's Ghost

by Brad R. Torgersen

Brad is one of those guys who you simply cannot help but like. He gives far more than he should (as witnessed by his presence here, despite all his other commitments) and always goes the extra mile. He's the 2009 winner of the prestigious Writers of the Future contest, has been published in Analog as well as the InterGalactic Medicine Show, and has been nominated for both Hugo and Nebula awards. His breakout novel, "The Chaplain's War" (2014, Baen) put him on the radar in a huge way. And if that isn't enough, he's also a U.S. Army Reserve Chief Warrant Officer.

Brad's contribution to A Fistful of Credits, "CASPer's Ghost," takes us down the dark road of what humanity can do to itself, as well as some of the ancient technology lying around the Galactic Union left from over from a war many thousands of years ago. We're sorry it's the last story in the book, but we think we've saved the best for last.

Find out more about Brad at
https://bradrtorgersen.wordpress.com/.

CASPer's GHOST
by Brad R. Torgersen

The air of Echo Tango Six rippled like heat waves coming off an old Earth highway. A man didn't walk through it as much as he swam, and to that end, nobody without a powered armor suit could last more than a couple of minutes in Echo Tango Six's several-hundred-degrees Celsius temps, and hundred-plus atmospheres of pressure. Ordinary vacuum-proof technology just didn't cut it here. If there was a less hospitable terrestrial world on which to test cutting-edge technology, Theo Mathis wasn't aware of it. Not even Venus—back home—was this bad. Because Venus didn't come with a hostile enemy force eager to stake a counter-claim to Echo Tango Six's sole valuable resource.

"How do you figure the F11 got down here in the first place?" asked a woman's voice in Theo's ears.

"Supernova," Theo said. "Or at least that's the going theory."

"Duh," said the woman. "I know *how* F11 gets from the inside of brown dwarfs, out into the universe. But how did such a rich deposit wind up *here,* specifically?"

"Maybe we'll get the chance to find out," Theo replied.

"Cut the science chatter, Blue Nine, Blue Ten," commanded a stern male voice.

That was Chief Wixton. Theo's boss.

"Yessir," Theo reflexively replied.

"You're supposed to have your eyes on the new test unit we're putting through trials," the chief said. "We'll worry about planetary formation theory later."

451

Theo called up a window in his heads-up display, showing him the vital stats on the big Combat Assault System, Personal, suit that was trudging through Echo Tango Six's infernal atmosphere, just a few meters ahead. Like Theo's own CASPer, the experimental unit was fully automated and environmentally stabilized. It kept the pilot—or, at least, what passed for a pilot—safely protected from Echo Tango Six's heat and pressure, as well as the occasional acid rain storm that swept in.

Unlike Theo's CASPer, the experimental unit's pilot did not have a name. Just a designation: CB, for CASPer Biomechorg. Or Charlie Bravo, as the others in the platoon had taken to calling him—or her, or maybe *it?* Even Theo wasn't quite sure what to make of the hulking, largely silent automaton that marched in their midst. Charlie Bravo rarely said anything, and when Charlie did, it was often in text form. Very basic relaying of information. Like a computer probe. Though Chief Wixton had assured the platoon that Charlie Bravo was reliably Human at heart.

"Sent to us from top Company people," the chief had said, prior to the deorbit maneuver which dropped them down into Echo Tango Six's roiling, hell-like weather patterns. "The CB is a one-off. The first of potentially many, many more. But the Company suits won't make the decision to begin commercial production until or unless the first CB has been put through a rigorous live-fire trial.

"We got the contract on Echo Tango Six from the Zuparti—to investigate and secure a supposed deposit of F11. We know the Zuparti aren't the only ones interested in this find. Hostile contact is expected. Which means we get the CB for the duration of our time here."

So far, they hadn't seen or detected anyone other than themselves. They were gradually closing on the clump of F11 which orbital surveys said was embedded in the surface less than a kilometer ahead.

If the ride from space had been rough, plodding across the surface was proving rougher. Theo's CASPer was already complaining about temperature-related problems in both the joint servos and the coolant system radiator. In this cursed climate, there was nowhere for the suit's waste heat to go. All the suit could do was keep the occupant insulated from the worst of it.

Like Theo's suit, Charlie Bravo's was complaining of the same problems.

"I estimate we've got less than ninety minutes before things get genuinely dangerous," Theo said on the platoon tactical channel. As one of the platoon's resident brain men—whose job wasn't strictly limited to shooting—Theo was keenly aware of the fact that Echo Tango Six was taking all of the platoon's CASPers well beyond manufacturer-recommended operational parameters.

"The landing boat will pick us up well before then," Chief Wixton reassured. "All we have to do is go in, confirm the existence of the F11 deposit, secure a perimeter, then wait for Green and Gold Platoons to arrive."

"I hope the Zuparti are making this worth our while," said Blue Ten—Carla Giordano's slot in the formation.

"Beyond your base pay," Chief Wixton confirmed. "A verified F11 deposit gets us all a *very* healthy bonus. But don't go counting your chickens before they hatch, Blue Ten. First things first. Let's just *get* there, to start. Worry about the money later."

A crackling voice interrupted Blue Platoon's tactical conversation.

"Blue Chief, this is Silver Falcon, how do you read?"

That was Director Bufordson, who was Wixton's boss. Not a soldier—at least, not anymore. Bufordson had left his uniform in his locker a long time ago and was one of the suits now. Albeit a suit who still deigned to go out with the grunts on contract jobs. There weren't very many in the Company who ranked higher than Bufordson. He was sitting in the operational control center aboard the gate-capable mothership in synchronous orbit.

"Silver Falcon, this is Blue Chief, I copy you, over," said Wixton.

"How's the CB holding up so far?" asked Bufordson.

"Oh, as well as any of us, sir. One of my smart boys guesses we've got an hour and a half before problems with the CASPers get truly serious—including problems with the experimental unit. I'll keep you apprised of any changes."

"Good. Good. Any sign of opposition yet?"

"Not a thing, sir. Any sign up top?"

"If there is a competitor on this planet, their base craft is hiding somewhere other than here. And we've not detected any foreign signals, either encrypted or unencrypted. Perhaps our Zuparti contact was wrong? If the F11 deposit is *not* here, we could be poking around down there for nothing."

"I sure hope not, sir. For all the trouble we've gone to, I'd hate to think we have to eat a contract."

"The Zuparti would still owe us base operational and attrition costs, but I agree with you—it would be a huge waste of our talents. Give me a fresh update as soon as you find something conclusive. This is Silver Falcon, out."

The signal from orbit dropped, and the platoon was back to talking amongst themselves.

Except for Charlie Bravo, who merely rattled off a mundane series of surface observations: ambient temperature, estimations of surface rock density, and so forth—and in text form only.

The group kept pushing forward. Moving slowly. Trying hard not to overtax their CASPers to the point of requiring a premature pullout. Silver Falcon wouldn't be happy if he had to send Green or Gold down before it was their turn.

"Blue Chief, this is Blue Two," said a male voice.

"I copy you, Blue Two. What's it look like up ahead?"

"Soupy as hell," said the platoon's scouting expert, Adzil Abner. After Wixton, Adzil was the next merc in command—the equivalent of a senior non-commissioned officer, if one bothered to pay attention to the old Earth rank systems which had existed before first contact with the Galactic Union.

"Yah, I think we all know that," Chief Wixton retorted with irritation. "We pay you to find out things I *can't* already see for myself."

"My suit's sensor suite is pretty fouled up in this climate, Blue Chief. Infra and ultra are practically useless. Both radar sets give me readings which are inconsistent with each other—I'm pretty sure that's the heat, messing with the equipment—and long-distance visual is a wash."

"What about passive comm detection?" Wixton asked.

"That seems to be working okay, but I've got silence on this side."

"Push forward, then. The second your situation changes—especially if the F11 detection matrix pings—you holler. So far the suit-to-suit comm doesn't seem particularly degraded. Though that could change fast if our opponents spring some countermeasures on us."

"What if we spring ours on 'em first?" remarked a different female—Blue Sixteen, one of the two CASPer troops with active electromagnetic jamming and scrambling capability. She could wreck the hell out of an enemy comm network, while leaving Blue Platoon's comm clean as a whistle.

"Let's hope we get that lucky," Wixton said. "Now step it up a bit, please. We don't want Blue Two getting too far out in front. In fact, Blue Five and Blue Twenty, take a forty-five to Blue Two's trajectory, and give me some eyes on our right and left."

"Roger, boss," came the twin replies, as two CASPer units split off and began to slow-lope out in front, but perpendicular to each other, with the main group in a tactical file headed more or less up the middle of their original path.

Theo felt sweat form on his hands. And not from the heat. He was still relatively new to mercenary life. To date, he'd participated in just three prior contracts, none of which had required him to do much more than garrison-style security in the wake of actual fighting. This was the first time Theo had gone in with the vanguard. And he had Charlie Bravo to look after on top of everything else.

Several minutes ticked by in relative silence.

Then—

"Blue Chief," said Blue Five.

"Copy you," Wixton replied. "Find anything?"

"Not sure, Chief," replied Blue Five. "Did Silver Falcon brief you on any prior inhabitants of this wonderful little world we're on?"

Blue Chief laughed out loud.

"No," he finally said, recovering. "I am fairly certain nobody—alien, or indigenous—has ever lived here before."

"Then why the hell am I looking at the entrance to what appears to be a subterranean tunnel?"

The whole platoon stopped short at once. All, except for Charlie Bravo, who kept moving ahead.

"Blue Zero," Theo said over the tactical, "this is Blue Nine. Come about and stand fast, please."

ROGER, said the text in Theo's field of view.

On the wedge-like tactical display, showing a real-time view of the whole platoon—plus the three scouts moving in front—the little dot for Charlie Bravo, suddenly came to a halt.

"Thank you," Theo said.

"Repeat your last?" Wixton asked Blue Five.

"I don't know what else to call it, Chief. There's this ramp leading down to about five meters subsurface, and a big circular pressure door at the bottom of the ramp. I'm standing right in front of it, if you want to patch through to my cameras."

The whole platoon suddenly got a Tri-V-view of what Blue Five was seeing. Sure enough, it looked like a pressure door. Big enough for two CASPers to pass through, standing on each other's shoulders.

"Copy," said Wixton. "All Blue Platoon members, close and group on Blue Five's present location. I want a three-three defensive perimeter immediately. Is that understood?"

The lot of them *rogered* their understanding, and diverted course for the discovery their comrade had made.

Before long, half of Blue Platoon was arrayed in a jagged half-circle around the ramp Blue Five had talked about, with a second jagged half-circle up on the surface above. Blue Chief pulled Theo and Charlie Bravo down to where Blue Five was carefully examining the pressure door's exterior—seeking any sign of power or a control board that might allow the platoon to gain entry.

"It's not Union-standard," Blue Five said, "or I'd have found a place to jack my CASPer in by now. I *can* tell you the alloy is carbon-molecule reinforced. Very durable construction technique."

"It's old," Theo remarked.

"How can you tell?" asked Wixton.

"Look at the runnels cut into the face of the metal. Echo Tango Six's acid rain has been washing across this artifact for a long time."

"He's right," Blue Five said.

"So it's . . . pre-Union?" asked Wixton.

"Maybe," Blue Five remarked. "We don't know for sure. We'll have to get inside."

"Any sign of the F11 deposit that brought us here in the first place?"

"No," said Theo. Like the others, he had dropped from orbit with a special sensor built into his CASPer's usual tactical suite. If there was an F11 deposit under them, it should have registered by now.

Blue Chief seemed unsure of himself.

He activated the channel to orbit.

"Silver Falcon here," said Wixton's superior.

"Sir, I'm sending up something you oughta see. Need your recommendation on how best to proceed. One of my kids down here thinks this thing might be pre-Union technology, but that's just a guess. Do we investigate further? Or stick to the original plan?"

A few moments of silence, then Bufordson's voice replied, "Who the hell builds anything on the surface of a Godforsaken ball like *this?* Copy you, Blue Chief. Understand you've got something highly unusual on your hands. Any luck getting the door to open?"

"Negative, sir. Though I don't know if we ought to bother trying for too much longer, before we—"

The channel to orbit suddenly cut out with an ear-splitting squeal.

"Dammit," Wixton barked, his CASPer straining on its mechanical legs, as he tried to reorient his comm system for better signal capture.

"Inbound! Inbound!" yelled one of the other platoon grunts—it sounded like Carla. Her signal was weak and echoing. Whatever had blocked the Chief's orbital conversation was making a mess of their tactical channel, too.

Theo's stomach suddenly jumped into his throat.

"Security," Blue Chief snapped, "Give me a report. Where are they coming from?"

"Everywhere!" shouted Carla's voice.

"We can't see anything," Wixton said. Which was true. The whole platoon was tied together with a sensor-share network which would show them on their tactical display where the bogeys were approaching from and in what number. But the display had gone blank—not even the familiar signatures of the platoon were registering.

"Line-of-sight response," Wixton ordered, as his CASPer began to charge back up the ramp, with Blue Five close behind. "Are we taking any rounds yet?"

The platoon channel was a squelched mess, but Theo saw the exhaust trail of a CASPer-launched missile lance overhead and detonate beyond Theo's constricted horizon. At the bottom of the ramp, there wasn't much Theo could see or do. Lacking specific instructions, he hesitated. Should he stay at the bottom, with Charlie Bravo dutifully at his side? Or take Charlie Bravo up to where the shooting had started?

Without being told, the experimental unit suddenly bolted.

"Hey!" Theo yelled, but it was too late. Charlie Bravo raced to the top of the ramp and disappeared as two more missile trails appeared in the impossibly-thick air.

Theo felt the *thump* of an explosion through his armor. Nothing on the radio yet. That shockwave had traveled directly up his legs, from the ground.

"Hell," Theo breathed, and followed Charlie Bravo up the ramp.

The security perimeter had collapsed in on itself. Blue Platoon was fighting savagely—in pairs—as what appeared to be hundreds of *things* swarmed around them. Theo looked this way and that, until he saw Charlie Bravo going *mano a mano* with one of the bogeys. It definitely wasn't a CASPer from a rival mercenary team. Rather, each of the bogeys seemed to be a pile of animated rock. No head, no hands, no feet, just a mass of sand and stones that lashed out with appendages of sand and stone. When one of those hits connected, Charlie Bravo got knocked down pretty hard. Only to leap back up again, and continue the melee.

Not that the CASPer's weaponry seemed to do much damage. Theo watched as Charlie Bravo put a missile right into the middle of one of the bogeys. The thing blew apart in a hail of fragments. But then, directly beneath where the enemy had exploded, a new one seemed to rise directly out of the ground to assume its dead companion's place.

With comm out, there was no way to talk to Charlie Bravo, or anyone else.

Theo stood, dumbfounded, simply watching, until suddenly one of the bogeys noticed him, and the fight was on.

Theo hit the ground hard, the bogey directly on top of him, smashing away at the chest of Theo's CASPer with battering-ram blows. Theo pulled his legs to his pelvis and kicked up and out, hurling the creature away. But before he could get to his feet again, a second creature was on him. Then a third. All of them dumbly hammering with curved arms that slammed into the CASPer's armored hull like a pile driver.

Then Charlie Bravo was there, sweeping the bogeys off Theo and pulling him unceremoniously to his feet. Together they began targeting bogeys in tandem, launching missiles and MAC rounds, watching the enemy burst into bits with each successful hit. But it didn't seem to matter. The enemy reformed the instant they were destroyed, and their total number seemed to be increasing.

Another *thump* shook Theo to the core, matched with a simultaneous flash of light. When the auto-blackout on Theo's screen cleared, he could see where one of the other members of Blue Platoon had been destroyed—the CASPer had exploded ferociously.

No sign of Blue Chief. Nor Blue Two for that matter.

Thump! Thump! Thump!

"We're getting creamed," Theo yelled, not caring if anyone could hear him. He and Charlie Bravo stood back to back, kicking and punching, as well as launching additional missiles.

A damaged CASPer suddenly emerged from the fray, and grabbed Theo's CASPer by the arm. For an instant, Theo recognized Carla's suit markings, then she was dragging him back down the ramp, with Charlie Bravo fighting on their flank. Carla seemed to be transmitting something, but the comm was full of static. Finally she aimed a finger at the pressure door at the bottom of the ramp.

It was open. If only just.

A figure seemed to be beckoning through the door.

Theo and Carla ran for their lives. Charlie Bravo seemed to instinctively know what to do, and he followed them, with the bogeys close behind.

They cleared the aperture just as it snapped shut again, crushing two of the bogeys in the process.

And they were in total darkness.

* * *

"Human," said an odd voice through Theo's CASPer's speakers.

He slowly sat up, the motors of his joints audibly complaining. He quickly ordered a full systems check and realized his CASPer had been fairly mauled in the battle. With both missile magazines near empty, and the armor plating having been almost completely pounded to pieces, the mechanisms underneath were slow to respond to his movements—numerous systems glowed yellow on his display, or blinked red if they were completely deadlined.

The only good sign was the temperature was far less than it had been outside. Even if the pressure itself was still over seventy atmospheres.

"Who are you?" Theo said through his helmet's mic pickup. "Carla? Charlie Bravo? Hello?"

Charlie ordered his external lamps to illuminate. Only one of the three flickered to life.

A Jivool—in self-contained battle armor—stared down at Theo through the creature's helmet visor. Like Theo's suit, the alien's suit appeared to have been righteously trashed, with similar physical battle damage. The bear-faced creature didn't have an expression Theo could recognize, but its point-to-point Union-universal tether seemed to be working just fine. The Jivool's mouth moved, and Theo's CASPer's computer translated.

"Your companions are alive," it said, "though I cannot be sure about the odd one. He seems more machine than flesh. Your female is presently unconscious, but her suit is functioning. You are the first living creatures I have seen in almost five cycles."

"Blue Platoon," Theo said, trying to struggle to his feet. "We've got to help the others."

"There is *no* help for them," the bear-like being said. "Just as there was no help for my own company when we landed here."

"Let me guess," Theo said. "You were the competitors that our Zuparti client warned us would be waiting?"

The Jivool seemed to grunt, then closed its eyes.

"I suppose it was inevitable that another mercenary outfit would be dropped here. We too were sent to secure a suspected F11 deposit, though not by a Zuparti. At that time, we expected no resistance, other than the hostility presented by this planet itself. The—" the next word the Jivool spoke did not translate "—surprised my unit entirely. We were not far from here and upset to discover the expected deposit of F11 was not forthcoming when a horde of those *things* boiled up out of the ground. Our weapons were far superior, but they would not *die*. My people . . . we fled, until I alone stumbled into this ancient structure. It was purely by luck I discovered the archaic radio signal control commanding the outer aperture to open and close. The *things* . . . they seem unable to penetrate the walls of this place. It is *thing*-proof."

"Where exactly *is* here?" Theo said, turning to reach his hand across to where Carla's CASPer lay on its side. Using the connector in his suit's wrist, he temporarily linked suit-to-suit with her to confirm the veracity of the alien's words. Then he did the same with Charlie, whose systems all checked out, but who had not as yet begun to move.

"We will discuss that in a moment. But first, I must ask: are there additional Humans who will come?"

"Yes. If Blue Platoon does not report in, or is destroyed, our leader in orbit will send down two other platoons."

"They will also be destroyed. *Nothing* which is not original to this planet is left intact. The *things* see to it. They not only murdered my company, they ripped apart and devoured our vessel."

"What did your people in orbit do about it?"

"Our vessel *was* our ship from orbit. Again, we did not expect hostilities. We landed as a whole. Over one hundred of my people died. I salvaged the few power cells I could, whilst fleeing here, and that was the end of us."

"The . . . things that attacked. What are they?"

"I do not know," the alien admitted. "I suspect very much they are a native form of life to this world. Not organic in the way you and I would understand. They did not evolve to live on a planet you or I could call home. This is *their* world. And though they are primitive, they would seem to be perfectly capable of ensuring no foreign presence survives here. Almost as if the planet itself dispatches antibodies to destroy an infection."

"Is that what we are?" Theo asked, somewhat incredulously.

Carla groaned and began to stir, her voice coming across the suit-to-suit.

"Lord," she said shakily, "I feel like someone spun me through a double spin cycle."

"That's an understatement," Theo said.

"We the only two who made it?" she asked.

"Us and Charlie. Plus this...other guy."

"I've never seen a Jivool in person before."

"Me neither. He says his company got here before us and was wiped out just like Blue Platoon got wiped out. He saved us."

"What for?" Carla asked, sitting upright and staring at their new companion.

"What would be the point in letting you be killed?" the big bear-alien said, using its suit-to-suit with Theo to talk to them both. "There would be no profit in it. While we remain on the surface of this cursed world, we are made allies by circumstance."

"No argument from me on that count," Theo muttered. "How the hell are we supposed to get out of here?"

"I have been pondering that very question," the Jivool said.

I KNOW HOW, a text flashed across Theo's visor.

"Charlie?"

I KNOW HOW, the text repeated itself.

"Okay," Carla said. "Just what the hell is going on with our experimental CASPer? Charlie, no offense, but none of us are even really sure what you are to begin with, okay? Are you drone? Programmed at Company headquarters?"

NO. I AM ME.

"But what the hell is a 'me' in your terms, Charlie?" Theo asked.

I JUST KNOW THAT I AM ME. AND I KNOW THAT WE CAN GET OUT OF THIS PLACE. GO BACK TO ORBIT. I HAVE DONE IT ONCE BEFORE.

Theo stared at Carla, who simply stared back.

The Jivool seemed startled.

"How is this possible?" the alien asked.

YOU HAVE BEEN HERE LONGER THAN I WAS, ORIG-INALLY. YOU MUST KNOW ABOUT THE LOWER LEVELS.

"Yes, I have discovered multiple levels," the alien admitted. "Some of which can be reduced in pressure and temperature, to the point that I can remove my helmet if I wish."

WE MUST GO THERE. I WILL BE ABLE TO SAY MORE WHEN WE ARRIVE.

* * *

It took them almost an hour to cross through five different pressure locks, each one similar to the first. At each stage, the pressure dropped substantially, until finally they were in an environment which more or less mimicked Earth-relative pressure. After closing the door on the fifth lock, Theo was surprised to see his external atmosphere sensor showed a rapid gas exchange taking place, as nitrogen and oxygen were flooded into the new compartment to displace the carbon dioxide which had dominated before.

When the sensor showed green, Charlie texted the words, OPEN MY COCKPIT.

Slowly, Theo complied, while Carla used her suit lamps—two of three had survived the massacre—to give Theo enough light to see by.

The emergency release on the side of the cockpit worked just like on a normal suit. But the form revealed—when at last the canopy rotated upward—proved to be anything but normal.

Carla audibly gasped. This time, she was heard via comm. Whatever the things on the surface did to distort transmission, it apparently didn't register this deep in the ancient complex.

"You find me ugly," Charlie said, his voice a curious and vocoded monotone.

Theo and Carla opened their cockpits and the Jivool removed its helmet. There was an instant of held breath—none of them quite sure if they could trust what their suit sensors said—then they inhaled with relief. Not only was the atmosphere life-sustaining, it was pleasantly cool to boot.

"Jesus," Carla said, staring at their odd compatriot. "You look like . . . you look like there was barely anything left of you when you were put back together again. What the hell *happened* to you?"

"I cannot say for sure," Charlie said, his facial expression neutral. Almost all his face appeared to be scar tissue, save for his eyes, which seemed quite Human, although they blinked slowly at regular intervals, which became somewhat unnerving.

"What does that mean?" Theo asked.

"Do you know the phrase 'déjà vu'? That is perhaps the best way for me to describe it. I know nothing beforehand. Yet, all of this—as it happens in the moment—is immediately familiar. Landing on the surface. Spreading out in formation. Getting attacked by the creatures above. Even retreating to this old pre-Union structure. I know I have done it all before."

Charlie's words were translated for the Jivool through its helmet, which it held in both gargantuan, gauntleted hands.

"Why didn't you *warn* us?!" Carla yelled. "We got wiped out up there!"

Charlie's face remained void of emotion.

"I didn't know we would be attacked until the attack happened. Then it instantly felt like a replay of a very similar attack. When . . . *Bronze* Platoon was destroyed."

"Bronze Platoon?" Theo said, quickly looking at Carla, who shook her head: she didn't know anything about it.

The Jivool spat some growling, deep-throated consonants and vowels which churned out the other end of Theo's helmet speakers as, "How can we trust that this is the truth?"

"That passageway," Charlie said, aiming the arm of his CASPer in the direction of a long, dark corridor which branched off from the pressure lock holding area in which they now huddled. "I know it has three more passageways branching at its end. Two of which are sealed. One is open. The Jivool has been here, too. He can attest to this."

Theo and Carla looked at their alien companion.

The big bear's upper lip quivered slightly, then he spat more consonants and vowels.

"That is correct. During my initial reconnaissance of this place, I discovered the passageways as your cyborg has described. Though I detected nothing of prior Human habitation. This structure was not created by Human hands, nor by Human minds."

"That's because it is . . . it is . . ."

Charlie's face pinched with an expression of frustration—the first time he had shown any emotion at all.

"I am sorry," he finally said. "I can *feel* the memory. It is there. But I cannot call it to the surface."

"Maybe if we keep moving," Theo said, "it'll come back to you. We obviously can't stay here."

As a group, they moved out. With the Jivool leading the way, followed by Carla, then Theo, and Charlie trailing behind. Occasionally, Charlie's face would pinch with renewed frustration, and he would stop for a moment, his lips moving to form noiseless sounds. Then his face would resume an expressionless mask, and he would begin walking again—the boots of his CASPer clanking noisily alongside the racket made by the others.

"What is he?" the Jivool asked as they walked.

"We were told Charlie was a prototype," Theo said. "He dropped with us as a form of 'field test' but that's all I was told. I had no idea he was . . . fully integrated like he is. There seems to be precious little of his original body left. I don't know why a genuine cyborg conversion was necessary."

"Maybe the part we see is the only part that made it," Carla said. "If he's right, he must be the only survivor from a prior contract dispatched to this world."

"Yeah, but why the hell keep us in the dark during mission prep?" Theo asked. "If they put a whole platoon here before, and lost the manpower, it makes no sense that we—Blue, Gold, Green— didn't know about this disaster beforehand. Certainly Chief Wixton should have known about it. And while he can be a pain in the ass, I don't think he's the kind of man who'd ever hold out on us."

"If the channel to orbit wasn't still blocked, we could ask Silver Falcon."

"If Silver Falcon knew about this...well, I am not going to make any assumptions. I just want to...whoa!"

The group suddenly stopped short, along a stretch of corridor which had opened up on one side, showing a magnificently-sized subterranean hall of columns. The forest of curiously-shaped pillars stretched into the dim distance, illuminated only by their CASPers' lights.

"Like a giant-sized Greek temple," Theo remarked.

"How deep are we, anyway?" Carla whispered to no one in particular, as she stared into the far distance.

"At least 300 of your meters," the Jivool said. "And there are spaces beneath us, much larger still. I had only just begun to explore them all when my system began to weakly detect your comm signals above. I rushed back the way we came in time to open the top-most outer door and see your Blue Platoon being destroyed."

Charlie stared out at the titanic columns.

"Beautiful, isn't it?" Carla said.

"Boosters," Charlie simply replied.

"Come again?" Theo asked.

"They are not what they at first seem to be," Charlie said. "Each cylinder is in fact a launch silo. Almost all of them are empty. But a few are not."

"Launch silo?" the Jivool said. "For what, precisely?"

"Ground-to-orbit craft," Charlie said.

"How do you know this?" the alien growled.

"I know it, because it's the way I got back to orbit the first time. I am just *now* remembering. Only . . . only . . ."

Charlie's pinched expression was pronounced, as he looked down at the floor.

"Goddamit," Theo said, "What happened?"

Charlie looked up, his eyes suddenly filled with an intense pain. Small drops of fluid leaked from his eyelids, and ran unnoticed down his scarred face.

"The creatures . . . they only wounded me. It was the ride back into orbit which killed me."

"You mean *almost* killed you?"

"No. Killed. My CASPer was wrecked, and almost out of power. By the time I got down here, I had to abandon it. I found and climbed a gantry next to one of the silos. Up on top, I found a way to unlatch the door to the inside, which in turn took me to an empty payload bay. When I closed the payload bay hatch, the craft initiated an automated launch sequence. The G forces were...they were...I should be dead."

"I can't believe pre-Union technology would survive so long and still be working," Carla said. "I mean, I'm not a brain like Theo, but even I know machinery breaks down eventually, no matter how sophisticated it might be."

"Do not underestimate what the elder races were capable of," the Jivool grumbled. "Even my species, which has had much more time to study them, does not understand everything about the pre-Union era. We only know there was a great war, fought with terrible weapons of amazing power and scale. Not all of these weapons were destroyed at the war's end. Perhaps this whole underground complex is merely a giant missile battery, to be used to surprise an enemy space fleet?"

"But why put your battery at the bottom of a pressure-cooker hell-hole?" Theo asked.

"What better place to hide such a battery?" the Jivool said. "It would be the last place any sane species would think to check. War can turn desperation into brilliance."

"Well, yeah. Brilliance that doesn't help us at all, if what Charlie says is true. Even if we can find one of these vehicles intact and get it to launch like Charlie says, we won't fare any better than he did."

"We have the CASPers," Carla said. "Charlie didn't have his. Not the first time."

"I'm still not even sure I *buy* Charlie's story," Theo said. "What reason would the Company have had to land Blue Platoon here in the first place? Knowing we were being sent into a death trap? Even if Silver Falcon is a suit, he's not a cold fish. The Company doesn't throw away its people like that."

Charlie was now leaning against the corridor wall, punching a gauntlet into the wall over, and over, and over again.

"I am dead…I am not dead…I am dead…I am not dead," he said, repeatedly.

"He's in hell," Carla said quietly so only Theo could hear. Or so she thought.

Charlie suddenly whirled around and glared at them. His whole face was pink, as well as moist.

"I am the ghost of a man who should not have lived!" he yelled, his mechanized throat making a digital warbling sound as he shouted the words. "I cannot remember who I really am! I cannot remember why I was really here! I cannot…I cannot…I cannot…

Charlie sank slowly to his knees, his fists balled on either side of each hip, while tears ran freely from eyes which were clenched shut.

"Come on," Theo urged quietly. "Let's go see if there are any full silos which might help us."

* * *

The search took hours as they wandered from one stupendously-sized column to the next. And the next. And the next. It was difficult to keep track. Every silo looked the same. And the few times Carla or Theo or the Jivool climbed a gantry, they discovered the interior had been left empty.

Then, as Theo began to worry about their CASPer power supplies running low, they stumbled across something remarkable.

It was another CASPer, an older Mk 7. Even more battered than their own. Lying on the ground, its cockpit locked open. Its power had died long ago, but there was still a name stenciled on the CAS-Per's shattered breast plate.

"Broussard," Theo said, reverently reaching out with his gauntleted hands to attach a suit-to-suit connection. He didn't have enough power to do much more than reawaken the abandoned suit's computer, but it was the only real chance they'd had so far to get some concrete answers.

Within a few moments, the surviving data in the abandoned suit had been transferred to Theo's. He closed his cockpit and used the Tri-V displays to quickly cycle through the abandoned suit's log file.

"Your name is...Christopher Broussard," Theo pronounced. "You were *Chief* Broussard, in charge of Bronze Platoon, which landed on Echo Tango Six approximately...four Earth years ago. Plus or minus a couple of months. You were sent to discover if rumors of an F11 deposit were true and found this pre-Union installation instead. The creatures on the surface attacked just prior to you broadcasting your findings. You were the only survivor."

Charlie Bravo stood motionless, his mouth silently repeating the name Theo had spoken. The former chief was lost in his own world.

Carla pulled Theo aside, with the Jivool in hearing range.

"I still can't figure it out, though," she said.

"Which part?" Theo asked dryly. "There are several."

"This place," she said, spinning on a heel, her arms outstretched. "How could any race construct this complex, when the surface is lethal in several different ways?"

"You mean the things?"

"Them, and the environment."

The Jivool had a thought.

"Perhaps the pre-Unionists brought the creatures with them. A form of feral life which, bred in an environment similar to this, might thrive? And provide a natural, active defense against intruders once the silo system had been installed? That way the weapons are triple-protected against outsiders. A near guarantee that nobody could deactivate or disable the battery. If the pressure does not crush an expedition, the temperature will cook it. All else becomes food for the things."

"They *wanted* this!" Charlie—Chief Broussard—suddenly shouted.

"What?" Theo said, quickly walking back to the cyborg's side.

"I'm getting it. Now. The tornado of fragments in my head...it's slowing down. The Company...they didn't know what they had down here; they just knew it was something very, very important. Something they could use. Maybe sell? Maybe reverse-engineer? Biological or technological, it didn't matter. We—my platoon—never sent up a full report. We only gave them images of the pressure door to the underground. Back in orbit, a few days later, they had my corpse, and the pre-Union spacecraft which launched me. An almost irresistible mystery."

"But why send you back?" the Jivool asked. "And in such a compromised condition after so much delay?"

"And not *tell* us about it," Carla reemphasized.

"I don't know," the cyborg admitted.

Theo looked around at the nearby silos. "There is one sure way to find out."

* * *

The payload bay contained no visible controls. No readouts. No Tri-V devices. Nothing to indicate the bay could be used to control the functioning of the ancient spacecraft in any meaningful way. If and when it finally went up, Theo, Carla, Broussard, and the Jivool merc survivor would be purely at the mercy of its wholly unknown programming.

Assuming the launch didn't fail halfway.

Or bust apart right there in the tube itself.

Lacking couches, straps, crash nets, or anything else to secure themselves to the bare metal deck, the two Humans, one alien, and one cyborg simply laid down on their backs, with their cockpits closed and helmet fastened, while Theo reached over and manually pulled the hatch shut. Which left them in complete darkness—there were no portholes—to contemplate their ultimate fate.

When several moments passed with no light, or any sound, Carla began to grouse.

"We picked a dud," she said. "Just our luck."

"I don't even know if we can get the hatch back open," Theo muttered.

"Wait," the Jivool suddenly said. "Can you hear that?"

"Hear what?" Theo asked.

"Hang on!" Broussard shouted.

Theo was suddenly flattened to the deck, his system's speakers *blooping* little alarm noises at him, regarding the sudden and stiff amount of acceleration he was experiencing. An ordinary trip to orbit might subject a Human to three or four Gs, at the very most. But when the CASPer detected force in excess of twelve Gs, it was programmed to know the occupant was in serious danger of not only blacking out, but suffering permanent physical damage, or even death.

Nobody could say anything. Or scream. They simply lay where they were, practically cemented to the floor by the raw power of the motors working beneath them. Motors which had been built an untold number of years ago, and which had sat in undisturbed stasis for this one moment—when four refugees would use the craft to blast their way up out of the cauldron of Echo Tango Six, and back into blissful, cold, empty space.

Where Silver Falcon was waiting for them.

* * *

Theo vaguely remembered coming to. He hurt. All of him hurt. His vision was blurred. His ears were ringing. And his stomach was unhappy to be introduced to microgravity so quickly after having been pancaked across the bottom of the pre-Union booster's payload bay.

It took many minutes for all three Humans aboard—even the man who was mostly a machine—to get their wits about them.

Outside? Impossible to tell what was happening. Since the craft had no windows and there were no display panels with which to discern what might be happening, they simply had to wait. And wait. And wait.

Until, at last, they felt the gentle nudging on the hull which told them somebody or something had come along to secure them. Probably a small boat from the Company mother craft.

More waiting.

Until the hatch was cut open—Human torches, very noisy and bright—and a squad of space-suited techs popped in.

"Please tell me nobody was stupid enough to send down Gold or Green," Theo wheezed, as he was carried in his CASPer out of the ship.

"No," said one of the techs. "Silver Falcon was gnawing a fist off, trying to decide what to do, when we picked up the booster over the planet's pole. It took a bit of work to intercept you, but now that you're back, I can assure you, nobody will go back down to the surface until Silver Falcon gets a full report."

"The Jivool—"

"We'll take care of the alien. He might represent our rivals, but he also presents an opportunity to perhaps win a few points with those very same rivals. Who knows? There may come a time when we're working the same contract, on the same side."

* * *

Silver Falcon's master suite was luxuriously decorated with all the best Earth accoutrements money could buy, including a huge natural rock water fountain which took up practically one whole wall—and was made possible only by the spinning torus that looped around the Company mother craft's main body that ran centerline through the torus's middle.

Ridiculous and gaudy, Theo thought. Especially for a man who'd worked his way up from being a shovel head in the front ranks.

But then, maybe that was the point? Maybe to remind people—or even himself—just how far Bufordson had come in his 67 years of life.

Theo and Carla were seated in front of Silver Falcon's desk. At their side, riding on a robotic carriage, was Chief Broussard. Removed from his former CASPer, he seemed to be regaining his memory at a rapid clip, now that he was back in familiar territory and seeing familiar faces.

Especially Silver Falcon's.

"You goddamned prick," Broussard said, putting as much emotion into his vocoded voice as he could.

Silver Falcon merely cleared his throat uncomfortably and looked at his former top chief, who had commanded his former top platoon.

"It was nothing personal, Chris," Silver Falcon said. "When they found you in orbit the first time, they told me you were too far gone. Except that some of your memory might be saved if we acted quickly. I demurred. Once they had what was left of your brain tied into the basic cybernetics, though…well, you were a drooling idiot. I told them to pull the plug. It would be cruel to let you linger like that. Except you kept remembering little nuggets, here and there, to the point that the psych people told me that association was the key to you getting it all back. Sights. Sounds. Smells. Even getting you back to the actual world where it all occurred in the first place."

"So, you used me like a piece of meat?"

"Who was stone dead when we found him, yes."

"Would you use one of your own kids in the same way?"

"Dammit, Chris, that's not fair! You were *dead*. I told them initially to let you *stay* that way. Alright? They kept telling me, 'Oh no, there's something there still, it's not really the person, but we might get some details.'"

"Why not immediately go back down to the surface?" Theo asked.

"Where my best platoon vanished without a trace?" Silver Falcon said, somewhat incredulously. "Young man, you may not realize it, but losing an entire platoon with no answers put me in a terrible position with my superiors in the Company. There had to be an accounting, and they weren't going to spend any more blood or treasure on the matter until that accounting was given. They washed their hands of Echo Tango Six…until the Zuparti client came along, and gave the Company a sufficient financial incentive to go back."

"You mean, to drop us into a blender," Carla muttered.

"What good would it have done to warn you? Hmm? We didn't understand what had happened the first time; I'd pried nothing coherent out of Chris's revived brain, and the client was paying well enough that the Company committed not just one, but *three* fresh platoons to the effort so that there *would* be backup in case anything went wrong, and we had to roll in the cavalry.

"They didn't even want me on this contract in the first place! But I told them it *had* to be me because I was there the first time. And I had to write all those letters to all those families with all those death pensions attached. I *had* to know what happened. And I also had Chris—or what passed for him—along for the ride. Sending him back down seemed like the only real shot at getting something concrete. For the sake of his legacy."

"You could have told us the truth about him," Theo said.

"Like hell, kid. He wasn't any good as a chief anymore. He barely remembered enough to function as a low-level squad grunt. He didn't even remember his own goddamned name, okay? He was blank. Except for the blotches that weren't. I hoped that putting him back on the surface, in a tactical situation, would help gel some of those blotches back together. And I was *right.*"

"Well, congratulations," Broussard said sarcastically.

"Fuck you, Chris. If you really are back—and I mean *back* back—you may be sitting in this chair someday soon. Then you can judge me. Until then? Be thankful you're alive, through a string of miracles even I can't entirely believe."

The cyborg was silent.

"So," Theo said. "What happens to us now?"

"First of all," Silver Falcon said, "you all get bonuses. Very, very hefty bonuses. Attached to some very generous time off. Then? Well, now that we actually know what we're dealing with on Echo Tango Six, we have to consider our options. There's a whole pre-Union base down there. Intact. Nobody has looted, messed with, or destroyed any of it. Since the F11 claim did not pan out, and the Company has taken a substantial hit on overhead—from the reduced contractual severance—my superiors are eager to recoup their losses."

"And you?" Theo asked. "What do *you* get out of it?"

The older man rubbed his hands at his eye sockets.

"We've lost two platoons on Echo Tango Six. Almost 60 good, hard-working, professional men and women. When we build a memorial to these people, I want it to be because they paved the way for something truly groundbreaking in Human history. A milestone. That pre-Union missile facility down there may or may not be the greatest discovery in Human history. But I want us to sure as hell find out. To decide whether or not the price—very high, very painful—was worth it. So we can tell their spouses, their parents, and their children that they were heroes. Is that good enough for you, son?"

Theo considered. "Yeah. Maybe."

"Good. Because I want you back down there. And her too. And even Chris, despite the fact he's hating me today. We can't afford to stall. The Jivool survivor you picked up will be only the first of many of his kind to come—assuming their client is still interested. I want to make sure that missile base is in Company hands—Human hands! So that there can be no doubt whatsoever that we've got the claim. To technology rights. To spinoff development. To academic and xeno-archeological fees—assuming we can protect and pacify the surface enough to let researchers go down.

"Besides, having you with Green and Gold will help them save lives too. What do you say?"

Theo looked over at Carla, who stared back at him.

"Crazy enough to try it again? This time, knowing what we're in for?"

"If the paycheck is big enough," she remarked dryly.

"I can guarantee it *will* be," Silver Falcon said, smiling for the first time.

# # # # #

About the Editors

A bestselling Science Fiction/Fantasy author and speaker, Chris Kennedy is a former school principal and naval aviator with over 3,000 hours flying attack and reconnaissance aircraft. Chris is also a member of the SFWA and the SCBWI.

Chris' full-length novels on Amazon include the "Occupied Seattle" military fiction duology, the "Theogony" and "Codex Regius" science fiction trilogies and the "War for Dominance" fantasy trilogy. Chris is also the author of the #1 Amazon self-help book, "Self-Publishing for Profit: How to Get Your Book Out of Your Head and Into the Stores."

Find out more about Chris Kennedy and get the free prequel, "Shattered Crucible" at: http://chriskennedypublishing.com/

Located in rural Tennessee, Mark Wandrey has been creating new worlds since he was old enough to write. After penning countless short stories, he realized novels were his real calling and hasn't looked back since. A lifetime of diverse jobs, extensive travels, and living in most areas of the country have uniquely equipped him with experiences to color his stories in ways many find engaging and thought provoking.

Find out more about Mark Wandrey and get the free prequel, "Gateway to Union," at http://www.worldmaker.us/news-flash-sign-up-page/

Four Horsemen Titles

Cartwright's Cavaliers

Asbaran Solutions

Winged Hussars (coming soon)

The Golden Horde (coming soon)

* * * * *

The following is an
Excerpt from Book One of the Revelations Cycle:

Cartwright's Cavaliers

Mark Wandrey

Available from Seventh Seal Press

eBook, Paperback, and Audio Book

Excerpt from "Cartwright's Cavaliers:"

The last two operational tanks were trapped on their chosen path. Faced with destroyed vehicles front and back, they cut sideways to the edge of the dry river bed they'd been moving along and found several large boulders to maneuver around that allowed them to present a hull-down defensive position. Their troopers rallied on that position. It was starting to look like they'd dig in when Phoenix 1 screamed over and strafed them with dual streams of railgun rounds. A split second later, Phoenix 2 followed on a parallel path. Jim was just cheering the air attack when he saw it. The sixth damned tank, and it was a heavy.

"I got that last tank," Jim said over the command net.

"Observe and stand by," Murdock said.

"We'll have these in hand shortly," Buddha agreed, his transmission interspersed with the thudding of his CASPer firing its magnet accelerator. "We can be there in a few minutes."

Jim examined his battlespace. The tank was massive. It had to be one of the fusion-powered beasts he'd read about. Which meant shields and energy weapons. It was heading down the same gap the APC had taken; the tank was heading toward Second Squad, and fast.

"Shit," he said. He had to stop them.

"Jim," Hargrave said, "we're in position. What are you doing?"

"Leading," Jim said as he jumped out from the rock wall.

* * * * *

Find out more about Mark Wandrey and "Cartwright's Cavaliers" at: http://chriskennedypublishing.com/imprints-authors/mark-wandrey/.

* * * * *

The following is an
Excerpt from Book 1 of The Kin Wars Saga:

Wraithkin

Jason Cordova

Available from Theogony Books

eBook, Paperback, and (soon) Audio Book

Excerpt from "Wraithkin:"

Prologue

The lifeless body of his fellow agent on the bed confirmed the undercover operation was thoroughly busted.

"Crap," Agent Andrew Espinoza, Dominion Intelligence Bureau, said as he stepped fully into the dimly lit room and carefully made his way to the filthy bed in which his fellow agent lay. He turned away from the ruined body of his friend and scanned the room for any sign of danger. Seeing none, he quickly walked back out of the room to where the slaves he had rescued earlier were waiting.

"Okay, let's keep quiet now," he reminded them. "I'll go first, and you follow me. I don't think there are any more slavers in the warehouse. Understand?"

They all nodded. He offered them a smile of confidence, though he had lied. He knew there was one more slaver in the warehouse, hiding near the side exit they were about to use. He had a plan to deal with that person, however. First he had to get the slaves to safety.

He led the way, his pistol up and ready as he guided the women through the dank and musty halls of the old, rundown building. It had been abandoned years before, and the slaver ring had managed to get it for a song. In fact, they had even qualified for a tax-exempt purchase due to the condition of the neighborhood around it. The local constable had wanted the property sold, and the slaver ring had stepped in and offered him a cut if he gave it to them. The constable had readily agreed, and the slavers had turned the warehouse into the processing plant for the sex slaves they sold throughout the Dominion. Andrew knew all this because he had been the one to help set up the purchase in the first place.

Now, though, he wished he had chosen another locale.

He stopped the following slaves as he came to the opening which led into one of the warehouse's spacious storage areas. Beyond that lay their final destination, and he was dreading the confrontation with the last slaver. He checked his gun and grunted in surprise as he saw he had two fewer rounds left than he had thought. He shook his head and charged the pistol.

"Stay here and wait for my signal," he told the rescued slaves. They nodded in unison.

He took a deep, calming breath. No matter what happened, he had to get the slaves to safety. He owed them that much. His sworn duty was to protect the Dominion from people like the slavers, and someone along the way had failed these poor women. He exhaled slowly, crossed himself and prayed to God, the Emperor and any other person who might have been paying attention.

He charged into the room, his footsteps loud on the concrete flooring. He had his gun up as he ducked behind a small, empty crate. He peeked over the top and snarled; he had been hoping against hope the slaver was facing the other direction.

Apparently Murphy is still a stronger presence in my life than God, he thought as he locked eyes with the last slaver. The woman's eyes widened in recognition and shock, and he knew he would only have one chance before she killed them all.

He dove to the right of the crate and rolled, letting his momentum drag him out of the slaver's immediate line of fire. He struggled to his feet as her gun swung up and began to track him, but he was already moving, sprinting back to the left while closing in on her. She fired twice, both shots ricocheting off the floor and embedding themselves in the wall behind him.

Andrew skid to a stop and took careful aim. It was a race, the slaver bringing her gun around as his own came to bear upon her. The muzzles of both guns flashed simultaneously, and Andrew grunted as pain flared in his shoulder.

A second shot punched him in the gut and he fell, shocked the woman had managed to get him. He lifted his head and saw that while he had hit her, her wound wasn't nearly as bad as his. He had merely clipped her collarbone and, while it would smart, it was in no way fatal. She took aim on him and smiled coldly.

Andrew swiftly brought his gun up with his working arm and fired one final time. The round struck true, burrowing itself right between the slaver's eyes. She fell backwards and lay still, dead. He groaned and dropped the gun, pain blossoming in his stomach. He rolled onto his back and stared at the old warehouse's ceiling.

That sucked, he groused. He closed his eyes and let out a long, painful breath.

* * * * *

Find out more about Jason Cordova and "Wraithkin" at:
http://chriskennedypublishing.com/imprints-authors/jason-cordova/

* * * * *

Made in the USA
Middletown, DE
17 June 2017